the
Book
Charmer

the
Book
Charmer

KAREN HAWKINS

Gallery Books

New York London Toronto Sydney New Delhi

G

Gallery Books
An Imprint of Simon & Schuster, Inc.
1230 Avenue of the Americas
New York, NY 10020

First Gallery Books hardcover edition July 2019

GALLERY BOOKS and colophon are registered trademarks of Simon & Schuster, Inc.

For information about special discounts for bulk purchases, please contact Simon & Schuster Special Sales at 1-866-506-1949 or business@simonandschuster.com.

The Simon & Schuster Speakers Bureau can bring authors to your live event. For more information or to book an event, contact the Simon & Schuster Speakers Bureau at 1-866-248-3049 or visit our website at www.simonspeakers.com.

Interior design by Jaime Putorti

Manufactured in the United States of America

10 9 8 7 6 5 4 3 2 1

The Library of Congress has cataloged the trade paperback edition as follows:

Names: Hawkins, Karen, author.
Title: The book charmer / Karen Hawkins.
Description: First Gallery Books trade paperback edition. | New York : Gallery Books, 2019.
Identifiers: LCCN 2019004356 (print) | LCCN 2019007480 (ebook) | ISBN 9781982105556 (ebook) | ISBN 9781982105549 (paperback)
Subjects: | BISAC: FICTION / Contemporary Women. | FICTION / Family Life. | FICTION / Romance / General.
Classification: LCC PS3558.A8231647 (ebook) | LCC PS3558.A8231647 B66 2019 (print) | DDC 813/.6—dc23
LC record available at https://lccn.loc.gov/2019004356

ISBN 978-1-9821-3566-9
ISBN 978-1-9821-0554-9 (pbk)
ISBN 978-1-9821-0555-6 (ebook)

To Cap'n Hot Cop, who sat with me on a snowy day
in front of a roaring fire in the music room of Blantyre,
a romantic Gilded Age mansion in the Berkshires,
debating plot points for *The Book Charmer*,
the book of my heart.

Nate, you are my magic.

Sarah

DOVE POND, NC
JULY 21, 2001

On the Saturday after her seventh birthday, a book spoke to Sarah May Dove. If she'd been older, she might have been surprised or even shocked, but as she was only seven and still a stubborn and devoted believer in Santa Claus, the Tooth Fairy, and the Easter Bunny, she didn't even blink.

In fact, after a moment's thought, she decided that books always spoke inside the quiet of one's head, although usually only while being read. So hearing a book speak didn't faze her in the slightest.

Besides, she was a Dove, and everyone knew the Dove family was special. Every chance her mom got, she proudly pointed out that when the Doves had seven daughters, as they did now, good things happened to their hometown of Dove Pond.

Mom wasn't just bragging; history had proven this true. In 1735, a seventh Dove daughter was born to the Dove family. When Jane Dove, the fourth oldest daughter, turned seven years of age, the town was suffering under a severe, crippling drought. Jane, a softhearted child who loved animals, cried at the thought of all the thirsty farm animals. As her tears fell, clouds gathered, and it began to rain. From then on, every time Jane cried, it rained. It was said that whenever local farmers wanted it to rain, they would bring Jane onions. And when they wanted sunshine, they brought her cake.

In 1829, another seventh daughter arrived. The oldest, Mary Dove, was said to have hair the color of spun gold and a propensity for finding lost jewelry, much to the delight of the townswomen. One hot summer day, while wading in the creek that wandered through town, Mary kicked over a rock and uncovered a large gold nugget. Thus began the Dove Pond gold rush. The gold rush lasted a remarkable thirty-two years, long enough to whip up a building frenzy that left behind the marble-fronted town hall, eight brand-new brick buildings on Main Street, a new school, and several streets of stately homes, all of which still stood today.

Sarah, her sisters, and her mother lived in one of those houses, a sprawling structure with so many creaks and leaks that it couldn't keep out the smothering summer heat no matter how many window air conditioners they added. Because of this, every Saturday through-out the summer, Sarah and her sisters retreated to the deliciously cool air-conditioning in the Dove Pond Library.

Sarah loved those trips to the library. As she was the youngest by five years and had no interest in either makeup or boys, the only things her sisters cared about, she filled her days with books. Every Saturday, after their mother dropped them off, Sarah's sisters would cluster around the fashion magazines, whispering and giggling, while she roamed the aisles alone looking for books about dragons.

Sarah wished with all her heart that dragons were real instead of existing only between the pages of certain books. Fortunately for her, there were lots of books with dragons. Although only seven, she'd been reading since she was three, a fact her mother told anyone who would listen. Sarah was a voracious reader, and she'd found friends hiding between the pages of books. For her, the trips to the library meant more than the refreshing burst of air-conditioning. They were life.

On the Saturday after her seventh birthday, ignoring her sisters' giggles as they clustered around one of their stupid magazines, Sarah headed for the Young Adult section. She had just walked past the glass display case that contained relics explaining the history of Dove Pond, when a dusty, paper-rattled voice rang out.

Read me.

The words echoed inside her head, without true sound, yet with a presence so keen that Sarah stopped in her tracks, her gaze locked on the glass case.

A small book propped in the center of the case rustled impatiently. *Read me* now.

Sarah dropped her backpack on the floor and walked to the case. She placed her hands flat on the cool, smooth glass and stared at the book, an old cracked-leather journal that rested among some other early artifacts in a display about the founding of Dove Pond.

She knew this particular book, even though she'd never seen it outside of the case. It had been written in 1702 by Charlotte Dove, the seventh daughter of the founding family of Dove Pond and one of Sarah's ancestors. Every Founder's Day, portions of it were reprinted in the local paper. Sarah knew the oft-repeated passages well, especially the few paragraphs where fourteen-year-old Charlotte Dove described in breathtaking detail the exact moment the Dove family had crossed the crest of Black Mountain, North Carolina, to look down into the green valley below. There they'd seen a single pond glistening in the morning sun like a sapphire set on a bed of emerald velvet and had decided that here was where they'd stay.

And so Dove Pond had been born.

There's more to the story, the book said.

"Like what?" Sarah asked.

You'll know when you read me.

Sarah considered this. She was allowed to check out only two books at a time and they had to last her all week, so she had to be very careful which ones she picked. "You're very small."

I have eighty-seven pages.

Which wasn't many, especially as it was handwritten. She could read that in a few hours. "Are there dragons?"

No. The book's sharp irritation was evident even through the thick glass.

Sarah dropped her hands from the case. "I want a book with dragons."

The book fluttered with irritation. *Read me,* it repeated sharply. *You* have *to.*

If there was one thing Sarah Dove didn't like, it was being told what to do. With six older sisters, that happened way too often as it was. So instead of agreeing to read the book, she said, "No, thank you," and turned to leave.

A boy she knew from school stood not four feet away, staring at her.

Blake McIntyre was a year older than Sarah. Whenever her sisters were anywhere near his older brother, Carter, who was a senior in high school, they became giggly and weird, which annoyed Sarah so much that she took it out on Blake whenever she saw him. It would have been more meaningful to take out her irritation on Carter, but he was never around. Meanwhile, she saw Blake on the bus every day, and so she teased him mercilessly.

He looked past her to the case and then back. "Who are you talking to?" Despite his bold tone, his face burned bright red.

"I'm talking to myself. Who else?"

He shifted from one foot to the other, his book bag hanging heavy on his shoulder. After an awkward moment, he said in a stiff tone, "I never talk to myself."

She shrugged. "That's because you wouldn't listen."

He scowled. "You don't know that."

She offered a scoffing smile, one she'd learned from her oldest sister, Madison, who seemed to instinctually know how to cut a person to the quick. "Don't I?"

His face turned an even brighter red. After an awkward moment he muttered something under his breath, and then, with a final, confused look from her to the case and back, he left.

The book barely waited for him to leave before it hissed, *Open the case. It's not locked.*

"Nope." She scooped up her book bag from where she'd left it on the floor. "I need a book with dragons."

You'll be back! the book whispered angrily. *Wait and see! You* need *me!*

Sarah ignored it and headed upstairs to the Young Adult section. She was happy when she reached the books she really liked, the ones that didn't snap at her but instead told stories of dragons and swords and girls who made things happen.

For the next month, every time Sarah returned to the library, the book fussed at her. First it would demand, then it would beg, and when that didn't work, it would snarl and fume. Irked by the book's insistence, Sarah started using another path to reach the stairs to the Young Adult section, avoiding the display case altogether.

As the weeks passed, Sarah discovered she could hear other books, too, although their voices were silkier and whisper-soft. They weren't demanding like the journal, but instead tried to tempt her.

You'd enjoy reading me, a very pretty book with a red cover told her one Saturday.

She thought about that. "Do you have dragons?" she asked.

No, but there's a unicorn on page 142.

She liked unicorns, but not as much as dragons. Sarah mentioned this to the book, and because it was much politer than the journal, the book sighed its regret. *Another time, then,* it said. *When you're tired of dragons.*

Which would never happen. "Of course," Sarah replied politely as she moved down the shelves.

Later that day, sitting in the back seat of the van with her book bag in her lap, Sarah asked her sister Ava, who was closest to Sarah in age, if books ever talked to her.

Ava snorted rudely. "No, but I wish plants could." Ava was always growing something. Their backyard was filled with flowers, all because of her. Mom said Ava had a "green thumb," which was true. Ava's thumb, like the rest of her hands, had a faint green tint. "It's grass stain," Ava had said. "From working in the garden." But Sarah didn't believe her. They were Doves, after all.

She looked at Ava now and wondered what it would be like if flowers could talk. After thinking about it (and remembering that some plants had thorns and prickers and could cause itchy rashes), Sarah decided she'd rather have books talk to her than anything else. Well, all books except one.

When they reached home, Sarah—always the last one out of the van—waited for the screen door to bang closed behind her annoying sisters before she hefted her book bag over her shoulder and went around the porch to the backyard. No one would miss her until dinner, and she couldn't wait to read the books she'd checked out of the library.

As she walked by the rusty swing set, she glanced to the house next door where Travis Parker lived. She and Trav had been in the same class since kindergarten, and he was her best friend. He wasn't home this summer, as he was staying with his grandpa at his farm outside of Atlanta. She wished Trav were here, because she'd tell him about the talking book and how rude it had been. He'd probably laugh at her, but that was okay. She laughed at him, too, so it all worked out.

She stopped to kick off her shoes, sighing happily as her toes sank into the cool, soft grass. Stuffing her shoes into her backpack, she hurried past Ava's flowers where they lined the path to the huge, sprawling willow at the very back of the yard.

Hundreds of years old, the tree rose into the sky and then bent over to trail its leafy branches in the shallow creek that wandered across the back corner of the yard. Sarah loved this tree and she was pretty sure it loved her, too.

With a quick glance at the house to make sure none of her sisters were watching, Sarah slipped behind the tree to her special place. The back of the trunk had been hollowed out by a long-ago lightning strike. Over the years, the wood had been worn smooth by rain and wind until, when she sat against the trunk, it fit her perfectly and hid her from view.

Sarah opened her backpack and reached in for one of her books . . . and then frowned. In her hand was the cranky journal, its cracked-leather cover rough under her fingers. "How did you get here?"

Does it matter? I'm here, so read me.

The note of satisfaction in its voice irked Sarah. "No." She put the journal aside and dug into her book bag, searching for the two books she'd checked out, both about dragons and elven warriors. After a moment, she looked at the journal. "Where are they?"

Not here. So read me.

For a wild moment, Sarah thought about throwing the old journal into Sweet Creek. But one look at the cracked-leather cover and yellow-edged pages made her reluctant to abandon the idea. It was an old, old book, over three hundred years old, and was important to the town, which was why it had been on display in the case. *Maybe that is why it's so cranky. It's old and it was forgotten. That would make me cranky too.*

With a deep sigh, she picked up the journal, placed it on her lap, and spread her hand over the leather cover. She'd only meant to feel the cracked leather, but to her astonishment, words and pictures flew through her mind. She saw a graceful but ink-stained hand writing the words in the journal using a quill dipped in ink. She saw sunsets and sunrises and a long, long trip on a creaky wagon. She saw the glimmer of a silver lake in the middle of a green valley, and a tree crashing to the forest floor on its way to becoming the floorboards for a house. She saw a blue-eyed boy with hair the same color as hers looking back over his shoulder and smiling, and a group of men straining against ropes tied to a wall as it was lifted into place in a building she recognized as the First Baptist Church.

She saw all of this and more at a breathtaking pace, her hand growing warmer as the pictures grew more vivid, more real. Faster and faster they came until, finally, her head aching slightly, she yanked her hand from the cover and stared down at her burning palm.

The book whispered a reluctant apology.

She curled her fingers over her palm and knew the book had been right. "I need to read you."

Yessss.

Sarah settled against the tree, opened the book, and soon became lost in the scribbled words. And as she did so, she saw her town the way Charlotte Dove had seen it in 1702. Sarah saw Dove Pond being born and then growing one building at a time. She saw people who came and stayed. People who fell in love and married, had children, and then grew old and died. She saw each and every moment Dove Pond had existed, even beyond the pages of the book, and as she read the journal, she realized that she lived in a place like no other.

It was there, under the dripping limbs of the weeping willow tree, on the grassy banks of Sweet Creek, and deep within the pages of her ancestor's journal, that Sarah May Dove fell in love with her hometown.

Later, when she was older and had time to think about it, she'd realize that was what the book had wanted all along. But at the time, she was merely lost to the drama, the excitement Charlotte Dove had spilled onto the pages, along with the beauty of the people who'd made Dove Pond live.

Sometime later, the screen door slammed. "Sarahhhhh!" Her sister Madison, who was as bossy as she was long legged and tall, yelled again. "Dinnnnnerrrr!"

Sarah rubbed her eyes. How long had she been reading? It couldn't have been long, because the book only had eighty-seven pages, and yet the sun was much lower than when she'd first sat down.

"Sarrrrahhhhh!" Madison yelled again, more sharply this time. Sarah's mom said something from inside the house, and after a pause, Madison disappeared, the screen door slamming closed behind her. She'd be back, though. Madison wasn't the sort of person who quit.

Sarah closed the book and hugged it against her chest. The words, invisible but vibrant, soaked through the cover. If she closed her eyes, she would see the story once again, as if she were still reading.

A faint breeze arose, rustling the grasses and lifting the scent of the damp evening air, fireflies just beginning to dance across the yard, as if offering to lead her home.

Read the rest, the book demanded.

"I will," Sarah said. "But after dinner when no one will bother me." She picked up her book bag, slid the book inside, and then stood, her legs stiff. "I promise."

She couldn't stop now, and both she and the book knew it. Later, while everyone slept, she'd crawl deep under the covers with her flashlight and read until the middle of the night, devouring every last word the way a starving person would a meal, savoring each bite even while ripping furiously into the next one.

But for now, she shouldered her book bag and slipped out of her hiding place into the cooling evening. With the book muttering irritably from her bag, she followed the line of fireflies across the yard and went inside.

Grace

"I'm a good girl. I'm a good girl. I'm a good girl." Grace Michelle Wheeler whispered the words under her breath from where she sat beside her sister in the back of their caseworker's car. Grace said the words a lot, hoping against hope they'd come true. But somehow, they never did.

If Grace had been a good girl, her mother wouldn't have left her and Hannah on the church steps and then run off with Rob, the greasy-haired man from the corner Fast Mart who smelled like old burritos.

If Grace had been a good girl, neither she nor Hannah would be where they were now, sitting in the back of their caseworker's car, on the way to yet another foster home.

If Grace had been a good girl, they'd never have to worry about food to eat, or a place to live.

Grace met Miss Wanda's gaze in the rearview mirror. The caseworker's damp round face puckered with disappointment. "You're too old for such behavior. Why, you're going to be in the fifth grade when school starts back."

Grace jutted out her chin. "I'm not sorry."

The caseworker flushed. "You should be! You have to do better. You *have* to."

Grace knew she had to do better. But no matter how good she was, how careful she was, things happened. Things she couldn't control. At the last place, she'd gotten into a fistfight with the Hendersons' redheaded son, Mark. If he'd made fun of her, she'd have ignored him, because she was used to that sort of thing. But this time he'd been mean to Hannah, and Grace had seen red.

Grace saw red a lot. Sometimes the color floated above her, not hot as she'd always thought anger would be, but icy and frozen, a blast of frigid air waiting to drop on her head and freeze her mid-flight. And when it happened, when the red enveloped her and threatened to trap her in place, she fought, swinging hard fists and kicking with all her might. This time, she'd smashed Mark's fat nose until it bled. He'd sobbed like the stuffed marshmallow he was until his parents had come running and pulled her off him.

Through the fading, icy haze, she'd heard Mark denying he'd done anything wrong. Grace had a history of lashing out, so she hadn't offered a word to defend herself, knowing it would be useless. Besides, she couldn't blame the Hendersons for taking their son's word over hers. They were only doing what real parents were supposed to. She hadn't been surprised when they'd called Miss Wanda and demanded that Grace be moved to another home, although they hoped to keep Hannah.

Everyone wanted to keep sweet, blond-haired, blue-eyed Hannah, and no one wanted wild, brown-haired, brown-eyed Grace. When Miss Wanda had explained that Grace and Hannah were sisters and had to be together, the Hendersons had let them both go. And so, here they were. Homeless again.

The miles sped by outside the car window, and Grace pressed her fist against her aching stomach. She knew what was ahead. There'd be another home with different rules from the last, rules she and Hannah were somehow already supposed to know. And another school with whispering girls and mocking boys who'd notice their choppy haircuts and hand-me-down clothes and regard them as losers. And teachers who would frown at such late, end-of-the-year transfers and shake their heads when they realized how far behind both girls were. That was the price one paid for moving schools: being either too behind or too ahead. It was always one or the other. And not being accepted was the price one paid for not already belonging. There was no cure for it. It was how it was, and how it would always be.

Suddenly tired, Grace leaned her head against the window and saw that Miss Wanda was looking in the rearview mirror at Hannah. The caseworker's face softened until it reminded Grace of fresh-baked bread.

People always did that when they looked at Hannah. While Grace fought her way through life, her hair tangled and her fists tight, Hannah floated along on a silver cloud, her feet never muddy, her hair as silky smooth as her smile. She never allowed other people and their harsh words to affect her. Grace was proud her little sister was able to keep the muck of their life from splattering onto her smiles.

For Grace, Hannah was everything. And so long as Hannah loved her, Grace would find the strength to deal with the rest of the stuff they had to put up with. They were a family, the two of them, and no one could change that. When Grace grew up, she'd take care of them both. She'd get a job, one with a desk and folders and Post-it notes, and she and Hannah would have enough food and the best clothes and house that money could buy and they'd live together forever.

Miss Wanda turned the rusty Honda onto a long, narrow dirt road. The car bumped along the drive, kicking up enough dust to dim the morning sun. When they reached the end of the road and parked, the dust settled around them, coating the car in a reddish haze.

Grace craned her neck to look out the window. A chipped, white-painted house sat in a yard packed with flowers of every kind and color, captured in place by a crooked white picket fence. Three mutts pressed their noses through the slats, tongues lolling as they panted heavily.

Miss Wanda opened their door and then waddled to the trunk to get their duffel bags while Grace helped Hannah with her seat belt. They climbed out of the car into the moist, humid air.

Grace held Hannah's hand, which was hot and a little sticky from the peppermints Miss Wanda had given them when she'd first picked them up.

"Good lord!" Miss Wanda huffed as she hauled their bags from her trunk. "Grace, what's in your bag? It weighs a ton."

Grace didn't answer. Up until a year ago, everything she'd owned hadn't been enough to fill her bag more than a third of the way full. But now it was stuffed with important things she'd started collecting for when she and Hannah had their own home. The things weren't new, but Grace would replace them after she got her first paycheck. Right now, inside the duffel bag were two slightly stained mugs rescued from a trash can at school, two forks and spoons taken from a church dinner when no one was watching, and a dented pot she'd found in the weeds behind a parking lot while waiting for Mrs. Henderson to finish a meeting. There were other things, too—a forgotten beach towel she'd found in a moldy box in the Hendersons' garage, a shiny canister that had once held dog biscuits but had been thrown out when the seal had stretched, and other items, all ready for when she and Hannah were old enough to strike out on their own. Grace wished that time was now.

Face red from exertion, Miss Wanda dropped the duffel bags beside the car and took a deep breath. "There. We're unloaded." She proffered another fake smile. "Smell that fresh air? This is much better than being in the city, isn't it? I think you'll like living with Mrs. Giano."

Grace stared past her to the house, which, despite the cacophony of flowers in the yard, had a tired, baked-in-the-sun air. "That's not a house. It's a shack."

Miss Wanda flushed. "Grace Wheeler, you shut your mouth! Mrs. Giano may not be as well-off as some of the other foster parents, but she has a sufficient income and is very good with the children she takes." The caseworker hesitated and then added in a defensive tone, "I've known Mrs. Giano since I was a little girl. In fact, I'm the one who talked her into being a foster parent. We grew up in the same town, and while she may be a little different, she's kind and smart and . . ." As Miss Wanda's voice trailed off, her gaze moved to the house. After a moment, she added in a murmur, as if talking to herself, "She's special."

Unimpressed, Grace looked at the yard, where the flowers crowded toward the small house as if trying to climb in. One vine had even managed to find a hold on the peeling paint of a clapboard wall and looked like it was tapping on the window. The dogs panted loudly in the quiet, watching them through the cracks in the faded wood fence, their wagging tails stirring the flowers.

Everything was unfamiliar and awkward and new. Grace was tired of new. She wanted something familiar and comfortable, although right now, she couldn't think of anything that was either of those. The urge to run shivered through her. "No. We don't want to stay here."

"Want? Lord, child, you'll be lucky if you're *allowed* to stay. Mrs. Giano's very picky about who she takes."

"She gets to pick?"

Miss Wanda cut Grace a hard look. "They *all* get to pick. Mrs. Giano only allows certain children to stay with her, and then not many. In fact, it's been almost a year since she's had any." The caseworker eyed the open window before adding in a low voice, "We're to go to the porch. Mrs. Giano will come and look at you there."

Grace's chest burned. She knew what Mrs. Giano would see, and it wouldn't be good, at least not for Grace. The red frost hovered overhead. The uncertainty made things worse, freezing her blood while angry, icy strands shot through her body. "I don't care if she looks at us." Grace raised her voice. "*I'm* going to be looking at *her*, too. And I might not like her, so—"

"*Grace!*" the caseworker hissed. "Stop it! If this doesn't work, then—" Miss Wanda cast a meaningful glance at Hannah.

The world stuttered to a sudden halt, locked in place like a too-sharp picture. Grace, still holding Hannah's hand, choked out a ragged "No!"

Genuine pity flashed across Miss Wanda's plump face, the tears in her eyes more frightening than anything she'd said. "I'm sorry, Grace, but that's the way it is. And it's your own fault. This is the third placement in less than a year. My supervisor has had it. I had to beg her to let us try this. This is your last chance."

Hannah looked up at Grace. "What does she mean?"

We'll be separated. I'll go to the group home, and you'll be placed with a family, and we'll never see each other except for holidays, if even then. And you'll grow up without me and we'll no longer feel like sisters, even though we are. That was what Grace should have said. She never lied to Hannah. You didn't lie to the people you loved. But the horribleness of losing Hannah froze Grace's tongue and she could no more answer than she could think.

Her terror must have shown, for Hannah's expression softened into a faraway look as if she had gone to a better place. Humming softly, Hannah began to turn away, her fingers slipping from Grace's.

Loneliness swamped Grace and she gripped her sister's hand tighter. "It will be fine," she said desperately.

Hannah looked back at her, doubt clouding her usually clear blue eyes.

"I *promise*, Hannah." Whatever happened, she would never part from Hannah. Never. *I'll be good. I'll be good. I'll be good.* A huge pressure settled on her chest, the cold red cloud hanging so low that it fluttered over her, tugging painfully. Ignoring it, she looked Miss Wanda right in the eye. "Hannah and I will *make* Mrs. Giano like us."

Relief flickered across the caseworker's doughy face. "Good. That's exactly what needs to happen. I'll do what I can, but it's really up to you." Her gaze softened. "This is a wonderful home, although you'll be changing schools again. Still, you can always make new friends, can't you?"

It wasn't a question, so Grace didn't answer. She didn't have friends. She had nothing in common with the girls in her classes. Their worlds consisted of things Grace had never known, things like birthday cakes, homes they were never forced to move from, and parents who loved them. They didn't know or understand her world, what it felt like to go hungry, to be left alone for days at a time only to be placed into a foster system that tossed her about like a ball in a game. And she was fine with that, because she had Hannah, who was both Grace's sister and her best friend. That was all she needed. Just Hannah.

"Let's go, girls!" Miss Wanda smiled her too-sunny smile as she picked up the duffel bags, grimacing once more at the weight. She swung Hannah's lighter bag over her shoulder and lumbered to the gate, the other bag bumping heavily against her shin. She flipped up the latch and opened the gate. "Go on in."

The dogs crowded forward, tails wagging as Grace and Hannah walked past Miss Wanda and into the small yard. The caseworker closed the gate and then led the way up the cracked concrete sidewalk to the porch, chatting breathlessly and exclaiming over Mrs. Giano's excellent cooking and how much they'd like having so many pets.

Hannah released Grace's hand, cooing at the dogs as she bent down to welcome wet kisses. She loved animals. At times, Grace wondered if her sister loved them more than people. Grace wouldn't blame her if she did.

They climbed the stairs to the porch. It was a rickety place, the porch, but someone had tried to make it pretty. The wood-slatted floor had been painted an ocean blue, and two white wicker chairs filled with plump, colorful pillows sat beneath a window. A small metal table stood between them and held two books, their pages yellowed with age.

While Hannah continued to coo at the dogs, Grace wandered toward the books. She didn't like to read, but as school detention often consisted of writing lines over and over while seated at a cubicle in the school library, she'd seen the title of this one before. It was *James and the Giant Peach*. The second book was fatter, intimidatingly so, the words *Little Women* scrawled over the cover in sweeping gold letters. Grace wondered how little the women were. Were they just short, or were they fairy-size? She hoped they were fairy-size.

Miss Wanda dropped the duffel bags onto the wood porch and fanned her red face with a limp hand. "Good God, Grace, your bag feels like you've got rocks in there. I—" She sniffed the air and instantly brightened. "Bacon! Mrs. Giano must be fixing breakfast."

Grace's stomach growled, but she ignored it and picked up the fat book. She opened it and was surprised to find that it smelled like cake. She wished she could sit in one of these cushioned chairs and read about little, tiny wo—

The screen door banged open and Mrs. Giano stepped outside, a fat orange cat following her.

Mrs. Giano was small and not so young, although her movements were quick like a wren's. She wore a dress printed with so many flowers that if she'd fallen in her own yard, Grace didn't think they would be able to find her.

"Good morning!" Miss Wanda pulled the book from Grace's hand and put it back on the table, then collected Hannah. The caseworker pushed the girls in front of her, her hands as heavy as sandbags on their shoulders. "These are the girls I told you about. Girls, this is Mrs. Giano."

The woman walked toward them, the smell of bacon and pancakes wafting with her. She was short, with black hair so vivid it couldn't be real, and dark, piercing eyes that seemed to see everything at once. Her cat walked with her, ignoring the dogs that were now falling over themselves trying not to make eye contact, as if the fat house cat was a lion in disguise.

"Good morning." Mrs. Giano's voice was as colorful as her clothing, syrup-slow and rich. She stopped in front of them, hands folded, one brow lifted, no smile on her pointed face. "And what are your names?"

"This is Grace. She just turned ten. And this"—Miss Wanda thrust Hannah slightly forward—"is Hannah, who is seven years old."

Mrs. Giano eyed Hannah for a long moment, and Grace waited for the inevitable gushing.

But instead, Mrs. Giano crossed her arms over her narrow chest and said nothing.

Miss Wanda's smile faltered, and she said in a hopeful voice, "Hannah is a wonderful child. Everyone says so. She's never in trouble and has very good manners."

Mrs. Giano bent to examine Hannah more closely.

Hannah returned the look, her distant smile never changing.

Mrs. Giano straightened. "Lord, but you are trouble, aren't you?"

Miss Wanda's eyes widened.

But Hannah's smile just grew. "What's your cat's name?"

"Theo."

"I want to pat him." Hannah reached out her hand.

The cat arched, hissing.

Mrs. Giano didn't look surprised. "Perhaps another time."

Hannah shrugged and turned her attention back to the dogs.

Miss Wanda blinked rapidly. "Mrs. Giano, Hannah is never trouble. It's Grace who—" The caseworker caught herself. "But she promises to be good this time. And she will, won't you, Grace?"

Mrs. Giano's dark gaze moved to Grace.

Grace lifted her chin and stared back, desperately wanting to say something smart or funny that would make this woman like her enough to let them stay. But the more Grace wanted it, the angrier she became.

She hated this.

Hated the feeling she had to plead for food and a place to live.

That she had to beg to exist.

To even breathe.

The longer she and Mrs. Giano locked gazes, the madder Grace got, and the lower the red frost came.

"Stop glaring!" Miss Wanda hissed, her hand tighter on Grace's shoulder.

But Grace couldn't. She was locked in battle, and she wouldn't—couldn't—give up.

Something silky wrapped around her ankle. Startled, she looked down.

Theo blinked up at her as if he understood how worried and furious she was, and how confusing it was to feel both of those things at the same time.

He butted his head against her ankle and purred loudly.

"Well, well." Mrs. Giano smiled. "Theo likes you."

Grace didn't know what to say. She watched the cat twisting around her leg, and she was afraid to pet it for fear it might hiss the way it had at Hannah.

"Mrs. Giano, please," Miss Wanda said in a breathless, desperate tone. "Give them a chance. I promise they're both good girls. Grace just needs a steady home life and she'll—"

"*Pssht.* I can see the girl myself." Mrs. Giano's gaze moved from Grace to the small table where the books rested. "I saw you with the book. So you like to read, do you?"

For a moment, Grace—so desperate for acceptance—thought about lying, but somehow Mrs. Giano's gaze no longer felt so challenging. "I don't like to read," Grace admitted. "I'm not very good at it."

A sliver of a smile crossed Mrs. Giano's narrow face. "You'll get better with practice. I promise."

I promise, the woman had said. That meant Grace would be around longer than ten minutes. A tiny sprout of hope bloomed in her heart, but the frosty haze over her head rippled a stern warning. She'd hoped before and it hadn't helped. She knew from experience that hoping was dangerous and painful.

Don't give in, she reminded herself. Her jaw tightened, and she said in a sharp tone, "I might never like to read, even if I do practice."

Miss Wanda puffed out a muted, anxious noise.

Mrs. Giano's gaze narrowed and then slowly moved from Grace's face to the red frost that hung over her head. The woman's expression softened and she tsked. "That's not good for such a little one, is it?"

Grace didn't know what to say. No one had ever acknowledged the cold mist that followed her. And certainly no one had looked worried about it. "It won't leave."

Mrs. Giano nodded slowly. "It will take some work, but we will make it go away."

Miss Wanda frowned, obviously confused. "Mrs. Giano, what—"

"I'll take them."

Grace's chest eased as air rushed in.

The cat meowed loudly, as if echoing his owner.

Miss Wanda said in a cautious tone, "*Both* of them?"

Mrs. Giano shot the caseworker a hard, impatient glance. "Of course, both." She turned to Grace and Hannah. "Call me Mama G. That's easier than 'Giano.' Now, come in and have breakfast. I made scrambled eggs, bacon, and biscuits. All of us should eat, except"— she pointed a finger at one of the dogs—"you. You stole some of my bacon from the counter, so you will eat last."

The dog, a spotted mongrel with one ragged ear, didn't seem surprised to have been singled out. In fact, Grace thought he looked almost embarrassed. Ears down, tail hesitantly wagging, he went to the end of the porch and lay down in a spot of sun as if resigned to his fate.

Inside, a bell dinged. "Ah. The biscuits are ready."

As soon as Mama Giano mentioned "biscuits," the air was filled anew with the rich scent, as if it had been waiting inside for its cue.

"I'd better get them before they burn. Come on in." The screen door slammed behind her as she disappeared into the cool darkness of her home.

Theo, his green eyes locked on Grace's face, wound back and forth around her legs as she stared at the door, her heart aching in a new, unfamiliar way. She wanted so badly to believe everything she'd seen so far. That this place might really be different. That she and Hannah had finally found a place to stay that would last longer than a few months.

Life had taught Grace that that was unlikely, even impossible, but her bones ached with how so, *so* much she wanted it to be true.

Miss Wanda puffed out a heavy sigh of relief. "That went better than I'd hoped, although—" Her gaze flickered to Hannah, and she seemed on the verge of blurting out something. But after a moment's struggle, she shook her head and forced a bright smile. "I'll get Hannah's bag. Grace, you can carry yours."

Grace left the cat and got her duffel bag, half dragging it beside her, the pot clanging against the cups. She moved slowly, lingering so that she was well behind Miss Wanda and Hannah.

As soon as the screen door closed behind them, Grace dropped the bag and looked around. The cushioned chairs beckoned while the fluttering breeze played with the nodding flowers. The scent of bacon and biscuits made her stomach ache with something other than sadness.

The cat sauntered around the now-dozing dog and came to sit beside Grace. He leaned against her, warm and fluffy, his orange silk fur soft against her leg. The slow twitch of his tail and the deep purr rumbling from his chest made the moment sweet.

Grace closed her eyes and lifted her face to the spill of sunlight that slanted under the porch roof. "We are going to be okay," she whispered.

For once, she wasn't saying it to make herself or Hannah feel better.

This time, she meant it.

Calm settled over Grace, unfamiliar and rare, yet as warm and comforting as a towel fresh from the dryer. It wrapped around her, easing her heart and softening her anger.

It would be years before she figured out what the delicious feeling was, but every day after, she would remember it as clearly as if it were still there. For it had been in that moment there, on the porch of Mama G's small, weathered clapboard house as it baked in the morning summer sun, a fat cat leaning against her leg, that Grace discovered what it felt like to come home.

CHAPTER 1

Grace

DOVE POND, NC
MAY 16, 2019

"Are we there yet?" Daisy asked.

"No," Grace said for the eighth time, her eyes locked on the moving truck that slowly rumbled along in front of her Honda. Every side of the ancient truck bore the words MCLAREN'S YOU NEED TO MOVE WE CAN DO IT, LLC.

Mama G, in the front beside Grace, looked over the seat at Daisy. "We just passed the 'Welcome to Dove Pond' sign, so it won't be long now."

"We've been driving *forever*." Daisy slumped, twirling her ponytail with restless fingers, a habit she'd picked up during the past few difficult months.

Daisy was a precocious child, this daughter of Hannah's and an unknown boy from her high school. Even at the tender age of eight, Daisy was an odd, old-souled sort of kid, all elbows and knees, blurting what she thought no matter how bold or ill-advised. She was smart too, perhaps even brilliant, according to her test scores, and she could read well above her level, devouring books the way most kids her age devoured cartoons. Despite that, the child made only mediocre grades, as she was easily distracted, she and her restless mind. *Just like her mother.*

Grace looked at Daisy in the rearview mirror, noting the blond hair and crystal-blue eyes. *Oh, Hannah, you would be so proud of her.* Grace's throat tightened and she forced herself to focus on the truck they followed.

Mama G looked up from her knitting to admire the large maples and elms that dotted the streets. "I love these trees." She sighed happily, then returned her attention to the mittens she was making.

Shortly after Grace and Hannah had come to live with Mama G, she'd taken up knitting, saying it "calmed the nerves." Grace thought that was strange, because no one had a more peaceful spirit than Mama G. Over the years, she'd made hundreds of scarves and mittens, most of which had ended up in Grace's room, as Hannah had never liked them.

Grace glanced over at Mama G now. Her once-graceful hands were liver spotted and gnarled, but they never stopped moving. Normally, Mama G's rhythmic knitting sent a flood of calm through Grace, but today it did nothing.

Right now, everything felt useless, empty. *Broken.*

Grace swallowed the lump in her throat and applied the brakes as the moving truck slowed in front of her. "We should be turning onto Elm Street soon."

As if in answer to her prayers, the truck's signal flashed and the vehicle slowly turned.

"Almost there." Grace admired the rows of elms that shaded the road. "Our new house is at the end of this street." *New* meaning "recently rented." She silently ticked through her Things That Must Be Done list: unpack, register Daisy for school, find a caretaker for Mama G—the list seemed endless, and she winced to think about the shrinking amount left in her bank accounts. The events of the past few months had murdered her savings. But by Grace's careful calculations, if they lived frugally over the next year, they would have enough for a down payment on a small house in Charlotte.

The thought of returning to Charlotte calmed Grace. For the past five years, she'd worked at a large financial company in one of the city's trendier areas. She'd been happy there and, until the craziness of the past few months, she'd never thought she'd leave.

But she'd go back, and this time she'd take Mama G and Daisy. It wouldn't be easy, but it would happen. She would make sure of it.

Behind her, Daisy leaned against her window and stared at the houses rolling past. The street was long and wide, the sidewalks shaded by the towering trees. The quality of the houses perched along the way gave Grace hope. Huge and ornate, the grand old lady houses flaunted a variety of pastel colors. Windows glinting in the afternoon sunshine, they gazed at one another with sleepy, lace-fluttered windows and wide, white-trimmed porches.

It looks like a safe neighborhood, and these houses—wow! Perhaps this will all work out. Hope blossomed, so Grace—ever cautious—tried to tamp it down, hugging her worries like a shield.

"I like these houses," Daisy said. "I bet they have ghosts. They look like the right kind."

Grace looked at Daisy in the rearview mirror and saw her niece's nose pressed against the window glass. "There is no such thing as ghosts."

Her mouth instantly tight with anger, Daisy said in a sullen tone, "How would you know?"

Grace had to clamp her mouth over a sharp reply. Just a week ago, Mama G had warned Grace to pick her battles with Daisy, and this wasn't a hill worth dying on.

It still hurt, though. And Grace was never sure if she was giving up some sort of authority by not reprimanding Daisy about things like tone of voice and eye rolls. *I don't know a darn thing about raising kids. Not one. Yet now, here I am.*

Until two months ago, Grace's position in Daisy's life had been "Favorite Aunt" and nothing else. Grace had loved being the FA, who breezed into town like Mary Poppins, beloved by everyone as she bestowed presents and took Mama G and Daisy on all sorts of fun adventures. *Those were the days*, she thought wistfully. But things were different now. *Everything has changed.*

Daisy muttered to herself, "I *like* ghosts."

Grace tightened her grip on the steering wheel. It was silly to argue about something as ridiculous as ghosts, but she didn't want Daisy afraid to sleep at night because of every old-house thump and creak. For all of Daisy's bravado, she was a sensitive child and suffered from her own overactive imagination.

"Ghosts can be very nice," Mama G said in a thoughtful tone. "The ones I've met were, anyway."

Daisy leaned toward the front seat as far as her seat belt would let her. "You've met ghosts? Were they—"

"She's joking, of course," Grace interrupted. She wished Mama G wouldn't encourage Daisy's flights of fancy.

"Mama G, tell Aunt Grace you aren't joking," Daisy said in a belligerent tone. "Tell her that you've seen ghosts."

Grace swallowed a sigh. Parenting was damned hard. If you weren't being scoffed at, you were being challenged. But then again, maybe it was only difficult because she sucked at it. Part of the problem was that while she wasn't really Daisy's mother, Grace'd also lost her standing as the Favorite Aunt. Right now, neither she nor Daisy was quite sure what Grace was, except inexperienced.

Loneliness swamped Grace, seeping into her soul like icy water. Growing up, no matter how badly life had treated her and Hannah, they'd had each other. Even when, at seventeen years of age, rebellious Hannah had run away, leaving four-month-old Daisy with Mama G, she'd kept in touch with Grace. Grace had been in college, neck-deep in tests and papers and fighting for her place on the dean's list, but she'd been ridiculously grateful for Hannah's scarce text messages and rare phone calls, even though 90 percent of them had been requests for money. Still, those tiny contacts had made Grace feel that she and Hannah were still a family. But more than that, they'd allowed Grace to pretend that things were okay. That Hannah was okay, even though she wasn't.

Two months and eleven days ago, Hannah had died, her life burned to a crisp by her own wild spirits. And Grace, still pretending things were "okay," hadn't been ready. There was a hole in her life now, one she didn't know how to fill. Somehow, in losing her sister, she'd also lost all the hopes she'd been clinging to that, with time and love, Hannah would stop wandering the world like a lost soul, chasing dangerous men and even more dangerous thrills. That one day, she'd come home, realize how much she missed Grace and Mama G, and how special Daisy was, and she'd welcome them all back into her life. That they'd finally become the family Grace had always so desperately wanted them to be.

Hannah's death had left Grace aching, angry, and empty. But it was even harder for Daisy. The little girl had loved her beautiful but distant mother with an obstinate, uncritical passion. For weeks after the funeral, she'd refused to go to school, staying in bed unless forced to get up, arguing about everything with everybody. It had taken all of Mama G's considerable influence to convince Daisy to return to her classroom. But once there, the child had been sullen and silent, ignoring her friends and teachers alike. She did no homework and when the time came to take a test, instead of answering the problems, she filled the paper with drawings of furious dragons spewing fire. Had her previous grades not been so high and her teachers so understanding, she might have failed.

The school counselor had warned Grace that the next few months, and perhaps longer, would be difficult and that it would be normal for Daisy to continue to "act out," at least for a while. Despite the warning, Daisy's sudden flares of anger and her stubborn refusal to accept Grace as a parent had made a difficult situation even worse.

But more than anyone else, Grace understood anger. What was difficult was seeing the sheer pain that lurked behind every sharp word that tumbled from Daisy's mouth and being unable to do anything to help.

Grace gripped the steering wheel harder, torn between a growing anger at Hannah for being so careless with herself, even though it had cost others, and also desperate to tell her how much she'd been loved. *Everyone loved you, Hannah. Everyone except you.*

"Ghosts aren't always bad, you know," Mama G mused aloud as she pulled a length of yarn from her knitting basket.

"Mama G, please. Don't."

Mama G nodded. "I know what you're thinking, but ghosts are nothing like the silliness people put in horror movies. Ghosts aren't scary at all. They're just wisps of lives gone by. Shadows, really."

"What do they look like?" Daisy asked before Grace could change the subject.

Mama G stopped knitting and pursed her lips. "Sometimes they're a faint shape. And sometimes they're just a memory that flickers out of the corner of your eye."

"I'm going to meet one," Daisy announced. "I'm going to find out how she died so I can help her find her murderer."

"Most ghosts weren't murdered," Mama G said calmly, pulling more yarn from her basket. "Most died in their sleep."

Grace knew what would happen now. Daisy, always too excitable, wouldn't be able to sleep and it would be Grace, and not Mama G, who'd have to handle it. "Ghosts don't exist," Grace repeated firmly. *"At all."* She wished the moving truck would find the house. It was barely creeping along, and she had no wish to continue this conversation.

Mama G didn't look up from her knitting, but said under her breath, "Well, well. *Someone* is in for a surprise."

"It's not going to be me," Grace said baldly. "Mama G, the likelihood of— Ah! Here we are!" *Thank God.* She slapped a smile on her face and was about to say something ridiculous like *Welcome home!* when the house came into view.

Grace's hopes were instantly and viciously smashed.

Although as beautiful and gracious in design as its neighbors, the house at the end of the driveway was a faded shadow of the others. The pale lavender color was now more gray than purple, the wide porch was crooked, and much of the delightful trim she'd seen on the other houses was missing, the paint chipped and peeling. Grace was reminded of a jaded old woman wearing a faded housecoat, her worn smile marred by missing teeth.

"I bet this house has ghosts," Daisy said.

"Oh, I'm sure there's more than one," Mama G agreed as she stored her knitting in her basket.

Dear God, please keep me from screaming. Grace drove past the moving truck, which had pulled close to the walk, and parked her car beside a large, rusty RV that sat at the rear of the driveway near a garage with a deeply dented door. She put the car in park and stared up at the house, noting the thick moss that clung to the roof.

Mama G patted Grace's hand where it rested on the steering wheel. "The car's still running."

"I know." She wondered what would happen if they just stayed where they were, locked safely away. The car wasn't large, but it was big enough to sleep in if they lowered the seats and had pillows and blankets and—

"Look!" Daisy opened her door. "There's a tire swing in the tree in the front yard."

Mama G nodded. "I saw that. You'll have to give it a try and see how high you can swing."

"Daisy, wait." Grace leaned forward and tried to see the swing. "Don't get on it yet. I want to be sure it's safe before you—"

It was too late. Daisy had already jumped out and was headed for the swing.

"I'll get her." Mama G climbed out of the car and started to follow Daisy but then stopped. She leaned down to look at Grace, where she sat glued in the driver's seat. "Come inside. It may need a little work, but it's a lovely house."

"It's a wreck," Grace said flatly.

Mama G smiled, although it was a tired, worn effort. "Grace, I know this is difficult for you—"

"For all of us."

Mama G's gaze softened. "Right now, life isn't fair for any of us. We're all three mad at life, at all of this change—maybe even at Hannah."

Grace's throat tightened.

Mama G sat back in the passenger seat and placed her hand over Grace's. "You have to let it go. All of it—your anger, your worries, your fears. Daisy is counting on you. And, as much as I hate to add to your problems, so am I."

Grace grasped Mama G's hand and squeezed it. "I owe you a thousand years of being counted on."

Mama G smiled sadly. "Unfortunately, I think you're about to pay them all back at once. But we have to move forward, sweetheart. And we can't do that if we hold on to what was."

"I'm not holding on to anything."

"Not on purpose, perhaps. But you are in other ways. And so am I, and so is Daisy. It's tough letting go of something you only thought you had, and that's what Hannah was—she was a maybe. A possibly. A perhaps. She knew how to make people hope that she was more than she was ever willing to be."

Grace didn't think she'd ever heard a better description of Hannah. Still, it was who Hannah was, who she'd always been. Tears burned Grace's eyes. "She never came to visit and rarely called, but I miss her. It's so weird. It's—" She swiped the tears from her eyes.

"I know." Mama G patted Grace's hand. "Everything is going to be all right."

"I wish I believed that."

Mama G chuckled. "Always the skeptic, aren't you? Even when you were a child. But look. We came to Dove Pond for a new start. If we decide to, we'll find happiness here. I know we will. This town is . . . well, it's different. And this is where we're supposed to be. I'm sure of it."

Her throat too tight to answer, Grace managed a short nod, although she wished she felt sure about something—anything, really.

Mama G sighed and pulled her hand from Grace's. "Come in when you're ready." She slid back out of the car and started to straighten, but then hesitated.

Grace's heart sank anew at the flicker of uncertainty in Mama G's usually serene face. It took all her strength not to let her voice break as she said softly, "You were going to see to Daisy. She went to the swing."

Mama G's face cleared. "Oh yes. Daisy." She nodded as if that was all she needed to hear, but her face was pink with embarrassment. With a few mumbled words, she walked away, the car door hanging open in her wake.

Grace bent over the steering wheel and rubbed her aching temples. Mama G's memory was getting worse. A month ago, Grace had found her standing in the middle of the road in front of her own home, the mail clutched forgotten in her hands as she looked around, confused and unaware that she was less than forty feet from her front door.

Warm, humid summer air swirled inside from the open door. Grace closed her eyes, remembering the neat, wonderful life she'd led only a few short months ago when she'd stupidly thought she had figured out life, success, happiness—everything. But all that had changed with one phone call from a weeping Mama G, whose every other word had been "Hannah."

Grace had gone back to Mama G's house and together they'd organized the funeral and tried to untangle the mess that had been

Hannah's life. While there, Grace had slowly realized that Mama G wasn't herself. She kept forgetting things, items had been left in odd places, and doctor's appointments were made and missed. After finding Mama G looking so confused in front of her own house, Grace had taken her to the doctor, who'd confirmed that the always-strong, never-wavering Mama G was showing signs of Alzheimer's.

Grace's heart, already broken by Hannah's death, had shattered. Mama G was the rock Grace had built her life upon. And now, quite suddenly, it was Grace's turn to make things work and to take care of not just Mama G, but the recalcitrant Daisy as well. Grace only hoped she was strong enough to do both.

At first, she'd hoped she could pack them up and take them to Charlotte with her, but it had taken no more than ten minutes of honest face-the-music thought for her to realize that she couldn't continue to work eighty hours a week as a financial analyst, raise a devastated and angry Daisy, *and* take care of Mama G, all at one and the same time. No matter how many times Grace ran the numbers, the reality was grim but clear.

So, broken but unbowed, Grace had quit her dream job, cashed in her retirement plan, paid off her lease, and moved back home to look after what was left of her small, tattered family.

She needed a new job, of course, something with far more flexibility than her previous position. While she'd been searching, one of Mama G's cousins, a sharp-tongued woman by the name of Mrs. Philomedra Phelps, had called Grace and offered her the job of Town Clerk Level 1 for Dove Pond, North Carolina, Mama G's old hometown. The position was well below Grace's skill level, but offered the flexible hours she desperately needed. Attached to the offer was the rental of Mrs. Phelps's own home at a ridiculously low amount, as she was retiring to Florida.

Grace hadn't wanted to move, for the salary was dismal. But two days after Mrs. Phelps's phone call, a big storm had blown through Whitlow and Mama G's ancient house had sprung what seemed like a hundred leaks. Almost every pot in the house had been called into service to catch the water as it dripped through the eaves and dissolved the ceiling plaster, raining wet, soggy clumps onto Mama G's furniture and rugs. When the repairman came to assess the damage, the burly man had reluctantly informed Grace that the old, rickety clapboard house was past fixing.

The day after this bleak news, the dementia specialist overseeing Mama G's care made a chance comment that brought Grace back to Mrs. Phelps's offer. While discussing treatment options, the specialist mentioned how she'd taken her own mother back to her hometown after she'd been similarly diagnosed and that it had seemed to ease the decline, at least a little.

The doctor hadn't offered the comment as a cure, and indeed, she hadn't mentioned it more than once, but the words had caught Grace's attention. After a long and sleepless night, Grace had called Mrs. Phelps and accepted the job.

And now, here they were, moving from Mama G's worn-out house and into another ramshackle eyesore in the picturesque town of Dove Pond.

Grace wished for the thousandth time that this was all a dream and she'd wake up to everything the way it had been, that Hannah was alive and Daisy not so angry, Mama G's memory not chipping away like old paint, and—

Someone knocked on the window. Two men peered at her through the glass. The big man in gray overalls was mover Ricky Bob McLaren, his brown hair slicked to one side as if his comb only worked in one direction. She knew who he was because of the large patch on his shirt. At his side was his helper, a short, round, bearded man with the name TOMMY emblazoned on his much smaller patch.

Ricky Bob pointed to the truck, then to the house, and then back to the truck.

Tommy, as if helping his boss, mimicked the movements, but in an exaggerated fashion.

Grace rolled down the window. "Yes?"

Ricky Bob held out his hand. "We'll need the house keys."

"Mrs. Phelps should still be home." Grace turned off the car and climbed out. "I'll find her. She—"

"There you are," spoke a brisk, sharp voice, followed by a clanking noise that gave Grace visions of Scrooge's Marley. From around the moving truck, a squat, iron-haired woman in a flowered shirt and khaki shorts appeared. She leaned heavily to one side, carrying a tote filled with bottles of margarita mix and tequila, which clanged with each step. The old woman scowled at Grace. "You said you'd be here by three."

"I said we'd be here *around* three," Grace corrected, adding a smile to soften her words. "It's barely three thirty."

"Which is thirty minutes late. I have hours to drive and a schedule to keep." The woman walked past Grace, the bag of bottles hanging dangerously close to the cracked driveway.

Ricky Bob and Tommy scrambled to get out of her way, scattering like chickens seeing a fox.

Grace swallowed a sharp retort. "The moving men need the house keys."

Mrs. Phelps rolled her eyes. "The doors are unlocked."

"Thank you," the men mumbled as they hurried off.

Grace watched as they made their way into the house, glad to see Mama G and Daisy leave the swing and follow them inside. Grace felt safer knowing they were indoors.

Mrs. Phelps clanked her way toward the ancient RV. "I never lock the doors and Ricky Bob knows that, but then he's an idiot." She set the tote on the ground beside the passenger door of the rusty vehicle. "He was a sight smarter when he was fifteen, if you can believe it. But not now. Too much football. That boy's had more concussions than most people have had colds."

"I was told he was a good mover."

"Better than most, providing you keep the instructions simple." Mrs. Phelps looked Grace up and down. "My, look at you. Where are you going that you're so dressed up?"

Grace looked down at her sundress and sandals, both of which were better suited for a day out in Charlotte's tony Myers Park district than here in tiny Dove Pond. "It's part of my strategy to win the world. You know—dress for the life you want, not the life you have."

"If you dress like that in town hall, you'll be the only one seeing it. The mayor only comes in for a few hours a day, if that. So, other than tax season, you'll be pretty much alone." Mrs. Phelps opened the passenger door, placed her tote on the floorboard, then slammed the door closed. "That's it, then. I'd better get on the road. I scheduled a pee break at seven o'clock, as I should be near Atlanta by then, and you don't want to get caught in traffic and need to pee."

Grace managed to keep her smile, but barely. "You're very organized. That bodes well for my taking on your old job. I'd like to talk about that, as the job description was vague. To be honest, I'm not exactly sure what the town clerk does."

"Every damn thing," Mrs. Phelps said baldly. She walked around the front of the RV to the driver's door, Grace following. "You'll process business licenses, voter registrations, and tax and fee payments. You'll figure it out."

Grace hoped the older woman was right. "I'll call if I have questions. But before you leave, about the house. It's . . . um. Not good. It's in worse shape than I expected."

Mrs. Phelps stopped by the driver's door. "She's solid. Everything works. As we discussed on the phone, I left some of the larger pieces of furniture for you. The rest is stored in the garage, so if you decide you want to use it, just help yourself. You're welcome to it."

"Thank you. I'm worried about the porch, though. It looks crooked."

Mrs. Phelps fixed her icy button-bright gaze on Grace and lifted her thick eyebrows. "That porch has been crooked as long as I've been breathing, and it hasn't fallen off the house yet. So long as you don't load it up with a hundred or more fat people, it should stand for another hundred and fifty years." Mrs. Phelps regarded Grace with suspicion. "You don't plan on doing that, do you? Load it up with fat people? When we spoke on the phone, you said you weren't a partier."

"I'm not, and I don't plan on loading the porch with anyone. I—" Grace bit off the rest of her sentence and took a steadying breath. "I would like to have someone check it out."

Mrs. Phelps looked as if she wanted to argue, but a quick glance at her wristwatch made her snap out a reluctant, "Fine! There's a business card for the Callahan brothers in the kitchen drawer by the stove. They own a handyman business and can fix just about anything. Call them and have them look at it. If they think something needs doing, they'll know who to bill."

"Great. Thank you."

Mrs. Phelps opened the driver's-side door, revealing a large, cracked-leather captain's chair. She hauled herself inside, plopped into the seat, and slammed the door before saying out the open window, "As I told you on the phone, everything is included in the rent but yard care. Better watch that. If you don't keep it up, you'll have one of the Dove sisters on your ass about it, and you don't want that."

"The Dove sisters?"

"They live there." Mrs. Phelps nodded up the street.

Grace turned to look. Two houses from them sat what must have been the largest house in Dove Pond. Painted a bold mauve and decorated with more than a usual amount of ornate white trim, it towered over its not-so-small neighbors. But it was the yard that stole all the glory. The grass was a deep, velvety green like that of a golf course, but it was a mere background for the hundreds—no, *thousands*—of flowers that bloomed in meticulously kept beds around the house, down the walkway, around each tree, and along the street. "That belongs on a movie set," Grace murmured.

"They keep the place up," Mrs. Phelps admitted in a grudging tone. "Unfortunately, they're busybodies and will notice if you don't mow."

Grace imagined white-haired crones with hooked noses yelling about the height of the grass and demanding that people pick up after their pets. *Great.* "I can't abide rudeness."

"They aren't rude. More likely to kill you with kindness, which annoys the crap out of me even more than rudeness. And they're always watching." Mrs. Phelps eyed the mauve house with obvious distaste. "I don't see 'em now. Probably at work. The oldest is never home, as she has her own business. But the youngest, Sarah, is the town librarian, and she's always at the fence between her house and the one next door talking to Travis Parker. He lives there." Mrs. Phelps nodded at the smaller, neat-looking yellow house that served as a buffer between her house and the Doves'.

"I hope he's a good neighbor."

"Not bad," Mrs. Phelps said, although she didn't seem happy about it. "Although I can't stand his damn motorcycle, which he drives like a bat out of hell. He has long hair and tattoos up both arms, but he's a veteran, so I guess that's okay. The house used to be his father's, who died a year or so ago. Trav mostly keeps to himself, which is good."

Well, that didn't sound too bad. Except for the motorcycle. She hoped it wasn't too noisy.

"Damn it, look at the time! I've got to go." Mrs. Phelps started the RV, which belched a puff of black smoke before settling into a rumbly hum. "Call if you have more questions. You have my number."

"I will. Did you say goodbye to Mama G? She was in the front yard when you came out."

Mrs. Phelps's face softened. "We spoke. She seemed fine at first, talking about the house and the memories she had of it, but then I asked why you all had moved here, and she couldn't remember. Like it had just slipped out of her mind, a big thing like that."

"It's been happening more often."

"Inna was always the smartest one in the room, too. It's hard to see her like that. She could make me laugh, even when I felt like the world was about to end." Mrs. Phelps's blue eyes grew shiny and she fished in her pocket for a wadded tissue. "It's not so obvious when you talk to her on the phone, but in person . . . Damn." She wiped her eyes and blew her nose before saying in a husky voice, "Take care of her, will you?"

"I will. I need to find someone to watch after her when I'm at work."

"Linda Robinson." Mrs. Phelps tossed the tissue into the empty ashtray. "She's good. Her husband, Mark, works at the post office, so just go in and ask. He'll put you in touch with her."

Grace nodded. She tried to think of something else to ask Mrs. Phelps, but nothing came.

This was it, then. And yet Grace hated to let the old woman leave. As prickly as she was, once Mrs. Phelps left, the move to Dove Pond would be official.

Finite.

Permanent.

No, not permanent, Grace told herself briskly. *I have a plan, and if everything goes right, then in a year we'll move to Charlotte and start fresh.*

She took a deep breath. It felt good to have a goal for the future firmly in mind. It allowed her to look past the dreary, harsh realities of her present-day situation, and focus on a brighter and better future. Still, her feet didn't move away from the RV. "Good luck in Florida."

"Thanks." Mrs. Phelps looked down the tree-lined street. "I'm going to miss this place. I'd stay here, but my kids moved away, so . . ." She straightened her shoulders as if pushing off pounds of regrets. "Can't spoil my grandbabies unless I'm there. My daughter's mother-in-law has already moved there, and she's had free rein for far too long."

"Ah. You're going to stop her."

"Stop her? Hell no! I'm going to join her. Two grandmothers are better than one. Evelyn is a hoot, too. We plan on joining a line-dance class together, maybe even try belly dancing." Mrs. Phelps chuckled. "My daughter won't know what's hit her."

"I'm sure she'll be glad you're there."

"She'd better be. This move is costing me plenty." Mrs. Phelps revved her engine and removed her arm from the window. "Enjoy Dove Pond!"

Grace stepped back. "We will. We'll take care of—"

But she was speaking to the side of the RV, as Mrs. Phelps was already moving. The old woman maneuvered the creaky vehicle past Grace's Honda, around the moving truck, and then—with a speed that belied its massive size—whisked the lumbering vehicle down the drive.

Grace had never been more jealous of a rusty old RV in her life. What she would have given to speed away from this derelict house and the dismal year that lay ahead. *If it weren't for Daisy and Mama G, I'd pay someone to take my place. Or I would if I could afford it.*

But she couldn't, which was why they were here now, she and Mama G and Daisy, all three of them washed up onshore, shipwrecked victims in Hannah's destructive wake. *Oh, Hannah, why did you—*

"Grace?" Mama G appeared from around the moving truck, her brow furrowed with worry. "The movers are asking where to put things and I don't know what to tell them."

Grace took a deep breath and forced a smile. "Let's go see what they need." She slipped an arm around Mama G's thin shoulders and they walked back to the house.

Once inside, she settled Mama G and her knitting onto a lumpy, peach-colored divan that had been left in the front sitting room and then went to speak to the movers.

As Grace walked through the rooms, she took stock of their new home. The inside of the house matched the outside—both were lopsided and faded, with hints of long-ago grandeur. The floor was made of wide pine planks that had been scuffed by the rubber and leather soles of a thousand feet. At one time, the plastered walls must have been a golden color, but over the years, in places where the sun hit, pale yellow patches had bloomed. The light fixtures were wrought-iron relics of a time gone by and in need of a thorough cleaning. A wide staircase with a decorative handrail arose from the foyer to the second floor, and Grace could hear Daisy's quick footfalls overhead as she went from room to room. Here and there were the large, surprisingly ornate pieces of furniture Mrs. Phelps had left in the house—the long, peach-colored divan Mama G was now perched upon, a pair of green-velvet-covered chairs that looked as if they belonged on a movie set, and a cupboard that filled one corner of the sitting room all the way to the ten-foot ceiling.

Grace joined the moving men where they stood beside the cocoon of tape and blankets that protected her dining room table.

"It won't fit," Ricky Bob announced. "At least not with that in here." He nodded to a huge walnut buffet Mrs. Phelps had left behind. The monstrosity lined one wall and looked more appropriate for a castle.

"We can put the table against the far wall." Tommy scratched his jaw. "But it'll be tight, so your funk shoe might be off-kilter."

Ricky Bob snorted. "Tommy, I done told you about a million times it's 'fang sway,' not 'funk shoe.'" He stripped off the tape that held the blankets in place over the table's delicate surface and then he and his assistant folded the cotton covers and placed them in a neat pile. "I suppose we could move this buffet to another room, if you want."

Grace picked up the blankets. "It's huge, so I doubt it'll fit anywhere else. Just leave it there. The table will be fine against the wall."

"Interested in selling those blankets? I can pay you five dollars each and help you make back the money they cost you."

Grace's arms tightened around the covers. "No, thank you. I'll need them when I move again. We're only staying a year."

Ricky Bob looked surprised at this, but soon he and Tommy headed back out to the truck while Grace stashed the blankets inside the built-in corner cupboard in the living room. When she finished, she returned to where her table sat, the late-afternoon sun slanting over the gleaming mahogany. She trailed her fingers over the satiny surface, glad to see that it had survived the move unscathed.

The dining room set had been her first purchase after she'd gotten her dream job. It meant a lot to her, although Ricky Bob was right— it was too big for this room. She placed her hand flat on the glossy waxed surface, the wood warm against her fingers. If she were smart, she'd sell this table and get something smaller. But she couldn't give it up. She'd given up so much already. Too much.

A flash of red appeared at the corners of her eyes, and she gritted her teeth against it. It had been years since she'd had to fight her demons. Mama G's love and calmness, along with the steady drumbeat of success, had done much to banish the red-hot anger that used to consume Grace. But Hannah's death had brought a hint of Grace's fury back, and she hated it.

Daisy ran down the stairs, her tennis shoes bouncing off each step. Grace left the table and went into the sitting room, happy to find her niece twirling at the bottom of the steps, her mood lighter than before.

From the divan, Mama G tapped her foot as if she could hear the invisible music. "Lord, child, you do like to dance."

Encouraged, Daisy danced faster, looking just like her mother, blond and serene. But where Hannah could look right through you until you felt lonely and cold, Daisy's gaze was personal and direct, even when she was mad at the world.

Panting from her exertions, Daisy plopped onto the floor beside Mama G. The little girl leaned her head back and, still breathing hard, reached up to touch the sunbeam that poured through one of the front windows, as if trying to catch the golden dust motes that spun in the light.

Grace smiled, caught in the unexpected peacefulness of the moment. Daisy was a warrior, this child of misfortune whose father had denied her and whose mother hadn't been able to do more than hug her and leave, over and over again until they'd all been exhausted. But that had been Hannah—she'd disengaged from her pain until there'd been nothing left of her to give to her own child. *Or anyone else.*

Ricky Bob and Tommy thumped back and forth through the house, arguing with one another the entire time. They carried in side tables, an armoire, boxes of Daisy's books, and finally a plump blue recliner that clashed horribly with the vibrant green chairs Mrs. Phelps had left behind. "Please put it here." Grace pointed to an empty spot beside the fireplace. As soon as the recliner was in place, Grace patted the armrest. "Look, Mama G. Your favorite chair."

Mama G didn't need two invitations. "That divan is as lumpy as a stack of firewood." She settled into the chair with a sigh of relief, her eyes twinkling as she smiled up at Grace. "You'd think with all the padding on my ass, I wouldn't need such stuffed cushions, but lord, this feels good."

Daisy, who'd brought Mama G's knitting basket, giggled.

Even Grace had to laugh. "We all deserve comfortable chairs."

Mama G smiled indulgently. But as Grace watched, the older woman's smile slipped, and she looked around the room as if searching for a memory that had just skittered out of sight. "We are . . ." Her voice, which used to be so crisp and firm, started to quaver, much like her hands. "I used to know this place."

Grace patted Mama G's shoulder. "We're in Dove Pond at Philomedra Phelps's house. She just left. Remember?"

Mama G blinked. "Oh. Oh yes." She surveyed the room as if seeing it for the first time. "I hope she'll cook us some spaghetti. I never could make sauce the way she did, although mine's pretty good."

"Your sauce is better than good," Daisy said. "It's perfect."

The loud rumble of a motorcycle outside caught Grace's attention. She left Mama G and Daisy talking about the merits of spaghetti sauce and went to the front window.

Grace pushed aside the lace curtain. Sunlight lit the front yard, gleaming through the trees to sprawl in golden patches on the green grass. The rumble drew closer, and a red-and-silver streak flashed down the street. The bike slowed and then turned into the driveway next door. *This must be Travis Parker.*

Grace leaned forward so she could see him a little better. Broad-shouldered and as powerfully built as a cage fighter, the man wore a white T-shirt and jeans with effortless ease. He parked the bike next to his walkway, kicked the stand into place, and climbed off. He removed his helmet and long, dark hair spilled almost to his shoulders, in odd contrast to the harsh lines of his face. *Oh great, of all the neighbors in the world, I get Khal Drogo.*

He pulled his hand impatiently through his hair, hung his helmet on his bike, and then walked toward his house. He paused as he neared the door and turned to stare across his yard, as if looking for something. The sunlight hit his face and she caught sight of a thick red scar that ran up his neck to disappear under his five-o'clock shadow on one cheek.

I wonder what happened? A motorcycle wreck, no doubt.

He cupped his hands to his mouth. "Killer!" he yelled.

Killer? Alarmed, Grace looked in the direction he stared, waiting to see the hellhound worthy of such a name.

The man called again, more loudly this time. But nothing happened, and after a moment, he shrugged and went inside.

So that was her neighbor. And Killer, too. *If that dog comes even close to Daisy, we're going to have some words.* Mrs. Phelps had said Travis Parker was the keep-to-himself type, and Grace could only hope the old woman was right. Judging from the deeply carved lines on his face, the khal didn't look as if he was what one might call "good-natured."

She was starting to turn away from the window when a blue pickup truck pulled into the drive that curled up to the Dove house. Intrigued, Grace pushed the curtain farther back and was surprised to see that the woman who climbed out of the truck wasn't an ancient crone at all, but was Grace's age or perhaps even younger. The woman had dark blond hair that was tied in a messy braid that flopped over her shoulder, and she wore a floaty, gauzy dress and sandals.

She reached into the back seat, pulled out a stack of books, and used her shoulder to shut the truck door. She'd just started up the walk toward her house when she stopped and looked down at the books and began scolding them as if they were alive.

Grace blinked. *Good God. I'm surrounded by loonies. Biker Khal Drogo next door and hippie Hermione Granger in the house after that.*

The woman patted the top book on the stack and started up the flower-lined walkway to her door. She'd just reached the steps when, with a sudden swivel, she looked directly at Grace. A delighted smile broke over her face, and she waved.

Startled, Grace jumped back and released the curtain, her face hot. As she turned, she found Mama G's gaze locked on her.

"See something interesting?"

"No," Grace lied.

"You should go and say hi." When Grace shook her head, Mama G tsked. "Change never hurt nobody, child. You know that. It's those who can't or won't change who lose."

"I'm hungry." Daisy put down the ball of yarn she'd been winding for Mama G and stood. "I know what I want for dinner."

Relieved by the distraction and hoping to extend Daisy's rare good mood, Grace said, "Let me guess."

Daisy smiled, for the moment looking so much like her old self that Grace's heart lifted. "Okay," Daisy said. "Guess."

"Spinach?"

"No!" Daisy shook her head and then spun in a circle while Mama G's knitting needles settled into their familiar clicking. "Guess again."

Grace pretended to think, relishing this moment of the not-angry Daisy. "Boiled eggs?"

"No, no, no!" Daisy spun a little faster. "Guess *again*!"

"Liver and onions?"

"No, no, no, *no*!" Daisy tilted to one side, too dizzy to stand as she plopped at Mama G's feet, panting heavily. "Pizzzzzaaaaaa!"

Mama G looked up from her knitting. "Pizza?"

"You like pizza," Daisy assured her.

Mama G's smile disappeared, and she said sharply, "I know I like pizza. My momma used to make the best pies. In fact . . ." Mama G looked around the room. "She and my aunt Penelope would make pies in this very house every Sunday night. Philomedra and I would set the table and we'd have the neighbors over and there'd be wine and— Oh, it was so much fun!"

Grace's heart lifted. Perhaps coming back to Mama G's hometown would do her some good, after all. Here, far away from the tatters of their old life, maybe they could find a new one, a better one, one where the world wasn't ripped in half by the black hole where Hannah used to be.

"Pizza, huh?" Grace threw up her hands as if conceding a victory to the others. "Fine. Pizza it is." With a smile, she went to quiz the movers on the best place to order a delivery. After all the troubles she, Mama G, and Daisy had weathered, they deserved the best pizza Dove Pond had to offer.

It wasn't much, but it was a start.

CHAPTER 2

Sarah

Sarah pulled the huge ring of keys from her pocket and unlocked the door of the Dove Pond Library's book-drop box. She lowered the big metal flap, the heady vanilla old-book scent tickling her nose and making her think of cookies and cake and hours spent under the willow tree in her backyard, reading until the sun slid out of sight.

Sighing happily, she pulled the books out, stacking them on the rim. She had to lean way in to reach the last one, and the second her fingers closed over the cover, the book spoke.

Kym Brummer, the book said thoughtfully, as if the name had just occurred to it.

Kym, the nine-year-old daughter of Miriam Brummer, the principal of Sweet Creek Elementary, was a voracious reader. Sarah looked at the book, which had a picture of a horse with the title *My Friend Flicka* printed across the top. "I read you when I was in elementary school," Sarah murmured. "You think Kym might enjoy you, do you?"

Oh yes, the book replied. *She likes horses.*

"We all do at that age," Sarah said drily as she placed the book on the top of the stack. "She has two books due this afternoon, so I should see her today. I'll make sure she finds you."

The book rustled in thanks.

Sarah patted the book. How she loved being the town librarian. It was odd to think that just a few short years ago she'd had the worst job in the world, selling ads for the *Dove Pond Register*. The position had offered little pay and no future, especially for someone who was never comfortable asking people for money. Selling was not her thing. But books? Oh yes. Books were her thing. And although she'd known that for a long time, it had still taken a while for her to figure out where she belonged.

Four years ago, Dove Pond's long-serving librarian, eighty-nine-year-old Nebbie Farmer, had walked out of her house without the necessary clothing one time too many. The day after Nebbie's chilly stroll down Main Street, Mayor Moore and the Dove Pond Social Club threw the biggest retirement party the town had ever seen. Nebbie, pleased by the large turnout, had gotten happy-weepy as people came, hugged her, ate cake, and shared "Do you remember when Nebbie . . ." stories. There were quite a few of these, as Nebbie had never been what one would call a "conformist."

After the party, Nebbie's daughter drove her mom to the nearby town of Glory, where the retired librarian became the newest resident of the vaunted and well-loved Glory Assisted Living Center. Within the first week, Nebbie had joined no fewer than seven clubs and had found two new best friends, both of whom enjoyed sitting in the buff just as much as she did.

The week after Nebbie's retirement, Mayor Moore listed the librarian's job in the classified section of the *Dove Pond Register*. Sarah, knowing her time at the *Register* was coming to an end one way or another, had half-heartedly applied. She'd had no hope of getting the position, as she was sadly underqualified; she had no experience and her degree was in poetry rather than library science. But to her shock and wonderment, after a cursory interview, she was hired. Later, while drunk as a skunk at the Fourth of July parade, Mayor Moore had let it slip that she'd been the only applicant.

Sarah hadn't cared. She'd gotten the job and loved everything about it—the beckoning smell of the books, the neat rows of shelves, the whispers of a thousand friends who knew her better than her own family. Even the cool, dark basement held treasures, accessible only by the use of two special keys. There, carefully preserved between plastic sheeting, rested the entire dusty history of Dove Pond. As soon as Sarah touched the first ancient document, a land grant dated 1708, which had crackled with age and excitement, she knew she was right where she belonged.

And now, here she was, four years later, getting ready to open the library doors for another exciting day. Still kneeling, she'd just closed the metal door of the drop box and locked it when a fat black cat rubbed against her ankle, pressing so firmly that she teetered for a precarious moment.

"Siegfried!" she admonished as she put a steadying hand on the sidewalk. "You should warn a girl."

Siegfried arched his back and then began to walk in counterclockwise circles.

One.

Two.

Three.

He sat back down, meowing plaintively.

Sarah's smile slipped and she stood, staring down at the cat. It was the sixth day in a row that Siegfried had turned his counterclockwise circles. And he wasn't just doing it in front of the library, but in front of each and every door as he walked down Main Street.

He looked up at her now, mewling loudly.

"You feel it, too, don't you? Something is going to happen." Something good, she hoped.

And oh, how she hoped.

Despite the promises Charlotte Dove's journal had whispered so long ago under the willow tree, the good luck portended by Sarah's birth had yet to materialize. In fact, to look at the number of shuttered businesses on Main Street, things were rapidly going in the opposite direction.

The thought made her want to weep. Her beloved town was dying right before her eyes and she had no idea what she was supposed to do to stop it from happening. She looked down the street, noting how the awnings that hung over the once-bustling businesses had, over the years, gone from vivid red to a washed-out pink. The flowers that filled the large cement pots were straggly and tired, while FOR RENT signs hung in every third or so doorway. Even the sidewalk had dulled from a once-blinding white to a worn-looking gray.

Dove Pond needed the Dove family magic more than ever. And yet nothing had happened to save the town. Nothing! With every passing day, Sarah felt more like a failure. Expectations, even inherited ones, could weigh on one's shoulders like bags of cement if they were unfulfilled. There were days Sarah's back ached from it.

The cat meowed again, louder this time. Sarah moved the stack of books to her other hip for balance, then bent down to pet the poor creature. "I'm worried, too, Siegfried."

"That cat is nothing but a pain in the ass."

Sarah looked up to see Mrs. Jo Hamilton approaching, her wide-brimmed hat flopping with each step. A widow, she was as wide as she was tall, and closer to ninety than to eighty. As notorious for her colorful wardrobe as for her outspoken opinions, she wore a flamingo-pink suit that set off her ebony skin while a bright blue purse hung from her wrist. She clutched an elaborately carved wooden cane, while a huge, summer-perfect hat sat perched atop her black-dyed hair. Trailing behind her on a red leash was her very fat, very lazy bulldog, who went by the ridiculously appropriate name of Moon Pie and always had a different-colored ribbon around his neck. Today, he was sporting a bright if bedraggled purple bow.

Moon Pie stood behind Aunt Jo, panting while he carefully avoided any challenging eye contact with Siegfried.

"Aunt Jo!" Sarah said. The elderly woman was one of Dove Pond's oldest residents and had long been a Dove family friend. With a smile so sweet it was impossible to see it without returning it, Aunt Jo was Sarah's favorite person in the world. "You're all dressed up this morning. What's the occasion?" Sarah wished she had hats like Aunt Jo's. The older woman decorated them herself with a wide array of silk flowers and colorful ribbons. The hats always made Sarah think of fancy teas and the Kentucky Derby.

"I'm going to church. I've been promoted to deaconess and it's my first official meeting."

"Congratulations! When did that happen?"

"Sunday night. But don't be too impressed. No one else would do it. I was just the slowest-moving hippo and our new pastor is a damn cheetah. If you hesitate, you're lost."

Everyone had heard about Preacher Thompson, newly arrived at the First Baptist Church. Although he'd been there less than two months, he'd already caused a mountain of upheaval. "I hear he's a bit unconventional."

"If you only knew. He has no appreciation for the history of our church. Why, he wants to paint the whole building bright blue so people will notice it. Can you imagine?" She puffed out her disbelief. "How could they not notice our church? It has a *bell.*"

Moon Pie barked as if he agreed. Then, apparently exhausted by that small effort, he dropped to the warm pavement, where he stayed, panting heavily.

"Blue is my favorite color," Sarah admitted.

"I'm not talking about a soft, *pretty* blue. I'm talking bright, *obnoxious* blue. Blue the color of a swimming pool at a high school."

"Ugh."

"I know, right? Now, a nice, light, crisp blue, that I could see. I could support a pale yellow, too. I could even go green, if the shade was right. But *bright* high-school-pool blue? No."

"I can't imagine it." The First Baptist and the First Methodist churches were the only two churches in Dove Pond and each actively poached members from the other, a practice enthusiastically encouraged by the two preachers, who were by nature of the town's shrinking population sworn, if polite, enemies. "You know, Aunt Jo, if you're unhappy—and I can see why you would be—there's another perfectly good church in town, and we'd love to have you."

"Shut your mouth! I've been going to First Baptist since before you were born. It's where I was baptized and wed, and all my children were baptized and wed, and it's where I plan to have my funeral, too."

"Even if it's been painted high-school-pool blue?"

"Even then, although if it is that horrible color, I might just ask that everyone go into the service through the back door. The trees will cover up most of that ugly blue then."

Sarah laughed. "I hope your preacher doesn't get his way with the paint color."

"Me too. I'm beginning to suspect Preacher Thompson is colorblind, to like such a horrible shade. Still, he's worth putting up with. That man is as handsome as the day is long. Zoe Bell says he looks like Idris Elba's younger and sassier brother."

"Zoe knows men."

"She does. And she knows we've a winner in our new preacher, so I'm staying, even if the building gets painted black with orange flames. Sermons go faster if I have something nice to look at."

"That's one thing your preacher has over mine. As much as I love Preacher Lewis, he's not what I'd call easy on the eyes." Preacher Lewis was plump, bald, and a bit of a mess when it came to his clothing. Sarah didn't think she'd ever seen him when he didn't have a mustard stain on his shirt.

Siegfried meowed loudly, which caused Moon Pie to growl as if nervous.

Aunt Jo eyed the cat with disfavor. "What's wrong with him? He's meowing like he's about to give birth to a dozen wildcats."

"He's uneasy, and so am I." Sarah hesitated and then said, "Aunt Jo, I think something is about to happen."

"Happen?"

"Here. In Dove Pond."

Aunt Jo's warm brown eyes lit up. "The Dove family good luck? Is that it?"

"I hope so. I've seen signs. I'm not sure, but—"

"It's about damn time!"

"Don't I know it," Sarah said fervently. She hoped she was right. She was a Dove, darn it, and the journal had foretold that she'd be pivotal to saving their town. Where was the promised good luck? She'd been waiting so long, and she couldn't help but worry that her friends and neighbors were starting to question the Dove family lore.

Meanwhile, she was left waiting, each day adding to the growing worry that somehow she'd already messed things up.

"Tell me about these signs," Aunt Jo said. When Sarah hesitated, the old lady rapped her cane on the sidewalk. "Spit it out! I'm almost ninety years old. This ticker can't take suspense."

Sarah laughed. "Then I'd better say it fast, because I don't want Preacher Thompson coming after me because I smote down his best deacon."

"He's about to find out what a good deacon is, and it's not going to be pretty." Aunt Jo moved a little closer. "But enough about the church. Tell me about these signs you've seen."

"Okay. But just know that I could be wrong about this. I hope I'm not, but I could be." Sarah looked around to make sure they couldn't be overheard. "The first sign came from Siegfried."

Aunt Jo's face fell. "That mangy cat is one of your signs?"

Moon Pie sneezed, and it almost sounded as if he were trying to keep in a laugh.

"Yes," Sarah said earnestly. "He's been walking in three counterclockwise circles in front of every door on Main Street for almost a week now."

"Every day?"

"And every door."

"Oh! Well. That's something, then." Aunt Jo looked impressed. "Even for a cat."

"There's more," Sarah said. "The flowers in the town planters keep changing colors."

Aunt Jo's eyes widened. "*All* of them?"

"No, just the ones on this end of town." Sarah wondered yet again what that meant. "Which makes it even more suspect."

Aunt Jo looked at the flowers across the street in front of town hall and then eyed the planters that staggered down Main Street. "They're all purple."

"They are now, but every once in a while, the ones on this end of the street will be blue or pink or some other color. Then, a few hours later, I'll look again, and they'll have changed back."

"Lord help us, you're giving me chills." Aunt Jo looked eagerly at Sarah. "What else?"

"There's one more thing. Yesterday at noon, the town fountain started running again."

Aunt Jo gasped. "That fountain hasn't run in almost fifty years!"

"I couldn't believe it, either. And it started up on its own. I know because I mentioned it to Mayor Moore and he didn't even know it was running again."

"Praise the Lord! I *knew* it would happen sooner or later!" Aunt Jo's voice held all the awed hope that Sarah felt. "Sarah Dove, we are seeing the beginning of the famed Dove family good luck! Your momma would be so proud."

"I hope I'm right and that's what's going on," Sarah said fervently. "Something good needs to happen to this town. It feels as if it's fading away, right in front of me."

"I know. Money's tight, businesses are failing, and people have been moving away like rats jumping from a sinking ship." Aunt Jo shook her head, her hat flopping decisively. "Cowards, all of them."

"They don't have a choice. They can't stay without a job, especially if they have kids."

"I know, I know. Our youth program at church is just pitiful. There's maybe three couples young enough to have children, and they don't seem to be trying. I suggested we have an oyster bar for Sunday dinner, just to urge things along, but Preacher Thompson didn't want the smell in the church."

"He has a point. Besides, it's not easy to get fresh oysters this far inland unless you're a restaurant and have connections."

Aunt Jo sighed. "It's a damn shame, but no one stays put nowadays."

"Most of my sisters have left, too." Only Sarah and Ava remained. After college, much to Sarah's chagrin, her older sisters had scattered to the wind, following better jobs and unworthy boyfriends away from Dove Pond. "They have to come back," she said firmly. "Our family belongs here." The books she held murmured in agreement, and she wondered if they knew more than she did, or if they were merely being supportive.

"I hope so, I— Oh!" Aunt Jo waved at the police cruiser driving past. "There's Sheriff McIntyre. He's just now back from that conference in Atlanta, isn't he?"

Sarah's heart fluttered, but she refused to look. "Was he out of town?" She tried to keep her voice from sounding as if she cared, even a little.

"Yes, he was, as I'm sure you already knew." Aunt Jo looped Moon Pie's leash over the handle of the drop box and came to stand a little closer. "He paid for the training and the trip himself, too. I know, because his momma has been bragging about it, saying he's the perfect public servant and should run for mayor."

Sarah didn't answer, and Siegfried, offended by the bright red leash now hanging near his head, meowed his complaint and left, swishing his tail as he went, stopping to turn three times in the doorway of the antique shop before moving down the street to the next door.

Aunt Jo sent Sarah a sly look. "I never expected the town's richest bachelor to become the town sheriff, but of course, you probably knew long before the rest of us that Blake McIntyre wanted to go into law enforcement. After all, you two dated once."

"A long time ago, and I wouldn't call it dating." Sarah managed a shrug. "I've hardly spoken to him since."

Which was true. Mostly. From the day all those years ago when Blake had caught her talking to Charlotte Dove's journal, they had avoided one another. That had lasted all the way through middle school.

But when they'd reached high school, Blake had started pursuing her with a doggedness that had caught everyone's attention. Sarah, a late bloomer and far too engrossed in her books to want a boyfriend, had ignored him so thoroughly that his friends eventually started calling him Blake the Invisible.

All that had changed at the beginning of her junior year. When they'd returned to school that fall, she'd discovered that over the summer Blake had grown three inches taller, his shoulders were broader, his light brown hair magically lightened by the sun, and his smile—which had always been his best feature—newly dazzling. To her astonishment, Sarah had found herself suddenly, instantly, and deeply in love.

But the damage had already been done. The years she'd spent ignoring Blake had been promptly returned tenfold and he'd repaid her for the public humiliations she'd so unthinkingly heaped on his head by never again looking her way.

Sarah should have left well enough alone, but she was too caught up in her own emotions to make a good decision, and the more Blake refused to speak to her, the more crazed about him she'd become. *Crazed* was the right word, too. "Terrible teen hormones," she muttered under her breath.

"What?" Aunt Jo asked, her bright eyes locked on Sarah's face.

"Nothing. I just remembered I have a meeting this afternoon. That's all." As far as Sarah was concerned, the entire Blake episode had been one big horrible mistake, which had culminated in a night she refused to think about even now. The past was dead and gone and there was no benefit in reliving it. The books on her hip hummed in concern and she absently patted the top one.

Aunt Jo tsked. "I wish you'd talk to that boy. At least try to be friends."

"I do talk to him," Sarah said. "We're not enemies. We're . . ." Good God, what were they? They were nothing. And it was better that way. "It's been years, Aunt Jo. There's nothing there."

"I guess so," the old woman said, looking disappointed. "Your momma and I always thought—" Her gaze locked on something across the street. "Is that the new town clerk?"

Sarah turned. Grace stood by the door to town hall, staring at the planter as if she'd only just noticed it. She was dressed in a finely tailored gray suit with tan power high heels, complemented by a fashionable turquoise tote. With her dark hair pinned in a neat bun, Grace looked more like an actress playing a posh New York attorney than a small-town clerk.

"That's a nice suit, except for the color." Aunt Jo wrinkled her nose. "It's boring. She'd know better if she'd watch a few episodes of *Project Runway.*"

"But those shoes." Sarah looked down at her own blockish sandals where they peeped out from the hem of her lilac maxi-dress.

"I'd fall and kill myself if I tried to wear heels like she's wearing, but it might be worth it," Aunt Jo said with a sigh. "I hear she's reorganizing everything in town hall, getting things onto a computer, even."

"It needed done. When I paid my property taxes last month, Mrs. Phelps gave me a carbon copy receipt."

Aunt Jo sniffed. "I might be almost ninety, but even I know that's some 1950s stuff right there. As much as I love Philomedra—and I do, because she always makes me laugh—our town needed a new clerk."

"Well, we have one, and she seems very detail oriented. Or so I've heard."

Aunt Jo turned a surprised look at Sarah. "Haven't you met her already? She lives only two houses from you!"

"I know, I know." It wasn't because Sarah hadn't tried. She'd been to visit her new neighbors no fewer than three times, but each time she'd been met at the door by the charming but flustered Mrs. Giano, who always said the same thing—that Grace wasn't home, even though on at least one of those occasions, her car had been parked in the drive.

It was obvious to Sarah that Grace was avoiding her for some reason. The whole thing was regrettable, because Sarah was excited to have new neighbors. The elderly Mrs. Giano, who was Mrs. Phelps's cousin, reminded Sarah of a very small, wise elf, like those from one of her favorite books. Meanwhile, Daisy, with her heart-shaped face, Cupid's-bow mouth, and halo of blond hair, could very easily be a sullen fairy. When not swinging wildly in the tire swing that hung from the tree in the front yard, she stood staring over the fence at Trav's motorcycle as if she longed for a ride. And yesterday, both Mrs. Giano and Daisy had chatted with Sarah on their front porch for a full half hour when she'd brought them a welcome-to-the-neighborhood pecan pie.

But as friendly as the two were, Grace was the polar opposite. She hurried in and out of her house with her gaze locked straight ahead, as if afraid someone might try to engage her in a conversation. Someone like Sarah, who'd waved until her hand felt like it might fall off, and who hadn't gotten so much as a nod for her efforts.

And now, Grace stood across the street, staring at the planter in front of town hall as if wondering where she could buy one.

Aunt Jo jostled Sarah with her elbow. "Go over there and say hi."

"She doesn't want to meet me—or anyone, for that matter."

"Some people don't know what's good for them. Go talk to her. Find out everything about her, and then call me and Moon Pie and tell us what she says. We want to know who she is, where she came from, and if she has a church yet. I'm not a gossip, but this dog—well, you know how he is."

Sarah laughed and looked at Moon Pie, who was now sleeping on his back, sprawled across the sidewalk with his tongue hanging out one side of his gaping mouth. "Fine. I'll speak with her and then I'll call Moon Pie and tell him everything."

"He'll thank you when he wakes up. But you'd better go. Any minute now she'll head inside and you'll have to talk to her through the clerk's window, which would put an end to any sort of juicy tidbits she might accidentally drop."

"You're right. I'd better get over there. Thanks, Aunt Jo." Encouraged, Sarah waved goodbye and then hurried across the street.

She'd just reached the other side when she realized she was still carrying the stack of books. Well, she'd just have to take them with her; she couldn't let this opportunity slip through her fingers.

She hurried up the sidewalk toward Grace, who was still looking at the yellow flowers in the plant—

Yellow?

Sarah stopped and looked down Main Street. The rest of the flowers were purple. Only the flowers near town hall had changed.

What was so different about this end of the street compared to the other? She couldn't think of a single thi—

Grace.

The books resting against Sarah's hip shivered.

Good lord, it's her. The thought poured into Sarah's mind perfectly formed, as if she was reading it and not thinking it for the very first time. *Grace Wheeler of the flawless tailoring and distant disposition is important to Dove Pond.*

But important how? And to whom?

The books chattered in agreement, so loudly that Sarah was surprised she was the only one who could hear them. They rattled on and on, making wild, hopeful suggestions and talking over each other until she could only make out a few words here and there . . . *help . . . maybe . . . town . . . she . . . can—*

Shush! Sarah silenced their chattering, her temples aching from the rampage. Still, she wasn't angry. She was relieved.

It was finally happening.

Dove Pond was going to be saved after all, and—even better—lovely, generous Fate had sent Sarah a helper.

Sarah had to fight the urge to pump her fist in the air and dance around. Excited, the books rustled, and she had to scramble to keep from dropping them.

She'd just settled them back on her hip when she saw Grace turn from the planter and take a step toward the doors.

"Wait!" Sarah called out and then ran the last ten yards to where Grace stood.

Grace turned, her expression cool and distant. "Yes?"

Sarah smiled. "Hi. I'm Sarah Dove, the town librarian. I live two doors down from you on Elm Street. The mauve house?"

"Oh yes. Nice to meet you."

Sarah's excitement faltered at the coolness of Grace's tone. She shifted the books to her other hip. "My sisters and I inherited the house from our mom. Just my sister Ava and I live there now because the rest of them moved away after college."

A stiff smile touched Grace's mouth, but other than to murmur a polite "I see," she didn't add anything that could be interpreted as encouragement to continue the conversation.

Sarah refused to give up. "Ava owns her own gourmet tea business. She also does landscaping, so if you ever want someone to do your yard, I'm sure she'd be happy to take you on. My two oldest sisters have Ava and her crew drive to Raleigh every spring for their own yards because no one can do it like she can."

"I'll be sure to contact her if I need help."

"She's really good. My oldest sister, Madison, is as picky as they come, so if she likes something, it's got to be good. She's a doctor, you see. My other sister Alex is a veterinarian. They live only three houses away from each other, although they haven't spoken in almost five years. There was a man who— Well, you know how that goes."

Grace glanced at her watch.

Sarah should have stopped there. She knew it, and yet she couldn't. Instead, she heard herself adding breathlessly, "My other sister Ella trained in Paris to be a chef and now she owns her own pie company. But she comes home every Christmas and makes our dinner, which is good, because while I can cook, I can't make dishes the way she does. My other sisters are Cara—she's a computer genius and runs a matchmaking site that is making her rich—and Tay, who is an English professor specializing in ancient manuscripts and—" Noticing that Grace was ever so slowly moving away, Sarah clamped her mouth over the rest of her sentence. "I'm sorry. I was rambling. I didn't mean to."

"No, no. It's fine."

There was an awkward moment, and the silence Sarah had been fighting off fell between them with the thoroughness of a guillotine blade.

Oh God, I'm embarrassing myself. I should just leave. I'll tell her I've had too much coffee. That should wor—

"You have a lot of sisters."

There was something in Grace's tone—the tiniest hint of wistfulness.

"There are seven of us. I spent most of my childhood standing in line for the bathroom."

This time Grace's smile held some warmth. "There were only two of us and it was a morning fight to get to use the bathroom mirror. I can only imagine how crazy it must have been with seven of you."

"You don't want to know," Sarah said earnestly. She smiled in return. "I'm glad I finally got to meet you. Mrs. Giano said you've been working long hours."

Grace's smile disappeared. "When did you speak to Mama G?"

That's an unusual thing to call your mother. "I've been by your house a few times, but you weren't home, although . . ."

"Although what?"

"Your car was in the driveway one of the times I stopped by. I thought maybe you didn't want to be bothered. Mama G said you weren't there, though, so . . ." Sarah shrugged.

"I didn't know you'd stopped by. Mama G . . . She doesn't always remember things."

"She was very sweet. Your daughter is nice, too."

"Daisy is my niece, not my daughter."

"Oh. Is she your sister's child, then, the one you used to fight for the bathroom mirror? Or do you have brothers, too?"

"It was just me and Hannah." Grace's eyes darkened, and she looked away, her expression suddenly closed off.

Oh dear. Something happened there. Sarah hurried to change the topic. "I saw you looking at the flowers just now."

Grace's gaze returned to the planter and her brow creased. "It's weird, I could have sworn they were purple, but"—she gave an uneasy laugh—"I must be going crazy."

"No. They were purple this morning. I saw them."

"I'm so glad you noticed it, too. I thought I was losing my mind." She reached down and touched one of the yellow flowers. "What type of flower changes like that? I'll ask Lenny the next time I see him. He'll know what they're called."

Lenny Smith's official title was Director of Public Works, and he served as the town handyman and gardener. But as talented as Lenny was, Sarah knew he hadn't planted flowers that would change colors. This was Dove Pond magic.

The books agreed, shifting a little so that she had to grab at the top one to keep it from slipping off the pile.

"Those look heavy," Grace said.

"They are." Sarah grimaced. "I was just emptying the book drop box when I saw you, and I forgot I was holding them."

"You need to get those back to the library. I've got to go, too. I've hours and hours of data entry ahead of me, so—"

"Don't go yet," Sarah protested. In her excitement, she raised her voice the faintest bit.

It was obviously too much. Grace moved slightly. She didn't take a full step back, but it was enough to let Sarah know she'd seemed too demanding.

The books murmured a warning and Sarah swallowed the words she'd been about to blurt out, about how she'd waited for this day since she was a child of seven, about the ancient journal and its belief that the town would need to be saved and she would be the one to lead the way, about the various signs she'd witnessed in the past week that something big was about to happen, along with a detailed explanation of the Dove family history.

The books were right; now was not the time.

Sarah tamed her wide grin into a calm smile. "I just meant that it's nice to see someone new in town. You just got here, but I think you'll like it. Dove Pond is a special place."

Grace's gaze drifted past Sarah to the street beyond and there was a hint of regret in her voice as she admitted, "It's a pretty town."

Sarah followed Grace's gaze. It was early-summer warm today, which meant it was neither too hot nor too cool. The sunshine heated the sidewalks and reflected off the curbs, while slightly tattered awnings fluttered in the breeze across the row of storefronts. It was a beautiful day, and Dove Pond was showing her best, if somewhat faded, colors. "Picturesque, isn't she?"

"Very. It's too bad I don't plan on staying long. A year, if that. But I'm sure I'll enjoy it while I'm here."

What? Sarah shook her head. "You'll be here longer than a year."

Grace cut Sarah a hard look. "No," she said flatly. "I won't be."

The books murmured their disagreement, while Sarah swallowed a sharp answer and had to settle for an unsatisfactory, "Well . . . we'll see, won't we?"

She and Grace stared at one another, neither of them willing to bend.

The soft breeze fluttered between them, as if looking for a way to bridge the widening gap. Sarah's lilac maxi-dress flapped around her legs, while Grace's stiff suit barely moved.

Regret filtered through Sarah's stubbornness. *I'm making things worse, me and my unruly tongue. I'm going to chase her away before she's even settled in.* Sarah took a steadying breath and said, "Look. I'm sorry. You'll stay however long you want, of course. I'm just—" She managed an awkward laugh. "I'm just happy to see a new family in town."

Grace's expression remained frozen.

Sarah added, "One day, when you have some time, I'll show you around."

Grace looked down Main Street. "I'm pretty sure I've already seen it all."

"Oh, I wasn't talking about the buildings. I meant I'd introduce you to the people. That's what makes Dove Pond what it is, the people and their stories."

"Stories?"

"Everyone has a story. That's what makes us who we are." Sarah pointed to the town square. "See that statue behind the fountain? That's Captain John B. Day. He was a war hero in World War II. Or so the townspeople thought in nineteen fifty-five, when they put up the monument."

Grace shot a curious glance at Sarah. "The townspeople just *thought* he was a war hero?"

"Yup. It turns out he never made it to the front. He was just in charge of the kitchens at Fort McClellan in Alabama. But when he came home, he knew a lot of war stories because of all the soldiers who came through that camp. The Days are great storytellers, every one of them. And while Captain John never specifically said the stories were about him, people thought he was just being humble."

"No one asked him outright?"

"Nope. And if you'd ever heard a Day tell a story, you'd know why. The Days can spin yarns that seem so real that if one of them told you a tale about a blizzard, you'd get frostbite even if you were standing in your kitchen on the hottest day of the year."

Grace laughed. "That's something, all right. But this statue . . . after the town discovered the truth, why did they keep it?"

"The Days convinced the town council that food was an important part of the war effort. They said his biscuits were really, really, *really* good. Plus, his family offered to pay for the statue, so no one was out any money."

Grace eyed the statue. "He was quite a handsome man."

"That didn't hurt." Sarah grinned. "Such is life in a small town."

For the first time, Grace returned Sarah's smile. "Apparently so."

Encouraged, Sarah added, "The old town records are kept in the library basement, so I know more about Dove Pond than most people. You should come over and— Oh! There's Kat Carter. She's coming out of the post office right now."

Grace's gaze followed Sarah's nod. A tall brunette wearing huge sunglasses and a too-tight red dress sauntered toward a low-slung white Audi roadster.

Sarah could tell Grace was intrigued, because she shifted a little closer. "Kat's a Realtor and a member of the Dove Pond Social Club," Sarah explained. "She has the Carter gift."

"Gift?"

"Carter women can smell when a man has money."

Grace looked impressed. "That's a handy talent."

"Very. Men fall wildly in love with the Carter women too. Like they can't help it. Kat's mom has been married four times, all to rich men."

"So, the ability to make wealthy men fall in love with you and marry you doesn't come with the ability to stay married."

"Kat's mom, Ella, changes husbands at about the same speed I change my living room couch. Maybe more. I've always wondered if the Carter gift is a curse or a blessing."

Grace watched as Kat slid into her car, every movement somehow sensual. "If the gift is a real thing, then why does Kat still have her maiden name?"

"Kat's got the gift, but she refuses to use it. She's found her rich man and he's crazy for her, but she won't have him."

"Poor guy."

"I know. His name is Mark Maclean. He owns ten gas stations, seven Chick-fil-A's, and a dozen or so high-end apartment buildings, all in Charlotte."

"He doesn't live here?"

"Not anymore. He visits a lot, though. And he asks Kat to marry him each and every Christmas. He's done it a different way each time, too, but she always refuses. She says marriage comes with a lot of responsibilities and she's not ready yet."

"How long has this been going on?"

"Since high school, about seventeen years now."

"Good lord. I'm surprised he's still waiting."

"I don't think he has a choice; she's a Carter and—"

The deep rumble of a motorcycle drowned out Sarah's voice as Trav rode by on his Harley. Sarah noticed that Grace's expression darkened as he went by.

As soon as she could be heard, Sarah said, "Have you met Travis yet?"

"No."

There was a grimness to Grace's mouth that worried Sarah. "I know Trav looks a bit rough, but he's not. He's a super-nice guy, just a little terse."

"My niece is taken with him, although I've warned her about bothering him."

Sarah had seen Daisy hanging over the fence between their houses and knew the little girl liked to watch Trav work on his motorcycle. "Trav lives alone now and says he likes it, but . . . I wonder about that sometimes. His dad died last year from complications caused by dementia."

Grace's gaze locked on Sarah. "Dementia?"

"Yeah, Trav took care of him to the very end, too. He— Oh! Over there!" Sarah inclined her head toward the hardware store. "See that man, the round one with fuzzy red hair?"

"The one in the wrinkled brown suit?"

"That's Wilmer Spankle. The Spankles and the Jepsons have been enemies since they bought property adjoining one another in the eighteen hundreds. No one remembers why they started fighting, not even them. But you'd never know it from how much they scrap today. And every generation, too. It's not a real town gathering if there's not a Spankle-Jepson fight in the church parking lot."

Grace's lips twitched. "I suppose I was wrong. There are a lot of sights in Dove Pond."

"More than you can imagine," Sarah said fervently.

"Apparently so. Tell me, who is that woman glaring at us from the café window? She's been watching us this whole time."

Sarah looked, and her stomach knotted. Of all the people in Dove Pond, there were only two she avoided. Most days, she was successful. But apparently today wasn't one of those days.

Grace had noticed Sarah's expression and couldn't have looked more curious. "You know her, I take it?"

Sarah hoped her face wasn't as pink as it felt. "That's Mrs. Emily McIntyre. The McIntyres are some of Dove Pond's wealthiest citizens. Her oldest son is a veterinarian in Raleigh, while the youngest is the sheriff here in town."

"McIntyre . . ." Grace's eyes narrowed. "There's a plaque on the town fountain with the McIntyre name on it."

"There are a lot of plaques in town bearing that name. The high school track, the park at the south end of town, the street up the hill, and yes, the fountain."

"Mrs. McIntyre must love Dove Pond."

Sarah could have told Grace that Emily McIntyre only loved what she owned, but now was not the time for negativity. "The park is beautiful. We should have lunch there one day."

But Grace's gaze remained on Emily. "If that glare is any indication, Mrs. McIntyre might be fond of the town, but she's not very fond of you."

Sarah forced a smile. "You're a good observer of the human condition. I'll tell you about that someday over a glass of wine. It's a long story and I—"

The town's squad car pulled into a space a few yards away and turned off. The door began to swing open.

"I have to get back to work. I—I need to get these books to the library to—" The words froze in her throat as Blake climbed from his squad car.

Grace appeared thoroughly confused. "What's wrong?"

All the air had left Sarah's lungs and she couldn't answer.

Blake looked the way he had since high school—tall and broad shouldered, his light brown hair as regimented as his uniform. He glanced her way for the merest second, just long enough for the old, aching desire to settle into Sarah's suddenly restless legs.

She should stay right where she was and pretend she didn't care. She knew that was what she should do, knew it as sure as she knew the sky was blue and Blake's eyes were a seductive green. Knew it as clearly as the sunlight on the window of the café where his mother was even now watching them, a faint sneer on her carefully lipsticked mouth.

The urge to run grew with each second, and Sarah found herself backing away, grabbing at the books on her hip just before they slipped out of her grasp.

Grace frowned. "Are you okay?"

"I've got to get back to work. If you're free, maybe we can have lunch tomor—"

Blake stepped onto the sidewalk. His shadow touched Sarah's.

She spun on her heel and raced across the street, the books clutched against her hip.

When she reached the library, she took the steps to the door two at a time, almost stumbling in her haste. As she unlocked the doors, Sarah could feel Mrs. Emily's blazing dislike burning a hole between her shoulder blades.

The doors banged closed behind Sarah as the calming smell of old books and the murmurs of various tomes welcomed her. Heart still racing, she closed her eyes and leaned against the wall while the cool, air-conditioned chilliness soothed her hot cheeks.

Forget them. Think about finally meeting Grace. That's what's really important—Grace and Dove Pond. It took a moment, but Sarah slowly regained control of her thoughts. Grace Wheeler was important to the salvation of Dove Pond, that much was clear. But how?

That question needed answering. Fortunately, Sarah knew where to start. Sometimes the only way to begin a journey to the future was with a gentle shove from the past.

She left the wall and set the stack of books she'd been carrying onto the return cart. Then she took out her keys and headed downstairs to the Dove Pond archives, where Charlotte Dove's cranky journal safely dozed in its glass case, far away from the damaging sunlight and unfiltered air.

The book had aged over the years and it slept more and spoke less. In fact, it had been more than a year since she'd exchanged more than a sleepy hello with it.

She unlocked the door, flipped on the lights, and stepped inside. Rows of shelves and cases filled the basement, the remnants of Dove Pond's long history. She walked past the boxes and bins and went instead to the far corner, where the journal dozed on an acid-free pillow she'd bought from a library supply catalog her first day on the job.

She softly tapped on the case, but the book slept on.

She waited a moment and then, impatient, tapped the glass a little louder.

The book stirred, grumbling as it reluctantly came awake.

"Hi, sleepyhead," Sarah said. "Are you up?"

What do you want?

Long gone were the days the journal wanted Sarah to read it. For all of Nebbie Farmer's expertise in the Dewey Decimal System, the previous librarian hadn't known how to care for an ancient book. And so the journal had been displayed near a sunny window, the glass case magnifying rather than reducing the harmful rays. Nebbie had also placed the poor book on colorful but acidic paper, which had slowly broken down the glue that held it together. The years of unintended neglect had left their mark and the journal's pages were now delicate, the leather cover laced with deeper cracks, the binding ragged and failing, and its temper—which had never been good—infinitely more curmudgeonly.

Sarah crossed her arms and leaned on the case, peering through the dim light at the journal. "I'm sorry to bother you, but I have a question."

The book grumbled, but she couldn't make out the words, so she continued. "There's a new woman in town and I think she's a sign that Dove Pond is about to be saved."

The book said something under its breath.

"What?" Sarah asked.

I'm not your personal seer, the book groused.

"Look, I just want to know how she's going to help. That's your job, isn't it? To explain how I'm going to meet my destiny? How I'm supposed to save our town?"

The book didn't answer, and after a moment, Sarah tapped her finger on the glass.

The book jolted as if reawakened.

"Her name is Grace Wheeler."

The book said in a sharp tone, *Ask another book! I'm sleeping.*

Sarah had to fight not to snap out something unpleasant. "Come on," she pleaded. "This is about Dove Pond, and that's what you're about. No other book here would know."

That's true, the book said grumpily. It sighed and then rustled, as if searching for an answer.

Sarah tried to contain her excitement. She tucked a strand of loose hair behind her ear and, as the minutes lengthened, jiggled her foot impatiently under the case.

Finally, she could stand it no more. Just as she opened her mouth to ask her question again, the book spoke.

She's the one.

Yes! There it was. Confirmation at last. "I knew she was important! But what will she do? I know she's here to help me, but how?"

You'll know.

The book's flat tone suggested that was all the help it was willing to give. She bit back a frustrated sigh and said, "Come on. Just explain what you mean and I'll leave you alone."

No.

She supposed she was lucky it had taken the time to say what it had. "Fine. I'll make it work. It's not ideal, having an assistant, because I always thought I'd be the one to do all the work when the time came, but hey, I've never been one to turn down help, so—yes. This will be great. But I hope she hurries and does whatever she's supposed to do, because she's not planning on staying long."

The book, which had been drifting back asleep as she spoke, suddenly focused its attention on her. *What?*

"I spoke to her not five minutes ago and she says she'll be here a year, if that, and no more."

She has to stay.

"Has to? Like . . . forever?"

Yes, forever. The book couldn't have sounded more irritated.

"But why? I mean, once she's helped the town, she can leave, because I'll still be here."

She has to stay forever.

Sarah gave an uneasy laugh. "I wish she would, because I'm sure she's nice once you get to know her, but I can't just make someone stay in Dove Pond who doesn't want to. I couldn't even get my sisters to stay, and I know them."

She. Has. To. Stay. The book hissed each word, punctuating them as if with a hammer.

Sarah grimaced. "That's not going to be easy."

The book didn't answer but muttered about "silly people" as it settled deeper into its cushion. Soon, the only noise coming from it was a faint snore, and Sarah knew it was done for the day.

"Well, I guess that's that." She straightened, absently staring down at the old journal as she thought about the situation. Of course, she was ecstatic that things were going to turn around for Dove Pond. That was the best news ever, even if she didn't know exactly how. And despite talking to the book, she still didn't know why or even how Grace was important, which was frustrating, to say the least.

But progress was progress and Sarah refused to see this new development negatively. Things weren't happening exactly the way she'd envisioned, but then again, what in life did? She should be happy to have a helper, even a reluctant one. "I'll just have to convince her to stay."

From upstairs, Sarah heard footsteps and the faint echo of a child laughing. She looked at the clock and realized it was almost time for Children's Hour.

Feeling more hopeful than she had in a long time, Sarah patted the case one last time and left the archives, locking the door behind her. Soon, she was too busy to dwell on the events of the morning, although every once in a while, she'd stop what she was doing and smile. It was finally happening. Dove Pond was going to be saved.

CHAPTER 3

Trav

Travis Parker lived his life one moment at a time. He didn't do it because he was a believer in any weird-ass, meditate-like-a-guru, hinky way of life. He did it because he'd found peace in simplicity. According to Don, his therapist at the Veteran's Administration, that was a good way to live, especially now that Trav had turned the corner of his long fight with PTSD and was finally starting to feel more like himself.

As the late-afternoon sun slanted down Main Street, Trav rode his motorcycle through town. The roar bounced off the red brick buildings, so loud he could feel it in his chest. His bike might be too loud for some people, but for him the roar was a release. He revved the engine as he rode, the deep-throated rumble as refreshing as a plunge in an icy river.

He turned off the street and headed home, the sun casting shadows through the leafy trees, so different from the grim, sandy vistas he'd seen in Afghanistan. Those, he didn't miss, but he did miss the men in his unit. He kept in touch with those who'd come home, but it wasn't the same. Everyone had moved on—they had lives and families. And in a way, so did he.

Fortunately for him, he had good friends, and for now, they were all the family he needed. Trav glanced down at his watch and grimaced. Although it was late in the day, he had to get home so he could change and head to the garage. Another hour under the hood of Joe Baldwin's slick red Corvette and it would be back in top shape, and Trav had promised Joe the work would be done today.

Growing up, Trav had hated working on cars. Perhaps it was because Dad had owned a garage. If there was one thing a teenage male didn't like, it was being predictable. Because of that, even though he'd worked in Dad's garage all through high school, Trav had never once considered becoming a real mechanic. He'd been something of a star in his small universe, the first-string quarterback and valedictorian. So naturally, he'd wanted something bigger, something that didn't already have his dad's fingerprints all over it. Instead, Trav had gone to college, where he'd majored in mechanical engineering, imagining himself developing the next fighter jet or working on some other equally exciting project. Later, he'd enlisted, still searching for a life of adventure.

Now, the last thing he wanted was excitement. Working in the garage was peaceful. There was a simple beauty within those cool, concrete walls with their organized bays where broken things came in, he and the other mechanics fixed them, and then they went home. There was no pain involved. No emotions. No fear or blood or sand or anything ugly. There were just cars and trucks, and peace. He worked there five and a half days a week alongside two full-time mechanics, a shop manager, and a part-time bookkeeper. And because he was now the owner, Trav enjoyed an optimum mixture of both control and challenge. Not too much of either.

He benefited from that balance. Gone were the days when he had the urge to drop to the floor every time he heard a loud noise. When his blood boiled because someone accidentally cut him off on the freeway or pushed in front of him at the grocery store. Now, if he could just find a way to sleep, he'd be completely back to normal. *Oh God, sleep. That would be nice.*

Trav turned his motorcycle down his street and glanced at the Dove house as he drove by, noticing that Sarah's truck wasn't in the driveway. She must still be at work, which was no surprise. She was the town librarian, which was the perfect job for her, as no one loved books the way Sarah did. *Which is probably healthy for the rest of us.*

He pulled into his driveway and parked his bike, noticing Killer lurking in the bushes. Killer had been his dad's cat and had slept at the foot of the older man's bed for years. After Dad died, Killer had tried to sleep at the foot of Trav's bed. But his tendency to toss and turn had irked the cat, who, after that one night, had returned to Dad's empty bed and stayed there.

Or that was where the cat stayed when he wasn't out wandering around. There was no keeping that crazy animal indoors and Trav had long ago given up trying.

Trav set his bike on the kickstand and then tugged off his helmet, his too-long hair tangling in the strap.

He muttered under his breath as he tugged his hair free. He knew he should get his hair cut, but sitting in a barber's chair made him feel tied down, the cape draped around him like a rope, holding him in place while someone he didn't know stood behind him with a blade. *No, thank you.* He could cut his own hair well enough to keep it shoulder length, at least. One day Trav would find the peace of mind needed to sit in that damn chair and get his hair cut. But not today.

Trav dropped his helmet into the saddlebag and looked around for Killer, but the cat was nowhere to be seen.

He started to turn back to his house and found his gaze resting on the Phelps house next door. It was quiet today, unusually so. Most days, when he came home, the little girl who lived there would hang over the fence and stare at his bike as if she thought it would stand up and turn into a Transformer. But today, she was nowhere to be seen.

Good. I hope she stays away. He didn't have time for little girls who stared, or for their cranky mothers who excelled at giving side-eye as if they thought he was a serial murderer. Scowling, he grabbed his keys and headed for the porch. Trav'd just stepped onto the sidewalk when a loud bang came from the garage, followed by a muted whisper.

Instantly, his heart raced and he crouched, his hands open at his sides, ready for the coming fray. He remembered the large wrench in his tool kit and wondered if he should get it. He was just getting ready to run to his bike when he heard a child's giggle.

Good God. He straightened, his heart thudding sickly against his ribs, his palms damp. He took a deep breath and then went to the garage, grabbed the door by the handle, and raised it.

The little girl from next door stood in the center of the garage, a small, waiflike figure holding a broom, an inexpertly swept pile of dirt in front of her. She wore a T-shirt with a sparkly picture of a pink pony on it, her muddy sneakers untied. Behind her, at the back of the garage, cleaning one of the windows, was her tiny, fragile-looking grandmother.

The old lady squinted at him as if trying to remember his name.

"What are you doing here?" His voice, still rough from the scare he'd had, boomed around the garage.

The old woman flinched as if he'd hit her, and instantly, he was contrite. He hadn't meant to startle her.

But Daisy was made of stronger stuff. She pointed to her broom. "What's it look like we're doing? We're cleaning."

She didn't call him stupid but it was there in her voice.

Trav didn't think he'd ever heard that much dry sarcasm from such a tiny person, and he had to fight a grin, which dispelled the lingering, unpleasant effect of being surprised. "I can see that you're cleaning, imp. Who let you into my house?"

He half expected the old lady to speak, but without saying a word, she'd turned back to the window she'd been washing.

"You'll have to ask Mama G," Daisy said. "She was already in here when I found her." She was little, this girl, smaller than she should be. Her blond hair was mussed and half falling out of a pink rubber band, as if she'd put it up herself and hadn't combed it first, which made her seem vulnerable somehow.

He crossed to where she stood. "However you got in, you should go home."

"Don't you want your garage cleaned?"

"No, thank you. Go home, Daisy."

Her smile was more of a smirk. "You know my name."

"I've heard your mom yell it about a hundred times now."

Daisy's smile disappeared. "Aunt Grace is not my mom." The words were sharp, tight, filled with meaning.

He shrugged, unable to delve into the feelings of a little kid when he was struggling to contain his own. "Just take your grandma and go. I—"

"Robert Parker? Is that you?" The old woman peered at him from across his garage, her dark eyes bright. "I haven't seen you in so long!"

Robert was Trav's father's name. "I'm sorry, but I'm not—"

"Don't you remember me? I'm Inna Phelps Giano." She put down the window cleaner and, damp rag still in hand, made her way to him, edging her way around his weight bench and weights.

As she moved, Trav's soul sank. She shuffled rather than walked, as if uncertain where her feet might land. He knew that walk. His father had walked like that the last year of his life, before dementia had stolen him away. *Oh, Dad. You deserved so much more from life.*

It still hurt a year later—even more than the explosion that had left Travis a cinder of his former self. Dementia was an unforgiving illness, one that stole hope and crumbled pride. And it was beyond sad to know that this tiny, elf-like, kind-looking old lady was suffering from it.

She beamed up at him now, as if she thought he could walk on water. "Oh, the fun we had when I babysat you."

Daisy frowned. "Mama G, you couldn't have babysat him."

"Oh, but I did. He was only this tall then." She put her hand even with her shoulder, her smiling gaze still fixed on Trav. "You remember me, don't you?"

Trav raked a hand through his hair. Damn it, but he couldn't let this poor woman down. After an awkward pause, he said shortly, "Yes."

Daisy stared at him, but he ignored her.

Mrs. Giano chuckled. "Oh, Daisy! Robert and his brother and I had such fun! I watched them after school in the afternoons and we played cards and rode bikes and, oh, all sorts of things." She gazed at him as if he were an angel. "You were such a good boy, and not nearly as mischievous as your brother."

People didn't usually look at Trav the way she was looking at him, trusting and amused, especially after he'd returned from the war with the angry red scars that marred his cheek and neck.

"Lord love you, you had such a good sense of humor." Mrs. Giano laughed softly. "I remember that cow. Do you?"

He didn't, of course, but he knew better than to argue. "Oh yes. The cow."

"You and your brother were always up to something. Daisy, I wish you could have been there the time they stole Preacher Landon's cow and rode it up the steps of the church. It was during a service, too, and the cow got so startled by all the people laughing at it that it ran right down the aisle, and then up the steps to the choir loft. It took eight of us to get her out of there."

Daisy eyed Trav with newfound respect. "Cool."

"Not really," he said shortly.

Mrs. Giano patted Trav's arm. "You had us all worried, thinking you might not grow up at all, what with your wildness, but look at you now! Although . . ." She frowned and put her fingers on his cheek. "What happened here?"

He jerked away. "It's nothing."

But it wasn't nothing, and he noticed how Daisy stared at his scar where it disappeared under his shirt, curiosity flickering over her face. Trav could already hear the questions—*What happened? Does it hurt? How far does your scar go?*

Dad had asked all of those questions and more after Trav returned from the burn hospital in Texas, and Trav—still bitter and hurting from more than his physical injuries—had refused to talk about it. Now it seemed stupid not to have at least let him know the basics. That wouldn't have been too much to ask.

God, he had so many regrets. Hundreds of them. Perhaps the biggest one was that he hadn't spent enough time with Dad. Trav wished for the millionth time that after college he'd stayed home for a while before rushing into the service. But like most young men, he'd been desperate to prove himself. He'd wanted a real challenge and by God, that's what he'd gotten.

After sailing through basic training and officer school, he'd been assigned to active duty in Afghanistan. There he'd commanded a squadron that oversaw crucial repairs to the war-torn electric grid. It had been a difficult, tough assignment, but he'd thrived on it. And when the time came to re-up for deployment, he'd signed back up without a second thought.

Maybe he should have given it a second thought, because ten months later, the week after Christmas, he and his squadron had just returned to the base after a week out running lines through some hard-won areas, when they were hit by an insider attack. One moment, he was walking toward the mess tent with a few members of his squad, all of them dirty and tired and ridiculously happy to be back on the base. And the next, there was shouting, gunfire, and an explosion that sent Trav and his men flying through the air. After that, all Trav remembered was the deep sear of pain and loss.

The memories came when he least expected them—when he least wished to remember them. And right now, even though he stood in the garage of the beautiful house he'd grown up in, the summer sun beaming through the branches and making patterns on the concrete leading into the garage, he saw very little of it. Instead, his mind bounced like a wrecking ball from bloody memory to bloody memory. He gritted his teeth and tried to stop his thoughts.

You're doing it right, living in the present, one minute at a time, Don had said not a half hour ago. *And you're healing, so don't rush yourself. When it's time to move forward, you'll do it without thinking.* Trav believed that. He trusted Don, who understood more than most. The counselor had lost both legs in Iraq and knew the fight well.

"Where did you get the scars?" Daisy's voice broke the silence.

"Daisy! That's not a polite question," Mrs. Giano said, although a flicker of warmth lit her eyes. She reached up and brushed the hair from his forehead as if he were a child. "You might not be able to fix a scar, but you could get that mop cut."

"I like his hair," Daisy said. "Whenever she sees him, Aunt Grace calls him 'Khal Drogo.' I think she's right. That's exactly who he looks like." Daisy shot a quick glance at her grandmother. "I mean, from what I've seen from pictures. I've never watched that show."

Trav knew a lie when he heard one, but he didn't say anything. She wasn't his kid, after all, so if she wanted to sneak-watch a forbidden show, who was he to say otherwise?

"Evelyn Kilgore used to do my hair." Mrs. Giano left his hair alone and patted her own mussed white curls. "She was such a kind lady and I was so sad when she died, although she'd been sick for such a long time. I—" Mrs. Giano's gaze locked on the rag in her hand and the words faded away. Her brows knit. "Why am I carrying this? Was I . . . What was I doing?" She looked around her as if suddenly unsure who or where she was.

Trav recognized the signs and said softly, "You were cleaning the window."

Her gaze locked with his, as if she were seeking an anchor. "Was I?"

"And doing a fine job, too."

Daisy pointed to the back of the garage. "You said the windows were dirty and that you wouldn't go home until they were clean."

Mrs. Giano looked at the window she'd just left and, now that she had a purpose, the confusion faded. "I'd better finish then, hadn't I?"

She turned and shuffled back to the window, completely forgetting Trav's too-long hair and ugly scars.

"Did you really ride a cow into your church?" Daisy asked.

He sent her an impatient look. "No, but apparently my dad did. His name is—was—Robert. That's who Mrs. Giano thinks I am."

"Oh." Daisy glanced at Mrs. Giano, who was humming as she cleaned the window, before turning back to Trav. "If your name isn't Robert, then what is it?"

"Trav. Look, you guys need to go home to your aunt."

The little girl's brows snapped down, the line of her mouth suddenly sharp. He felt sorry for her and whatever struggle she might be having, but he didn't have the energy or the knowledge to get involved.

Daisy said shortly, "Aunt Grace is still at work."

"Then who is keeping an eye on you?"

"Ms. Jane is watching us this week. She's only temporary until Ms. Linda can start on Monday."

"Linda Robinson?" At Daisy's nod, he said, "She's nice." He had no idea who Ms. Jane was, but Linda was a professional caretaker and had helped with his father during his last months. "I bet Ms. Jane is looking all over for you."

"No. She's having a fight with her sister, so she's on the back porch on the phone, arguing."

Trav took a step back so he could see out one of the garage windows. Sure enough, an elderly woman he now recognized as Jane Lewis, the organist at the Methodist church, was on the porch, talking on the phone and pacing back and forth, gesturing wildly. "That looks like some fight," he admitted.

"Her sister Louisa ate all their leftovers. Jane wanted to bring them here for lunch, but late last night, Louisa snuck into their refrigerator and ate them. Jane's mad because she didn't get any, plus Louisa's supposed to be on a diet."

Daisy spoke in the weirdly mature way that children who speak mainly to adults have. And yet, as mature as she sounded, she looked far too young to be standing here in his garage without a capable parent at her side.

Trav ran a hand through his hair. "I've got to change and get to work. Can you get Mrs. Giano home?"

"Nope," she said matter-of-factly.

"Why not?"

Daisy sent him an impatient look. "If I tell Mama G we have to go before she's done, it'll upset her and she'll cry. I can't stand it when she cries."

Trav looked over to where Mrs. Giano was scrubbing a once-dingy pane of glass. There were four windows in total. She'd already cleaned two of them, and she was about halfway through one of the remaining two. "Surely she won't mind leaving one for me to do?" But even as he said it, he knew it was unlikely. If Mrs. Giano's illness was anything like his dad's, she was becoming more stubborn as the days went by. That was how Dad had been, as determined as heck to hang on to his opinions when he could no longer hold on to his memories.

Trav sighed. He didn't know Mrs. Giano, but he knew he'd hate it if she cried. "I guess we'll have to wait until she's done. I have to change, anyway. When I get back, I'll help you get her home."

Daisy shrugged. "Okay."

He started to go inside but stopped at the door. "Why are you all cleaning my garage, anyway?"

"I don't know. She was doing it when I got here." Daisy leaned on her broom, looking far too cool for her age. "I jumped in because I figured it'd get her out of here quicker."

The kid had a point. "You're a smart one, aren't you?"

She eyed him as if he'd just said the most unoriginal thing in the world. Then she pointed behind him. "There's another broom by the door. Feel free to join in."

He had to quell the urge to remind her that it was his house, so he damn well knew where the brooms were. "I'm late for work, so you're on your own. Just finish up as soon as you can, okay?"

"Okay." Daisy's gaze wandered back to her grandmother. "She's not well, you know. She's sick, which makes her confused."

He didn't know what to say to that. "My dad had the same thing."

The little girl looked at him, her eyes the bluest of blue and as innocent as a kitten's. "Where is your dad now?"

Trav rubbed his neck where his scars pulled. Damn it, *this* was why he hated talking to people. Because then they needed things— answers, thoughts, help, *stuff*—and he was in no position to offer any of those. He supposed the only thing he could do was tell her the truth. After a long silence, Trav said shortly, "He died."

Daisy nodded as if she'd suspected as much. "Mama G won't die from this. She's going to get better."

No, she wasn't, but this wasn't his war to fight, so Trav just shrugged, wishing it didn't make him feel guilty. "I'll be right back. If she gets done before then, feel free to leave. I'll lock up."

Daisy went back to sweeping. "We won't be too long. She only has one window left now."

He mumbled an agreement and went inside. Once he reached his room, he quickly changed into his coveralls and work boots. As soon as he finished, he headed down the hall on his way to the garage but found himself stopping at his dad's bedroom door.

Although Dad had been gone for over a year, Trav hadn't touched the room. He should have, because this was the master bedroom and it had a large private bath, which would be more convenient than staying in his old, smaller room and using the bathroom down the hall. But the thought of going through his dad's personal things seemed wrong somehow. *I don't have to do anything now. I'll do it when the time is right.*

Still, he felt guilty, because Dad had been a stickler about neatness. He'd drilled his own habits into Trav's head, which had made Trav's move into the army far more effortless than it might have been. Dad had kept his shop the same way he'd kept the house—so clean and organized that the mechanics used to joke about being able to eat off the shiny concrete floor. But all that had changed when Dad had gotten sick.

After the explosion that had torched him, Trav had been assigned to a burn hospital in Texas. After eight long months, he'd finally been released. He'd arrived home a hollow shell of himself, barely able to stand upright, the puckered skin on his back and shoulder aching as if still on fire, the pain medications leaving him numb and out of touch. But even through all of those distractions, he'd been shocked at the condition of Dad's house. The dishes were undone, the beds unmade, piles of mail sat forgotten on tables and in chairs. But more astounding were the Post-it notes.

There were dozens.

Pink, blue, and yellow, they were all over the house, labeling everything from the food in the fridge, to which buttons on the remote adjusted the sound, to when various medicines were due. Dad had even written notes to remind him to feed Killer. There were Post-its on the bathroom mirror, the refrigerator door, the doorframe near the key hook, and just about everywhere else.

Some of the Post-its had lost their adhesion and had drifted to the floor and lay abandoned under chairs and tables and in corners, where they'd faded and curled, collecting dust, their duties forgotten along with them. Yet despite the Post-its, Killer's water bowl was still empty, food still rotted in the fridge, and Dad's important medicine sat untouched in labeled vials in his bathroom cabinet.

Other things had changed, too—Dad's walk had become less certain, just like Mrs. Giano's. He shuffled slowly, almost as if he were a thousand years old instead of fifty-six.

But Trav didn't fully understand the depth of Dad's illness until they went to the shop one brisk morning. Trav had hoped that things would be better there, that perhaps Dad was just depressed, living at home alone. But things were worse at the shop. The place was devoid of customers, dirty rags and buckets of grimy oil sat in the corners of the once-pristine garage, the office was stacked with unfiled papers and unpaid bills, and the shelves in the parts room were empty. Shop manager Arnie Gonzalez was the only employee left, as the other two mechanics had moved on after Dad had repeatedly forgotten to pay them. According to Arnie, most of Dad's prized customers were now taking their cars thirty minutes away to a repair shop in Swannanoa.

It took almost two weeks, but Trav had finally convinced Dad to see his physician, Doc Bolton. Trav would never forget the exact instant Doc said the word *dementia*. He could still see the deep, genuine sadness in Doc's worn face, and the stubborn denial in Dad's. That had been a horrible day, just one of many more horrible days that were yet to come.

Trav rubbed his face and turned away from Dad's bedroom, trying to silence the crackling feel of loneliness the room left him with. *Just one day at a time*, he told himself. *Just one fricking day at a time.*

He'd just reached the kitchen when he heard a noise in the living room. Frowning, he made his way there.

Mrs. Giano stood in front of the shelf beside the TV, a dust rag in her hand, one of Dad's trophies in the other.

She looked up as Trav came into the room. "Ah, there you are. I was looking at your trophies. So you're a bowler."

"Those are my dad's."

"Your dad's?"

"Robert Parker. He was my dad." Trav waited, wishing he knew her well enough to know when she was lucid. "He used to live here, remember? You used to babysit him."

A startled look came over her face and her gaze moved over him and then down to the trophy she held. "Robert was your father," she murmured, as if trying to comprehend that fact. After a moment, she looked back at him with a faintly embarrassed smile. "Well, then, I never knew your father was a bowler."

Relief swamped him as he realized she'd understood him. "Dad didn't start bowling until I was in college, but he must have been pretty good, as he was on the premier league."

She put the trophy back and looked at the other awards. "Are any of these yours?"

"No."

"Well." She finished dusting the shelves. "You deserve some trophies, too. You should find a way to get some."

Although he was glad she was feeling better, he wished she would leave. He was used to being alone when he was here, and he was just now realizing how much he prized his privacy. He rubbed his neck where the scar pulled, suddenly tired. "Look, Mrs. Giano, I appreciate your help but—"

Daisy popped her head around the front door. She looked from Mrs. Giano to him and then back. "What's going on?"

"I was just telling Mrs. Giano that it's time she left, as I have to go to work."

Daisy came inside and shut the door. She looked around, her glance touching on every item in sight.

"You should both go home, *right*?" he said impatiently.

She dragged her gaze from the pictures of him when he was a kid that Dad had arranged along one shelf and shrugged. "Sure." She wandered to where Mrs. Giano stood and touched one of the trophies. "Do you bowl?"

It was obvious he was going to get no help from Daisy, the imp. "No. As much as I'd like you both to stay, I've got to get to work."

"Then go," Mrs. Giano said. "We'll lock up when we leave. I— Oh dear. That mirror is smudged." She went into the hallway, where a mirror hung on the wall over a low table where Dad used to drop his wallet and keys when he came home.

"We'll go as soon as she's done," Daisy announced.

Trav turned to find her sitting on the big leather recliner that dominated the room. "Don't sit there. That was my dad's chair."

"So?"

"So get out of it," he snapped.

Her eyes ablaze, Daisy locked her gaze with his and deliberately reached down and popped up the footrest.

"Dam— I mean, stop that!" He went to the chair and lowered the footrest. "Get up."

The little girl glared at him, but after a hostile moment, she stood. "You're sort of a pain."

"You don't even know." He put his hand on her shoulder and directed her toward the door. "Go home and take your grandmother with you. You'll be missed soon, and I don't want your aunt marching over here thinking I've kidnapped you or worse."

Daisy looked interested. "You think she'd do that?"

"Yes, and I wouldn't blame her. No one is going to believe you all showed up just to clean an already clean house."

"The windows in the garage were—"

"I know, I know. The garage was dirty, I'll grant you that. But the house is clean."

"Cleaner than ours," Daisy admitted. She tilted her head to one side. "Are you afraid of Aunt Grace?"

"No."

"You should be. She can be mean. Sometimes she yells."

"I yell too. More than I should."

Daisy leaned against the chair. "You don't have any friends, do you?"

He frowned. "I have friends. Lots."

"You have one," she said. "In all the time we've lived beside you, I've only seen you talk to Sarah Dove."

"You've only lived beside me for two weeks," he pointed out, and then felt like a fool for even engaging her in this conversation. Still, he couldn't help but add, "I meet most of my friends away from the house at a place called Po Dunks, where they don't allow kids." Which wasn't exactly true, although he'd never seen any there. "Besides, you can't really be alone when you live in Dove Pond. If I sneezed outside this house in the morning, by lunchtime at least seven people would have heard I was catching a cold."

She grinned. "Sounds like a pain."

"It can be." He realized Daisy was watching him, so he asked, "How come you don't have any friends?"

"We're not staying, so why would I bother? Aunt Grace says that as soon as we can afford it, we're going to move to Charlotte, where she used to live and—"

A staccato knock sounded at the door.

Travis could feel the irritation in each rap. "There's your aunt."

"That was an angry knock," Daisy noticed.

"Great."

Daisy never moved from where she stood leaning on the forbidden chair. "You'd better let her in or she'll yell."

Of course she would. He went to open the door.

Grace stood at the threshold, Jane standing behind her, looking sheepish.

He'd seen Grace before, usually marching to or from her house. She was small, like her mother and niece, but she made up for her lack of size by walking as if she were at the head of a very large, very aggressive army.

She didn't even bother with a greeting. "Have you seen—" Her gaze had already moved past him and locked onto Daisy. "There you are!" Relief and irritation flashed across Grace's face. "What are you doing here?"

"Mama G wandered over, so I figured I'd better keep an eye on her."

"I can't believe you—" Grace stopped and looked at Trav. "Excuse me, but would you mind stepping out of the way? I can't speak to her with you in the middle."

"Sure. It's my house, but—yeah. Do whatever you want." Trav stood back. "You might as well come in. Everyone else has."

Without giving him a second glance, Grace walked past him. "Where's Mama G?" she asked Daisy.

"In the hallway," the little girl said sourly.

"Thank God you're both okay. Why did she come here?"

"She said the garage windows were dirty and they were bothering her, so she came over to clean them."

"To be fair," Trav inserted, "Mrs. Giano did a great job on those windows."

He was rewarded with a look of chilly disdain from Ms. Grace. For some reason, that made him happy, so he grinned in return.

Mrs. Giano, hearing her name, poked her head into the living room. "Grace! You're home early."

"It's not early. Why did you leave the house without letting Ms. Jane know where you were going? We've been so worried about you!"

Jane, who'd stayed on the porch, waved weakly at Trav. "I'm so sorry about this. I was outside for only a few minutes, and when I came back, they were gone."

She looked as if she might cry, so Trav said, "It's fine. Really it is. I was giving them time to finish whatever they thought needed doing. Next time I'll just come and get you."

Mrs. Giano folded the dust rag into a neat square and placed it on the coffee table. "I suppose we're done now."

"Mama G, why—" Grace caught herself and took a deep breath. When she spoke again, her voice was smooth and silky, not a trace of stress in it. "It's time to come home. Dinner will be ready soon."

"I hope we're having biscuits." As Mrs. Giano walked past Trav, she stopped and looked up at him. "I'll leave the rest of the cleaning to you."

"I'll get right on it."

"Clean this first." She placed her hand over his heart, her hand surprisingly warm through his coveralls.

He stared down at her, not knowing what to say. He was six feet three inches tall, and she was barely five feet flat, if that, and he easily weighed twice what she did, if not more. And yet at that moment, he felt as if he were a child of three, and she a giantess with dark eyes that could see into his very soul. "I need to clean my heart?"

"There's too much worry in there. It clouds things." She chuckled. "Sometimes you just have to scrub out all the silliness and let the sun in."

"Life isn't that simple."

"Isn't it?" She patted his chest. "Think about it, will you? But not too much."

"Mama G," Grace said, embarrassment obvious in her voice.

Jane slipped her arm through Mama G's and led her out the door to the porch. "Time to go home."

With a final smile at Trav, Mrs. Giano allowed Jane to lead her away.

Daisy rubbed her nose as she eyed her aunt. "I'm in trouble, aren't I?"

"You know it. You shouldn't have left the house without telling Ms. Jane where you were."

"I didn't have time. Besides, she was on the phone and—"

"Daisy." Grace's voice cracked sharply. She cast a self-conscious glance at Trav and then said in a tight voice, "We'll talk about this at home. Let's go."

"But I—"

"*Now.*"

Daisy hunched her shoulders. "Fine. But I'm not going to say I'm sorry. I was *helping*." With that, she marched out of the door after Mama G.

Grace turned back to Trav and said stiffly, "I'm sorry for the intrusion."

"It was no problem," he lied.

"I'm sure it was. I don't know what got into Mama G. She doesn't usually wander off like that and I—" Her voice broke, a sob caught in her throat.

Her gaze flew to his and he recognized every emotion that flickered through her brown eyes—fear, sadness, and embarrassment that she'd let her feelings show. He knew all three of those emotions and knew them well.

This rigid-seeming woman wasn't nearly as icily cool as she liked to project. For some reason, he found that reassuring. He rubbed his neck where his scar tugged. "My dad had the same thing as your Mama G. Or something like it."

She swiped at her eyes, her cheeks pink. "I'm sorry to hear that."

"It wasn't easy. Look, I don't know you or Mrs. Giano or Daisy, but . . . I know things are tough right now. But they'll get better and you'll find a way to handle them. Not completely, but some." He wished he could offer something more comforting than that, but he couldn't lie. It was a piss-poor way to make someone feel better, to promise that things wouldn't be quite as bad as they were now, but it was all he had.

She nodded once and then set her shoulders back, and just like that, the softness he'd glimpsed was gone. "Thank you," she said in a cool tone. "I appreciate you taking care of my family. I'll make sure they don't bother you again."

"It was nothing," he repeated.

She proffered her polite smile and then turned on her heel and left, walking as swiftly as she could without actually running.

Trav stood in the doorway and watched her go, wishing he knew what to say, but nothing came to him. Not one damn thing.

His visitors were gone and he was free to go to work. And yet he stood where he was and watched until they were all safely back inside their house.

CHAPTER 4

Grace

Grace carefully balanced her coffee cup as she unlocked the lobby door. The door, ancient and wooden, with etched glass panels, creaked as she swung it open. She let it close behind her and then set her cup on the top of a water cooler so she could flip the GONE TO LUNCH! WE'LL BE BACK AT ____! sign to OPEN! That done, she collected her cup and made her way behind the counter to her desk.

The Dove Pond town hall had been built in the mid-1800s and—from what she could tell—had never been remodeled. The counter and windows were of smooth, aged oak, and set with two wrought-iron-framed cashier windows, ornately decorated as Victorians were wont to do. The floor was of wide pine planks that had been scuffed to a glorious golden shine. The whole thing reminded Grace of the banks she'd seen in old western movies.

She surveyed her desk, an ugly 1970s monstrosity decorated with chipped faux wood and flanked on both sides by heavy filing cabinets. More filing cabinets lined the wall behind her desk and filled the basement, too—dozens of them. To her irritation, she'd quickly discovered that Dove Pond had barely entered the computer era, so the office was awash with paper. The next time she went to a job interview, her first questions would be, "Are you a Luddite?" and "Does the term 'computer' give you hives?"

She hooked the toe of her shoe in the handle of one of the bottom drawers of her desk, tugged the drawer open, dropped her purse inside, then pushed it shut.

The bang must have awoken Mayor Moore, for he soon lumbered out of his office, grinning sleepily. "Ah! Miss Wheeler! Back from lunch, are you?" Gone was his mussed, ill-fitting gray suit and too-long tie, and in their place were a floppy flannel shirt and too-big blue jeans. The mayor was a rounded, large-boned man with thinning gray hair, his thick eyebrows hanging over pale blue eyes that twinkled constantly.

He brightened on seeing the coffee cup in her hand. "I see you went to the Moonlight Café. They make the best coffee this side of the Mason-Dixon Line."

Although Grace's new boss flashed a perpetual smile, he still managed to irk her. She'd never met anyone so deeply determined to avoid work. That, she'd discovered, was her real job—to make sure he didn't have to do his. She eyed his flannel shirt. "That's a bit casual for a public speech, isn't it?"

"I'm not going to the Kiwanis meeting, after all. I already informed their president, Mark Robinson, that something came up. He said he understood."

"I've only met Mark once, but his wife, Linda, watches my mother and niece." Hiring Linda had been one of Mrs. Phelps's best suggestions, and she was infinitely better than the elderly and inefficient Jane, who—although a sweet and kind lady—didn't have the force of personality necessary to keep Mama G and Daisy corralled.

Grace would never forget pulling into the driveway last week and seeing Jane standing alone on the porch, looking stricken. The few minutes it had taken them to figure out where Mama G and Daisy had gone had been some of the longest of Grace's life. The open garage door at Mr. Parker's house and a random comment by Jane that Daisy seemed fascinated with their next-door neighbor's motorcycle had sent Grace rushing to her neighbor's door.

She bit back a grimace at her own pettiness for having mentally labeled him as untrustworthy merely because he had long hair and rode a motorcycle. He'd taken good care of Mama G and Daisy during their visit and, from the little Grace had seen, his house was ridiculously charming. He wasn't a barbarian at all.

Grace glanced at the drawer that held her purse and cell phone, and resisted the urge to text Linda and check in. But as Grace had left them just a few hours ago, such a text would make it seem that she didn't trust Linda. And she did. So far, anyway.

Sheesh, parenting and caretaking were so much harder than she'd thought they would be. No one had explained to her that she'd be constantly worried, her imagination churning out worst-case scenarios with devastating details as if she'd suddenly become Stephen King's muse.

"You're lucky to have Linda," the mayor said. "She's an angel, and her husband, Mark, isn't bad, either. When I told him I'd rather come to the Kiwanis meeting next month instead of this one, as it'll be warmer then and the fishing not quite so good, he understood. He's a hunter, so he has excellent seasonal awareness. Speaking of which, I should go. The fish are waiting."

She set her coffee on the corner of her desk. "Not to be critical, but don't you owe it to the citizens of this town to work at least forty hours a week?"

"I worked late last night for the town hall meeting, so I'm taking some time off." He chuckled. "Town hall. Why, it was just me and Mr. Cramer, who always comes to complain about the buzzing streetlamp outside of his home."

"Can't it be fixed?"

"It doesn't buzz; that's just his excuse to visit. I always take him out for coffee and ice cream after the meeting, and he likes that." The mayor beamed. "A good man, Cramer, if a little crazy. But every election year, just like clockwork, I can count on him to put up hundreds of signs for my campaign. Why, he'd plaster the whole town if I let him."

"It doesn't sound like your town halls are very productive."

"That's sort of the point, isn't it? If you have people coming to your town halls, then you've already made a mistake. But if no one comes, you're good to go." He winked, walking past her to the office supply closet.

She followed. "I didn't realize we got comp time."

"Oh. Sorry, but you don't. But you *do* get overtime, so that's good." He stopped near the closet and beamed as if he'd just given her the best news in the world.

Grace had to fight the urge to knock the smile off his face. When she'd first met him, she'd thought his good humor was sincere, but she'd quickly realized he was one of those people who could look you right in the eye and tell you the worst news possible—*you're fired*, or *your mother died*—and his smile would still be locked in place. "I'm glad to know there's overtime. I have at least six months of paperwork that should be logged into the computer, and perhaps more. I can come in on Saturdays and start—"

"Easy there! There's overtime, but you can't *use* it."

"What?"

"It's just for emergencies like tornados or earthquakes."

"But the paperwork is so far behind. I need to—"

"Oh dear, look at the time! The fish will wait for me, but you—" His smile deepened. "If you don't hurry, you'll be late."

"For what?"

"The Dove Pond Social Club." The mayor blinked. "Surely I put that on your schedule?"

"There's nothing on my schedule today."

"Oops," he replied cheerfully. "You'd better get a move on, as they meet at the library conference room in five minutes. You'll enjoy working with the club. It's such fun."

"Fun or not, I don't have time for a social club. The tax notices are ready for mailing, there's a stack of invoices that should be sent out this afternoon, I'm trying to get the last six months of parking tickets—"

"Whoa! Miss Wheeler, the social club isn't just fun. They plan the festivals. Or rather, *you* plan the festivals with *their* help."

She could only stare at him. "Festivals? With an *s*?"

"We have two," he announced proudly. He counted them off on his fat, sausage-roll fingers. "The Apple Festival and the Spring Fling. Sadly, you missed the Spring Fling, but the Apple Festival happens the first weekend in October and is ready for your special touch."

"I don't have a special touch when it comes to planning events, especially festivals. I don't think I've ever been to one."

"They're wonderful events and there are parades and craft booths and—oh, all sorts of things. You'll enjoy planning them. It was one of Mrs. Phelps's favorite duties. Surely she mentioned them?"

"Not a word."

"Oh. That's surprising."

Wasn't it, though? Every day brought a list of things Mrs. Phelps hadn't mentioned, none of them good. "I don't know the first thing about festivals. You need to find someone else to work with this club."

"Oh, don't worry! There's a folder full of notes, and the other social club members know everything else." His smile brightened as if he'd just solved all her problems. "They're a good group, as good as it gets. You'll love working with them, and they love, love, *love* our festivals."

"Then let them do it. I won't stand in their way."

The mayor laughed as if she'd told a good joke. "You'll be wonderful. Mrs. Phelps thought so. When she hired you, she said you'd make the festivals better than ever. And if there's one thing I trust, it's Mrs. Phelps's ability to spot talent. She has a gift with that."

Grace bit back a snarky comment. She and Mrs. Phelps had spoken so few times that it was unlikely the ex–town clerk had divined anything about Grace other than she was desperate for a job.

Mayor Moore snapped his fingers. "Oops! I haven't given you the festivals folder, and you'll need it for the meeting." The mayor walked back past her to his office.

She went to his door and watched him shuffle through the stacks of folders piled on his huge desk. "What exactly happens at these festivals?"

He moved a stack of gray folders and began looking through the blue ones that had been resting underneath. "Oh, you know, the usual. A parade with floats, craft booths, cotton candy and caramel apples, maybe a talent contest or a beauty pageant or some such thing. It varies from year to year."

She winced. What a difference a few months could make. Instead of heading meetings where millions of dollars' worth of financial decisions were made, she was now recording traffic fines, sending out tax notices, and planning vapid, town-wide prom parties. She was capable of so much more.

"Where is that file? I don't know where it could have gotten t— Ah! There it is." Mayor Moore removed a bulging folder from a stack balanced on one corner of his desk and handed it to her. "This is an important job; more so than you might realize. Our local businesses count on our festivals to help them make it through the slower months, and lately . . ." He waved a hand as if to bat away a fly.

"What's that mean?" She waved her hand to mimic his gesture.

His smile slipped, but only for a second before he raised it back into place. "Nothing. It's just that our attendance has gone down a little."

She tightened her grip on the faded folder. "Define 'a little.'"

"Something like, oh, forty-two percent."

He'd mumbled those last few words, but she still heard them. "Good lord. That's almost half!"

"Which is why I'm delighted you're going to be working on it. We need fresh blood. I wish you could have seen how things used to be in the old days when tens of thousands of people wandered our streets." His expression grew dreamy. "They ate and drank our food and beverages, bought flags and crafts and quilts and—God, just about everything. They were like locusts, and when they left, not a hot dog or a pot holder was left in town, and the cash registers were full. Festival goers spent money like water."

"I hear a lot of past tense in those sentences. How many years in a row has attendance been going down?"

"The last ten or so. Maybe longer."

"Let me get this straight: you want me to reverse a ten-year trend in one year," she said flatly.

"Oh, it may take you two. I'm not expecting miracles here. But I'm sure that if anyone can do it, it'll be you. As I said, Mrs. Phelps is never wrong. Not about people, anyway."

Riiiight. Grace had yet to tell him she would only be here a year—not that it mattered. No one could change a ten-year trend in a single year, not without a huge infusion of new talent and cash, neither of which she saw in this office. Just to be sure, she said, "I assume you'll be committing new funding?"

"If I only could. There's no extra funding, not this year." The mayor's smile widened, and he said in a false, breezy tone, "But I'm sure you won't let us down! Just come up with some fresh, new ideas, and delegate the implementation to the planning committee. That way you won't be stuck doing everything yourself."

As if it would be that easy. But she guessed she had no choice. *What have I gotten myself into?* "Who is on this committee?"

"Social club," he corrected as he led the way out of his office and headed back to the supply closet.

She followed him, plopping the fat folder on her desk as she walked past.

"There are eight—oh, wait—make that seven people besides yourself, all community leaders." He paused by the closet. "Mrs. Hopper is no longer a member. She resigned last year because she didn't get her way regarding the parade theme. She wanted to call the Apple Festival parade the March of Very Fat Santas."

"Santa in the fall?"

"Exactly. Plus the 'fat' part seemed as if it might be a sort of fat shaming, too. Whatever you do, you don't want the social media mob after you. The club told Mrs. Hopper no to her fat Santas, and she upped and quit. She has a thing about Santas. If you ever go to her house, you'll see what I mean. There are hundreds of them in her living room alone."

"All year-round?"

"Oh yes. She lives on Maple Street. You can tell her house by the Christmas lights, which are on all year." He pulled a fishing rod from behind the closet door and then crossed to the large file cabinet in one corner of her office, where he opened the highest drawer and pulled out a tackle box. "All the information you need is in that folder: every purchase ever made, every parade lineup ever planned, every special guest who's ever attended—you name it. Mrs. Phelps was a very thorough record keeper." He opened the tackle box, pulled out a floppy hat decorated with an assortment of fishing hooks, and donned it. "There. I think that's it." He refastened the lid and, carrying the pole and box, walked past her toward the door to the lobby.

She followed him. "Mayor Moore, you can't go now. I have so many questions. I don't know—"

"Don't worry. I'll be back in time to sign the weekly paychecks at five. We can't forget those, can we?"

"Mayor, I—"

But he was gone, the door swinging closed behind him.

"Damn it!" Grace told the door. She wished she could kick something, but she was wearing a pair of expensive shoes that she could no longer afford to replace.

She dropped into her chair and crossed her arms, wondering if throwing her stapler might release a little of her irritation. But no, that was childish, and no matter how much this position irked her, it was putting food on the table and a roof over her family's head. She needed this job and needed it badly.

Between the ever-collapsing walls of her unimportant, low-paying, tiny job, the relentless progression of Mama G's illness, and Daisy's continued refusal to accept her as a parent, Grace had never felt so weighted down. It wasn't that she thought of Daisy and Mama G as burdens; she loved them too much to ever think of them that way. But their survival and quality of life rested squarely on her shoulders and no one else's, and today she could feel every square inch of that responsibility. Worse, she was beginning to wonder if she was up to it. As a kid, once she'd reached Mama G's house, Grace's life had changed. She'd never again failed at anything except for one key goal—taking care of Hannah and keeping her safe. That one thing had been beyond Grace's abilities, and now here she was, trying to take care of two people instead of one, neither of whom particularly welcomed her efforts.

Grace sighed and rubbed her temples. Was this why Hannah had abandoned Daisy at Mama G's all those years ago and run away? Because she couldn't handle the feeling that her every move, her every decision, would impact, and perhaps ruin, Daisy's life? *Oh, Hannah, you should have asked for help. We'd have been there for you. But to just dump her like that and then leave. It hurt her. I still see it in her eyes.*

Grace's throat tightened, and a deep flash of rage burned her throat. In some ways, she understood Daisy's anger and knew that most of it was directed at her mom. To be honest, they all had reasons to be angry with Hannah, although no one more so than Daisy.

The clock on the wall chimed the hour and Grace shot it an impatient look. With a sigh, she stood. Hannah might not have been able to live up to her responsibilities, but Grace could and would. She was more than capable. *Now, to deal with this ridiculous festival.*

She collected her things, realizing with dark humor that she was late for a meeting she didn't want to go to, where she was supposed to plan an event she didn't want to attend, while making nice with people she didn't want to know. *People like Sarah Dove.*

Grace grimaced at her own grumpy thoughts. Sarah had stopped by the house several times since their conversation in front of town hall last week, and while Grace had been polite, she hadn't encouraged the woman, either. As nice as Sarah seemed to be, she obviously wanted to be more than mere acquaintances. But right now, Grace had no time for anyone other than her own family. They were her one and only focus.

The clock seemed to tick louder, and Grace yanked her thoughts from the darkness of her past, scooped up her coffee, and grabbed the fat folder from her desk. Muttering to herself about bosses who didn't do any work, she fixed the door sign, moving the plastic hands to show that she expected to return in an hour.

She started to leave but then paused, staring at the sign. Surely it wouldn't take a whole hour. "*Delegate*, he said," she muttered aloud. "I'd delegate the whole damn thing if I could."

She stood where she was for a long moment, staring blindly at the sign while her mind locked onto a truly unique idea.

Could she?

Why not?

She smiled. *Delegation is the key.*

Grace moved the hands on the sign to indicate she'd only be gone fifteen minutes. "That's better." And with that, she locked the door and left.

CHAPTER 5

Sarah

Sarah watched Grace walk across the street, her notebook held to her like a shield, her heels striking the asphalt with enough force that, had it been warmer, they would have left marks.

What a mess.

It was the fourth, or perhaps fifth time Sarah had thought that in the last five minutes. And it was all because of the tightly controlled woman right now fleeing the scene of carnage she'd created.

Well . . . to be fair, "carnage" was a bit harsh. "Fiasco" was more accurate. "Disappointment" worked, too. "Deep disappointment" worked even better.

Zoe Bell and Nate Stevens came out of the library and joined Sarah on the top step. Nate had been a classmate of Sarah's oldest sister, Madison, and had even dated her in high school for a short time, which could be said of most of the good-looking guys she went to school with. He was tall, handsome, auburn-haired, tanned, and perpetually dressed in flannel. As owner of the local Ace Hardware, he had access to a lot of signage, which made him a valued member of the Dove Pond Social Club and pretty much every other organization in town.

He watched Grace on the other side of the street, striding up the sidewalk as if she owned the place. "That was interesting."

" 'Interesting' doesn't begin to cover it." Zoe watched over the top of her sunglasses as the door swung closed behind Grace. The vice president of the First People's Bank, Zoe was dark-haired and elegant, a dead ringer for a young black Audrey Hepburn. She knew it, too. In celebration of her self-aware Audreyness, Zoe wore expensive vintage everything and, by Sarah's reckoning, owned no fewer than a hundred pairs of cat-eye sunglasses.

Zoe shifted the faded folder she held to one side and slid her sunglasses up so they rested on her head. "I have to give her credit. She's efficient."

"Efficiently devastating," Sarah said sourly. "Someone needs to tell her that wasn't cool."

"It won't be me," Nate said. "I know a tank when I see one, and that woman would as soon roll over you as wave hello."

"She was mighty," Zoe said. "At one point, I had to fight the urge to salute."

"We all did," Nate agreed, his blue eyes twinkling.

"Tank or not," Sarah said, "we can't let what happened at that meeting go unchallenged."

"Don't look at me." Nate went down the few stairs to the sidewalk. "I'll support whatever you guys decide, but I'm not going against that force of nature."

Zoe eyed him with a thoughtful gaze. "Really? You'll support whatever we decide, no questions asked?"

"Yup, because I know I'm leaving this fight in capable hands—all of yours." He backed away as he spoke. "Meanwhile, I've got to get back to work."

"Afraid?" Zoe demanded, although she smiled as she said it.

"Terrified," he admitted. "Just let me know when the next meeting is, and I'll be there."

Sarah nodded absently. "Someone will send an email."

"Perfect. See you all later." He gave them a friendly nod and headed down the street toward his store.

Zoe moved down a step so that she could watch him go. As soon as he was out of earshot, she murmured, "He knows how to wear those jeans, doesn't he?"

Sarah sent a frustrated look at Zoe. "You haven't changed since high school."

Zoe shrugged. "We all have our hobbies."

Sarah rolled her eyes, although she wasn't all that irked. She liked Zoe. Or she did now. In high school, Sarah hadn't known how to handle Zoe's barbed humor. Now Sarah rather enjoyed it. "Not to disrupt your designated hobby time, but we've an emergency on our hands. What should we do about it?"

Zoe didn't stop watching Nate's departure. "I'm not sure yet, but I'm thinking."

"Think fast," Sarah ordered.

The library door creaked open and Ed Mayhew came outside, squinting in the afternoon sun and looking a bit disoriented. "Was it me, or did we just see a hundred and fifty years of tradition toppled in less than five minutes?"

"One hundred and fifty-seven," Sarah corrected. Ed and his wife, Maggie, had moved to Dove Pond from Asheville eight years ago to open Paw Printz, the best (and only) pet store in town. Convivial and creative, the couple had quickly become two of Dove Pond's most active residents. Short, paunchy, and pale, Ed reminded Sarah of his dog, an elderly dachshund named Peggy Mae. Fortunately, Ed's disposition was better than that of Peggy Mae, who'd either bitten or tried to bite just about everybody in town.

"What a meeting." Ed raked a hand through his salt-and-pepper hair, leaving a good bit of it standing on end. "Maggie had her hopes up that the new town clerk would know how to turn the festival around. We all did. But that—" He shrugged helplessly. "Hell, I don't even know what that was."

"It was painful," Zoe said.

"Like being kicked in the teeth," Ed agreed. He sighed. "I guess I'll head back to the store, but I'll tell you what—I'm not saying a word about this to Maggie. She'd just go on a tear, and I don't have the energy to listen."

"We should all keep this to ourselves," Sarah said. "I'll have Erma add that to the minutes email. No talking. The last thing we need is a bunch of rumors swirling around town. In the meantime, Zoe and I are going to find a way to fix this."

"I hope you can." He shook his head. "Hostile takeovers and dark secrets. We've turned into the Real Housewives of Dove Pond. Just let me know when everything is settled."

"We will," Zoe said.

"Good. I'll see you at the next meeting, then." He frowned. "There *will* be a next meeting, won't there?"

"Of course," Zoe said sharply.

"And soon," Sarah added.

"Then I'll be there." He nodded goodbye and headed across the street.

Sarah watched him, noticing that he walked right by the planter in front of town hall without so much as a glance. Apparently, she was the only one who'd noticed that the formerly purple flowers had faded to a pale, sickly green as Grace whisked past.

It was becoming more and more obvious that Grace's presence in their town meant something monumental, and yet no one else seemed to have realized it. It was all Sarah could do not to announce it from the rooftops, but she knew from long experience that it was best to let people discover things for themselves. Besides, such an announcement would raise questions, and Sarah didn't have answers. Not yet, anyway.

"That was complete and utter baloney!" Erma Tingle announced as she stepped through the doors. A short, square woman with brown skin, she wore her iron-gray hair in the same style she'd sported since she graduated from Dove Pond High forty-two years ago. "I'm going to speak to Mayor Moore about this. I bet he'll have something to say about Miss Wheeler's decision to ditch her responsibilities."

"Good luck finding him," Sarah said.

Zoe added, "He'll be out fishing by now. Besides, he won't do anything. You know how he hates confrontation."

"Well, we have to do something!" Erma said. "I've never seen the like. She just came in, took the roll so she could mark us all present, announced we needed a new chairman, and then called a vote on the first person who offered to do it. Then she dumped her folder and left. She was in that room all of"—Erma looked at the notes she'd taken—"three minutes."

"It was shocking," Zoe agreed, absently smoothing the bent corner of the fat folder she held.

"And *you*!" Erma poked Zoe's arm. "*You* raised your hand the second she asked who wanted to be chair!"

"I regretted it as soon as I did." When Erma stared at her in disbelief, Zoe rolled her eyes. "You can't think I *want* to be the chair. I don't even like coming to the meetings. You know that."

Sarah had to admit that was true. "She does complain about it a lot," she told Erma.

"See?" Zoe said. "But I couldn't say no to a leadership opportunity. She waved the chairmanship position in front of me like a red flag. It was right *there*."

"So you jumped at the bait," Erma said, looking disgusted.

"I'm weak! It's all the bad training I've had. My father has said over and over and over, 'Zoe, you're a Bell, act like it.' 'Zoe, never refuse an opportunity.' 'Zoe, always be in front, no matter the cost.'"

Erma snorted. "I don't know why you listen to him. Your father also thinks there's a good chance the world is run by lizard men. I'm on some sort of email list he's set up since he retired, and he keeps sending out videos that look like they were made in someone's mother's basement with an old camcorder."

"He's got too much free time now, but we all know he made the bank what it is today." Zoe grimaced. "I can't help myself where he's concerned. It's ingrained, like going to church. I know I won't go to hell if I skip one Sunday, but the thought of my dad's face when he sees that empty pew makes me sick to my stomach. I feel the same way if I say no to a leadership opportunity."

The door behind them opened and Kat Carter came out, followed by Sarah's sister Ava. No two women could be more different. Kat was dark-haired, tall, and curvaceous, the kind of woman who, even while wearing jeans, looked as if she were about to get on a private jet to Paris. Meanwhile, Ava was short and never wore makeup, and her blond hair was tied back in a permanent ponytail. She was attired in her usual overalls and, as far as Sarah knew, hadn't worn heels since her prom. As different as the two were, Ava and Kat had been close friends since the fifth grade.

Ava stopped beside Sarah. "Is this the after-meeting?"

"Why weren't we invited?" Kat asked. She said in a lower voice to Ava, "Everyone wants to go to the after-meeting."

Sarah sniffed. "Only the cool kids are allowed at the after-meeting, so you're both out."

Ava broke into a grin, a brilliant lopsided affair that transformed her from tomboy gardener into a dazzlingly charming woman in the space of a second.

Sarah returned the grin. She and Ava had grown close since high school, and Sarah couldn't ask for a better roommate or sister.

Ava looked at Sarah now. "Any ideas of how to proceed?" The name of her business, AVA'S LANDSCAPING AND GOURMET SPE-CIALTY TEAS, was spelled out in colorful, flower-strewn letters on her overall pocket. It wasn't the most creative business name, but as Ava liked to point out, her creativity was better spent on her plants and brews than on the words printed on her overalls.

Sarah was proud of Ava's success. Ava was a master gardener, and everything she touched bloomed. It had been that way since she was a kid, and now her services as a landscaper were in high demand. Even more profitable was her side business providing the trendy shops in downtown Asheville with the specialty teas she made from the plants she grew in her greenhouses. Although they'd never talked numbers, Sarah was fairly certain her sister was making a small fortune.

"And you." Ava pinned Zoe with an accusing look. "You practically jumped out of your seat when Grace asked for someone to take her place as chairman."

"I know, I know." Zoe made a face. "I caved. But I'm going to take care of it. If I have to move heaven and earth, Grace Wheeler will lead our club once again."

"We need her," Sarah said.

"Badly," Zoe agreed.

"I don't know," Erma said in a skeptical tone. "Do we really want Grace in charge of our festival if she doesn't want to do it?"

"Yes," Sarah said firmly.

Ava's gaze locked on Sarah. "You know something."

Sarah nodded. She never could hide anything from her sister. "She's the right one for the job. That much I'm sure of." And she was.

Erma threw up her hands. "Fine. Get her back. We need a chairman, and if Zoe doesn't want the job—"

"I don't," Zoe said emphatically.

"Then Ms. Wheeler it is." Erma narrowed her gaze on Zoe. "I assume you've already got a plan in mind."

"I might. If Mayor Moore wasn't such a pushover, I would—" Zoe stared at the closed doors of town hall, her lips pursed.

"Uh-oh," Ava announced. "She's thinking."

Kat leaned closer to Ava to say in a low voice, "I've seen that look before. Zoe's in hunting mode."

Sarah could almost see the shiny cogs twirling in Zoe's sharp, edgy brain.

Suddenly, Zoe gave a cool, calculating smile, her hazel eyes sparkling. "Rest assured, fellow club members," she announced. "By this time next week, Grace Wheeler will once again chair our club."

"Voluntarily?" Kat asked.

"No, but she'll do it with enthusiasm." Zoe considered this and then amended, "Well, not enthusiasm. I can't promise miracles. But she'll do it with purpose."

"That's good enough for me." Erma surveyed Zoe with appreciation. "You look like your mom when you talk like that."

Zoe's smile flashed. "Thank you. She was as hard as nails, my mom."

Ava cocked an eyebrow at Zoe. "Need any help from us?"

"Not right now. I can handle the first part of this project on my own. Mayor Moore will be in the bank this afternoon to make his mortgage payment. I'll catch him there."

The hope Sarah had been feeling wilted when Zoe mentioned the mayor. "If you're expecting Mayor Moore to take care of this, you're going to be disappointed. He won't do anything. You know how he is."

Zoe's smile didn't waver. "I know exactly how he is. Wait and see."

"Fine." Sarah couldn't keep the doubt from her voice.

"If Zoe says it'll happen, then it will," Erma said. "But whatever you're going to do, do it quickly. We need to get Miss Wheeler up to speed on her duties as soon as possible or we'll be behind."

"Will do. I'd better get back to work. See you all later." Zoe turned on her heel, ready to head down the steps.

"Wait," Sarah called out. "I almost forgot." She hurried into the library, grabbed a book she'd set out earlier, and brought it back outside.

"Uh-oh," Ava said. "She's armed."

Sarah ignored her sister and thrust the book into Zoe's hands.

Zoe looked at it. "*Basic Italian in Ten Easy Weeks.*" She frowned. "I don't need this."

Erma peeked over Zoe's shoulder at the cover. "You'd better take it. Last week, she gave me a huge, hardback repair manual for my truck and it sure came in handy last night."

"Your truck broke down?" Ava asked.

"It did. Thank God I had that book."

"Wow." Zoe looked impressed. "You fixed it yourself."

"Lord, no. The transmission got stuck in neutral and if I hadn't had that book to use as a chock block, that damn truck would have rolled off into the ditch while I waited for a tow."

"Sheesh," Zoe said in a testy tone. "That doesn't count: you didn't use the book as a *book*. You'd have been in even better shape if she'd just given you a block of wood."

"It worked, and I was glad I had it. That's all I know." Erma checked her wristwatch. "I'd best be off. Missy Robinson is watching the shop, and she has clarinet practice in fifteen minutes. Take the book, Zoe. You'll be sorry if you don't." Erma waved and then left.

"I've got to go, too," Ava announced. "I'm supposed to meet someone about my rental house." About five years ago, as Ava's business had begun to grow, she'd bought a small cottage situated on two acres of land. She'd used the cottage as an office and had built two large, self-watering greenhouses behind it. But her business had grown in such leaps and bounds that she'd had to purchase another twenty acres at the edge of town that included a large farmhouse and a huge barn as well. Ava had moved her office to the farmhouse and now leased the cottage for a reasonable sum, although she kept the rights to the greenhouses, where she grew the more delicate plants she used for her teas.

"Are you renting to anyone we know?" Kat asked curiously.

"No. Her name is Sofia Rodriguez and she's new to the area. I'm hoping she'll work for me."

"You could use the help," Kat said. "If you're leaving now, I'll come with you. I parked beside your truck." Kat looked at Sarah. "I'm meeting Ellen Jameson. She's putting her house on the market. She took a job in Charlotte and it's too much of a commute."

Sarah winced. "She's lived here her entire life."

"She hates leaving, but she has no choice. Dr. Lynn retired and is closing his office, and there are no other nursing positions in this area. She tried to get a job in Asheville, but she needed a day shift because of her kids, and there weren't any, so Charlotte it is."

Zoe didn't look happy. "I hate that."

"Me too," Kat admitted. "But it is what it is. I'll see you all at the next meeting." With a wave, she and Ava left, walking together to the library parking lot.

Zoe didn't wait for them to get out of sight before she held out the book. "I'm not taking this stupid book. No one in Dove Pond speaks Italian and I'm not going to Italy."

Sarah shrugged but made no move to reclaim the book.

Zoe shook it. "Come on!"

"Nope."

"Just take it. I'm not going to read it."

Sarah shook her head.

"Good God, you are a stubborn woman, do you know that?"

"I do. I'm rather proud of that fact."

Zoe rolled her eyes and slid the book on top of the fat file. "You are just as weird now as you were in high school."

Sarah grinned. "Thanks."

"You— Ugh!" Zoe regarded Sarah narrowly. "Tell me something. You seem awfully determined to see Grace Wheeler take her place at the helm of our little club. More than the rest of us. What do you know that the rest of us don't?"

Sarah briefly toyed with the idea of telling Zoe about the signs she'd seen that Grace was going to help save Dove Pond, but then thought better of it. Zoe wasn't the type to buy into something she couldn't touch, so Sarah just shrugged. "Our town needs her. *We* need her. You know how bad things are getting. You, of all people, can see that our town is in decline."

Zoe frowned. "And you think the festival income can patch that hole?"

"No, but—" Oh sheesh, how could she put this? "I think Grace can fix things for Dove Pond, and not just with the festivals."

"How? From what I've heard, before she came here, she worked with a wealth management firm. If there's one thing Dove Pond doesn't have, it's wealth."

"I don't know how it's going to work. I just know it can and will."

Zoe snorted. "You're an odd bird, Sarah Dove."

Sarah shrugged. "Thanks."

Zoe rolled her eyes and then headed down the stairs, stopping when she reached the sidewalk. "I'll stop by tomorrow and let you know what's going on. But first I need to do a dry run so I'll have an idea how far we'll need to take things."

"I can't wait to hear what you've come up with, although I'm sure it'll work. The only person in this town more stubborn than me is you."

A reluctant grin touched Zoe's wide mouth. "That's the truest thing you've said all afternoon. Now, if you'll excuse me, I have a date with the mayor that he doesn't know about."

"Go ahead. I've got to get ready for Children's Hour and I haven't picked a book yet."

Zoe waved as she left and was soon across the street, heading to the bank. When she reached the planter in front of town hall, she slowed, as if surprised by something. After a moment, she shrugged and continued on her way.

Sarah looked at the flowers. They were now mottled, partially caught between a weak green color and their former glorious purple, every bit as confused as the members of the social club. *Don't worry*, she told herself. *We'll get her back on track.*

Or so Sarah hoped. The way Grace had marched into their meeting and so quickly divested herself of her responsibilities was a setback. Even if Zoe did manage to get the mayor to put Grace back in charge of their festival planning, someone would have to make sure she understood the importance of their endeavors, not to mention the peril their little town was in.

But it was more than that. The journal had said that Grace had to stay in Dove Pond forever. And for that to happen, she had to care. She had to care about the town and its people, and she had to become a true part of Dove Pond.

That, apparently, was Sarah's job, and she had no idea how to make it happen.

Not yet, anyway. "But I'll find a way," she muttered to herself as she went back into the lovely quiet of the library. "I have to."

CHAPTER 6

Grace

Grace parked her car beside the green pickup truck in her driveway, grabbed her satchel and purse, and headed up the walkway. What a lousy, lousy day. She'd hoped to spend at least part of her morning going through the annual budget, a copy of which she'd found in a dusty folder labeled STUFF, but she'd had no chance. The mayor had forgotten to mention until this morning that an important state tax report was due by five; no fewer than twelve people had showed up with various questions she couldn't answer about the new county business license requirements; and the phone had rung off the hook. It was a good thing she'd handed off the social club last week, because she had no time to plan a party or a festival or whatever they wanted to call it.

Still, Grace couldn't help feeling a tiny pinch of guilt for walking away from a responsibility, even one as frivolous as the Dove Pond Social Club.

She reached the porch and had just put her foot on the bottom step when Linda came out, the screen door slamming shut behind her. Large-boned, as broad of shoulder as she was of waist, Linda

Robinson looked more like a linebacker than a home care assistant. Grace smiled at her; she couldn't have asked for a better caretaker. "Hi, Linda. Sorry I'm late."

"Pssht." Linda's brown hair, thick and curly, framed her round, freckled face like a halo. "Ten or fifteen minutes isn't going to kill me. Besides, you were kind enough to call ahead and let me know, which is all I ask."

"I still feel bad. I tried to get out of the office, but the tax mailers went out a few days ago, so I had a ton of phone calls."

Linda clicked her tongue in sympathy. "No one likes to pay taxes."

"I don't either, but I like good public schools, drivable roads, and a fire department that can do more than make an annual calendar."

"I don't know," Linda said thoughtfully. "That calendar is pretty sweet. My daughter, Missy, bought six, one for her and five for her friends. The school won't let them hang pictures of bare-chested men in their lockers, so she and her friends cut out little outfits for them. I think they enjoyed that even more than the calendar."

Grace laughed. "If Missy likes the calendar, then it must be cool. I need to order a copy."

"You'd better hurry. They go fast. By the way, speaking of tasty treats, your momma had her dinner a half hour ago, but Daisy wouldn't eat. She's in the backyard right now, looking for crayfish in the creek."

"I'll make sure she gets her dinner. She gets hangry fast."

"So do I, which is why I'm heading home now. Mark cooks like an angel. He called a few minutes ago and said something about a roast he made from a recipe he got off some cooking show. I don't know what he said after that, because my stomach growled so loud it blocked my ears."

"I wish I had someone to cook for me."

"But you do. I left stew on the stove for your dinner."

"Thank you. That's very kind of you."

"It's not the same as having a special someone cook for you, though. When we first started dating, Mark made me a chocolate torte that almost gave me an orgasm. I knew I had to marry him then. I was *not* going to let a man who could cook like that get away."

"I might be tempted to chase after a man like that, too. Mama G used to do all the cooking, but I do most of it now and I'm not very good at it." It stung to admit she wasn't good at something, but well, there it was. "I'm learning. Or trying to, anyway."

"I'm sure you do fine. Do you mind walking with me to the truck? I'd like to talk to you about something."

All Grace wanted to do was go into the house, sink into a chair, and put her feet up. But Linda looked so concerned that Grace set her satchel and purse on the porch and then came back to fall into step beside her. "What's up? You're not going to quit, are you? Because if you are, I'm going to need a drink."

"I don't even know what the word *quit* means. No, I'm just worried about something and didn't want little ears overhearing." Linda glanced at Grace, and her face softened. "I know it's been a rough few months for all of you. I can see it in your faces. But the fact is, Mama G is not going to get better. She's going to be harder and harder to take care of."

"I know, but she's calmer here than she was in her home in Whitlow. She has so many memories of this house and she's not nearly as agitated as she was."

"Oh, honey, it's not Mama G I'm worried about." Linda stopped by her truck and turned to face Grace. "I'm worried about you."

"Me?"

"Yes, you. Look, I don't mean to pry, but becoming a new mother, even of a child as old as Daisy, is a lot of work and stress. And in addition, you're trying to deal with Mama G, and you have a new job—Sweetheart, you've got more plates in the air than you've arms. Do you have family or friends that live nearby? Someone you can lean on now and then?"

Grace briefly thought about arguing that she could handle all her "plates," but the genuine concern on Linda's face quashed the idea.

Linda was only saying what Grace had begun to think—that she was in over her head. "There aren't many members of our family left. Mrs. Phelps was the last of Mama G's relatives to live here and my sister, Hannah—" It still hurt to say *died*. As if in saying it, Grace was making it more final. *It's final enough as it is.* She shrugged. "Now there's just me, Mama G, and Daisy. But trust me, whatever happens, I'll take good care of them."

"I know you will, but you're going to need support. Emotional support."

"I can handle it. I'm sure of it."

Linda raised her plucked, pencil-thin eyebrows. "You think you can, I know. But do you understand what you're about to face? You're about to head into some deep, deep waters, the likes of which you've never seen. And from what I can tell, there's no one rowing your boat but you."

"I'm a good rower."

"I'm sure you are. But we're talking waves bigger than you. You're going to need more than one set of hands on those oars to make it, because believe me, before it's over, it's going to get tough."

Grace's stomach sank. "That's grim."

"Because it is. Look, I'm not trying to scare you, but I've been doing this job for almost twenty years and I've taken care of a lot of mothers and fathers who've fought the same battle Mama G is fighting. As hard as it is on those poor souls, it's harder on their children. It hurts like the deepest cut to watch your parents fade away. One of my clients said it was like trying to hold sand in her fingers; no matter how tightly she gripped, she couldn't hold it in place."

Fade away. That's exactly how it felt. Grace had to clear her throat before she could speak. "It's not easy, but I've faced rough water before. More than most people, in fact, so I know we'll find a way through this." They had to. She'd find a way. She'd always found a way, and she wasn't going to stop now.

Still, behind her thoughts hovered a shimmering, panic-colored cloud that she refused to examine too closely. *What will I do when*

Mama G no longer knows me? Because then I'll be alone. Really *alone.*

She'd have Daisy, of course, but they were still painfully new to each other in the role of parent and child, both struggling to figure things out. And even if they managed to jell into a real family, that didn't change the bald truth about Mama G. Her time with them was limited.

Tears flooded Grace's eyes and she clenched her hands into fists and wished she owned a punching bag. A real one. One she could beat the living daylights out of. *Time* was much too short of a word. And it got smaller still when you cut it down into countable hours, and then racing minutes, and finally into desperately minuscule seconds. Eventually, there was nothing left. That was what was happening to Mama G right now—she was being sliced away, one memory at a time, and it made Grace sick to her soul and so furious she could spit nails.

Linda put her hand on Grace's shoulder. "It's hard, I know."

Grace forced her dark thoughts away. As much as she liked Linda, the weight of her hand made Grace cringe. If she cried, she might never stop.

She moved slightly, and Linda let her hand drop back to her side. Grace managed to blink away her tears and keep her voice even as she said, "You're sweet to worry, but I'm going to be okay. I have to be. In a weird way, that helps."

Linda's smile seemed pained, but she threw up her hands. "Okay, then. I just wish you had more of a support team, that's all."

Desperate to change the subject, Grace said, "How was Mama G today?"

"Good. We only had one bad hour. She woke up from her nap irritated and then we couldn't find the remote for the TV."

"Did you find it?"

"Yes, in the bathroom sink."

"She keeps putting it in the weirdest places."

"Most likely she's having trouble remembering what it's for and she doesn't want to admit it, so she hides it. I've had patients get paranoid that people were trying to steal their things, too, although that doesn't seem to be the case this time." Linda opened the door of her pickup and set her bag on the seat. "Right now, Mama G's memory is like the ocean. It comes and goes, high tide and low tide. But each time, the beach erodes a little bit more."

"I see." And Grace did see, although she wished she didn't.

"When you find the remote or a spoon or a toothbrush or whatever stashed in the wrong place, that could be a sign that she needs help using it from now on."

"I'll pay attention."

"I know you will. What she needs more than anything right now is to know she is going to be okay. She needs to hear that as often as you can work it into the conversation."

Grace tucked her hair behind her ear. "I've been trying to do that, but I'll amp it up."

"You're doing great. I hope I didn't upset you by saying something. I just don't want you to get burned out. I— Oh! I almost forgot. There is some good news."

"Thank God. I could use some good news."

"Sarah Dove left you a book." Linda said the words in the exact same reverentially thrilled tone in which someone might announce, *You won the lottery!* "I left it in the kitchen."

Grace had to fight a "big deal" shrug. "That was nice of her but, to be honest, I think I've read just about every book there is on Alzheimer's. When Mama G was first diagnosed, I bought them all."

"It's not about Alzheimer's. It's fiction." Linda beamed as if that made more sense. "When I was in middle school, I checked that exact same book out of the library. I know it's the same book, because I accidentally splashed hot chocolate on it, and try as I might, I couldn't get the stain out. I thought Mrs. Farmer, the librarian at the time, might shoot me when she saw it, but she just shook her head and put the book back on the return cart."

Great. A stained library book. *That's just wonderful.* "I'm surprised Sarah sent me a book. I don't even have a library card."

"Sarah never worries about that. If there's a book she thinks you need, you'll get it."

"Really? How many books a year does she lose, doing that?"

"None. Trust me, she knows where her books are. More than that, they know where she is." Linda's pointed brows lowered the faintest bit, her gaze narrowing. "You *do* know about Sarah and her books, don't you?"

"She's the town librarian. What more should I know?"

Linda looked astounded. "Well, butter my butt and call me a biscuit! You've lived here for almost three weeks and *no one* has told you about the Doves? Not Mrs. Phelps? Not the mayor? Not *anyone*?"

"The mayor never tells me anything except that he's going fishing. Before she left, Mrs. Phelps did mention that one of the Doves—Ava, I think it was—would get mad if I didn't keep the yard up. But that's it." Well, there'd been a little more than that, but it had been odd and vague, and at the time, Grace had been focusing on other things, like trying to keep her sanity.

Linda tsked. "And here you are, practically next-door neighbors with Sarah, *plus* you're both in the social club, so you see her all the time, too, and yet no one has told you about her."

It looked like the Dove Pond town gossips were rather inept. Not only had they forgotten to share some sort of salacious tidbit about Sarah, but they also seemed to have missed Grace's departure from the social club, which was fine with her. "I've been working a lot lately, so I haven't had the chance to speak to many people, including Sarah."

"I don't care if you work a hundred hours a week—you should still speak to her. If it were me, I'd talk to her so much she'd ask me not to." Linda paused, as if collecting her thoughts. "You should know about this. The Doves are special."

"Special," Grace repeated, wondering where this was going.

"Yes. They founded this town, but more than that, they've kept it alive. And they're . . . well, they're special. Each in their own way, too."

"Wouldn't you say most people are 'special in their own way'?"

Linda shook her head emphatically. "Not like this. This is a kind of special you don't normally see. Take Sarah, for example." Linda leaned closer and said in a reverential tone, "Sarah Dove is a book charmer."

"A book . . . charmer?"

"She knows what book everyone should have."

Wasn't that the job of every librarian? Grace tried to keep her expression neutral as she murmured politely, "How interesting."

Linda made a face. "You don't get it. Look, just do yourself a favor; if Sarah Dove offers you a book, take it. You'll regret it if you don't. She once tried to give me a book about horseback riding, and I almost refused because I'd never ridden a horse in my life and never wanted to. But darned if a month later there wasn't a big ice storm and the roads were a mess and most of the cell towers and electric lines were down. I still had to go to work, though, as I was watching over Mr. Brockton and he wasn't doing well. So off I went. I got all the way across town when my car slid off the road and got stuck in a ditch near the Yorks' dairy farm. Have you met T. W. York yet?"

"I don't think so."

"You will. T.W. has more DUIs than birthdays, and he has to pay those fines in your office."

"He sounds like quite a character."

"He is. Because of his DUIs, he can't drive a car, so he rides his horse, Sandy Face, everywhere he goes. So when my car got stuck at the end of his drive, he showed up on Sandy Face, leading a saddled horse named May Belle the Furious. And wouldn't you know, he wanted me to ride that animal to the gas station to fetch a tow truck?"

"Did you?"

"I did, because I'd read that book Sarah gave me. And good thing, too, because May Belle the Furious was a pain in the ass. She almost bucked me off twice, and one time she headed off down some side lane and it was all I could do to get her to turn around and—" A loud buzz sounded. Linda pulled her cell phone from the top of her purse. "I've got to go. That's Mark. Missy's home and dinner's ready."

"You'd better hurry so it doesn't get cold." Grace tried not to look too relieved to be spared any more Sarah Dove nonsense. "I hope the roast is as good as you expect, or better."

Linda shoved her phone back into her purse. "I'm sure it will be. Enjoy your stew. And don't forget, whatever you do, read that book. I'm not kidding."

"I will," Grace promised, though she had no plans of doing any such thing.

Linda waved and was soon gone.

Grace returned to the porch and collected her things, glancing down the street to the huge mauve house. *Good lord, the Doves are an odd family. And what a weird town this is, to believe in book charmers and other nonsense.* Still shaking her head, she went inside.

"There you are!" Mama G was sitting in her favorite chair, knitting and looking so much like her old self that Grace smiled.

"Sorry I'm late." She placed her satchel and purse on the small table by the front door. "It was a crazy day at work. Phone calls from people not happy with their tax notices, and I'm beginning to think it'll take years to catch up on the data entry."

Mama G tsked as she pulled some yarn free from the ball in the basket. "Whoever heard of an investment group that can't even keep their own records up to date? I'd find someplace else to work if I was you."

"I don't work for—" She caught Mama G's expectant gaze and swallowed the rest of her sentence. "You're right. I should look for another job, shouldn't I?"

"They work you too hard." Mama G tugged some more yarn free and knitted away.

Grace sat on the edge of the green chaise across from Mama G and watched the old woman's hands, the needles clicking softly. It was peaceful sitting here, the sunlight streaming through the window while Mama G's needles clicked in time with the *SpongeBob* theme song that played from Daisy's room upstairs.

Grace glanced at the stairs. "Did Daisy come in? Linda said she was outside trying to catch crawdads."

"Daisy's outside at the fence, talking to our neighbor. She says he's a mechanic and his name is . . ." Mama G frowned, apparently forgetting that she'd already met Trav Parker. "I can't remember. His name is . . . was it Tom? No. Robbie. Not— Oh, it's Robert . . ." She brightened. "Yes. It's Robert, and Robert is a mechanic."

Grace arose and crossed to the window. Sure enough, there was Daisy, hanging over the fence as she watched Trav work on a large blue truck. He looked untamed, with his long hair and his muscled arms covered with tattoos. He finished working on the truck and reached up to release the hood stand. As he did so, the sun lit the side of his face and touched on his scars. Sarah had said he was a veteran. Perhaps that was where the scars had come from.

"Do you see Daisy?" Mama G asked.

"She's by the fence, as you said. I'm about to call her in." Grace opened the window and leaned out. "Daisy, honey? It's time to come in. It's dinnertime and you haven't eaten."

"I'm busy." Daisy hunched her shoulders and favored Grace with a "make me" glare before she turned back to the fence, both arms hooked over the top as if she were hanging there instead of standing.

Behind Grace, Mama G tsked. "She's getting lippy, isn't she?"

Grace pulled back inside and asked Mama G, "Has she been like that all day?"

"Just this afternoon. She gets bored, you know. I wish she had some friends."

So did Grace. She leaned back out the window and said to Daisy, "Linda left some stew for us on the stove. Come eat it while it's hot."

Travis wiped his hands on a shop rag, not sparing Grace so much as a glance, which irked her. There was something dark about him, Grace decided. Something harsh and unyielding. And it set off all sorts of alarms.

Uneasy, Grace turned to Daisy, who was ignoring her better than most teenagers could. She had her mother's rebellious spirit. After Grace and Hannah had moved in with Mama G, it had taken her a long time to teach them "the basics," as Mama G called them. Things like not interrupting others, waiting until it's your turn to go through a door, eating with your mouth closed, and other valuable social rules. Manners, some would have called them. A necessity, Mama G claimed.

Grace now realized how much patience it must have taken for Mama G to teach her and Hannah all of those things. Which is why Grace had smiled when Mama G admitted that Daisy was one of her most difficult projects. "More difficult than me?" Grace had asked. Mama G had thought about it and then said with a smile, "Well, almost."

Grace narrowed her gaze on Daisy now. "It's dinnertime. Come in."

Daisy remained hanging over the fence. She was like a colt, awkward yet graceful, all elbows and knees and smudge-faced scowls. Sometime today she'd slipped a pink tutu over her jeans, the back of it tattered and dirty.

I really need to order her a new one. "Daisy?" Grace said again, more sharply this time.

Daisy hunched her shoulders but didn't acknowledge Grace.

Trav slanted Grace a long, cool look, as if measuring her reaction. She swallowed the urge to snap out something cutting. There was nothing to gain in addressing her next-door neighbor, and she already knew from experience that losing her temper would just make Daisy dig her heels in deeper.

Grace silently counted to ten. Being a mother and a caregiver didn't fit her. She felt as if she were wearing a too-big jacket, the sleeves hanging over her hands so that she couldn't grasp the tools she needed to do either job correctly.

Grace had really believed that coming to this little town might give them all a fresh start. But while Mama G was at least a little better, Daisy wasn't. And all too soon, she would start the third grade at Sweet Creek Elementary School, which meant Grace had just a few months to motivate Daisy to do more on her homework and tests than draw fire-breathing dragons.

Daisy glanced over her shoulder to see if Grace was still waiting, the little girl's expression anything but warm. Under normal circumstances, raising a kid was a monumental job, but the difficulty increased exponentially when, instead of a fresh-off-the-line baby with no preconceived ideas or behaviors, someone handed you a saucy, nearly wild, furious eight-year-old prepacked with a righteous anger at life, one who believed in ghosts and fairy tales and other magical dreck that made real life a boring, bothersome place.

Grace put her hands flat on the windowsill. "Daisy." That's all she said, and she hoped she'd given it the same firm intonation Mama G used to use on her. She now knew it for what it was, a "mom tone," and in its stillness there was power.

Or so Grace hoped.

Daisy's expression didn't change one bit.

Darn it. Grace held her breath, refusing to back down. For a moment, she thought there might be an argument, but the silent standoff was broken when Trav picked up his bucket of tools and went inside. The garage door banged closed behind him.

Sullen, but without any reason to stay where she was, Daisy muttered something under her breath, turned away from the fence, and stomped down the side of the house toward the back door, the tattered tutu bouncing in rebellion.

Whew. Grace shut the window and yanked the curtain closed.

The kitchen door opened and then slammed. After a stilted moment, Daisy yelled, "You lied. Dinner's not ready."

Mama G looked up from her knitting and tsked. "She sounds mad."

"She can be mad. I wish she'd leave our neighbor alone."

"Why's that?" Mama G's knitting never slowed. "Daisy's keeping an eye on him. We both do."

Grace had been heading toward the kitchen, but that startled her and she stopped in the doorway. "Why?"

Mama G looked surprised. "Because he needs it."

Grace didn't know what to say. "You've been talking to him, too?"

"Not lately." The calm faded from Mama G's face and her needles slowed to a stop. "Or maybe I have talked to him since . . ." She frowned, and the lines between her eyebrows deepened.

Grace remembered what both the doctor and Linda had said. *Don't ask questions. Don't argue. It only upsets them. Stay positive. Be reassuring.* What they really meant was lie. Lie all day and every day, because Mama G no longer recognized the truth.

Grace's eyes burned. Truth was a funny thing. On its surface, it was all good, a measure of a person's character. But under certain circumstances, truth was a burden you spared someone else. A weight you carried for them so they could continue on, free from the pain of reality.

She suddenly remembered all the lies Hannah had told them over the years. Dozens, hundreds even. Had Hannah felt the same way? Had she told those lies because they'd made Grace and Mama G smile, relax, and stop worrying? Those lies had given them moments of peace even as they eroded their trust in her until there was no more. It was hard to love someone you didn't trust. In some ways, it was impossible, which was why lying to Mama G, even under a severe circumstance like this, felt like a deep, heartrending betrayal.

Mama G shook her head and started knitting again. "Are you making dinner? We should eat soon."

Linda had said that Mama G had eaten, but it wouldn't hurt her to have some more. She was growing much too thin as it was. Grace forced a smile. "I'll bring you a bowl of stew."

"I like stew. And don't worry about Daisy. She's a good girl, and that Robert Parker is a good man, too. A gentle soul, once you know him."

Grace didn't know who "Robert" was, but Trav Parker looked anything but "gentle."

Mama G plucked something from her yarn. "Cat hair. That Theo. He sheds so much, it's a wonder there's anything of him left. He's just a bag of hair, that cat."

Grace swallowed a sigh. Theo the cat had died years ago. She'd been fourteen at the time and had wept for a week. *Don't correct her*, Grace reminded herself. *Just accept. Why is that so hard to do?* "I'll bring you some stew."

"There's no need to bring it here." Mama G didn't even look up but kept plucking imaginary cat hair from her yarn. "I'll join you as soon as I'm done."

Her heart pained, Grace headed for the kitchen. The air was fragrant with the stew Linda had made and Grace wondered if perhaps Mark wasn't the only good cook in the Robinson household. "Mmm. That smells good, doesn't it?"

Daisy stood leaning against the door to the back porch, her arms crossed over her narrow chest. "I already told Ms. Linda that I don't like stew."

She's far too much like me, Grace thought, wincing. *Pick your battles, Wheeler.* "You know what? If you don't want stew, you can have a peanut butter and jelly sandwich, but you have to make it yourself. Just wash your hands first." Grace went to the pot on the stove and lifted the lid, the bubbling sound comforting.

Daisy stayed where she was, her blue gaze locked on Grace, although her chin was no longer tilted at that ridiculous angle. After a long moment, she asked, "Why don't you want me to talk to Mr. Trav?"

It's Mr. Trav, is it? At least she's being polite. "It's not that I don't want you to talk to him; it's just that we don't know him yet, and I want you to be safe."

"We know him. He's our next-door neighbor, has a motorcycle, and owns a cat named Killer." Daisy listed these things as if it was all anyone would ever need to know about Travis Parker. She added, "Killer is fat."

"Killer is a cat? I was expecting a dog."

"I hoped it was a dragon," Daisy admitted. "He's not a bad cat. A little cranky and he eats too much, but that's all."

Did the fact the man owned a cat mean anything? Did it prove he was good, or did it mean the opposite? *Did the Son of Sam have a cat? Did Ted Bundy? I can't remember.*

Grace pulled out two bowls and set them beside the stove. "What do you and Mr. Trav talk about?"

"Nothing." Daisy left the door and opened a cabinet by the fridge. She stood on her tiptoes, pulled out a cup, and then poured herself some milk. "He told me he only likes quiet people, so we don't talk."

"So . . . you just watch him work?"

Daisy nodded. "He said that if I watch and don't talk, I might learn something so that if your car broke, I might be able to fix it."

Grace's heart softened. That was kind of Daisy. She smiled and reached over to ruffle Daisy's hair. "I'd like that."

Yet more of Daisy's ire faded. She even looked a little pleased as she took a drink of milk. "I'm going to be a mechanic when I grow up. Mr. Trav is my friend now, and he could hire me."

That seemed a bit much, and although she was beyond happy to share a positive moment with Daisy, Grace didn't like the idea of her niece being friends with a grown man. "Well . . . I wouldn't call him a friend, exactly."

In a split second, Daisy's expression turned back to one of mulish anger and she smacked her cup down, milk splashing on the counter. "At least I have one."

Ouch. I've been stung to the quick by a child of eight. Daisy's words rang true and were all the more irritating because not ten minutes ago, Linda Robinson had implied the same thing. Good God, had someone

held a "Make Grace Get More Friends" meeting today? It was annoying. "You're right; I don't have any friends. I've been too busy working."

"You should talk to Mr. Trav, too," Daisy said. "He could be your
friend. He lives close, so you wouldn't have to drive to visit him."

"That's a good idea. I'll take it under consideration. Now, go wash
your hands and make your sandwich. The stew's ready, and Mama G
is going to join us."

Daisy had started for the door, but at this she stopped. "She
already ate."

"I think she wants more."

Daisy's gaze never left Grace's face. "She doesn't remember, does she?"
Grace shook her head.

Daisy frowned. "When will she start remembering again?"

The words caught Grace by surprise. *Never*, she answered in her
own mind, unwilling to say the word aloud.

She met Daisy's clear, hopeful gaze. The truth would utterly crush
Daisy's already bruised spirit, and Grace couldn't bring herself to say it.

She just couldn't.

So she said instead, "We'll just hope for the best. That's all we can
do. Now, go wash your hands. I'll get the peanut butter and jelly for
you."

After a moment's pause, Daisy accepted this and left.

Relieved, Grace shoved the painful thoughts away and dipped a
ladle into Ms. Linda's stew. Grace fixed two bowls, curls of steam rising into the air over each.

She put the bowls on the table and had just pulled the drawer
open to fetch two spoons and a butter knife when she saw the book
Linda had placed on the counter. It rested against the wall, almost
hidden by the breadbox.

Linda had said the book Sarah sent over was a work of fiction but
had failed to mention that it was also a classic. Grace knew this book.
She knew it because she'd first seen it on Mama G's porch all those
years ago.

It was an old book, dull yellow in color, almost mustard in tone. Linda's hot chocolate stain marred the lower corner below the title, which was written in a flowing font. Grace traced the words with her finger—*Little Women*.

She opened it to a random page, the familiar smell of old book rising to meet her. After she'd moved into Mama G's house, it had taken Grace two years to learn to read well enough to tackle the book, but when she had, oh, how she'd loved it. She'd loved it so much that after that, she'd read it over and over and over, as if she could never get enough of it. Meg, Beth, Amy, and Jo—especially Jo—had been Grace's friends more than any of the real girls at her school.

Grace paged through the book, smiling as the names of her favorite characters flew past. How had Sarah Dove known? She couldn't have, of course. *It's just a coincidence. A shot in the dark that landed. And who hasn't read this book? It's a classic.*

And yet, in the back of her mind, Grace could hear Linda saying, *If Sarah Dove offers you a book, take it. You'll regret it if you don't.*

Linda had acted as if reading the book would help in some way, which was baloney. It was a book and nothing more. And while it had been a wonderful book for a brooding, lonely child, it couldn't help Grace now. She closed the book and, after a moment's thought, dropped it into the breadbox and shut the door.

The kitchen door swung open and Daisy returned, her hands freshly washed. She began making her sandwich while Grace went to escort Mama G in for her second dinner of the night. Before an hour had passed, the book was forgotten.

CHAPTER 7

Trav

The nights were the worst. That's when his memories, bloodied and furious, howled in the blackness, ripping him away from the peace and rest he desperately needed and hurling him, sweating and frozen with fear, into the lonely, cold awake of night. Since he'd returned from Afghanistan, those dreams now defined his life. They reminded him of what he wanted to forget, forced him to relive the moments he hated over and over until he was held together by nothing more than the simple fact that he was too bloody stubborn to quit.

He rubbed his face, trying to scrub away the memories. God, how he craved sleep, the dead-to-the-world deep and dreamless sleep that left one feeling refreshed and awake, rather than exhausted and zombified. He craved it the way an addict craved a hit while going through rehab. It whispered to him, beckoning, only to slap him hard when he came close.

Cursing under his breath, Travis kicked off his sheet, the night air cool against his damp, naked skin. It had been 531 days since his life had changed—531 days since he'd slept more than two, maybe three hours at a time. So many days, and yet so few.

The clock in the living room chimed four and he sat up, relieved at the sound. He'd been awake well over two hours, staring at the ceiling and counting sheep and, when that didn't work, planning his day—anything but thinking about his dreams. When he couldn't sleep, he tried to stay in bed until at least four, as it gave him a sense of having a schedule, even when sleep wasn't part of it.

He got up and washed his face in cold water. He found some shorts, stuffed his feet into his Nikes, and went through the kitchen to the garage.

He flipped on the lights, which hummed loudly as if in surprise at his appearance. He ignored their insistent blinking as he raised the garage door to the dark and chilly air, which mingled with the gasoline-garage smell. The garage had benefited from Mama G and Daisy's cleaning spree. Inspired by their work, Trav had spent some time organizing the workbenches and going through the random boxes Dad had left stacked along one wall. Oil stains still marred the concrete floor, but the place was a lot neater than it had been.

Trav pulled a clean hand towel from a stack on the shelf over the washing machine and threw it over the arm of his treadmill.

"Exercise," his therapist Don from the VA had said. "It will help you sleep."

"How?" he'd asked, disbelieving.

"If you're physically tired, you'll sleep more and deeper. Plus, you'll produce the proper enzymes to enable your body to—" Don had grimaced. "Hell, don't ask me. Just try it. What do you have to lose?"

So he'd tried it. And it had helped, at least a little. He fell asleep better, even though his dreams didn't let him stay that way for long. The weights had also given him bragging rights when he hung out with his friends. Just last night he'd teased Blake mercilessly about not being able to bench-press his own body weight. There were benefits to not sleeping, a few, anyway, and he might as well use them all.

He hit the treadmill for a quick two-mile run, his usual warm-up before he lifted.

Killer came to sit in the kitchen doorway, watching Trav's run with an expression registering somewhere between overwhelming boredom and flat-out disgust. For some reason, the cat who thought it his God-given right to run around the house every fricking night between two and three in the morning, knocking things off tables and making all kinds of racket, felt 4 a.m. an unacceptable time for a workout.

The tabby swished his tail with disapproval before strolling to his bed in the corner and settling in, staring at Trav with an expression of total disdain.

Trav ignored the animal and finished his run. When he was done, he wiped the sweat from his face with the hand towel and crossed to his weight bench. As he went, he told Killer, "Why don't you do your run-around-the-house-like-a-crazed-hyena-in-the-middle-of-the-night routine while I'm working out instead of saving it for an hour before I get up? Then we'd be on the same schedule."

Killer got up, turned around once, and then nestled back into his bed, this time facing the wall, his back to Trav.

"Thanks. Same to you." Trav added weights to the bar and started the first set.

Killer wasn't the only one who didn't like Trav's exercise schedule. Trav's dad hadn't liked it, either. He'd never said a word about it, but Trav had seen the worry in his dad's eyes. Dad had never hidden his feelings well, which had been both a blessing and a curse as he began the long, slow, terrifying fall into dementia.

Trav gritted his teeth and added an extra set of reps to the set, pushing himself hard. His body was covered with sweat, his muscles aching in protest, but he pushed on, focusing on the here. The now. This moment. One minute at a time.

His arms trembled, yet he did one more rep. And then another. Until, exhausted, he could do no more. He lowered the weights to the ground and let his quivering muscles rest.

It felt good to work out. It cleared his mind and reminded him that there were things he could still do and do well. He wiped his face and neck with the towel, the rough cloth catching on the scarred ridges that lined his neck and the back of his arm and shoulder. The scarred skin was tight, tugging and painful as the nerves fought the thick scars and tried to reconnect. There were days he had to set his teeth against the burn caused by those aggressive nerve endings that flashed and flared like brutal bursts of fire under his skin. But as painful as it was, it was nothing compared to what it had once been. There'd been a time when he'd been in agony as old skin died and peeled or flaked away, leaving a charred morass of raw nerves exposed while new skin slowly crept in. The pain was bearable now, although it never truly left, but Trav had accepted that. Over the past few years, he'd learned to accept a lot of things, especially after Dad's diagnosis.

Those first months had been hard. Of course, Sarah had been a big help. The night after he found out what was wrong with Dad, she'd showed up at Trav's door with hot soup, some tea her sister Ava had made just for Dad, and a book on dementia. A lot of people in Dove Pond believed that Sarah and her sisters had special abilities, but that was just gossip and nonsense. The Dove sisters had hearts bigger than their heads. They cared more, perhaps, than they should, so their intuition was stronger than most. That was all it was.

Still, no matter how Sarah had known he needed the book, he'd stayed up most of the night reading it, making himself a to-do list as he went. When morning rose, so did Trav. And even though he felt barely healed himself, that very next day, Trav became the parent of his parent. He hired one of the ladies from church, Beverly Turnbull, a cheery, plump lady who'd known Dad for years, to come once a week to clean the house. Since Dad knew her, he didn't mind her puttering around. Then, claiming boredom, Trav had started taking Dad to work each morning and spending the day at the repair shop. Dad had always wanted Trav to take over the shop, so he'd been happy with the arrangement.

During that first week, while Dad sat in the office moving paper from one pile to the next, Trav and Arnie had developed a plan to get the garage back on its feet. Until that day, Trav had never thought about running the garage. That had been his father's job, not his. But things had to be done, and Trav was the only one who could do them. To his surprise, he found the same deep satisfaction fixing cars that he'd felt fixing complex electrical and water issues in Afghanistan, especially as word of the changes at the garage flew around town and their old customers returned.

As time went on, Dad became less able to function, and Trav quietly stepped up, eventually taking over the business. It was both the easiest and the most difficult thing he'd ever done. Easy because he knew without question that he was needed, and difficult because Dad's decline made the necessity painful.

Trav carried the heavy bar back to its stand, the faint morning breeze drying the sweat on his neck and shoulders. He still missed his father, although some days it felt as if Trav just had to turn around and he'd see Dad standing there in a flannel shirt, a fishing pole in his hand.

Trav looked at the fishing poles still leaning in one corner, his gaze moving to the broom that rested beside them. That made him think about the day he'd found Daisy and Mrs. Giano cleaning his garage, and he smiled. He was getting to know Daisy, as she spent a considerable amount of time hanging over the fence between their houses. He wouldn't say he liked her, because she was a kid, and he had no use for kids in his life, now or ever. But he had to admit she was sharp, and more often than not, he found her bare-bones view of the world refreshing.

Trav turned back to the weight bench just as Killer meowed loudly and sat up in his bed. The cat stared out the garage window.

Trav came to see what had caught Killer's attention. The house next door loomed in the darkness, the only light shining from an upper window over the porch. He wondered if that was where the Dragon Lady slept. That was his name for Grace, who was a brunette ball of tightly controlled ferocity. Trav had been a platoon leader, and he knew from experience that a person's walk told everything about them that you could want to know. And he knew from the way Miss Grace Wheeler strode to her car every morning, chin up and shoulders back, snapping the ground with her ridiculously high heels, that she didn't walk through life. She stormed.

She was the exact type of woman a man who wanted peace and quiet would do well to avoid.

Killer meowed louder yet, still staring at the lit window.

"You're bonkers," Trav told the cat. "There's nothing there."

Killer hopped out of his bed and hurried out of the open garage door.

In all the time Trav had known Killer, he'd never seen the fat, lazy animal hurry. Not once.

Curious, Trav followed the cat.

Killer crossed the driveway, ducked under the fence, and then disappeared into the yard next door.

"What the hell?" Trav muttered. He was just about to call for the cat when the upstairs window opened.

Mrs. Giano appeared. As he watched, she placed a small bowl on the windowsill and looked out expectantly. She wore a pale blue nightgown that caught the moon and made her glow, the light in her room making a nimbus of her thin, white hair. She looked like a feeble but glowing angel.

Killer meowed and then, with a graceful leap that belied his weight, leapt onto a low bush, and from there to a branch in a tree, and then to the porch roof. He then casually strolled to the open window and made himself at home on the ledge, lapping the milk as if he'd done it a thousand times before.

The old woman patted him as he drank, murmuring in a low voice. Trav moved closer.

"You were hungry, weren't you, Theo?" the woman said.

Theo?

"I warmed it for you, because I know you don't like your milk cold."

Killer drank as if he hadn't just ignored the food Trav had left him in the kitchen. When the cat finished, he licked his paws and then cleaned his face.

Traitor.

"Are you ready for bed?" the woman asked. Before Trav's bemused gaze, she lifted the fat cat off the windowsill and carried him inside, leaving the window open behind her.

Trav started forward to warn her, because he knew better than anyone how much his dad's cat hated being carried, but no screeching sound came from the house. Instead, after a long moment, the light clicked off and Trav was left in the dark, staring up at the window.

I'll be damned.

So Killer had a new home with an old woman who didn't know the cat's proper name, a Dragon Lady who could cut with a glance, and a busy little girl who seemed to think Trav was the cast of his own reality TV show. *Fine. You all can have him. I hope you know he's grumpy, ill-mannered, and fickle.*

Well, the window had been left partially open, so Killer could escape if he wanted. *I guess he's okay.*

Silence came from the dark room, and Trav suspected that Killer, now pretending to be "Theo," had curled up at the foot of the old woman's bed and gone to sleep, just the way he used to sleep at the foot of Dad's bed.

Trav rubbed his face with both hands to wash away the memories. Suddenly aware of the coolness of the night breeze on his bare shoulders, he went back into the garage. So long as Killer was safe, what was the problem? The cat wasn't even Trav's to begin with. Not really.

Still, as he stepped into his garage, he was aware that the house seemed even emptier than usual, as if he'd somehow lost something.

Scowling at his own maudlin thoughts, he picked up his weights and did two more agonizing sets.

CHAPTER 8

Sarah

"Stop staring," Trav said.

Sarah straightened from where she'd been leaning against the fence that separated her house from Travis's. "I wasn't staring. I was looking."

"Baloney. You've been staring at Mrs. Phelps's old house for an hour now."

"Half an hour," she corrected, watching him dry his motorcycle with an old beach towel. Although he was a few months older, over the years, she'd come to think of Trav as her little brother. Some of her friends, in particular the single ones, thought this a waste, because as far as they were concerned, despite his rugged appearance (and because of it for a few of them), he was an A+ catch. He had his own business and house; he was intriguingly quiet, which had created an air of mystery; and he was "damned easy on the eyes," as Zoe put it. But for Sarah, Trav was her best friend and that was enough. "It's been almost a month since the Wheeler family moved into Mrs. Phelps's old house. I believe we can now officially refer to it as 'the Wheeler house,' don't you?"

"Sure. Whatever. But if they see you staring, they'll think you're weird. Hell, I think you're weird and I've known you forever."

"Humph." Which was what Sarah always said when she knew she couldn't win an argument but didn't want to admit it. She took a deep breath of the lavender Ava kept planted along the fence, the scent soothing. It was too bad it didn't have the same effect on Trav, who'd always been the overthinking, too-serious type.

Trav's family had lived beside Sarah's for more than 170 years. She knew him so well that she couldn't remember the first time they'd met, and he was as much a part of her life as any of her sisters. She and Trav had been best friends from preschool all the way through high school, even after he'd been embraced by the popular kids while she'd been summarily ostracized.

She'd resented it at the time, although she should have expected it. In high school, Trav had been the trifecta of perfection—the star quarterback, homecoming king, and valedictorian. Sarah, meanwhile, had been the bold leader of a restless group of social pariahs who wore too much eyeliner and listened to angry bands while eschewing school, family, church, and pretty much everything else. Trav and his friends were called "promising" and "bright," while Sarah and her friends were called "trouble."

She didn't mind being an outcast, as she'd had more fun. No one expected much of her, and any sign of "good" (a passing grade or not getting sent to detention for an entire month) was greeted with enthusiastic acclaim, while kids like Trav were expected to do those things on a daily basis but without notice.

Sarah smiled. *Who'd have thought the rebel princess would grow up to become the town's upstanding, not-so-staid librarian?* She was rather proud of that jump in fortune. Of course, Trav would say he'd seen it coming, because even when she'd been a social outcast, he'd never stopped being her friend. They'd made an odd pair, the two of them and their weird friendship, but it had lasted over the years, during the death of her parents and his, until they were closer than ever.

She leaned against the fence once again, her gaze returning to Grace's house. Nothing moved, the lace curtains drawn against the fading sun. She sighed. "Grace is so frustrating."

"Why? Because she doesn't want to be your friend?" Trav went back into his garage and grabbed a bucket filled with rags and a can of wax. He returned and set the bucket beside his bike. "Not everyone wants to be friends. I don't."

"You're friends with me."

He shot her a hard look. "We grew up together. Neither of us had a choice."

Sarah could tell he was feeling especially surly this afternoon and wanted to be left alone, which she was determined not to do. He was alone far too often as it was. "At least admit you're glad Mrs. Phelps's old house wasn't left empty while she traipsed off to Florida."

"I'm glad they're quiet, but that's about it. I was worried Mrs. Phelps would rent her house to heavy metal types just to irk me."

"I wouldn't have been surprised. She is the meanest woman I know."

"Tell me about it," Trav said. "I went to pay my business tax last month and got there one minute after four. Seriously, it was *one* minute, and she still charged me the late fee."

"I'm sure she did it with a smile. One like this." Sarah wrinkled her nose and showed her teeth, trying to look like a rabid Chihuahua.

Trav grinned, picked up his bucket, and moved to the other side of his bike. "I wish I didn't have any neighbors."

"Even me?"

He pretended to consider this. After a moment, he shrugged. "You bring me dinner once a week, so you're okay."

"You're too kind. Come on, Trav. Neighbors are a good thing. And the Wheelers are already better neighbors than Mrs. Phelps ever was."

He set an empty can of wax to one side, fished a screwdriver out of the bucket, and used it to pry open a new can. "We don't know what kind of neighbors they are yet."

"Do they call the police every time you slam a door?"

"Not yet they haven't."

"Or throw the trash that blows into their yard into yours and then pretend they didn't, even when you saw them do it?"

He slanted her an irked look and didn't answer.

"Do they shoot at your beloved pet with an air gun whenever they see it outside—"

"Fine, fine," he admitted in a reluctant tone. "The new neighbors are a *little* better than Mrs. Phelps. But for the record, Killer is not a 'beloved pet.' He was my dad's cat, so I feel responsible for the mangy beast. That's the only reason he's here. He and I tolerate one another, no more."

"If you didn't love that animal, you'd have given him away. Lisa Tilden offered to take him. I heard her."

"Killer growls at Lisa. Besides, he'd just sneak out and come back here. He always does." Trav frowned. "Most of the time, anyway."

"He's consistent," she agreed. "It's good you kept him. Besides, I think Lisa was only offering to take him because she was hoping you'd notice her."

Trav muttered something under his breath and Sarah grinned. "I'm not telling her you said that. It'll break her heart; she's had a thing for you since high school."

He ignored Sarah and began polishing his bike with renewed vigor.

Still grinning, she looked past Trav to the dilapidated house beyond. "Grace and her family are special. Ava says the maple tree in the front yard loves them. She can tell because the leaves fall into a perfect circle with the stems pointing—"

"Stop," he ground out. "I don't want to hear what your sister thinks the maple tree 'feels,' or what books whisper to you, or what weird magic showed up in some pie your sister Ella cooked, or anything else about you and your weird family."

"You know it's true. You've seen things."

"Never while sober." He shot her a hard look. "If I believed that nonsense now that I'm a grown-up, I'd also have to admit that unicorns fart rainbows, and that's too far of a bridge to cross. All of you Doves have a bad case of NABS."

"What's that?"

"New age bullshit."

She laughed. "No. How do you *really* feel?"

He grinned and tossed the rag back into the bucket. "Reality, Sarah. That's all I'm interested in."

"Fine. Reality, then." Trav never admitted that he knew she had a special connection with books, and that was fine with her. She didn't need approval from her brother-from-another-mother. Just his friendship. "Here's some reality for you. Our new neighbor is exactly the type of woman you usually date."

"You don't know what type of woman I usually date," he growled. "I haven't been on a date since I got back."

That was true, although it wasn't because the women of Dove Pond hadn't tried. Sarah could name four right now who'd made fools of themselves trying to get his attention. "Admit it—she's your type. She's hot and she dresses well. All your previous girlfriends, at least the ones I knew, fit that same bill."

"It wouldn't matter if she was hot enough to strike a match, she has a kid."

"You don't like kids?"

"Nope." He began waxing the tank. A deep, lipstick red, it had so many layers of lacquer on it that it always looked wet.

"You can't dislike sweet, innocent children. That's inhumane."

"Children are fine so long as I don't have to see, hear, or talk to them. And I especially don't like the ones who stare at me over my fence as if they're planning on sneaking over it the first time my back is turned."

"You're talking about Daisy."

"Every day for two weeks now that kid has stood at that damned fence and stared at me. One day she'll jump it and come into my yard again."

"Again?" *Oho, what's this? He's met Daisy.*

He ignored her. "I know she'll do it, and she knows she'll do it, and when it happens, she and I are going to have a reckoning." He polished his bike with a fierceness that made Sarah raise her brows.

"Maybe you're approaching this wrong. Why don't you reach out to Daisy? See if she'd like a ride on your motorcycle since she stares at it all the time."

"No."

"Come on. Just take her for a short ride one day when you're not busy. It could help."

"Or not."

"Come on, Trav. You should get to know her. You might like her; she's not like other kids."

"How would you know what she's like?"

"I visited the Wheeler house a few times last week after work, so I've talked to her." And Mrs. Giano, too, who was just as charming as Sarah had suspected, if a bit vague at times.

"Does the Dragon Lady know about these visits?"

That was actually a pretty good name for Grace. Sarah shrugged. "I didn't ask anyone to keep it quiet, so I guess she does."

"You said you'd been visiting after work."

"So?"

"Three times, maybe? Like on Monday, Tuesday, and Thursday, when the library closes an hour earlier than town hall?" When she didn't answer, he smirked. "You've been visiting when she wasn't home."

Damn it. Trust Trav to figure that out. "Fine. I might have timed it that way. I want to get to know our Dragon Lady, but she's a little standoff-ish." Since the last meeting of the social club, Sarah had stopped by town hall no fewer than four times, and every time Grace had politely said she was "too busy to chat" but that she'd call when she "had a moment."

So far, no "moment" had happened. "She's not the warm and friendly type," Sarah said sourly. "So I thought I should get to know her family first."

Trav shook his head. "You're a troublemaker, Dove."

"No, I'm not. I just really, really want to be her friend."

"Why?"

That was the million-dollar question, wasn't it? Sarah didn't dare tell Trav that Charlotte Dove's ancient journal had announced that Grace had to—*must*—stay in town, as he would just scoff. Sarah decided a silent shrug was the only answer she could safely give.

"So you're trying to get to know her through her family. And let me guess—you sent her a book, too."

Sarah had, of course. Aware of Trav's dark gaze, she said in a lofty tone, "Maybe."

He gave a disbelieving snort.

She ignored it. Truth be told, she hadn't had a choice in the matter. The book had followed her for a week, showing up in odd places, and demanding to be delivered into Grace's hands. Sarah could have kissed Linda Robinson when she'd offered to deliver it for her.

"You'll never learn, will you?" Trav pulled a bottle of chrome cleaner from his bucket and set to work on the handlebars. "You're rushing things. A woman like that doesn't trust just anyone. She's a numbers person, a financial whiz, right? She quit her job with some huge firm in Charlotte to bring her mother—or rather, her foster mother—back to Dove Pond, where the old lady grew up, hoping to ease some of the effects of her Alzheimer's. Grace just got here, Sarah. And a month isn't that long of a time. Numbers people don't like being rushed, so back off."

Sarah frowned. "How do you know all of that?"

"You didn't?"

"Not all of it, no."

He looked suitably smug. "Well, well, well. I'm better informed than the town gossip. How about that."

"I'm not the town gossip," Sarah said with a dismissive sniff as she lifted up on her toes to see Grace's house better. "Spill. Tell me everything you know."

"Why should I?"

"Because if you don't, I'm going to march over there and tell the Dragon Lady you think she's hot. Well . . . I will as soon as she's home. Her car isn't in the driveway."

His smugness vanished. "You wouldn't."

"I would. And I'd be telling her the truth, because I've seen you look at her." To Sarah's amusement, his face reddened.

After a chilly moment, he said in a grudging tone, "You're a hard woman, Dove."

She flashed a smile. "Like a rock, Parker."

He threw the dirty rag into the bucket. "I'll tell you what little I know, but *only* because you feed Killer whenever I have to work late and *not* because you're trying to blackmail me."

"Just tell me what you know."

"Fine. First of all, she only plans on being here a year, if that."

"So she said, but she needs to stay longer." The words slipped out before Sarah could stop them.

Trav's eyebrows rose. "You don't have a voice in that decision."

"I know, but . . ." Sarah hadn't meant to say as much as she had, but it was too late to take it back now. "All I know is that Grace needs to stay in Dove Pond so she can accomplish"—Sarah waved her hand vaguely—"things."

"Like what?"

"I don't know, but whatever it is, she needs to stay here longer than a year." *Like forever.*

"She won't do it."

"She might," Sarah insisted. "Once she sees all Dove Pond has to offer, she'll want to stay."

Trav burst out laughing, which didn't help matters. "Good luck with that."

"Thanks." Sarah sent him an impatient look. "What else did you find out?"

"Her sister died a few months ago from an overdose."

"Dear God. I knew her sister had died, but I didn't know how or when." Sarah tried to imagine how she'd feel if she'd lost one of her sisters in such a way and found that she couldn't. She suddenly wanted to hug Ava. "That poor family."

"Apparently Grace's sister wasn't much of a mother, either, as she'd left Daisy in Mrs. Giano's care years earlier. According to my source, who heard it from someone who knows Mrs. Giano well, Grace and her sister had a troubled background. To compensate, Grace became too responsible, too focused on being perfect."

"That explains a lot."

"Meanwhile, her sister went in the opposite direction. She couldn't keep a job, lied constantly, stole money, abandoned her daughter at Mrs. Giano's for weeks on end, and then eventually left her there for good."

"And now Grace is responsible for both her niece and Mrs. Giano." This was so much worse than Sarah had imagined. "If something like that had happened to me, I would be so angry."

Trav's gaze moved to the Wheeler house. "I would be, too." He said the words in a low voice as if considering them for the first time. He shook his head and then turned back to his bike.

Sarah sent Travis a curious look. "Who's your source?"

He shrugged and started cleaning the headlight.

"Ah. It was Blake, wasn't it?"

"Maybe."

It took all her self-control not to turn red, but she thought she managed it well enough. She wondered how Blake had found out so much about their new neighbors, but then she remembered that his mother had been close to Mrs. Phelps, who was related to Mrs. Giano, so— *Yup. That has to be it.*

Sarah wished she could ask Blake directly what else he'd heard, but that would never happen. "The Incident" had dug a ditch between her and Blake that could never be bridged. It had ended not only their romantic relationship but their friendship as well. *And it was all thanks to my own stupid foolishness.*

Sarah shoved aside a mountain of old regret just as Grace's Honda pulled into the driveway. Grace climbed out, stopping to collect two grocery bags from her trunk. She wasn't wearing a suit today, and her dark hair was loose, her face partially obscured by a large pair of sunglasses.

"How old do you think she is?" Sarah mused.

"She'd have to have a college degree and at least a few years of experience to have a successful job in finance."

"Which makes her about our age, maybe a little more." Sarah was twenty-five, although she felt older. "I'd heard she had a crazy-good job in Charlotte. I bet the mayor was surprised she accepted the clerk position."

"I expect so. She's way out of this town's league."

"Hmm." Sarah wished she knew how to dress the way Grace did. It was a sleepy Sunday afternoon, but the woman was New York chic in a yellow sundress and a pair of white, strappy sandals. She should have been lounging on the deck of a yacht instead of carrying bags of groceries into a faded rental house.

"There's something about her." Sarah watched Grace disappear inside. "Don't you think?"

He shrugged but didn't argue.

Bang! The screen door slammed closed at the Wheeler house. Grace walked back to the car, this time with Mrs. Giano beside her.

Mrs. Giano fascinated Sarah. There was something old-world about her. Dressed in a flowered dress with a flowered shawl, the tiny old woman was so encircled by petals that it looked as if she were floating through a garden. She walked beside Grace a little unsteadily, clutching a large straw purse as if afraid someone would steal it.

"Damn."

Sarah glanced at Trav.

A bleakness had settled over him. At Sarah's questioning gaze, he said, "She reminds me of Dad. She's more unstable than when they first moved in; she's getting worse." With a regretful shake of his head, he picked up the bucket and headed into his garage.

Sarah watched as Grace helped her mother into the car and then turned back toward the house. "Daisy!" she called.

The screen door slammed again as Daisy came hopping out of the house with her shoes in her hand. She wore a pair of blue jeans and a powder blue shirt, a sparkling tiara nestled in her mussy blond curls. She danced rather than walked, whirling off the sidewalk and into the center of the yard, where, apparently delighted by the cool, thick grass under her bare feet, she started to twirl madly.

A sharp word from Grace stopped the girl dead in her tracks, her shoulders slumping as if she'd been denied air.

Trav came out of the garage, holding two open bottles of beer. He handed one to Sarah and followed her gaze back to where Daisy was now dragging her feet as she walked toward the car. "They're tiny, the lot of them," he said in an irritated tone. "Like yard gnomes."

"Like fairies," Sarah corrected as she took a cautious sip. "They're delicate, otherworldly fairies."

Trav snorted. "Delicate? The old woman maybe. But not the other two."

"You can't say that sweet little girl isn't delicate. Just look at her."

"That 'sweet little girl,' as you call her, can switch from being a chatterbox to a sullen brat in under a second. I've seen it happen. As for her aunt, she's hard as steel. Every once in a while, she'll slash you with a look that cuts to the bone."

"What? No criticism for poor old Mrs. Giano?"

"She's the worst. She's a cat thief."

Sarah blinked. "A what?"

"She entices Killer up to her house every damn night with a bowl of milk."

"So? You don't like Killer, anyway. I don't see why that—"

"It's still theft," Trav muttered. "It's the principle of the thing."

Grace opened the car door to the back seat, speaking sharply to Daisy, who was walking ever so slowly, dragging her feet through the grass in the most reluctant way possible.

Sarah couldn't hear Grace's words, but the effect was plain as day. Trav had been right when he'd said the little girl could change in an instant. Daisy's chin went up, her shoulders went down, and she snapped back an answer in a sullen tone that could have soured milk.

It might have been a normal reaction for a moody preteen, but it was startling coming from a mere child.

"She's a bit of a hellion, isn't she?" Trav said, taking a drink of his beer.

"Poor thing," Sarah murmured.

"Don't start." Trav finished the beer and tossed the empty bottle into the trash can, where it landed with a hollow clunk. He pulled his shiny black helmet out of a saddlebag and slid his keys from his pocket. As he did so, he shot an impatient look at Sarah. "Stop looking as if you want to adopt that girl. She already has a family."

"Does she have any friends? I've never seen any other kids over there. Have you?"

"How would I know? I don't watch them."

Sarah raised her brows and waited.

He scowled. "No, I haven't seen any other kids over there."

"That's what I thought. I wish Grace would bring Daisy to the library for story hour. There are a bunch of girls about her age who come every week."

"Don't get involved."

"I have to. Trav, that family belongs here."

"You don't know that."

"But I do. I really do."

His brows lowered. "How?"

She shrugged, knowing he'd scoff if she told him the truth. "I just have a feeling about it, that's all."

"You're ridiculous, you know that?" He tugged on his helmet and adjusted the strap. "I'll bet you they leave the second their lease runs out. If I'm right, you'll cook me a pan of lasagna once a month for a year."

"And if I'm right and they stay, then you can wash *and* wax my truck once a month for a year."

"You're on, Dove." Trav swung his leg over his bike and lifted it upright. He slid the key into the ignition and a second later the engine roared to life, echoing loudly.

Grace had just closed the car door behind Daisy, but now she turned toward them, obviously irked at the roar.

Trav had noted Grace's scowl, and he answered by revving his engine again, the noise so loud it rattled against the houses, bouncing like an invisible ball.

Grace slid her sunglasses to the tip of her nose and looked Trav up and then down, all with a flat, unimpressed air, as if she were examining him for defects and found more than she could count. And then—using only her middle finger—she slowly slid her sunglasses back into place.

Sarah laughed. "You've been burned, Parker," she yelled over the engine noise.

Trav sent a fuming glare at Grace, who had already turned away and was climbing into her car. She shut the door with extra force, and a moment later, the car backed out of the drive and disappeared from sight.

Trav stared after them, scowling. Then, muttering furiously to himself, he backed his machine into the street and, with a smooth twist of his wrist, took off.

He revved his engine as he rode by Grace's empty house, the sound as defiant as it was loud.

Sarah watched, smiling.

"Good lord, but that motorcycle is loud."

Sarah turned to find Ava climbing out of her truck in the driveway. "I didn't hear you pull up."

"You can't hear anything when he's revving that bike." Ava joined Sarah at the fence and eyed the beer in her hand. "Since when do you drink IPAs?"

"It's Trav's. I was just being polite."

"Give it to me. He'll never know."

Sarah grinned and handed the beer to her sister. "I had an interesting discussion with him. I'm starting to think our uptight, gravely wounded, and too-private-for-his-own-good neighbor isn't as immune to the Wheeler family as I thought. That makes me happy."

"You're a romantic. Too bad Trav isn't." Ava took an appreciative drink of the beer. "To be honest, I can't see Trav with a girlfriend who has both a kid and a sick mother. He's not domesticated enough for that kind of responsibility. And Grace seems as if she'd only date an executive type of guy, someone with a fat IRA account and a briefcase full of savings bonds. As much as I love him, that's not our Trav."

Sarah sighed. "No, it's not."

Ava took another drink of her beer, her gray-green gaze curious. "Have you asked the books?"

"Repeatedly. They're being stubborn. They've always been that way where Trav is concerned. He's not a big reader, you know."

Ava made a face.

"I know. I'll never understand how that's even a thing. In all the years I've known him, only one book has asked to visit him, and that was when his dad got sick."

"It's frustrating." Ava cast an expert eye over the closest lavender plant, using the toe of her boot to push some of the white gravel back around the base. "I know the feeling, though. I've been trying to develop a tea to help Mrs. Perez with her arthritis, but I can't quite figure it out."

"We can only do so much," Sarah said regretfully.

"True." Ava took another drink. A bee buzzed nearby and she watched it land on a lavender bloom. "Bees love lavender. So do butterflies."

"Do you think it would work on reluctant town clerks?"

Ava laughed. "Maybe. Mom always said you'd catch more flies with honey than vinegar." She finished her beer. "I'm heading inside. Are you hungry? I was thinking of warming up that broccoli-and-chicken casserole for dinner."

"I'll make a salad to go with it."

"Sounds good. And, Sarah, don't worry about Grace. You'll figure it out. I know you will."

At one time, Sarah and Ava hadn't been particularly close, but now Sarah didn't know what she'd do without her sister. "Thanks. I needed to hear that."

"It's just the truth." Ava smiled. "Let's go fix dinner."

"I'll be there in a minute."

"Good. I'm starving." Ava left, crossing the lawn toward the front door, the empty beer bottle in her hand.

Sarah stayed by the fence, her gaze returning to the Wheeler house. Mom was right about honey catching more flies, but Sarah didn't think honey would have much of an effect on Grace. Sarah might have better luck with cake. A nice, yummy coffee cake made with pecans and sour cream and—

Sarah straightened. Maybe that was the answer, as simple as it was. Who could say no to fresh, warm coffee cake?

It was a ridiculously small idea. But all big plans began with a small step, and this small step was better than none.

Feeling hopeful, Sarah left the fence and headed inside, already wondering if she had all the ingredients to make some of her sister Ella's irresistible coffee cake.

CHAPTER 9

Grace

Grace eyed the misty gray morning with a sour glare. She hated Mondays. It always seemed that the first day of the week waited with sharpened claws, eager to shred one's hopes and dreams. The piles of mindless data entry work stacked on Grace's desk waiting for her to arrive supported this theory, and she scowled as she put her car into reverse.

She'd just begun easing her foot off the brake when the passenger door flew open and Sarah Dove stuck her head in. "Hi!" the librarian chirped as Grace slammed on her brakes.

Grace's irk factor flew up a few points. Under the best of circumstances, even with a good night's rest, she wasn't a morning person. She needed time, quiet, and at least two cups of coffee before she could face the day with anything close to a smile. And so far, she'd had none of those things.

Last night, a few hours after going to bed, she'd been awakened by the sound of Mama G calling, "Theo!" over and over. Still half asleep, Grace had grabbed her robe and padded downstairs, where she found the front door ajar. Mama G stood outside on the porch in her nightgown, a bowl of milk in her hands.

Alarmed, Grace had followed. "What are you doing?"

"I'm looking for Theo. He hasn't come for his milk."

Still bleary-eyed and slightly irritated at being awoken, Grace had said in a sharper tone than she'd meant to use, "That's ridiculous. Theo's been dead for years. Now, come inside."

The words and tone had an instant effect, none of it good.

"Dead?" Mama G's voice had quavered with hurt.

Grace, instantly contrite but too tired to think, had nodded. "For years now. Let's go inside. You're just confused, and it's damp—"

"No." Mama G's expression had turned mulish and she'd backed away. "I just saw Theo yesterday; he's *not* dead. He's fine and he's hungry. I know he is." Before Grace could answer, Mama G turned and hurried down the steps, unsteady in the dark, the milk sloshing from the bowl and dribbling down her nightgown.

For a shocked and horrified moment, Grace had thought Mama G might fall, but at the last minute, she'd regained her balance. She'd stopped at the foot of the porch stairs to glare up at Grace. "I *have* to give Theo his milk. I've been waiting for hours, but he hasn't come home." Mama G looked across the front yard to the road. "Maybe I should put the milk by the road. He used to sleep in the mailbox. Made Mr. Horner so mad."

It had taken a solid twenty minutes of reasoning and then pleading, but finally Grace had managed to get Mama G inside with a promise to leave the milk on the porch for the missing "Theo." Still, the incident had left Grace shaken. If she hadn't woken up when she had, Mama G might have wandered off, and Grace had no illusions what might happen then. Just thinking about it made her sick to her stomach.

After she'd gotten Mama G back to bed, Grace had tossed and turned, unable to sleep, every creak of the old house making her bolt upright. It had been well after four in the morning when Grace had finally fallen asleep.

This morning, as soon as the alarm went off, Grace had forced herself to get up. While trying to stay awake in the shower, she decided to tell Linda what had happened and see if she had any suggestions for keeping Mama G from wandering out of the house after everyone was asleep. Tin cans tied to doorknobs? A bell of some sort? A house alarm?

To her relief, Linda had a number of helpful suggestions, the easiest and quickest of which was to put a lock high up on the door, out of Mama G's reach. Grace had called the Callahan brothers, the handymen Mrs. Phelps had recommended before she'd left, and explained the situation. To Grace's relief, one of them had promised to stop by this afternoon and install the lock.

Now, a mere hour later, feeling exhausted and as if she'd been run over by a semi, she faced the humid morning with a headache that had made her eyes want to cross.

So when Sarah beamed at Grace from the passenger door, looking fresh and well rested, and smiling widely as if morning was something to be celebrated and not merely survived, all Grace wanted to do was spew morning venom.

Fortunately, before Grace could open her mouth, Sarah shouldered the door aside and thrust a tumbler of coffee under Grace's nose.

The rich scent of hazelnut curled with the steam from the opening in the cup's cover, and Grace's soul sighed in relief. She put the car in park, then took the tumbler between both hands and held it as reverently as though it were a holy chalice.

"I'm glad I caught you." Sarah, burdened with a heavy book tote, a paper bag, and her own cup of coffee, slid into the passenger seat and closed the door. "I thought we might ride together." She dropped her tote on the floor beside her feet, slipped her cup into the nearest holder, and placed the paper bag onto the console between them.

The smell of vanilla and cinnamon filled the car, mingling with that of the coffee. "What's that?" Grace couldn't keep the hope from her voice.

Sarah opened the bag, and Grace's mouth watered at the fresh-baked smell.

"It's coffee cake," Sarah said. "It's my mom's recipe, although my sister Ella changed it a bit, and now it's even better."

She sipped the coffee. Rich, slightly bitter, with just the right amount of cream, it poured over her tongue and warmed her from head to toe. She took another sip, stunned into submission.

Grace looked at the bag and then at her cup. She could give in to her lesser impulses and refuse to drive Sarah and her delicious snacks to work and deprive them both of a pleasant drive and some much-needed coffee, or she could indulge them both and accept the gifts and the company.

While thinking through her options, she absently took another drink of the coffee. "God, that's good."

"Enough cream? I had to guess, but I thought since I take cream that you might, too."

It was too early to follow such a questionable line of reasoning, so Grace just said, "It's perfect. I'm not even exaggerating. *Perfect.*"

Sarah grinned, her expression far too bright for this time of the day. "Coffee is the elixir of life."

Grace was too busy savoring the hot perfection in her cup to answer.

Sarah reached into the paper bag and pulled out some napkins. They were party size and had HAPPY BIRTHDAY written on them in garish pink. She placed one on Grace's knee. "I hope you don't mind driving today. It dawned on me last night that we should carpool. We live almost next door, and we work right across the street from each other. We can save time and gas."

Grace didn't want to carpool, especially not with a freakishly happy morning person, which Sarah obviously was. But the coffee that had warmed her fingers had somehow also managed to unfreeze her soul just enough that she managed to murmur a polite "It would be environmentally sound." She took another sip and decided that a ten-minute drive with Sarah (if it was even that long) wouldn't be so bad. *Just for today,* she told herself. *But no more.*

Sarah pulled two pieces of coffee cake wrapped in parchment paper from the bag and handed one to Grace.

It smelled like warm brown sugar, spicy cinnamon, and sweet vanilla. Grace unwrapped her piece of cake, broke off a corner, and popped it in her mouth.

She almost moaned. *Oh God, the cake is as good as the coffee.* "My gosh, I can't even," Grace said. *Maybe we could ride together two days a week.* "It's delicious."

"Thanks. I can bring you the recipe if you'd like."

"I could never get this result. Baking isn't my thing."

"It's an easy recipe. If I can bake this and not mess it up, anyone can."

Grace tried not to gobble the cake down, but it was that good, plus it was just one slice. And a small slice at that. *Almost a sliver*, she told herself as she finished it.

Sarah licked an errant crumb from her lip. "When my sister Ella lived at home, we had a booth at the farmers' market every Saturday. People would come from as far away as Asheville for her coffee cake."

"I can see why." Grace wiped her fingers on a napkin and dropped it and the empty parchment back into the bag, wishing Sarah had thought to bring a few extra pieces.

"I'm glad we're riding together today." Sarah finished her cake and wiped her hands on a napkin. "I've been wanting to talk to you about the social club."

Great. That was the last thing Grace wanted to talk about. Coffee cake was one thing, chatting was another, and Grace realized that the quicker she reached the town hall parking lot, the quicker this conversation would be over.

She reluctantly replaced her coffee cup in the holder, put the car in reverse, and backed out of the driveway.

Sarah didn't waste any time. "Zoe and I were talking this morning and we hope you're not upset about what happened with the club."

Upset? Grace was ecstatic. "Why would I be upset?"

"I didn't think it was what you wanted."

But it was. She'd wanted to get rid of it, and she had. "I'm perfectly fine with the outcome." It had been a little over a week since Grace had handed the reins of the club to Zoe (actually, it had been more like "tossed and ran," but *still*), so Grace wasn't sure what Sarah wanted to hear her say.

Not that it mattered. What was done was done, and she was just glad she could now focus on getting the office organized. "The club couldn't be in better hands."

"That's what I think, too." Sarah beamed and dropped her napkin into the empty bag. "Whew, I was worried you'd be upset and here you are, perfectly fine!"

"I've been too busy to think about it. All municipalities have to migrate their tax records to the new state system by the end of the month, and Mrs. Phelps didn't bother to even start getting things set up, so I'm swamped."

"Maybe she just got behind?"

"Oh no. There's a Post-it on the folder that says, 'For the New Person—NOT ME.'"

Sarah winced. "That was cold."

"She apparently had tendencies."

"More than you know. And wow, did Mrs. Phelps hate computers."

"There are times I don't like them, either, but technology helps."

Sarah sipped her coffee. "Mrs. Giano was right. You take to challenges like a duck to water."

Surprised, Grace looked at Sarah. The woman's eyes were the palest gray green, almost silver in color, and it seemed as if they could see right through her. "When did you talk to Mama G?"

"I've been dropping by on my short days." Sarah pursed her lips. "I think it was Thursday that she told me you liked challenges. We were talking about the town, and the social club. I don't know if she understood it all, because she seemed distracted. She kept calling me Hannah." The pale green eyes locked on Grace. "That was your sister, wasn't it?"

The lulling effect of the coffee and cake faded as Grace's habitual morning ire returned in full force. "Yes." She snapped the word so that it had the sound of a drawer being slammed shut.

Sarah was quiet a moment. "Hannah is a pretty name."

Grace's hands tightened on the steering wheel. "I don't want to talk about my sister." *There. That should end it.*

"Okay." Sarah sipped her coffee.

For a moment there was glorious silence, and Grace was just starting to relax when Sarah said, "It's funny how having a sister can define you."

Good God. "I said I didn't want to talk about it."

Sarah grimaced. "Sorry. But . . . I know it must have been hard. If you ever do want to talk about it, I'm here."

Grace frowned. "There's nothing to say."

Sarah nodded in sympathy.

Irked, Grace added, "Besides, Hannah didn't define me. Nor did I define her. Your relationship with your sisters is obviously quite different from ours."

"Maybe. I sort of think our family defines us whether we know it or not. I mean, look at me. I'm the youngest, so I got hand-me-downs of hand-me-downs. The only thing new I ever got to buy for myself was underwear." With a faint smile, she smoothed the soft, multicolored maxi-dress over her knee. "Which is why I love fashion so much now."

Grace wouldn't have called what Sarah wore "fashion," but she grudgingly had to admit that cool pastels worked with the woman's pale skin and ash-blond hair. Still, Grace could relate to the agony of having to wear used clothing. As a foster child, she and Hannah had worn more than their fair share.

But still, Hannah'd had no impact on Grace's current fashion sense. If anything, Hannah's wildness had sent Grace down her own, conservative, professional path. Hannah might have been happy wearing dirty jeans and torn T-shirts, but Grace had wanted something more substantial for herself, which was why she'd migrated toward conservative suits, the opposite of Hannah—

The thought froze in Grace's mind. *Oh God. Sarah's right. Hannah did define me.* Grace wondered what other ways her sister had influenced her life, and she was suddenly hit with the painful realization that whatever influence Hannah might have had, it was no more. She was gone, never to return. Sadness and loneliness swamped Grace with devastating suddenness, and she had to bite her lip to keep the tears from her eyes.

This was why she didn't want to talk about Hannah. Sarah's sisters were all still alive and well, so she couldn't understand how grief could sneak up on you, or what it felt like to go from being the oldest sister to not even being a sister at all. It was as if a hole had been cut into every childhood memory Grace possessed.

Sarah, evidently unaware of the effects of her words, sipped her coffee. "By the way, did Linda give you the book?"

Grateful to be talking about something other than Hannah, Grace said, "What book? I don't— Oh. *Little Women.* She did." As far as Grace knew, it was still in the breadbox. "That was very thoughtful of you, and while I appreciate that you took the time to send it, I don't have time to read it. I would have returned it already, but I keep forgetting to bring it with me."

Sarah waved her hand. "Keep it as long as you want."

Grace fake-smiled. "That's okay. I read it as a child, and I'm not really interested in it now."

"Hmm. Maybe it's interested in you."

Grace's smile faded. How on earth was she supposed to respond to that? She remembered Linda's awed expression when she'd talked about Sarah Dove and her books. *This whole town is weird, and I'm not going to be a part of it.* So she said shortly, "I'll bring the book back to the library tomorrow."

"Sure." Sarah's clear gaze never wavered.

Oddly self-aware under such a direct look, Grace turned the car

onto Main Street. The morning sun slanted over the red brick buildings and brightened the faded awnings.

"I love mornings," Sarah said with satisfaction. "Thank you for the
ride. It was much more fun than driving by myself."

"No problem." Only it had been. Why had Sarah brought up
Hannah? *And when will it stop hurting?* But it was more than that.
Hannah's death didn't just hurt; it was beginning to make Grace
angry. Hannah'd had so much to live for—her daughter, Mama G,
and Grace had all loved her and would have done anything for her.
With each day that passed, Grace was beginning to wonder if her
sister had ever loved any of them back.

Grace pulled into the town hall lot and parked.

Sarah made no move to collect her things. "See you here this afternoon at five?"

"Why— Oh. Right. You'll need a ride home. Doesn't the library
close early on Mondays?"

"We close at four, so five will be fine. I need to reshelve the day's
returns, and afterward, I'm going to run down to the Moonlight
Café and order a take-home dinner for Trav."

"Trav. You and he are—"

"Noooooo." Sarah grinned. "Lord, but I'd love to see his face if he
heard you say that. We've known each other since we were kids. I just
keep an eye on him now that his father is gone."

"Daisy is taken with him. I hope he's someone safe for her to
know."

"He's safe. He's a really, really good person. Kids are drawn to him
and he hates it, which makes them like him even more. I think it's
because he's so brutally honest. Kids like that, you know." She smiled
at Grace. "Daisy seems like a great kid. You're doing a wonderful job
raising her."

"Mama G has raised her so far. My sister wasn't a good parent.
To be honest, she wasn't that good of a sister, either." It felt oddly
relieving to say that out loud. "Hannah left Daisy with Mama G

years ago, so when Hannah died, not much changed for Daisy. But Mama G's illness . . . that's changing a lot of things, and it's been hard on Daisy."

"It sounds hard for all of you."

"It is. I wish I knew how to make things easier for Daisy, but . . ." Grace shook her head. "Why don't kids come with directions, like dishwashers and blenders? Life would be so much easier."

Sarah laughed. "You're not the only one who's wanted that. Which is why there are a thousand books on child raising."

"And I've read them all. Seriously, when I realized I'd be raising Daisy, I ordered every book on child rearing I could find. I can quote statistics and psychological theories out the wazoo, but none of that helps when you're trying to get them to eat their brussels sprouts. To be honest, I feel like I'm guessing as I go."

"Our parents probably felt the same. What makes it more complicated is that every child reacts to things differently. My poor mom had to figure it out seven times."

Grace sent Sarah a curious glance. "For not having any kids yourself, you seem to understand them pretty well."

"Not really. But the library hosts a children's story hour, so I see most of the kids in this town every week, and you wouldn't believe how varied their tastes are. Some of them like adventure books, some like fantasy, some only read manga—it's crazy how many different books I have to keep on the shelves. Every kid is different."

"Yeah, well, if you think their taste in books is varied, you should ask them what vegetables they like."

Sarah grinned. "I'm afraid to. But hey, Daisy doesn't look any the worse for wear, so you must be doing something right."

"Thanks. I hope so." In Grace's old job, if she made a mistake, she could potentially lose millions of dollars for their investors. She'd thought that was a lot of pressure until she'd accepted the responsibility of raising a kid. Now if Grace made a mistake, she worried that she could mess up her niece's life forever. It almost didn't bear thinking about. Grace undid her seat belt and opened her door. "Thank you for the coffee and cake."

"You're welcome. Thank you for the ride." Sarah began collecting her stuff.

Grace climbed out of the car, pausing to reclaim her satchel and purse.

Sarah hoisted the heavy tote over her shoulder. "Ugh. I've got to stop taking so many books home with me."

"I should be taking home some work, too, but I've been trying not to."

"Oh, these books aren't work." Sarah patted her bag as she made her way to the sidewalk. "They just like to visit."

Well. That was special. And borderline crazy. "They're your friends, the books."

"You could say that. But they're not friends like us."

"We just met; I'm not sure that counts as 'friends.'"

"Oh, we're going to be friends, you and I. Good ones. The kind who go to each other's funerals."

Grace had to laugh. "There's no way we could go to each other's funerals. That's physically impossible."

Sarah grinned. "You don't believe in ghosts, I take it."

"No, I don't. Mama G does, though. At least ghost cats. She's been seeing our old cat who died years ago."

"Ohhh. I think I just got a shiver."

"Yeah, well, it's just her imagining things, that's all." Grace locked the car and joined Sarah on the sidewalk. "You don't *really* believe in ghosts, do you?"

"I believe in possibilities. And that's one of them."

Possibilities. Grace thought about this and realized she hadn't believed in those for a long, long time. "Have you ever seen a ghost?"

"No," Sarah admitted regretfully. "Which is too bad. They say the library is chock-full of them, but I've never seen one."

"If I ever saw one, I'd run away."

"That would make a short horror film." Sarah's pale eyes shimmered with humor, and she framed her hands as if setting a film shot. "First frame: you, walking down the street."

"In heels. Horror films always show at least one person running in heels. If they're Louboutins, I'd be willing to make that sacrifice."

"In heels it is. Second frame: a ghost pops up."

Grace pretended to scream, although she didn't let any sound escape.

"Exactly, but louder. Final frame: you, running away."

"'The End.'" Grace started walking toward town hall, Sarah falling in beside her. "There'd be production issues, though. If I were running from a ghost, there's no way a cameraman could keep up."

Sarah laughed. "Did you ever notice that ghosts in movies are always angry? Either someone built a house on their grave, or their final wishes weren't honored, or their mother made them wear weird clothing as a child— Lord, in movies ghosts are angry about all sorts of things. But it's that anger that makes them scary. When people are angry, they're scary, too."

Grace couldn't argue with that. "Maybe that's why I'm a little cautious of our neighbor. He always looks mad."

"Trav is a grump, but he's really a marshmallow-inside sort of guy."

"Why does he scowl all the time? I don't think I've ever seen him smile."

Sarah's expression sobered. "Afghanistan changed him. He was injured pretty badly and his platoon lost quite a few men. I don't know anything more than that, because he won't talk about it."

Grace hadn't made any real effort to speak to Trav. In her zeal to protect Daisy, Grace had done nothing but glare at him. *I judged him on his hair and tattoos and I shouldn't have.* "I saw the scars on his neck."

"The ones on his shoulder and back are worse." Sarah sighed. "He doesn't sleep well, you know. Every morning when I get up, his lights are already on, no matter how early it is. I keep an eye on him when I can, which isn't often." Sarah slipped Grace a side-glance. "Did you leave a lot of friends behind when you moved here?"

Grace stopped at the crosswalk that led to the library. "I worked ten- to twelve-hour days, so I didn't have time for friends." *And I don't have time now.*

She looked down the street where the summer sun warmed the pavement, little curls of mist rising into the morning air. Pockets of mist still lingered in corners and hovered over the damp grass in the park, making the morning-bright street soft and pretty, like a painting.

It really was peaceful here in this small town. But enough was enough. Soon it would be time to return to the real world, where she could start making her mark and planning a grand future for Daisy and, while she could, Mama G. Grace offered Sarah a polite smile and stuck her hand out for a shake. "Thank you again for the coffee and cake. They were amazing." They'd also made the day somewhat brighter. At least a little.

Sarah's smile faded at the sight of Grace's hand poised for a businesslike handshake, but after a slight hesitation, she accepted it. "It was my pleasure." She flashed a smile and adjusted her tote on her shoulder. "And look! I have enough cake left for the social club meeting this afternoon."

"They will enjoy that," Grace said absently as she fished the keys to her office from her purse. "Well, it's been fun. See you later this afternoon for the drive home. At five, right?"

"I'll see you before then— Oh! Someone is waiting at the library."

Grace followed Sarah's gaze to the library steps. "Looks like you have an early customer."

"That's Lisa Renfro. She called yesterday and asked me to set aside the new Mary Alice Monroe book for her. But I need to give her a book about craft beer too."

Grace eyed the thin, rather prim woman standing impatiently in front of the library. She wore a dull blue dress and flats, and her face was twisted as if in a perpetual frown. "She makes craft beer?"

"Oh no. Lisa's a teetotaler. I know because she goes to my church and tells everyone that she never drinks."

"Then why does she need a book on craft beer?"

Sarah grinned. "I have no idea. Yet. But I've got to let her in. See you this afternoon." She took off across the street, calling out to Lisa as she went.

Grace shook her head. She didn't understand Sarah Dove at all. Not even a little. When they drove home that afternoon, Grace would make it clear that, while it had been nice to share their ride, she couldn't continue to carpool. Getting Mama G and Daisy ready in the morning before Linda came was enough of a challenge without the added pressure of knowing someone was waiting on her.

I'll miss the coffee cake, though. Grace continued up the sidewalk to town hall, noticing that the flowers in the planter were now a lovely deep purple. That was her favorite color so far. *I need to remember to ask Lenny what type of flowers those are.* Grace reached down to unlock the door, but to her surprise, it was already open.

That was odd. She was always the first one to arrive in the morning. Mayor Moore rarely sailed in until after ten.

Curious, she walked into her office. The door had no sooner swung closed behind her than Mayor Moore appeared in his doorway. He was a mess, his hair standing on end as if he'd raked his hands through it a million times. His jacket was gone, and his tie hung undone and forgotten around his neck. Both his shirt and his suit pants were sadly wrinkled.

She frowned. "Did you sleep here?"

"What? I— No. I mean, I did, but only this morning. I was awake the rest of the time."

"I never see you this early." She put her satchel beside her desk, opened the bottom drawer, and dropped her purse in it. "Is something wrong?"

His smile, which had seemed forced, now looked both forced and frozen. "We need to talk." He gestured toward his office door. "Come in and have a seat."

"What's happened?"

His frozen smile grew more strained. He managed a fake laugh to match it. "You're direct, I'll give you that."

"Which you must be used to. I only met Mrs. Phelps once, but she didn't strike me as the sort of woman to beat around the bush."

His smile sagged, and he muttered something under his breath that sounded like "Beat around the ear, is more like," before he said in a mournful tone, "Please come in. This is important. I know you've got a lot of work to do—"

"So you've noticed."

"You say it a lot, so of course I've noticed." He didn't seem to realize he'd just lit her fires yet again. "Look, we've an emergency. A bad one."

And of course, he would want her to fix it, whatever it was. She reluctantly followed him into his office and sat in the chair across from his desk. "What's the emergency?"

His chair creaked as he dropped into it. "Something has happened. Something I've—" He raked a hand through his hair, leaving yet more of it standing on end. "I don't even know how it started or who suggested— I guess it doesn't matter. But I—I mean *we*—have to stop it, and fast."

"Stop what?"

He put his elbows on his desk and steepled his hands, eyeing her the way one might look at a caged tiger. "I've been the mayor for twenty-three years now. I've been through five elections and won them all."

"Congratulations." She noted his steepled hands and supposed he'd seen that gesture in a movie, for it rang as hollow as a spoon banged against an empty bowl.

"I ran good campaigns. Put up signs, made visits, spoke to the churches, the Kiwanis, the Shriners—to just about anyone who would have me. You never stop running for office, you know. It's a twenty-four-seven deal." Some of his stress disappeared behind a soothing cloud of self-congratulations. "Even now, I go to the churches for their events, hand out candy at the festivals, and I always, always kiss every baby I see, although"—his smile slipped a little—"that's not as easy as it sounds."

Probably not. She waited, but he didn't speak, seemingly lost in a mental list of all the babies he'd kissed and the issues that had arisen. "Mayor? You said there was an emergency. So far, I'm not hearing anything bad."

"Oh!" He blinked. "Sorry. I was just thinking. But you're right. The emergency. And it is one, so . . ." He wet his lips as if they were dry. "I've run all of those campaigns—all of them successful. Next year, I'm up for reelection." He looked at her meaningfully. "You can see where this is headed."

No, she couldn't. "I'm going to need a little more information."

"Of course. Of course." He nodded as if he'd wisely known she would ask. "I don't know how, but I never saw this coming, and I usually have my ear to the ground, looking for just this sort of thing." He took a deep, troubled breath. "Over the past week, I've heard rumors. Vague at first, but then I saw for myself that . . . Ms. Wheeler, we have a situation. A *dire* situation."

God, grant me patience! Can he talk in more circles? "What are we talking about here? Plagues? Locusts? Or have we moved straight into deaths of firstborns?"

"This is no joking matter!" he snapped, his perpetual smile seeming permanently lost. "Ms. Wheeler, we have a dire situation, one that only you can solve."

"Me? How?"

"The social club."

What? Suddenly, the cake and coffee from this morning took on a sinister meaning. "What about the social club?" She left so much frost hanging from each syllable that she was sure he could have chipped ice from them.

He winced and visibly shored himself up before saying quickly, as if by speaking fast, he might not upset her, "You have to reclaim the chairmanship of the social club."

"No."

"Yes. I don't know what happened at that meeting, but—"

"You know exactly what happened at that meeting. I told you about it the same day, and you laughed and said, 'Well done.'"

He flushed and waved a hand. "You said something, but I didn't really understand what had happened. That you'd given the chairmanship to Zoe Bell."

"Yes, you did. I very plainly said—"

"Then I didn't listen!" He took a shaky breath and pressed his fingertips to his temples as if afraid his head might explode. "Look, Ms. Wheeler. I need you to go to the social club meeting and take back the chairmanship."

"I can't. Zoe Bell is the chairman and that's that."

"I know who is the chairman. *That* is the problem." He raked his hand back through his hair, looking as if he were contemplating ripping out what remained of it by the roots. "Of all the people to give the chairmanship to, she is the *worst.*"

What was going on? Grace felt as if she and the mayor were having two different conversations, hers in English and his in Dothraki. "Zoe is the vice president of the local bank, so she has excellent contacts and must have good business sense. She seems very approachable and competent. She's the perfect choice to—"

"I don't want to hear another damn word about how perfect Zoe Bell is! You will go to the meeting this afternoon and take back the chairmanship!"

"I will not."

"You will, too!" He leaned forward, his face bright red, the veins on his forehead standing out. "You will chair the committee. You will plan the Apple Festival, and better yet, you'll pretend you enjoy it and smile so much people will think you, and everyone in this office, are huffing starter fluid!"

"And if I don't?" she asked stiffly.

His face reddened even more. "If you don't, I'll have to let you go." His voice squeaked on the last word.

She was so, so tempted to get up and leave. To just walk away from this job she didn't want and wished she didn't have. But life hadn't given her a lot of choices lately, and quitting wasn't an option.

"Ms. Wheeler, *please*. I don't want to fire you. I really don't. You've been an exceptional employee. Why, I've never seen the records in such good shape and you've only been here a few weeks! But . . . look, I am an elected official first and foremost."

"So?"

"So—" He glanced at the open door, climbed to his feet, and closed the door. When he came back, he dropped into his chair like a bag of wet sand, his shoulders slumped. "If you don't take back the chairmanship, I could lose my job."

"How?"

"Someone will run against me in the next election. That has never happened."

"Wait. No one has *ever* run against you? Not once?"

"No," he admitted. "Well, there was talk one year that Mr. Philbin, who owned the Seed and Feed store down on SR 20, might run, but fortunately, he died before he could get enough petition signatures."

"Fortunately?"

The mayor flushed. "You know what I mean. But now there's talk that someone else is considering a run."

Who could possibly be running for mayor that had anything to do with the— *Oh no.* "Zoe Bell."

He nodded miserably.

"You've got to be kidding me."

"She's going to do it." He edged forward in his seat. "Last week, I was at the bank standing in line to make my mortgage payment and I heard her telling one of the clerks that she'd hired a company to do some market research on a special project."

"And?"

"When she saw me, she shut up and then hurried away as if upset I'd overheard her."

"She could have been talking about anything."

"The next day, I saw her in the post office asking Mark Robinson how much it would cost to do a mailing. A *mass* mailing of *all registered voters.*"

"Oh."

He nodded. "See? I saw her again in the drugstore two days after that, and she was buying clipboards and pens."

"So?"

"She'll need to do a petition in order to get on the ballot," he said impatiently. "And she acted very odd when she saw me. I was still hoping that maybe I was wrong, that it was just a set of coincidences. But then, this weekend, my worst suspicions were confirmed. There is no doubt about it now."

"What happened?"

"I saw her in Kat Carter's yard. Kat lives across the street from me. They had two signs stuck in the yard, and they were comparing them and talking about them. The second they saw me, they grabbed them up and tried to put them in the trunk of Zoe's car, but Kat dropped one and I got a clear look at it. It said, 'Zoe Bell for Mayor: A Fresh Start.'" He shook his head as if trying to shake the vision from his eyes. "We can't have that. The Bells are a Dove Pond institution. If anyone in the Bell family ran for mayor, even their cat, they'd win."

"That's an exaggeration."

"No, it's not. Half this town owes them money, so they're well-funded enough to buy any election they want to. And you made things worse when you let Zoe take charge of the social club. She'll claim that's experience."

"Organizing a festival and running a town—that's not quite the same thing."

"Voters don't know that. It's the perfect platform on which to kick me out of office. I have no doubt she'll throw the best Apple Festival we've ever had and then walk around it, handing out flyers and kissing babies and acting as if the entire thing was her own private election party." He cursed under his breath. "We have to get that chairmanship back." He turned an accusing glare toward Grace. "*You* have to get it back."

"How?"

"You're going to march into the social club meeting this afternoon and reclaim the damn thing. Tell them you didn't know what you were saying because you were sick, or hallucinating from hunger, or you'd just hit your head on a filing cabinet, or— Damn it, I don't care what you say, just get the chairmanship back!"

"I can't."

"You must. This is war, Ms. Wheeler. And I'll be damned if I'm going to let a Bell, even a pretty one, steal my job."

"I hardly think running against you for public office in a fair election is 'stealing.'"

He clasped his hands together, his anger disappearing as pure desperation appeared to set in. "Ms. Wheeler, *please, please, please.* Do it for me and I'll—I'll give you some extra days off or—or order you a brand-new desk. Maybe, if I move some things around in the budget and we don't do Christmas decorations this year, I could give you a little raise and—"

"Whoa! No, sir. That's out-and-out bribery and it's illegal. Besides, I'm not going to be the cause of the town not having Christmas. That's just wrong."

His shoulders slumped, his watery blue eyes sadder than those of any puppy she'd ever seen. "What am I going to do?"

"Why don't you run for office for real this time? You know, find some issues that would appeal to the voters?"

He looked at her as if she'd suggested he cut off his own head and hang it on one of his fishing hooks.

"Not your thing?" she said drily.

"It wouldn't help. It's like I said, the Bells have a lock on this town. There aren't enough issues in the world to overcome that huge advantage."

She nodded as if she agreed, although she didn't. But to be honest, he already looked beaten. Despite herself, she felt sorry for him. As weak as he was, he was a nice person. A little selfish at times, but she'd bet he'd never said "boo" to a fly.

He needed a festival, then fine, she'd do it. But she wasn't about to commit to accepting more work without getting something back. She thought about it for a long moment, then finally she said, "Friday afternoons off."

Hope bloomed on his florid face. "That's possible, I suppose."

"And until we're caught up, you'll do four hours of data entry a day."

He blinked. "I beg your pardon?"

"*Every* day."

"Now, wait a minute—"

"I'll take back the festival committee, and you'll catch up on the data entry each and every morning."

"Then what will you do in the mornings?"

"My job. I have tax records to record, licenses to file, voter records to keep up to date—" She shot him an impatient look. "You know my job description."

He was silent a moment. "I have to do *all* the data entry?"

"Every last keystroke."

He sank back into his seat. "I can't do that! I'm the mayor, not the town clerk. Data entry is your job."

"And running an election is yours."

"I can't do the data entry. I'd have to be here every morning and—" He shook his head, looking like a toddler who'd been denied a lollipop. "No."

"Fine." She stood. "If you don't need anything else, I'll be getting to work. I'd offer to help with your campaign signs, but I'll be too busy doing data entry."

She made it all the way to the door and had her hand on the knob when he called out, "Wait!"

She turned around and crossed her arms.

"Fine, fine," he said, looking as petulant as Daisy. "I'll do the stupid data entry."

"And my half day off on Friday?"

"Two hours, but just for this month."

"Three hours every Friday until Daisy starts school."

"Look, you're already getting—"

"Say yes or I walk."

He grumbled under his breath, looking furious, but after a moment, he gave a curt nod. "Fine, fine. Whatever you want. Just don't leave Zoe in charge of the festival."

"Done. I'm not entirely sure how I'm going to convince her to give it up—she really wanted the job. Her hand shot up the second I asked for volunteers."

"I'm sure she about jumped out of her seat. Zoe Bell might be pretty as the day is long, but she's hard as nails under that painted surface. She's her father's daughter, that one."

Ah, but Grace was Mama G's daughter, which was even better. "I'll figure it out. Do you know what time the meeting starts?"

"Three."

"Good. That'll give me almost seven hours to prepare, won't it?"

"There you go!" Mayor Moore thumped his desk with his fist as if stamping his approval. "You go and show them that Zoe Bell is not the only one in this town who is tough as nails. I believe in you, Grace Wheeler. This is war, and I know you won't let me down."

Grace thought of a thousand things she could say in response, none of them polite enough to air. "I'll bring the data entry folders to you now."

His smile faltered. "Can't we start tomorrow? I was planning on fishing."

"If you start now, you can leave at lunch and fish all afternoon." Ignoring his pout, she returned to her desk and gathered the huge stack of folders and carried them back to his office. It took her the better part of an hour to get him started, as he knew nothing of the new computer system, but he eventually figured it out and, with much grumbling, began the tedious work.

She returned to her desk, admiring how empty it looked without the stacks of folders weighing it down. What should she do first? If she'd had the folder from the festival, she'd have started going through it and developing a thorough to-do list, but she'd given the folder to Zoe at the last meeting. Grace supposed that the least she could do was a quick run-through of the festival funding. Fortunately, the current town budget would have that information.

Where had she seen the annual budget? Ah, yes. It had been filed under STUFF. She shook her head at Mrs. Phelps's lack of organization and reached into her satchel for the keys to the filing cabinet. As she did so, she found something bulky and heavy resting on the keys.

Frowning, she pulled it out, and was surprised to find the book *Little Women*, the same one she'd left in the breadbox over a week ago. *How in the heck did this end up in my satchel? I didn't— Ah. Mama G.* Just yesterday Grace had found Mama G's hairbrush stuck in a fireplace vent. She still wasn't sure what was happening with that.

Grace found her keys and dropped the book back in her satchel, then tucked it beside her desk. She wasn't surprised Mama G had latched onto this particular book. She was living more and more in the past, and *Little Women* was a reminder of their home in Whitlow.

Grace rose and unlocked the file cabinets. She found the budget and carried it back to her desk. As she sat down, it struck her that the mayor's information about Zoe Bell's run for office seemed rather . . . convenient. A niggling suspicion made her wonder if something was off about the entire situation. But what?

She replayed the conversation in her mind, remembering the short meeting where Zoe had jumped at the chance to be the chair. It all fit, but still . . . Her gaze absently dropped to her satchel, the book's mustard binding in bright contrast against the dark leather.

When Grace and Hannah had first arrived at Mama G's house, every night before bed, Mama G had read *Little Women* to them. Hannah, who'd never been a reader, would fall asleep after the first few pages, but Grace had been absorbed by the antics of the lively March family. The sisters were close and loving, the mother kind and caring. Even when they fought, as they sometimes did, they only came to love one another more. How Grace had wanted a family like that. Even now she could repeat long segments, especially the plays that Jo and her sisters loved to perform for their mother and—

The plays.

Grace stared at the book, her mind locked on a fascinating idea. The idea firmed up and crystallized, so clear she could almost see it.

She reached into the satchel and pulled out the book, leaving it on her lap as she stared at it. *They couldn't have*, she told herself. *There is no way.*

But they had. She was as sure of it as if she'd witnessed it herself. "Holy machinations, Batman," she whispered to herself. "What a pack of small-town connivers."

She didn't know whether she was more irritated or amused, but after a moment, she dropped the book back into her satchel.

Well, well, well. This was going to be an interesting meeting.

Shaking her head, she flipped open the budget file and grabbed a notepad so she could write down the festival information. She'd just finished listing the line items that had to do with the festival when, as a matter of habit, she absently scanned the rest of the page, adding up the sums.

She hadn't gone far when she frowned.

That couldn't be right.

She pushed her notepad to the side and pulled out her calculator. For the next hour and a half, she added up numbers, over and over, turning through the pages and occasionally getting up to pull other files from the cabinet and compare their numbers to those in the budget.

Finally, her desk covered with a raft of opened files and papers, she leaned back in her chair and let out her breath in a long whoosh. Surely this was wrong. It had to be.

There was only one person who would know. She stacked the papers together, slid them back into their folders, and carried them into the mayor's office.

Ten minutes later, she returned to her desk, holding the folders close and walking slowly as if she were wading through molasses.

It was true. All of it.

She sank into her chair, put the files on her desk, and stared at them, her mind racing a hundred ways to Tuesday.

Mayor Moore was right about one thing: it was war. But it wasn't the war he'd thought it would be. Worse, Grace was pretty sure it was one that she, and everyone in Dove Pond, would lose.

CHAPTER 10

Sarah

Erma Tingle looked at the clock over the door of the library conference room. "Where is she?" She turned a glum look on Zoe.

The younger woman snapped shut her compact mirror with which she'd just touched up her red lipstick. "She'll be here. Wait and see." She sat at the head of the room, her legs crossed at the ankle and resting on the table.

Sarah rather liked the red soles of Zoe's shoes. While Sarah never wore high heels, she decided that if she did, she'd want some with red soles. She pushed the plate of coffee cake to the middle of the table so that it was more reachable. "Anyone want more cake? There're two more pieces."

"No, thank you." Kat looked at Ava. "That was hard to say. I could eat that all day."

"I'll have another piece." Nate slid some cake onto a napkin and pulled it across the table until it rested in front of him.

"If no one is going to have that last piece . . . ?" Ed looked around the table.

"Forget the damn cake," Erma said in a waspish tone. She leaned forward, favoring Zoe with a suspicious look. "You're sure Grace'll be the chairman?"

Zoe gave a smug smile. "Oh, she'll be the chairman all right."

"I rode to work with her this morning," Sarah said. "I asked her if she was okay with the way things had turned out with the social committee and she said she was, but now that I think about it, I'm not sure she knew. Zoe, when did you do the sign trick?"

"Saturday morning."

"Ah. I bet she didn't know." And Sarah had been so glad Grace hadn't been mad. "I bet Mayor Moore didn't say a word until today, the idiot."

Nate eyed Zoe curiously. "What sign trick?"

Zoe smiled. "You don't need the details. Just rest assured that I used wile and deception. They are my two biggest attributes."

"That's rather terrifying," Nate said, although he looked more intrigued than anything else.

Erma snorted. "Zoe, girl, I wouldn't brag about that."

"I don't know," Ava said, musingly. "They can be very effective traits to have."

Kat agreed. "Especially when used together."

"I just hope Grace gets here soon." Ed Mayhew finished the last piece of cake and opened his bottle of water. "We've got a new shipment of dog collars coming in at four and Maggie will need help get—"

The door flung open.

At first glance, Grace looked much as she had this morning—neatly encased in a tailored power suit with the hemline just so, her dark hair pinned into a neat bun at the nape of her neck. But that was where the "usual" ended. Her gaze, usually so guarded, blazed from within as if the fires of Hades lit her soul. She walked across the room, a stack of multicolored files gripped tightly to her chest.

Sarah had to fight the urge to stand up and cheer. Angry or not, this woman was going to save them all. *I know it. I just know it.*

Grace cast her fiery glance around the table. Erma gulped, and Ava, who always seemed amused whenever drama happened, gave a silent, appreciative whistle. Ed looked as if he might make a lunge for an open window, while Nate became busy adjusting his watch. Only Kat offered a greeting, a cautious wave hello.

Sarah stood. "Grace, how nice to see you. We didn't expect—"

"Stuff it." Grace dropped her folders on the table where Zoe sat, her feet still resting on the surface. "Nice shoes. Now move."

Zoe dropped her feet to the floor and collected her purse and notepad. "Of course you'd want the head seat. That makes sense." She patted the fat folder Grace had given her before. "I'll just leave this here so you—"

"Go sit down." Grace cut her an icy look. "And for the love of heaven, stop pretending."

Zoe grinned. "Who's pretending?"

Sarah had to admire Zoe's chutzpah. She didn't seem at all fazed by Grace's scorching fury.

Grace dropped her stack of folders on the table and eyed Zoe. "Not even going to deny it, are you?"

Zoe shrugged. "Why bother?"

"You are a piece of work."

"Thank you." Zoe couldn't have looked more pleased. "I decided it's for the best if we just get it out in the open and move on. Besides, it's obvious you've figured things out. I knew you would."

Nate leaned close to Sarah and whispered, "What the hell's going on?"

"Just watch," Sarah whispered back.

"You thought right," Grace said flatly. She pointed to the opposite end of the table, to the empty chair by Nate.

"Yes, Madame Chairwoman." Zoe took her things and strolled to the seat, sitting down with a gracious smile.

Nate looked as if he wanted to laugh but was afraid to.

Grace stood beside her chair and eyed her committee. "You all won. I'm here."

Sarah wasn't sure what to say. "Congratulations" seemed off target, and sympathy was uncalled for. She realized everyone was looking at her, so she smiled as she sank into her seat. "Welcome back! However it happened, we're glad you're here. We've a lot of work to do, so maybe—"

"Stop. Before we go any further, you all owe me an apology."

Nate's brows rose. "For . . . ?"

"She's talking to Zoe," Erma told Nate in an undertone. "I think she is, anyway." Erma raised her voice. "Zoe, what did you do?"

"Wait a minute." Grace examined the face of each member. "Not everyone was in on this."

"Just some of us," Sarah admitted.

"Not in on what?" Ed appeared bewildered. "What did you all do?"

"You didn't know anything?" Grace asked.

"I didn't. I mean, I knew they were going to get you back, but I figured they were just going to ask."

"Don't look at me, either," Erma said. "I have no idea what's going on. I was just told you'd be back. That's it."

"Well, well, well." Grace placed her hands flat on the table and leaned forward. "Miss Bell, do you want to tell them?"

Zoe pursed her lips. "I think it would be better if you did. You are in charge, after all."

"Fine." Grace took her seat. "As some of you apparently don't know, for one short week, Miss Zoe Bell ran for mayor of our lovely town."

Ed, who'd been taking a sip of water, choked.

Erma thumped him on the back. "Easy, Mayhew. She's kidding."

"I'm not kidding." Grace arched a brow at Zoe. "Am I?"

Zoe's lips quirked, but she managed to suppress her smile. "I might have run for mayor . . . a little."

Ava chuckled.

Grace looked at her. "What's so funny?"

Ava bit back her grin. "Zoe doing anything 'a little.'"

"It defies belief, doesn't it?" Grace replied. "And that's what got me to thinking. Mayor Moore has held his job for over twenty years and he's never once been challenged. Not once. I asked myself why that was, and then I realized that the job is boring and no one but a dedicated fisherman would want it. Zoe, I don't know you well, but I'll wager that you don't fish."

Zoe pursed her lips. "That's a fair assessment."

"So I was supposed to believe that all of a sudden, right after you agreed to take on the chairmanship of this committee—"

"Club," Ava corrected, wincing when Grace cut her a withering glance.

"Whatever you want to call it," Grace said in a cool tone. She turned back to Zoe. "You wanted me to believe that right after you took on the chairmanship of the social club, you *also* decided to run for a crappy job no one wants. You, the vice president of a bank."

Kat tsked. "Zoe, how could you be so greedy? Isn't one job enough?"

Grace shot a hard look at Kat. "You were part of it, too. I know you were."

Kat flushed and looked down at her notepad as if suddenly realizing she needed to write something very important but couldn't remember what it was.

As uncomfortable as the present situation was, Sarah had to admire how well Grace was stating her case. *She's a natural leader.*

Grace's attention returned to Zoe. "Somehow, over the course of one week, Mayor Moore *accidentally* heard you discussing polling while he happened to be at your bank, he *accidentally* caught you discussing a mass mailing to 'all registered voters' with the postmaster, *and* he *accidentally* got a glimpse of one of your proposed yard signs when Kat, who conveniently lives across the street from him, *accidentally* dropped it right as he walked past."

Nate eyed Zoe with appreciation. "You did all of that?"

Erma looked stunned. "In one week?"

Zoe smiled. "Brilliant, wasn't it? I knew he'd stop at nothing to keep me from running for his office, including order Grace to take back the social club."

"It worked!" Sarah tried not to sound too happy as she confided, "If the sign trick didn't push him over the edge, we were going to leave some signed petition-to-run forms in the copier at the drugstore. Mayor Moore goes there every morning on his way to work to buy a chocolate milk."

"How would he know something was left on the copy machine?" Ed asked.

Ava raised her hand. "That was going to be my job," she said, obviously pleased to have been included. "I was going to be there making flyers for a plant sale, and just as he passed the copier on his way to get his milk, I was to open the lid and pretend to be irked to find Zoe's petition there. I was to mutter her name out loud and then toss it into the trash."

"He was already getting paranoid," Zoe added. "We knew he'd wait for Ava to leave and then he'd look in the trash to see what she'd thrown away."

"Wow," Nate said. "You guys did a whole *Ocean's Eight* thing. I'm impressed."

Ava made a face. "I was really looking forward to playing my part, but we didn't have to do it, as the sign trick worked so well."

"He looked ill," Zoe said with satisfaction.

Kat chuckled. "It was almost too easy."

"What was your slogan?" Ed asked curiously.

" 'Zoe Bell for Mayor: A Fresh Start.' Ava thought of that."

"It was better than Sarah's," Ava said. "She wanted 'Out with the Old.' "

"That was too obvious," Kat agreed.

Nate cast an admiring gaze around the table. "Machiavelli, move over. Zoe Bell and company have arrived."

"Excuse me." Grace's voice cut through the air. "Are you all through congratulating each other? Because if you are, we've got work to do."

"Of course, but ah . . . don't you want to know why we wanted you back so badly?" Sarah asked.

Grace's cool gaze came to rest on her, and the faintest tinge of regret hit Sarah. She'd worried Grace would be upset. Actually, that wasn't true; she'd *known* Grace would be upset, which was unfortunate but necessary. But now, before they progressed, amends must be made. She cleared her throat. "Grace, I know you're mad, and you have every right to be, but we had a good reason for what we did."

"Really?" Grace's tones were clipped into single letters.

Sarah winced. "We need your help. We all want the festival to be bigger, better, something it hasn't been in a long, long time. We need strong leadership for that to happen."

"And we couldn't just ask," Ava added, "because you would have said no. That was obvious from the last meeting. You didn't want to do it."

"Heck," Erma said flatly. "You didn't even want to be here. That much was plain."

Grace eyed them for a moment. Finally, she sighed. "You're right. I would have said no."

"So we did what we had to do," Sarah said. "Which is when Zoe came up with The Plan."

"Well, it worked," Grace said sourly. "And I'm here, although you may wish I wasn't before the meeting is over."

Sarah's happiness slipped a bit. What did that mean?

Grace looked around the table. "Before we talk about the festival, we need to talk about something else. Something much more important."

"The festival is important," Erma protested.

Grace's gaze slid over her without stopping and then returned to the stack of folders in front of her. "We need to talk about the town's financial standing."

Nate shrugged. "Okay. What about it?"

"It's bad," she said.

Sarah winced. "The town isn't doing as well as it should. We know that."

"'Not as well as it should'?" Grace gave a curt laugh. "That's an understatement."

Ava frowned. "What do you mean?"

"It's bad. Much worse than you know."

"Ah," Zoe said, nodding. "I wondered how long it would take before you looked."

"Looked at what?" Sarah asked, growing even more concerned.

"Grace has seen the town's financial records," Zoe said.

"I have." Grace spread her hands flat on the table in front of her. "I went through the accounts this morning and what I saw was . . ." She shook her head. "It was bad."

Erma frowned. "You work in the mayor's office and you just today saw the accounts?"

"I've only worked there a month, plus I deal with the revenue side rather than expenditures, so the overall summary doesn't hit my desk. But today I decided that I should take a look at the festival funding before I came to the meeting, so I pulled out the town budget records."

"How far back did you go?" Zoe asked.

"The last ten years. It was grim."

"Does Mayor Moore know about this?" Ava asked.

"I spoke to him and he knew the gist, but no more. He's filed the exact same budget request every year since he's been in office."

Sarah blinked. "It's never changed?"

"Not once."

"God, that man is lazy!" Ed said with disgust.

Grace didn't argue. "The town's accountant does an annual audit, but the mayor hasn't familiarized himself with the details."

"That's some A-class avoidism there," Nate said.

"Tell me about it." Grace eyed the committee. "Here's the deal. I'm willing to come back and chair the committee, but on my own terms."

"Which are?" Sarah asked.

"I don't plan on staying in Dove Pond for more than a year. I've made no secret of that, but I want to be up front about it. I moved here from Charlotte, and I'd like to move back once I can afford it."

"One year?" Kat frowned. "That's not long."

"No, it's not. But before I leave, while I can't solve the issues plaguing the town, I can at least get you moving in the right direction. And in order for that to happen, this committee will have to do more than just plan festivals."

"Festivals are good for our economy," Erma said stubbornly.

"For one weekend, yes, but it's not enough. This town is drowning in its own debt, and if we don't do something soon, it'll be caught in such a downward financial spiral that it'll never recover."

"Spiral?" Ed swallowed loudly. "It's that bad?"

"It's that bad," Grace said.

"But how?" Erma asked, her voice choked. "I mean, I know people have been leaving and some businesses closed, but that happens every now and then. The economy can't always go up, you know."

"It's more than that," Grace replied. "I spent the past few hours thinking this through. Dove Pond doesn't have a town board of directors or a council, or anything like that, so if the mayor won't address a situation, that leaves the social club or no one."

Silence filled the room. Sarah wondered if Charlotte Dove's journal knew about this. The cranky old thing had to, and yet it hadn't uttered so much as a word to her.

Zoe clasped her hands together and rested them on the table in front of her. "What do you want us to do?"

"We need to plan something more important than the Apple Festival. Something that could help the town."

"Like?" Ava prodded.

"A business outreach. We need to invite potential business owners to town, let them see Dove Pond the way you see it. The way Sarah sees it. And we need to convince them to invest in the town. In you. In this community. And fortunately for all of you, if there's one thing I know how to do, it's sell an idea to a business."

And there it was. The reason Grace had come to Dove Pond. Sarah had been wondering what Grace could do for their town that Sarah couldn't, and now she knew.

"Geez." Kat pushed back from the table. "Look, I don't mean to be a killjoy, and I really want to help, but I only signed up for this committee to plan festivals. I didn't sign up to do business outreach, or whatever you call it."

"Neither do I," Nate said.

Ava hadn't stopped staring at Grace, and now she asked cautiously, "You think it will really help Dove Pond?"

"It can," Grace said without hesitation. "If we do it right, it could save the place."

"And there's no other way?" Ava asked.

"No," Grace said.

Ava shrugged. "Then we don't have any choice."

"Great," Kat muttered. "How much more work will this business outreach be?"

"A lot." Grace tapped the stack of folders in front of her. "Before we go any further, let me explain how Dove Pond got into this position to begin with. That will help you understand why an outreach program is the only way to turn the tide. After that, we'll make some decisions."

Several people glanced at Sarah, as if seeking her opinion. Such was the burden of expectations. She nodded. "Let's do this."

"I'm in," Zoe said.

"Me too," Ava agreed. "I'm curious to know why things have gotten so bad, although it's no secret the town's fortunes are sagging."

"That's true," Kat admitted. "We see it every time we walk down Main Street."

"It's more than that," Zoe said sharply. "Grace isn't kidding when she says our town is dying. The bank used to have over a hundred business accounts, and now we've less than forty, and some of those are inactive."

"It's tough to make it here," Ed said. "If it weren't for the pension I get from the twenty-two years I worked for the paper mill, Maggie and I couldn't live off what we make from the pet store. It wasn't that way when we first started, but now . . ." He shook his head.

"You all sound like the voices of doom," Erma huffed. "Dove Pond is experiencing a downturn, but so are a lot of other places. Give us a year or two and things will turn around. They always do, and the mayor knows it. In the meantime, we should focus on the festivals, as is our duty, and nothing more."

Nate grimaced. "Erma, it's more than a mere downturn. My revenue has dropped every year for the last four years, maybe five. I know yours has, too, because I've heard you complain about it."

Erma sniffed.

He raised his brows.

She flushed and snapped, "Fine! My revenue *has* dropped. And yes, the town is in trouble. But what can we do to fix it? We're just eight people!"

"Eight smart, capable, determined people," Grace said. "Before I moved here, I worked for a financial group in Charlotte that helped companies facing bankruptcy reorganize into leaner, more profitable models. Then we'd set up a smart, effective investment structure to help them plan for expansions and upgrades down the road. I'd think that if a business could do that, so could a town."

Sarah looked at the ceiling. *Fate, thank you for sending this woman to us.*

"First things first," Zoe said. "Technically, I'm still the chairman until we vote for Grace's return."

Sarah raised her hand. "I make a motion to accept Grace's conditions, whatever they may be, and that she be reinstated immediately into the position of chairman."

"I second that," Nate said.

"All in favor?" Zoe asked.

Everyone said "aye" except Erma.

Zoe raised a brow. "Is that a nay?"

"No," Erma blustered, looking miserable. "I vote yes, of course I do. I just wish I understood things better."

"That's why we're having a two-part meeting." Grace flipped open the top folder and pulled it forward. "First, I'm going to explain how the finances of the town have gotten so upside down."

"How long will that take?" Ed asked.

"A half hour. Perhaps a little more, depending on how many questions there are."

"Okay." He pulled out his phone. "I'd better text Maggie and let her know I won't be home for a while."

"Do that," Grace said.

Ava eyed Grace curiously. "What's the second part of our meeting?"

Grace paused and Sarah could feel the tension even from across the table. "We'll discuss that after we hold the vote to cut the festival budget."

"*What?*" Sarah couldn't believe she was hearing this. "But the festival is what we do. It's why the social club exists."

"We have to have the festival," Erma said, her face flushed.

"We're still having it," Grace said impatiently. "But it'll be a stripped-down version."

Ed shook his head. "No way! We barely have enough to do a decent job as it is."

Grace's cool gaze locked on him. "Need I remind you that there will be no Dove Pond Social Club if there's no Dove Pond? We have no choice. We're going to gut the festival budget and use the money for an outreach program where we invite potential businesses to visit our town."

Erma sniffed her outrage. "I will not vote to remove any money from the festival budget!"

"Maybe we shouldn't have a festival at all," Zoe said. When Erma looked shocked, Zoe added regretfully, "It's an expense. It hasn't been a moneymaker for years."

"We're still going to have it," Grace said. "The mayor has demanded that much, at least. But we can only afford a scaled-back version."

"How scaled back are you talking?" Kat asked.

"A few booths, maybe a parade, some hot dogs and balloons, but not a lot more."

Ed's face had turned a dull red. "I don't like this. And neither will Maggie."

"Some of my best memories are of the festivals." Ava looked sad. "I'd hate to see it get pruned back like that."

So did Sarah. "Grace, surely there's money somewhere else?"

"I'm afraid not. I looked through the budget several times and there's no other money. Here. I'll show you what I mean." Grace pushed the pile of folders forward. "There's one for each of you."

From where she sat, Sarah could see the name of each committee member on a cover. Everyone reached for their folder.

"The top page is a summary of the town's financial situation," Grace said. "Behind that is a list of tasks regarding a new, coordinated effort to reach out to some businesses. The tasks on that list need to be completed before our meeting next week."

"Whew." Nate ran his finger down his list. "*All* of this needs to be done before next week?"

"All of it," Grace repeated firmly.

"We'll do it," Zoe said, casting a challenging gaze around the table before looking back at Grace. "What do you plan to do with the funds you take from the festival account?"

"The majority will go into high-quality printed materials expounding the many benefits of moving a business to Dove Pond. After that, we'll host some coffee hours in town hall and, hopefully, schedule tours of available business properties."

"Printed materials, pah!" Erma scowled. "You want to beg businesses to come here."

"Not beg. Sell. I want to sell them on this town, the low cost of rentals, the high education level, and"—Grace's gaze moved to Sarah—"the people. That's a pretty impressive package of benefits."

"It's a special place," Sarah said, although at the present moment she was feeling far from hopeful.

"Well, I'm not going to do it." Erma pushed her folder away. "Not without the festival. We should honor tradition, and the festival is tradition. Having such a tiny little event with nothing but hot dogs and a parade would rile people and make them lose faith in the town more than they already have."

"That's true," Kat said.

Ava and Nate nodded.

Ed put his cell phone away. "Maggie's glad we're still having the festival. I didn't tell her about the cuts, though. She's going to be furious."

"Look," Grace said. "We have to do what's good for the town first, and what's good for the festival second."

There were grumbles and mumbles, but no one outwardly disagreed with her.

Grace continued, "Let's talk about the town's financial situation. You need to understand what's happened."

Sarah opened her folder. The top sheet held a pie chart featuring the town's annual costs and expenses. The red far outmeasured the green.

Grace went to the whiteboard that covered one wall and picked up a marker. "Some of you may have seen the budget summary the mayor hands out during department budget request time."

Sarah tapped the budget summary. "It doesn't look anything like this."

"That's because it only has expected income compared to annual expenditures. It doesn't include outstanding long-term debt."

"Hold on." Zoe's brows lowered. "He cherry-picked it?"

Nate made a disgusted noise. "Mayor Moore is a piece of work. He fudged the real figures."

"Look, I'm no fan of the mayor's," Grace said. "But things were bad at least a decade before he got into office. That said, his inability to face facts allowed the situation to worsen. If you look at that first chart, you'll see what I mean. Here's what's happened." She drew a big circle on the board and launched into a detailed explanation of the town's financial woes.

Sarah listened carefully. Basically, there were old, strung-out loans made necessary by everything from flood damage fifty years ago to the two bridges that led in and out of town, to recent street improvements that had gone over budget. In addition, there were squandered surpluses in healthy years and a too-conservative investment plan, all weighed down by the more recent effects of a reduced tax base.

Sarah, never a whiz with numbers, kept up until Grace began talking about debt-to-income ratios. That had most of the committee members looking lost except for Zoe, who muttered under her breath about "high-risk foolishness" while taking copious notes.

Grace finally capped her marker. "That's it. Every loan. Every bond issuance. Every mistake."

Sarah glanced around the table.

Erma stared at the pie chart as if she feared it might leap off the board and devour them all.

Ed, Ava, and Kat appeared caught between shock and outrage.

Nate tugged on his shirt collar over and over, as if he was too hot, while Zoe had retreated even more deeply into the report, her pen zipping down rows of numbers as she re-added the columns.

Sarah was the only one left with anything that felt remotely like hope. Dove Pond was in trouble, something she'd accepted years ago. And while the news was worse than even she'd expected, the answer to their problems stood by the whiteboard.

Grace dropped her marker back into the tray. "Any questions?"

Everyone shook their heads.

Sarah closed her folder. "Thank you for explaining everything."

"What a mess." Kat rubbed one temple as if it ached. "We've got to do something, and fast."

"I'll help in any way possible," Ed offered, though he didn't look hopeful.

"*If* there is anything that will help," Erma said sourly.

Ava closed her folder and pushed it away as if she wanted nothing to do with it. "What now?"

"Well, there's one thing I can do." Zoe flipped over the page she'd been writing on and started a list. "I'll research funding options. I have some contacts in other towns. I'll call them up and see what's to be done. There may be some state loans the town can apply for."

"I was hoping you would do that," Grace agreed. "We can meet tomorrow and talk about that some more."

"It's a date. Ten?" At Grace's nod, Zoe wrote the time on the top of her notebook and then tossed her pen back on the table. "I'll see what I can dig up before then."

"Thank you." Grace returned to her seat. "Which brings us back to the festival. As you can see, as much fun as the festival is—"

"It's tradition!" Erma snapped.

Grace inclined her head. "And as big of a tradition as the festival has been *in the past*, we have to use some of the funds for a program designed to attract more businesses to Dove Pond *to secure its future*."

Sarah scanned the budget sheet, looking for some other pool of funding, but she saw nothing.

Grace looked around the table. "All those in favor of moving half of the festival budget to a new business development initiative, say aye."

"Half?" Erma looked as if she might cry.

Ed didn't look any happier. "Why so much? Can't you make do with, say, a fourth?"

Grace shook her head. "We'll have to purchase potential client lists from local chambers of commerce, and those are pricey. Plus, printing costs are always high, and then there's the cost of bringing delegations to town and— It's all expensive. We'll need at least half of the festival budget to make this work, and even then, we're going to be stretching it."

"She's right," Zoe said. "I hate it, but I second Grace's motion."

"I'm voting no," Erma said sharply. "We can't cut the festival that much. We just can't."

"I vote nay, too," Ed said.

Grace looked at Ava.

She sighed. "Aye."

Nate shook his head. "Nay."

Kat bit her lip. After a moment, she nodded. "Aye."

Everyone looked at Sarah. She knew she had to support Grace, but oh, how she hated to see their beloved festival reduced in such a way. "There's no other way?"

"Not that I can see."

Sarah looked at Zoe, who shook her head. There was no help for it, then. "Aye," Sarah said.

"Damn." Erma wrote down the vote tally, looking as if she were writing an obituary. When she finished, she threw down her pen. "People are going to be mad."

"Very," Sarah agreed.

"We'll just have to explain things," Grace said.

Sarah frowned. "Grace, you said there were two parts to this meeting. What's the second part?"

Ed looked worried. "I'm afraid to ask."

Grace closed her folder. "This one is easy. I want to change the name of the social club."

Erma's mouth dropped open. "Is nothing sacred to you?"

"It's impractical. And with this new direction, we're no longer just planning social events. We're developing a plan to make our town more profitable, so we deserve an upgrade."

Ava eyed Grace with a fascinated look. "What are you thinking?"

"The Dove Pond Improvement Committee," Grace replied without hesitation.

"It's professional and describes our new purpose well," Zoe said. "I make the motion."

"I second," Ava said.

"All in favor?" Grace looked around the table.

Erma was the only one who didn't raise her hand.

"Passed." Grace began piling her papers into a neat stack. "Call me if you have any questions with the items on your task lists. I'll see you all back here next Monday at three. Until then, meeting dismissed." Grace stood and headed for the door.

"Wait," Nate called.

She stopped. "Yes?"

"It may take us longer than a week to get all of this done." He tapped his folder.

"No kidding," Erma said, looking at her list. "It'll take two weeks, at least. Maybe more."

"We need to move quickly," Grace said. "But fine. How's next Friday? That'll give you a couple of extra days."

Nate leaned back in his chair, and although he looked unconvinced, he said, "That'll help."

Grace nodded and continued to the door.

Everyone started talking. Nate leaned over to ask Zoe to explain something in the budget he didn't understand. Ed was already on the phone with his wife as Kat and Erma argued about the value of a business outreach. Looking concerned, Ava sat watching them all.

Sarah stood and hurried to the door. "Grace!"

Grace paused, one hand on the knob, her gaze cool. "Yes?"

There was nothing welcoming about that "yes." Sarah forced a smile. "I just wanted to say I'm glad you're here to help."

"You all didn't really give me a chance to refuse, did you?"

"We couldn't afford to. We need you. I didn't realize how much until now, but—" She took a deep breath. "We do."

Grace's expression didn't thaw.

"Look. I know you're mad."

"Wouldn't you be?"

"Yes. But not if I understood how important it was. Dove Pond is—"

"Look, Sarah. I'm going to do what I can. I'll be here for the next eleven months, but that's it. Whatever I can do in that time, I'll do. But after that, Dove Pond is your concern and not mine."

Sarah searched Grace's face for one sign—just one—that she cared about the outcome of their town, but she saw nothing. It was disheartening. *Forever*, the journal had said. *What if I've made her so mad that she's just that much more determined to leave?* Sarah's heart sank and she shifted from one foot to the other. "I guess I'll see you at five, then. For the ride home."

"Fine." Grace started to go, but then she stopped. "And for the record, I don't think we should carpool again. I've got enough things to coordinate as it is. I don't need another."

"Sure. I was going to make cranberry scones for our breakfast tomorrow. I'll just leave them at your house in the morning so you can get them before you leave and—"

"No! Sarah—" Grace looked at her, her mouth pressed into a flat line, her eyes sparkling with fury. "Don't."

Sarah recognized the anger and felt the rejection. She tried to think of something to say but couldn't. So she just nodded.

Grace wheeled and left, her heels snapping briskly on the library's wooden floor.

Behind Sarah, the committee buzzed like hornets stirred with a stick, and with a heavy heart, she returned to the table.

"It won't work," Erma said loudly.

"You don't know that!" Kat said. "We have to do *something*."

"But a 'business outreach'? I don't even know what that is! None of us do."

Ava collected her folder and stood. "I'm with Kat on this one. We have to do something and at least Grace has a plan."

"A bad one," Ed muttered.

"People are going to be pissed, too." Erma tapped the folder in front of her. "They won't care about any of this, I know they won't."

"They won't understand it," Ed added.

Erma frowned. "I won't be able to show my face at church again."

Nate looked at his folder as if it were a snake. "I can't believe the town is in such bad shape. I mean, I knew our revenue was down, but I had no idea about the loans. How did we not know about those?"

"They're old." Zoe shrugged. "And it's like Grace said—there's never been a town council or a board of directors or anyone keeping an eye on things. Just Mayor Moore, and he's been ignoring them and kicking them down the road for the next generation to pay."

"That needs to change," Erma said sharply.

Everyone nodded.

"At least now we know how things stand." Ava tucked her folder under her arm and slipped her pen into the front pocket of her overalls. "Knowledge is power, right?"

"I guess." Ed leaned back in his seat and rubbed his ear. "Geez, what a meeting. I feel as if I've been beaten with a stick." He looked around at the group. "Did you see your task sheets? They're color coded and there are check boxes beside each item."

A reverential look rested on Zoe's face. "Pure brilliance."

Kat closed her folder. "Color schemed or not, it's going to be a lot of work."

"How does the mayor keep a smile on his face?" Erma demanded.

"He's a fisherman," Nate said. "They live on hope."

Kat rolled her eyes and stood. "I just hope we can find a way to salvage Dove Pond."

Sarah looked at Zoe. "What happens if we fail?"

Zoe stood and collected her things. "I'd have to check, because our bank doesn't handle that type of thing. We handle solely private and business accounts and have no public-entity dealings at all. But I'd think the town might have to declare a state of emergency and ask the state for help. That would mean some short-term loans, which will help in keeping the garbage collected and such, but it would add to the town's long-term financial burden. After that, there will be cuts, services suspended, the elementary school could be folded into another in the county—" She grimaced. "It would be a mess."

"But now we have a plan of attack." Despite feeling wounded by Grace's anger, Sarah refused to give up hope. She just couldn't. "Come on. We can do this."

"We can at least try," Ava agreed. She looked at Kat. "Want some coffee?"

"Hell, yes," Kat said fervently.

"Wait for me," Nate said, joining them as they walked toward the door. "My head is spinning from all those numbers."

As they left, Zoe slung her purse over her shoulder. "Erma, you're right about one thing: people are not going to like this."

"They're going to raise hell is what they're going to do," Erma said. "And I don't blame them."

"We'll have to explain things to them," Sarah said.

"If we can," Zoe said. "I don't think Grace understands what that festival means to this town, but once word of this meeting gets out, she'll find out."

"I hope people will try to see this in a positive way. I mean, there's really no other choice."

"We can hope." Zoe slid on a pair of tortoiseshell cat-eye sunglasses. "I've got to go. See you kids around."

Ed and Erma took their folders and followed Zoe out, and soon Sarah was alone.

She went to the whiteboard, picked up an eraser, and wiped away the diagram. Grace was right. The town needed to expand, to increase, to attract new businesses and more people. But no matter how efficient her ideas were, Grace would never be an effective salesperson for Dove Pond until she understood it and loved it the way Sarah did.

Sarah dropped the eraser into place and went to collect her folder. She'd gotten Grace involved with the committee once again. That had been a success. But now, some way, somehow, she had to find a way for Grace to connect with their town and the people who lived here.

CHAPTER 11

Grace

The following Thursday, Grace was just locking the door of town hall when a deep rumble of thunder rippled through the air and rain began to pour. It sluiced through town in great sheets, spraying a fine mist onto the porch and pearling on her expensive suit. "Great." Muttering to herself, Grace fished her umbrella from her satchel, opened it, ducked under, and hurried down the sidewalk toward her car.

She'd only gone about ten steps when a big pickup truck rolled by. The fat wheels hit a deep puddle at the edge of the road and with a whoosh sent a wall of water raging toward Grace.

Grace only had time to tip her umbrella in the direction of the wave before it hit her, soaking her skirt and filling her shoes, and leaving her sputtering in outrage. She stood there, staring down at her sopping-wet clothes, icy red rage misting over her.

She didn't know how long she stood there, her umbrella still held in a defensive position that left her head uncovered while the rain poured down on her hair and shoulders, but slowly her vision cleared. She raised her umbrella and wiped the water from her eyes with a wet hand, suddenly realizing that Sarah stood on the sidewalk opposite.

The librarian wore a bright yellow raincoat with matching boots, and carried her usual tote bag, the umbrella over her head printed with a huge, happy ladybug.

Grace, cold and embarrassed, didn't move. Water continued to seep through her clothing and hair and ran down her face and shoulders, joining the rain. She was as wet as a drowned rat.

Sarah looked Grace up and then down, and then, without a return wave, she turned and walked away.

A moment later, Sarah drove her truck out of the library parking lot and, without sparing Grace a glance, sped off.

It was the perfect ending to a perfectly wretched week.

Grace couldn't blame Sarah for just leaving. Grace hadn't spoken to the perky librarian since the last meeting. In fact, the short ride home that day had been painfully silent for them both. After that, Grace had made no secret of the fact she was avoiding Sarah. It was childish and Grace knew it, but she'd felt a very real sense of betrayal by Sarah's effort to get Grace back into the chairman's seat. It was one thing for Zoe Bell and Kat Carter to pull such a manipulative prank. To be honest, Grace couldn't have cared less about them. But for some reason, it hurt that Sarah had been a part of it.

Grace sighed, suddenly so tired she could have cried. What a lousy, lousy week. Mama G's restless evening behavior was getting worse. She got up several times a night, and Grace with her. Each day had left Grace a little more tired than the night before. Then, this morning, while groggily brushing her teeth, Grace had suddenly remembered that Mama G had an appointment with Doctor Bolton at nine. Panicked, Grace had called the mayor and agreed to work until seven in exchange for coming in late, which meant she had to cancel her plans to take Daisy to a movie. That had put the child in a royally unhappy mood and had left Grace trying to do the impossible—to get both a fussy Mama G and a grumpy Daisy dressed, fed, into the car, and to the doctor's, all within thirty short minutes.

She'd managed to do it in forty-five, which was surely a record, even if it wasn't quick enough to get them to the appointment on time. Worse, Grace's temper, already piqued by her own forgetfulness, was further exacerbated when, once they reached the doctor's office, Daisy flatly refused to leave the car.

Despite knowing better, Grace had gotten into a shouting match with the testy eight-year-old that had upset Mama G so much her eyes had grown damp with tears. That had put an end to the argument, but even though Grace and Daisy had apologized afterward, Grace knew it was her fault things had gotten out of control. She was supposed to be the adult, and yet there she was, yelling as if she were Daisy's age.

Added to that, because of the argument, they were even later to Mama G's appointment, and while the office receptionist didn't say anything, Grace had felt that she was silently being judged, especially when she had to admit that, in her hurry to get out the door, she'd forgotten Mama G's morning medications. By then, Grace was so upset with herself that she missed most of what Doc Bolton said during the office visit, and once she got everyone back home and settled, she had to call him and ask him to repeat his instructions about the new medicine he'd prescribed for Mama G.

The whole morning had been muddled, disorganized, and regrettable, and the responsibility for it fell solidly on Grace's sagging shoulders.

How was it that she could walk into a complex financial situation, instantly see what needed to be done, and develop a comprehensive plan to fix things, but she couldn't get her own mother to a doctor's appointment in a normal manner or have a calm conversation with an eight-year-old? She was the world's worst caretaker and parent.

The *worst*.

Grace had finally reached the office at eleven, stressed out and depressed, only to find that the mayor was in a rotten mood, too. He felt he had reason to be as, in her absence, he'd had to answer no fewer than four unpleasant phone calls from furious citizens. Of course, Grace had known that cutting the Apple Festival budget would be unpopular. But she hadn't realized that the entire community would take the decision to heart in such a way, as if Grace hated their beloved town, or had some sort of evil vendetta against it.

As frustrating as it was, it was clear they blamed her and no one else. The day after the meeting, people had started treating her differently. When she'd stopped by the Moonlight Café for her usual morning cup of coffee, the waitress there, Marian Freely, who at seventy-eight had improbable auburn hair and always wore the reddest lipstick ever made, had poured Grace's coffee and taken her money without saying a word. Normally, Marian started talking the second Grace (or anyone else) arrived and didn't stop until they left, so her silence was shockingly pointed.

And it wasn't just Marian. Every chance they got, the citizens of Dove Pond let Grace know how much they disapproved of the committee's decision. Most of them shunned her, looking the other way when they walked past her on the street or saw her in town. But the worst were the ones who felt they should let her know in person what they thought of her decision. There had been a number, but the loudest among them, Ms. Jolean Hamilton, had marched into town hall just yesterday, accompanied by her little dog, Moon Pie. Ms. Hamilton had told Grace in no uncertain terms that the Apple Festival was the best thing to ever have happened to Dove Pond and that if Grace thought she could stomp all the goodness out of their beloved festival and then move away, she had another think coming.

Mayor Moore had been in the office for that one, and as soon as Ms. Hamilton and Moon Pie left, he'd wheeled on Grace and said, "*See?* I *warned* you about that!" and then he'd grabbed his fishing pole and tackle box and fled as if running from death itself.

To give him credit, he had warned her. The day after Grace had laid down the law to the Dove Pond Improvement Committee, the mayor had confronted her. Although he knew as well as she did that there was a sound reason for the festival budget cuts, he'd refused to admit it.

At first, he'd blamed the decision on "petty tyranny," repeating a phrase she was fairly sure he'd gotten from someone else, as she didn't think he totally understood the concept. Then he'd accused her of being in Zoe Bell's pocket and trying to get him tossed out of office.

It wasn't until Grace had slapped the spreadsheet with the town budget back on his desk and made him look through it yet again that he'd sullenly agreed that he could see no other solution. Not that he was convinced her business outreach plan would yield any benefits— oh no. But at least she'd forced him to see the truth of her reasoning, that they had to reinvest in the town before there was nothing left to invest in. He knew that the only thing worse than being the mayor of a town that had cut a beloved festival budget was being the mayor of a town that had declared bankruptcy.

A wind whipped down the street and she shivered as rain pattered loudly on her umbrella. She took a few steps toward the car, her wet clothes clinging uncomfortably, and then stopped. She was tired, too tired to cook. She glanced down the street to where the Moonlight Café sat, the windows glowing warm with golden light, the cheery red OPEN sign beaming a welcome. Daisy and Mama G loved the café's meatloaf. If Grace went now, she could pick up some to-go meals and be home in less than the time it would take her to cook something.

Grace headed back to town hall and, standing on the porch out of the rain, texted Linda to ask if she minded staying a little longer with Mama G and Daisy so Grace could pick up some dinner. She received a quick yes as well as a request for three roast beef to-go meals with green beans, garlic mashed potatoes, and gravy. Relieved, Grace was all too happy to comply, and she was soon on her way down the street to the café.

She pushed the wide door open, the welcome jangle announcing her entry as the delicious smell of hot coffee greeted her.

Every gaze locked on her, conversations stopping in mid-sentence, and glances quickly turned into glares, reminding her that she was currently Dove Pond's most gossiped-about pariah.

I wish I had on spurs so I could swagger through the crowd like villains do in westerns. But she didn't own spurs. Instead, she had on ridiculously high heels, which were now soaked. She dropped her wet umbrella into the holder by the door, hung her raincoat on a line of hooks that held other coats, tucked her wet hair behind her ears, and—as embarrassing as it was—attempted to wring the bottom of her drenched skirt onto the mat. Several water rivulets later, as un-soaked as she could get without the use of a towel, she straightened her shoulders and made her way through the silence, wending through the tables toward the counter, her heels making satisfyingly loud clicks on the old wooden floor, even if they felt squishy.

She saw a few faces she knew—Kat Carter sat with a man Grace had never seen, a handsome guy with the build of a linebacker but who was dressed as if he belonged in a New York penthouse. Kat caught Grace's gaze and she nodded, but stiffly, as if she felt forced to do so.

Grace returned the nod, irritated at how grateful she was for that small, although chilly, welcome.

Back in a corner, Doc Bolton sat reading the *Dove Pond Register*, a half-empty cup of coffee in front of him. He caught Grace's eye and smiled, his greeting much warmer than Kat's stilted one. Grace was so glad they'd found Doc. He was kind and thoughtful, and seemed to truly care about Mama G. He'd admitted that he'd lost a close friend to the same disease, and so had taken the time to learn as much as he could about it, and it showed.

Near the counter, she passed Maggie and Ed Mayhew, who sat laughing over something Ed was showing Maggie on his cell phone. Maggie saw Grace and the older woman's laughter disappeared, an accusing glare taking its place. Ed, meanwhile, flashed a short, awkward smile.

Grace returned the smile, feeling as welcome as an alligator in a fish pond as she slid onto one of the old-fashioned barstools along the counter.

A heavy man with a beard who sat at the end of the counter was working on the daily crossword in the *Dove Pond Register*, but he took the time to shift on his stool until his back was to her. She was fairly sure she'd never seen him before in her life, so the rebuke felt especially brutal.

Usually, the café was her favorite place in town. Small and cozy, it was decorated like most small-town diners, with a rich display of country kitsch that consisted of red gingham tablecloths, framed grain sacks, mismatched chairs, and jelly jars used as water glasses. It didn't hurt that the café also served the best coffee Grace had ever had. As corny as the place was, it had always felt right.

Or it had until the meeting last week. Grace slid the napkin dispenser close, took out a handful of napkins, and dried her face as well as she could.

The waitress Marian came through the kitchen door carrying a tray of clean coffee mugs. When she saw Grace, she gave a loud, disapproving "Humph!" and carried the tray to the far end of the counter, clinking the mugs especially hard as she put them away.

Coming here had been a mistake. Grace could see that now, but her pride wouldn't let her leave without doing what she'd come to do—get dinner for her family and Linda's. Grace pulled a menu from the stack tucked behind a napkin holder and pretended to read through the list of omelets, hiding from the other customers who sat nearby.

She'd been in Dove Pond for almost six weeks now, which wasn't that long. But somehow in that brief time, she'd come to enjoy being waved at, smiled at, and treated as if she was a part of something.

And now, to her surprise, she missed that.

A mug was slapped down in front of her and coffee poured into it.

She lowered the menu to find Marian standing in front of her, gathering the damp napkins Grace had used to dry her face. The waitress's bright auburn hair was piled on her head in something remarkably close to a beehive, her red-lipsticked mouth pressed into a straight, unhappy line. She was a remarkably colorful woman. Grace rather admired that.

"Thank you." Grace put the menu on the counter and reached for the coffee.

"Two creams, right?" Marian dropped them beside the mug along with a spoon.

"Yes. Thank you." Grace added the cream and then cupped the warm mug between her hands and cleared her throat. "I need six to-go orders."

Marian dug her notepad from her pocket and clicked her pen.

"Three meatloaf plates, and three roast beef plates. Fries and salads with the meatloaf plates, and green beans and garlic mashed potatoes with gravy for the roast beef."

Marian scribbled down the order. "That's a lot of food."

"The roast beef plates are for Linda Robinson and her family."

"I'll put extra rolls in Mark's. He loves our rolls." Marian tore the order from her notepad and turned to stick it on the wheel that hung over the pass-through window to the kitchen and spun the wheel around.

That done, she turned back to Grace. "It'll be fifteen minutes."

"Thank you."

"You're welcome." She dropped her notepad and pen back into the pocket of her apron and handed a dish towel to Grace.

Grace looked at the towel, not sure what she should do with it.

"You're dripping. I thought you might want to put it under your feet."

Grace looked down, and sure enough, a small puddle had formed where the water had collected at the hem of her skirt and was steadily dripping onto the floor. "Oh no. Thank you." She dropped the towel on the small puddle.

"You're welcome. Now." Marian leaned one sharp elbow on the counter. "You and I need to talk."

The other people sitting at the counter all stopped chatting and turned to listen in.

Tom Decker, a grizzled white-haired old man sitting three seats down from Grace, put down his cup as if he planned on taking notes.

Grace wished she didn't feel like a gladiator with a broken sword facing a pack of furious lions, but she was going to get what she was going to get. Besides, for the last week, she'd been explaining the reason behind the budget change to one citizen at a time. Maybe if she explained it to Marian, who was a notorious town gossip, the word would get out faster. She gave Marian a nod. "Fine. Let's talk."

"I hear you want to cut the festival budget."

"I don't *want* to, we *need* to. I know the festivals are important. I get that. But look at this town. While the café is doing okay, as it's the only restaurant left, Dove Pond isn't making it. Over a third of the businesses on this street are gone. We have to start planning for the future, which means investing money in attracting new businesses."

"I know." Marian leaned over and tapped a red-painted nail tip on the counter. "We need new business, but we also need our festivals, especially the Apple Festival. Surely you can find the money somewhere else."

The bearded man who'd been working on his puzzle nodded. "The Apple Festival is the town's oldest tradition."

Old man Tom took a slow sip of his coffee, looking at Grace over the rim of his cup, his gaze accusing.

She swallowed her irritation. "I don't want to get rid of the festivals. We just need to reallocate some of the funds for one year, perhaps two. Just long enough to see some payback from our outreach. You know, attract a few new businesses, get some new tax revenues, and then we can restore the festival budget and maybe even increase it. I don't know what you've heard, but I—"

"Hi, Grace." Kat slid onto the stool beside her. "Mind if I join you?"

Grace looked past Kat and saw the man she'd been talking to was now beside the door, tugging on an expensive-looking overcoat. He appeared mad, too, his jaw set, his mouth curved into a firm frown. Grace turned back to Kat. "Sure. I'm just waiting on some to-go orders and chatting with Marian."

"About the Apple Festival," Marian said grimly. "And why it needs to be fully funded."

Kat smiled at Marian. "Coffee, please."

"Fine." Marian sent a hard look at Grace. "I've got more to say about this."

At his end of the counter, Tom gave a decisive nod.

"Marian," Kat said in a dry tone, "I've known you since I was born and I would never expect you to drop a subject once you got your teeth in it."

"I'm not shy," Marian agreed as she placed a mug in front of Kat and filled it with hot coffee. "I was just explaining to Ms. Wheeler here that we need our Apple Festival."

"We're still having it," Grace repeated, feeling cold and wet and miserable. She hunched over her hot coffee and fought off a shiver.

Kat must have noticed, because she tsked. "How did you get so wet?"

"That puddle in the road near town hall. A truck drove through it right as I was walking past."

"It got you good."

"It was like a movie. A bad movie. I hope it was an accident, but I can't be sure. I seem to have made a lot of people angry."

"I'll say," Marian said as she set a small pitcher of skim milk in front of Kat.

"It sounds like Erma's been by." Kat looked over her coffee mug at Grace. "She's been making the rounds."

"I heard it from other people, too," Marian said in a sharp tone.

Kat snorted. "Yeah, well, the Soc—I mean, the Improvement Committee is going to do what we think is best for the town. That's all we can promise."

Marian sniffed. "If you cut the budget, there won't be anything left. It's already a quarter the size it used to be. Why, when I was a kid, the Apple Festival was the biggest event around here. People came from miles away. Back in the day, we had Ferris wheels and hot-air balloon rides and—oh, so much. Over the years, it's shrunk down until there's not enough left to cut, just booths and crafts and a few games. I can't see how—" A bell rang, notifying Marian that someone's food was up. She mumbled her irritation and left to fetch the orders, leaving Kat and Grace alone.

Grace rubbed her neck where it ached.

Sympathy softened Kat's expression. "They're being tough on you, aren't they?"

"You have no idea."

"I can imagine. Are you okay?"

"I'm fine," Grace lied, wondering why her eyes burned so much. "I take it people have been after you, too?"

"Yup, although they aren't blaming me."

"No, they're blaming me," Grace said tiredly. "I noticed."

"Sorry. You're new, so . . ." Kat shrugged.

"I know how it works. I was a foster kid once and I went to seven schools in four years. I was the new kid a lot and it always sucked."

At the end of the counter, Tom reached into his coat and pulled out a flask. He poured a goodly measure into his coffee cup and then caught Grace's gaze. He held up the flask in invitation.

She shook her head and he shrugged and returned it to his pocket, then began to sip his coffee with obvious relish.

Kat shot Grace a curious look. "I heard someone say Mama G was your foster mother."

"My sister and I lived with her since we were kids." Grace held her mug between both hands, soaking in the warmth. "You know, until

I started taking care of Daisy—or trying to—I never knew what a sacrifice Mama G had made, taking us in. She's a freaking saint."

"I don't know anything about parenting, except that I don't think I could do it."

"I don't think I can, either," Grace admitted. "It's difficult. Next time, I'm going to get a plant first, and see how I do with it. Then, if it's still alive at the end of a year, I'll move up to a fish. Then a parakeet. A cat. A bear. Finally, if all of those things are still alive at the end of a decade or two, I'll get a kid."

Kat laughed. "That sounds legit. But you can't be doing too bad with Daisy. Linda Robinson is at your house a lot. If you were doing something wrong, we'd all know about it."

"I'm bringing Linda dinner, so she's hardly an unbiased witness." Grace tucked her wet hair behind her ear. "By the way, thanks for joining me at the counter here and protecting me from Marian. That was nice of you."

"No problem. I've been telling everyone that we wouldn't cut the festival budget if we didn't have to, but it's an uphill battle."

"I didn't realize how attached everyone was to a simple street party."

Kat sliced her a critical glance. "It's more than that. It's a part of our history. And for some, a part of our future, too."

Grace thought about the shabby little town and then remembered the duffel bag she'd dragged onto Mama G's porch all those years ago. The odds and ends Grace had been collecting had all been junk, but they'd made her feel as if she had a future. Was that how the people of Dove Pond felt about their festival?

Sheesh. Everything was so complicated. She sighed and put down her coffee cup to rub her eyes and found herself battling a yawn.

"You look like you could use a nap," Kat said.

"When Mama G doesn't sleep well, neither do I. We had to install a lock on the doors to keep her from wandering off, and now every time I hear a creak, I jerk awake. It's hard to get back to sleep after that."

"Sundowners," Kat said with a knowing nod. "Trav's father had it. I remember him telling Sarah about it when I was hanging out with Ava at their house."

Grace had an instant picture of the four of them sipping drinks, maybe cooking a meal together, all of them laughing and sharing their lives as friends do. A twinge of jealousy pinched her. *That's ridiculous. I don't have time to parent Daisy, much less hang out with someone.* She turned her attention back to Kat. "I hope the task list I handed out at the meeting wasn't too much work."

"Not at all. I got through mine in just a few afternoons."

"You're kidding."

"Nope." Kat put her cup on the counter and watched the steam curl from it. "I have a degree in business management from Appalachian State. Making cold calls like that was an interesting exercise."

"That's handy to have, working in real estate as you do."

"You'd think that, wouldn't you? But I joined my mother's office, so we do things her way. She doesn't have time for statistics or business plans or anything like that." Kat made a face. "She thinks gift baskets and smiles will get her where she wants to go."

"But you don't."

Kat shrugged. "She sells a lot of houses, so I guess there's something in what she says. But whether she wants to admit it or not, there's room for improvement."

"I take it you've told her that."

"It didn't go over well. One day, I'm going to strike out on my own. But Mom's got a lock on the residential market here in Dove Pond. On this whole county, in fact. I'd have to move at least as far away as Asheville if I wanted to succeed." She gave a sour grin. "And since I really don't want to leave Dove Pond, here I am."

"You like this town that much?"

"I do. I grew up here and I know everyone." She grimaced. "Sometimes habits, especially comfortable ones, can hold you back. Which is why it was fun working on your assignment."

"I'm glad you enjoyed it. I suspect you'll be the only one."

Kat slanted Grace a curious look. "What gave you the idea to call all the businesses who've left Dove Pond?"

"It seemed the quickest, most direct way to find out where we've failed."

Kat nodded thoughtfully. "I learned a lot. People love this town and would move back in a heartbeat, but we don't have enough foot traffic. The communities outside of Asheville are full of big-box stores and outlet malls, and then you add e-sales on top of that—" Kat grimaced. "Small businesses get outpriced fast."

"And yet downtown Asheville is nothing but small businesses, all specialty shops, art galleries, and farm-to-table restaurants. They're doing well."

"Asheville has its own vibe, and the stores reflect that."

"Maybe we need to find a vibe of our own." Grace sipped her coffee. "The business owners who've left, they still had good things to say about Dove Pond?"

"A lot of good things. They loved the quality of life, the people, the community—they were all heartbroken to have left."

"Interesting. That's very helpful."

"Like I said, it was fun. I wrote a script, so I said the same thing to each of them."

"Nice." Grace eyed Kat with new respect. "Would you mind sharing that with the committee at our next meeting?"

"Sure. It makes me wonder why we can't—" Her gaze locked on something over Grace's shoulder.

Grace turned and just caught sight of a BMW as it passed by on the street outside, the steady rain beating down on the roof. She turned back to Kat. "Was that someone you know?"

Kat's gaze dropped to her coffee mug. "A little."

It was such a huge lie that Grace couldn't hide her disbelief.

Kat looked irked. "Fine. I know him. More than a little."

"I see. I suppose here is where I'm supposed to say something positive about relationships or whatnot, but honestly, I don't know a lot about them."

"You've never had a serious relationship?"

"I haven't had time. I worked my way through college and then had a full-time, seventy-hour-a-week job after that. And then my sister died and I became a parent, and then Mama G got sick—it's been a whirlwind of relationship nonstarters. I'm the poster girl for the woman you don't want to date."

Kat shook her head. "That's quite a list of too-busy-for-your-own-good life happenings."

"Fortunately, I'm perfectly happy on my own." Or so she'd been telling herself. "I just ordered takeout for dinner. That's one of my biggest skills as a homemaker, ordering out. I'm damn good at it."

"Don't knock it; that's a good skill to have. Did you get the meatloaf plate?" At Grace's nod, Kat tilted back her head and gave a blissful sigh. "My dad has homes in Paris, Lake Como, and Madrid, so I've eaten at some of the best restaurants in the world, but none can hold a candle to Jules's meatloaf plate."

Jules was the cook and owner of the Moonlight and was even now working her magic at the grill. "It's good meatloaf," Grace agreed, lifting her cup of coffee.

"Good? As our friend Linda Robinson would say, it's an orgasm level of goodness."

Grace, who'd just taken a sip, almost choked.

Kat gleamed with satisfaction, her brown eyes shimmering with humor. "Seriously orgasmic."

And in that moment, Grace understood the Carter gift. Sarah had said that the Carter women had the power to make men of wealth and power fall in love with them, and just now, Grace had caught a glimmer of it. Kat had the kind of brunette beauty commonly associated with 1940s movie stars, and the curvy, long-lashed, and sleepy-eyed sensuality one saw in pinup girls of a bygone era. But it was more than that. It was the warm and intimate way Kat looked at a person. It was as if everything she said was for you and you only. *Men would lap that up*, Grace thought. *And fast.*

Kat picked up her cup of coffee, her gaze moving back to the door. As she did so, a deep sadness erased the humor from her expressive face.

Grace wished she knew what to say, but nothing came to mind. This was where being a loner hurt; she didn't know what to say in this situation and, to be honest, a lot of other situations, too. *I should say something impersonal, something to distract her.* "To be honest, I'm beginning to question my decision about the festival budget."

Kat's gaze flew to meet Grace's. "Really?"

Grace looked around to make sure no one was listening and realized that Tom had moved a stool closer. She frowned at him before returning her gaze to Kat. To make sure no one could hear, Grace bent nearer and said in a low voice, "I don't want to say anything before the meeting, because it might get people's hopes up and I don't want to let everyone down again. But maybe reducing the festival budget wasn't the best idea. It's just that if we don't take the money from there, I don't know where else we'll find it."

"I know," Kat said glumly. "Zoe's already looked and she said the budget's too tight as it is."

Grace leaned back and sighed. "Maybe we could find sponsors for the festival. That would answer the problem, at least for this year."

Kat winced. "I don't like the idea of corporate sponsors. I don't think anyone else in Dove Pond would, either. It would lose its personality if you did that."

"The Apple Festival has a personality?"

"Lord, yes. Surely there's some sort of record in town hall that'll tell you all about it?"

"All I've seen is in that one folder from Mrs. Phelps. It has the event list, receipts, and flyers from the past few years, but that's it."

Kat's gaze grew thoughtful. "You should talk to Sarah. The town archives are in the library basement. I'm sure there's information on the festivals there."

Grace looked at her coffee mug. "Could you help with that? You could talk to Sarah tomorrow and then report at the meeting—"

"Hold on." Kat's gaze had narrowed. "What's going on? Why don't you want to talk to Sarah?"

"I don't mind talking to Sarah," Grace said.

Kat raised her eyebrows.

"Okay, okay. I think I may have made her mad."

"You can't make Sarah Dove mad. She's the nicest person in the world. The most positive one, too."

"Yeah, but apparently I'm not a nice person, nor a particularly positive one. And I was mad after that prank she and Zoe pulled to get me to take the chairmanship back."

"I helped, too," Kat said.

"I'm mad at you, too, then."

"You're still talking to me," Kat pointed out. "You're talking to Zoe, too. I saw the two of you sitting on that bench in front of the bank yesterday, going over some papers."

"Fine, fine. To be honest, I'm not mad at you or Zoe. I'm just mad at Sarah."

"It was Zoe's idea. Sarah and I just helped. Actually, I helped. Sarah didn't have much to do with it."

Kat wasn't saying anything Grace hadn't already thought. "I can't explain it to myself, much less you. It just bothered me more that she was a part of it. And then she wanted to carpool."

Kat waited.

So Grace added, "I didn't want to. So I told her no, but she kept showing up and . . ."

"And?"

"I left for work late so I wouldn't have to drive her."

"Oh."

"More than once."

Kat raised her brows.

"Okay, okay, I did it five times."

Kat flinched.

But Grace wasn't through. "And one morning, I may have dropped to the ground because I saw her coming and she may have found me there."

"On the driveway?"

"Yes. Laid out like a rug. It was so embarrassing."

"That was mean."

"I know! I'm horrible!" Grace covered her eyes. "I just couldn't—but she's so *happy* in the morning, and I hate that. But really"—Grace dropped her hand—"I didn't want her to expect stuff from me."

"Like what? A ride?"

"Oh, come on. You know how it is. You do something for someone once, and then they expect you to do it every day after that. So many people have expectations of me right now—Mama G and Daisy and work. I just couldn't handle one more."

"So tell her that. She'll understand."

"I know, I know. But it may be too late." Grace put her elbow on the counter and dropped her chin in her hand. "I saw her before I came here, and she didn't wave." Which had bothered Grace a lot.

Kat shook her head slowly. "I can't believe you made Sarah Dove mad. No one has ever been able to do that. She sees the best in everyone. I mean, it's uncanny."

Grace nodded miserably.

"You're a piece of work. I wish I could help you with this one, but you're on your own." Kat tilted her head to one side. "But can I point something out to you?"

"What's that?" Grace said glumly.

"You're exhausted. I can see it from here. And I know you feel like the world wants too much from you. God, I don't know what I'd do if I had your responsibilities. So you'd think that you, being a managerial sort, would do what you do best—collect a good team of people around you to tackle the problem. Sarah is exactly the sort of person who would bring you soup if you were sick, or sit with your niece when you had to work late, or bring dinner because you mentioned you were tired. She's the sort of person we all want on our team, and yet you've chased her off because she's too happy in the morning."

It sounded so petty when Kat said it that way. Grace sighed. She knew she was being ridiculous, but at the time, her actions had been an honest reflection of her feelings. "Look, even if Sarah and I carpooled, I wouldn't ask her to help with Daisy or Mama G or dinner or any of those things. That would be too much. I just met her. I couldn't ask for her help with something like that."

Kat rolled her eyes. "Boy, do you have a lot to learn about friendship."

"We're not friends."

"You would be, if you'd just try."

"What do you—"

The bell dinged. "Order's up!" Marian brought Grace's to-go order and stacked the dinners on the counter. "I'll put them in two bags. The one with the knot in the handle will be Linda's."

"I'd better get going." Kat stood and put some money on the counter. "Grace, do yourself a favor and apologize to Sarah. And then see what she has in that vault of hers about the Apple Festival. She'll be tickled pink to share it with you. She loves those old books and papers."

"You're right. I have to talk to her. I'll go tomorrow." Grace stood and pulled out her wallet. She paid the bill, collected the bags, said goodbye to Marian, and followed Kat through the café. "I suppose it won't kill me to have friends."

As they walked, Kat said over her shoulder, "You don't need scores of friends. You need only one . . . the right one."

The words tickled a memory somewhere deep in Grace's mind

and she stopped. Where had she heard them before? She couldn't quite— Oh yes. The quote hadn't been about friends, but about suitors. *You need only one . . . the right one.* She'd read those very words in *Little Women*.

The book kept popping up in her life in the most disconcerting ways. *I need to return that ridiculous thing to the library.* For a weird moment, Grace wondered if it would let her.

Grace realized that Kat was already at the door, so she hurried to catch up. She'd just hung the bags on a hook so she could pull on her raincoat when the door swung open and Trav walked inside. His hair was wet and slicked back, and he wore a damp T-shirt that clung to him in ways a mere T-shirt shouldn't. As he walked past her, he favored her with a dark stare as if irked to find her there.

She started to say something snarky in return, but a perky blonde wearing a too-low-cut shirt hurried past her. "Trav! There you are. I got a table over here." She linked her arm in his and practically dragged him away, cutting a hard look at Grace as she went.

Without sparing either of them another glance, Grace tugged on her raincoat, reclaimed her dinners, and pulled her umbrella from the stand. She went outside, Kat close behind. It was after-shower cool, everything looking washed and fresh.

"Lisa Tilden is a pain," Kat announced. "She's a massage therapist at some spa in Asheville, and a total flake. But wow, does she have it bad for Trav."

"It doesn't look like he's avoiding her."

"Chances are she invented some sort of emergency so he'd meet her. Where Trav is concerned, she's a desperate sort of woman." Kat sent Grace a curious glance. "You and Trav barely said hello. You haven't pissed him off, too, have you?"

"He's not much of a talker." She shrugged as if she didn't care, and indeed, she didn't. Much.

"I've always liked Trav. His father had the same illness as Mama G.

He might be of more help than you think." Kat leaned forward. "That means he would be another good member for your team."

"Maybe," Grace muttered. But Kat was wrong about this one. Mr. Tall, Dark, and Perpetually Scowling liked his privacy just as much as she liked hers, and that was perfectly fine. She glanced back at the café, where he sat with the clinging woman, and was surprised to find him looking at her. Their gazes caught and locked, and Grace had an instant impression of a spark, long and bold, arcing between them.

The image was so vivid she could smell smoke, and the soles of her feet grew warm. She wondered if the arc had burned the meals dangling from her hand but she was afraid to look.

Kat moved closer to Grace. "He is easy on the eyes, isn't he?"

Flushed, she turned away from the café, glad for the fresh air. "I don't go for the long-haired, tattooed type."

"Then you're missing out."

"Perhaps. It was nice talking to you, Kat."

"You too. I hope you find what you're looking for in the library. I'd sure like to be able to eat out without people fussing at me."

"You and me both." Grace, still uncertain why she'd imagined that bolt of electricity between herself and Trav, nodded absently. "See you tomorrow."

With that, she tucked her head and hurried home, refusing to look back.

CHAPTER 12

Trav

He clung to sleep, grasping at the wisps of a hollow dream as it was yanked away. He tried to clutch at it, hoping to stay asleep, but as the dream dissipated, he found himself wide awake, the light from the hallway hurting his eyes.

He rubbed his face, trying to remove the tiredness, and noticed it was still pitch-black outside. He wasn't sure what he'd been dreaming, but oddly enough, he could smell pasta sauce.

Homemade pasta sauce, like Mom used to make.

The memory was oddly real, and along with the scent of simmering sauce rich with oregano, he could hear the warm clank of a spoon hitting the side of a—

He sat up. It wasn't a dream. Someone was in his kitchen.

He was instantly on high alert, his skin prickling, his breathing shallow and brisk. He threw off the thin sheet and slipped from his bed, his heart thundering in his ears. He glanced at the clock that hung over the door. Four in the morning. He'd only gotten two hours of sleep, if that, and now he was furiously awake.

Silently, he yanked on his jeans and reached behind the door for the bat he kept there.

As quiet as the dawn, he made his way down the hallway, cautiously avoiding the board that creaked. His skin grew slick, and his stomach felt as if he'd swallowed a stone.

The lights were on in the kitchen, but nowhere else. He swung to one side of the door, against the wall, the hair on the back of his neck prickling, the bat raised and ready.

He waited, listening.

Something metal clanked, and a low voice murmured something indistinguishable.

He gathered himself and stepped into the kitchen, his gaze darting everywhere as—

"Robert, what are you doing with that bat?"

He blinked. And then blinked again.

Tiny Mrs. Giano stood before him. She was barefoot and dressed in her nightgown, an inside-out sweater hanging from her thin shoulders. Her hair, thin and white and curly, stood on end and caught the kitchen light until he could see her pink scalp between the strands.

She held out her hand. "Give that to me."

Give what— *Oh. The bat.* He still had it cocked back over his shoulder, ready to strike. *My God, I could have hurt her.* Suddenly sick, he lowered the bat. "I'm sorry," he choked out, his heart beating so hard he could feel it against his breastbone. "I didn't know you were—"

"Silly thing." She took the bat, jerking it from his grasp with a surprisingly strong yank, saying with a chuckle as if she were truly amused, "You Parker boys. Always in trouble, aren't you? And you, Robert, are the worst, because you know better."

Robert. She still thinks I'm Dad. He took a shuddering breath, his body weak as the rush of adrenaline left him. "Mrs. Giano, I'm sorry. I—"

Killer meowed.

Trav turned. The cat sat on the kitchen counter, licking a spoon. Trav noticed steam coming from a pot on the stove, the scent unmistakable; Mrs. Giano had broken into his house and was now making spaghetti sauce.

"Theo, you rascal! Get off the counter!" Mrs. Giano shooed the cat away. "He is so ill behaved, that one. I've been trying to cook dinner and he keeps interrupting me and—" Her eyes widened. "Robert! Where is your shirt?"

He looked down and his face heated. "Oh geez. I'll be right back."

She shook her head and waved him away much as she had the cat. "Get some clothes on, will you? You can't come to the table half naked. You know better than that."

"Yes, ma'am. I'll be right back."

"You'd better come back, because I'm going to need someone to set the table and it's not going to be me. I already did all the cooking."

"Yes, ma'am." He hurried to his room and found a T-shirt, stopping to slide his cell phone into his pocket before he returned to the kitchen.

She was standing by the stove when he reappeared, stirring the sauce, the bat leaning against the wall. "You can't hurry a good sauce. But it's almost ready. I just started the spaghetti."

She was so tiny, this woman, and she looked oddly at home standing beside his stove.

He found that he didn't mind that she thought he was Dad. In some ways, it made Trav feel a little closer to his father. Besides, it looked like he might get a home-cooked meal out of it, and that made it doubly worthwhile.

Killer, who'd made himself at home in one of the dining room chairs, watched Trav through half-closed eyes as if struggling to stay awake, but Trav knew the cat would be back on the counter if they turned their backs. "The sauce smells good."

She beamed at him. "It's my family's recipe. You always loved it, didn't you?"

From the smell of it, he still did. "Yes, ma'am." The pot of sauce bubbled merrily, and he noticed another pot on the back burner. Sticks of spaghetti rose out of it. *Ah, the spaghetti. That's going to taste goo—* A curl of smoke lifted from the pot just as the smell of burnt pasta hit him.

In two strides he was at the stove. He turned off the eye of the stove, grabbed a pair of pot holders sitting nearby, and pulled the pot off the back burner. The ends of the pasta were blackened, and some of them stuck to the bottom.

Mrs. Giano peered over his shoulder. "What happened?" Her gaze locked on the burned pasta. "Oh dear." She put a hand to her cheek and took an unsteady step back. "I forgot the water, didn't I?" Her voice wavered.

"No, it just boiled off." He opened the oven and set the pot out of sight, closing the door on the smell and the mess. He gave her an encouraging smile. "We need a bigger pot, anyway." He found another pot, put it on the stove, and pulled another box of pasta from the cabinet. "Five quarts of water."

"Four should do it," she corrected absently.

"Right." He filled the pot and turned the stove eye back on.

Mrs. Giano clicked her tongue. "Add salt and olive oil. I swear, haven't you cooked before?"

He was glad she'd already forgotten the burnt pasta he'd tucked out of sight. Dad had been the same way. He'd sailed along in his little bubble of long-ago memories, but at the first sign of forgetfulness, he'd wobble, uncertain, aware something was wrong. If Trav couldn't bring Dad back into the moment, his father would get upset, sad, and even angry.

Trav nodded toward the sauce pot. "Spaghetti dinners are the best."

As he'd hoped, that set Mama G wandering through her memories, sharing stories of spaghetti dinners she and her family had shared.

The water started to bubble. Trav added the pasta. "There. I'll set the table."

"Yes. You and your brother, your momma, and your dad. Oh, and we should add Grace and Daisy, shouldn't we? We can't forget them."

He nodded and went to get the plates. He shooed Killer away from the table and then set down the stack of plates. He made sure Mama G was busy before he pulled out his cell phone and texted Sarah.

Sorry to bother you, but I have an unexpected visitor. Tell the Dragon Lady her mother is here.

He didn't have to wait long for an answer.

Tell her yourself. Here's her number. And her name is Grace.

He frowned at the number. He hadn't wanted to talk to Grace directly. There was some sort of ill wind between them. An awkwardness that he couldn't quite overcome.

But it was more than that. Just yesterday, he'd seen her at the café, and when she'd looked at him something had happened. He couldn't describe it, but it had seared him from his heart to the soles of his feet. Afterward, he'd found himself thinking about her far more than he should.

God, I've caught a case of new age bullshit from Sarah. Scowling at himself for being so fanciful, he texted Sarah again. *Come on*, he typed. *Can you just let her know?*

The reply came quickly.

I'm asleep. You have the number.

Damn all difficult women. He guessed he would have to call Grace himself.

Should he call her or just text her? A text would be easier. And he could read it to himself before he sent it to make sure it didn't sound weird. That would be better than talking, where there was no do-over.

He thought about it a moment, and then texted: *This is Travis Parker. Mama G is here. You should come and get her.*

No answer came, so he waited, wondering if her phone was close enough to her bed to wake her.

After a moment, he added, *She is cooking spaghetti.*

He'd already hit send when he decided that was a stupid thing to write. She'd see what was happening once she got here. He grimaced at his foolishness and shoved his phone back in his pocket. Forget it. There was no taking it back.

"You're not setting the table," Mrs. Giano pointed out.

"Yes, ma'am." He set out the plates.

"Forks and spoons. We won't need knives."

He put out the silverware, keeping an eye on Mrs. Giano. Her eyes were bright and shiny, and she hummed as she stirred the pot. *She's happy,* he realized. *She's happy to be here with me.*

It had been a long time since anyone had been happy in his house.

His phone pinged, and he looked at it.

On my way.

There was a noticeable pause and then *Thank you. Sorry for the inconvenience.*

He muttered under his breath. It wasn't inconvenient. Not really. But he'd wait to tell the Dragon Lady that in person.

"Dinner will be ready soon." Mrs. Giano added a dash of oregano to the gently bubbling pot. "And this"—she held up the oregano bottle—"is not fresh. I've had to add twice the normal amount just to get it right." She shook her head at him. "You should keep fresh herbs. The jarred ones are bah!"

He nodded, because it was the only thing he could think to do. "Mrs. Giano, I—"

"Please. Call me Mama G. It's who I am." She sent him a sly look that sparkled with laughter. "Or it is when I need to be."

He couldn't help but smile. "Mama G it is, then." He walked past her and checked the bubbling water, stirring the pasta as he did so. "Is it ready yet?"

She came to look. "Hmm. Not yet. Another few minutes."

She lifted the lid on the sauce and waved her hand, wafting the scent of rich pasta sauce in his direction. "Smell that? It's gold."

It was at that. "It's nice of you to cook."

"My pleasure. Besides, I owe you for all the times you've fixed Mabel and wouldn't take a penny."

"Mabel . . ." he prompted.

"You know . . . Mabel! My Chevy. You've fixed her a hundred times, and you've never charged me, not once."

So Dad had fixed Mama G's car for free. Trav wondered how many other people Dad had done that for.

"I figured you'd need a good meal, living here all alone now as you do. Oh Robert, when I heard how Leigh died and left you and poor Travis, well, my heart just broke. I know how you loved her."

Trav realized that Mama G had moved in time from when Dad was young to closer to the present. Doc Bolton had once explained how that worked. *They don't operate on a time line. Days and events are fluid and they float between times, unfettered and unbothered until something jars them. Then they get confused, and become afraid, which they express with fear or anger. You have to let them know it's okay. Sort of travel with them from time to time, land where they land, be where they are, don't startle them.* It hadn't been easy, but over the months as he took care of Dad, Trav had gotten the hang of it.

He said now, "I can't wait to try your sauce. I'll get some parmesan for the spaghetti." He went to the fridge. "I hope you're hungry. That's a lot of spaghetti."

"I'll have a little." She smiled at him, and in that moment, her gaze cleared and her smile wavered. It was as if she'd just now seen him as he really was.

"You . . ." Still holding the spoon, she backed away. "You're not Robert."

Trav knew what was coming—the confusion, the embarrassment, the anger. To head it off, he said, "You make the best spaghetti sauce. Just the smell is making me hungry."

Mama G looked around her as if just now seeing the kitchen. She lifted her trembling, spotted hand to her hair and tucked a stray strand behind her ear. "I don't remember . . . How did I get here? I—"

"I invited you, of course," Trav said, keeping his tone soft but positive. "Why don't you sit down? The spaghetti you made is almost ready."

She looked at the bubbling pots. "I cooked all of this."

"Yes, and it smells wonderful." He took the spoon from her hand and placed it on the spoon holder on the stovetop. Then he took her elbow and gently led her to the table. "Come on, Mama G. Have a seat."

She sat down, her eyes now watery with unshed tears. "I don't know how I came to—"

The doorbell rang. *Thank God.* "I'll be right back. Don't move." He hurried to the front door, Killer following behind.

Trav reached for the door and realized he hadn't turned on the porch light. *Great. What a way to welcome her, making her stand in the dark.*

He flipped the light on as he opened the door.

Grace blinked up at him. She'd thrown on jeans and a T-shirt, her dark hair unbrushed. He'd never seen her so casually dressed and she looked younger and more vulnerable than he'd imagined she could.

Killer meowed and then rushed outside as if afraid he'd be tackled on the way, disappearing into the bushes.

Grace watched him and then turned back to Trav. "Where is she?"

"In the kitchen. I just got her to sit down."

"I'm so sorry." Grace shook her head, her brow creased with worry. "I didn't even know she was gone. I closed up everything when I went to bed, and she can't reach the lock because it's high, but somehow she did." Grace grimaced, obviously frustrated. "I'll take her home."

He stood to one side and pointed in the direction of his kitchen.

She brushed past him, and it was as if he could feel every step she took. Sparks raced through the floor and up through the soles of his feet.

I'm losing my mind, he decided. *Sarah would be so proud.*

He closed the door and followed Grace.

She stood near Mama G, who was still at the table.

Mama G smiled brightly. "There you are! I made spaghetti for Robert."

Ah. We are back to Robert.

Grace frowned. "It's very nice of you to cook, but we should let Trav—"

"Robert," Trav interrupted.

Grace's gaze flew to him.

"Robert already set the table," Mama G said, looking at the table with satisfaction. "We should eat while it's hot."

"Mama G, we should—"

"Grace." It was all he said, but it was enough. Her gaze locked with his and he was astonished at the depths of her deep brown eyes. He could fall into those eyes, he thought, and never surface. "We should eat."

"Of course we should eat," Mama G said, a touch testily. "I didn't do all of this work for nothing."

Grace opened her mouth but then closed it. "No arguing," she muttered under her breath. "Fine. We'll eat and then we'll go home."

"Of course we'll go home after we eat," Mama G said. "We can't stay here, in the Parker house, can we, Robert?"

"Not unless you're willing to do the laundry, too."

Mama G chuckled. "Dinner is all you're getting."

"You did all the work, so you stay right there and I'll serve." He picked up three plates and carried them to the stove.

Mama G opened her napkin and put it in her lap. "Grace, fix everyone a drink. I'll just have water. The doctor says I should drink more."

"Yes, you should." Grace looked at Trav. "Water?"

"Yes, please." While he filled the plates, Grace found the cupboard holding the glasses, and filled three of them with water and carried them to the table.

Soon, they were sitting, plates of spaghetti steaming in front of them. The light over the table streamed a round, golden beam over them and Trav wondered if they looked like a Norman Rockwell painting.

Mama G picked up her fork. "Isn't this cozy?"

The whole thing felt ridiculously strange. He'd eaten at this table by himself for over a year now. A long, lonely year. An emotion he didn't want to name rose up in his throat.

Grace, obviously determined to keep her time in his house short, twisted spaghetti onto her fork with brisk efficiency. "Eat, Mama G."

Mama G's gaze moved from Grace to Trav, and then to the plates he'd set out earlier that were empty.

The elderly lady's smile began to waver.

Trav cleared his throat and spun his fork in his spaghetti. "The Phelpses have always been friends of the Parkers."

Mama G's gaze turned back to him and her gaze refocused. "Our families have always been close. And oh, how I enjoyed your father."

Your father. Now she knows I'm not Dad. "You knew my dad well." God, but this was good spaghetti. He tried to find a comfortable topic that would occupy Mama G. "How did you come to babysit him?"

She pursed her lips. "How did I? Let me see . . . Oh yes! His mother knew mine. They set it up between them. Robert could be a terror and he and his brother had chased off more than one sitter. But he was good when I watched him. I've always known how to deal with troubled children."

Grace made a noise.

Trav found himself fighting a grin. *That one hit, did it?* He winked at her, which made her stiff expression soften. "I'm not bragging, but Dad wouldn't have called me a troubled child. I got straight As."

Grace rolled her eyes, but a small smile rested on her mouth, which made him oddly happy.

"So did Grace, eventually. But grades don't tell the whole story, do they?" Mama G's brow lowered. "I took care of a number of foster children, you know. Almost a dozen. I was always careful who I took."

That was interesting. "How did you pick which ones to take?"

Grace, who'd been toying with her spaghetti, looked up at this, her gaze locked on Mama G. "I've always wondered that."

"I had a method." Mama G took a sip of water. "I took the ones who needed me the most. Grace needed me. And at the time, I needed her."

"You needed me?" Grace gave an odd laugh. "I wasn't an easy child. No one needed trouble like that."

"There are no easy children," Mama G said calmly, adding parmesan to her spaghetti. "I thought you'd already figured that out."

Grace's gaze dropped to her plate, and she seemed to be thinking this through.

Suddenly, Trav felt as if he'd stumbled into someone else's conversation. He cleared his throat. "It takes a big heart to take in foster children."

"It does. But I've never regretted a moment. Some were harder to deal with than others. Some would stay for years, some for days, and you'd love them as well as you could. And then, when the time came, you'd pack their bags, kiss their foreheads, and send them back home."

"I can't imagine having to let them go like that." To be honest, he'd never considered it. "It must have been hard for both you and the foster kids."

"Foster angels," she said softly.

A crease appeared between Grace's brows.

"So much pain." Mama G shook her head. "You could see it in their eyes, hear it in their voices."

Grace cleared her throat. "I'm sure Travis doesn't want to hear about foster kids."

"Sure I do." He smiled at Mama G. "You gave those children a valuable gift."

"It wasn't one-way," Mama G said sharply. "We helped each other. I gave them stability and love, and they gave me hope and laughter, and much, much more." She put down her fork. "Let me tell you about Grace."

"No, no," Grace muttered. "Mama G, don't—"

Mrs. Giano looked surprised. "Why not?"

"There's no need. He doesn't want to hear this."

Oh, but he did. So much. "Please don't stop on my account."

Grace shot him a sour look, but he just grinned.

"He needs to hear this," Mama G said stubbornly. She locked her dark gaze on him, leaned forward, and said, "Grace is like you."

He had a fork of spaghetti halfway to his mouth, but he lowered it. "Like me?"

"She's angry, too. Angry at life. At fate. Which does one no good, you know. But when one has suffered, been left, abandoned, over and over and—"

"Mama G," Grace muttered, her face red. "Please. That's enough."

Trav had been a platoon leader for a couple of years, long enough to see through the facades of many of the men he'd led. The second he'd laid eyes on Grace Wheeler, he'd known she was strong, opinionated, and sharp-edged. It was in the way she talked, moved, spoke, and yes, even looked. And now he knew why. She'd come from a place of pain, and she'd fought her way free and was determined to never return.

He admired that. A lot.

"Of course, Grace has reason to be angry." Mama G picked up her fork, her gaze resting on Trav. "Just as you do."

Trav discovered that while he didn't mind Mama G talking about Grace, he did mind it when she talked about him. "No offense, but you don't know much about me."

"Ha!" She pointed her fork at him, her eyes narrowing. "Sleep eludes you the way a cat runs from a snarling dog."

He blinked.

"You don't sleep, so you get angry." Mama G turned her attention back to her plate and slowly twirled her fork in her spaghetti. "It's sad, but life is not fair. I sometimes think it was never supposed to be. Life is made up of moments, good and bad. But while you don't get to pick all the moments, you do get to pick which ones you cling to."

"It's not that easy," Grace said, her voice sharp.

"Let me tell you something, sweetheart." Mama G reached over and placed her hand over Grace's. "I once knew two children, two beautiful little girls, who'd experienced the exact same agonies in life. No difference at all. Parents who didn't care. A mother so selfish she couldn't do her job. Those girls were abandoned by adults who knew better. Then they were thrown into a cold and callous system and transferred from home to home to home and school to school to school, labeled as troubled by teachers and mentors alike, and cruelly mocked by the other children they met. And yet one would turn out good, and one bad. Why? Because one chose to cling to the dark moments, while the other one clung to the light."

"Oh lord." Grace sent an embarrassed glance at Trav. "It wasn't like that."

"Wasn't it?" Mama G patted Grace's hand. "Eat your spaghetti, dear."

Grace looked at Mama G's hand where it rested on hers.

Trav watched a gambit of emotions cross Grace's face—anger, embarrassment, worry—but behind it all was love. She dearly loved this strange, confused old lady.

Mama G turned her dark gaze on him. "Why are you so mad, young man? What makes you angry?"

Grace turned to look at him, the question reflected in her gaze.

"I don't know." He put down his fork, and although he hadn't planned to, he found himself answering her. "I'm more sad, I think. I guess that's most of it. I had men who looked up to me and counted on me and I thought I had things in hand. That they were safe. That we were all safe and—" He shook his head. "It was a myth. We were never safe."

"That's a hard lesson to learn," Mama G agreed serenely. "Life is full of surprises, and not all of them are good."

He couldn't argue with that. "So here I am, back home. I've been alone since my dad died, except for my friends. I guess I'm just waiting."

Mama G tilted her head to one side. "For what?"

He shrugged. "I don't know. But I'll figure it out."

Mama G nodded thoughtfully, and the silence, already heavy, lengthened.

But it was a peaceful silence. Trav found that he didn't mind this sort of quietness.

Grace stirred. "We should go. Mama G, are you done?"

"No, stay," Trav said.

Both women looked at him, various degrees of surprise in their eyes.

His face grew warm. He hadn't meant to sound so demanding, but damn it, he didn't want them to go. It had been so long since he'd had dinner in his kitchen like this, with people who made him feel as if he were a part of a family. Their family. And it felt . . . right. He felt safe. Alive. Connected. It was an odd feeling, and he wondered if Sarah might understand it better than he did. She came from a huge family, and few people were as attuned to the nuances of family life as Sarah. Maybe he'd stop by the library tomorrow and see what she thought.

Mama G nodded. "She has a lot of answers, doesn't she?"

Grace frowned, confused, while Trav stared at Mama G.

Good God, did she read my mind? Surely not. He pushed his plate away. "I don't know what you mean."

"Oh, I know things. I always have." She pushed her plate away as well, having barely touched the spaghetti. "I'm losing my memories but I think I might be gaining other people's. Has that ever happened to you?"

"No. Not that I know of."

"That's good. It's not much fun, you know. In fact, it's a little scary."

"Well!" Grace stood. "Thank you for having us. Dinner was delightful, but we should get home."

Mama G looked around, as if searching for a clock. "What time is it?"

"Time to go," Grace said briskly. "Dinner's over and we should get home."

"Is it late?" Mama G suddenly looked tired. "I'd like to go to bed."

Trav started to stand, but Grace threw up a hand. "That's okay. I've got this." She didn't spare him another glance as she helped Mama G from her seat.

Mama G went willingly, shuffling along as if almost too tired to walk.

Trav stood. "I'll walk you home. I—"

"No," Grace said sharply. "You've done more than enough." She had her arm around Mama G and they were already heading for the door. "Thank you," she said over her shoulder.

But as Grace opened the door, Mama G looked back. "You need to heal faster," she told him.

"Mama G—" Grace started.

"No," he said. "Let her talk."

Mama G looked from him to Grace, and then back. "You've both let your anger take over your lives, but it's time for that to stop." She locked eyes with Trav and then put her hand on Grace's shoulder. "One day, you'll need to be there for her."

Grace flushed. "Don't—"

"Shush." Mama G leaned toward Trav. "You and Sarah both. And Daisy, too. You will need to be there together. Do you understand?"

"Mama G," Grace muttered.

Trav, astonished at the sincerity in the old woman's dark gaze, nodded.

Mama G examined his face, looking for something. Whatever it was, she must have found it, for she broke into a huge smile. "You'll know when." She turned to Grace and patted her cheek. "Now we can go home."

And with that, she turned and shuffled out.

Grace sent him a pained look. "I'm sorry. That was . . . It was weird, but she's not—" She shook her head and then left, closing the door behind her.

Helpless to do more, Travis stood, staring at the closed door for a long, long time.

And then he went back to his plate of spaghetti and sat, the golden glow of the lamp overhead drawing a solitary circle around him and the empty table.

CHAPTER 13

Grace

The next morning, Grace sat in her car in Sarah's driveway and waited. It had taken a lot of discipline to get up early enough to be here, especially after Mama G's late-night run next door to cook dinner. "Spaghetti in the middle of the night," Grace muttered. "Who does that?"

Between Mama G's odd pronouncements and Trav's quiet intensity, it had been an uncomfortable dinner. Grace had to give her neighbor credit, though. He'd been more than kind and had gone out of his way to make Mama G feel safe and welcome, even after she'd started making prophetic statements like some sort of seer.

Grace leaned back in her seat and sighed. The whole thing had been unbelievably awkward. After she got Mama G home and back to bed, Grace had been too awake to sleep. And so she'd made herself some coffee, sat on the steps on her crooked porch, and did something she hadn't done in forever—she watched the sunrise.

It had been beautiful. The night had taken on a pinkish morning glow that had gradually warmed to an orange and then a bright golden hue as it lit the tree-lined street, burnishing leaves, catching the glisten of the dew, shimmering across puddles left by yesterday's rain, and highlighting the ornate trim work of the gorgeous houses. And as Grace watched the sun grow brighter and the neighborhood slowly come awake, she remembered what Mama G had said during their spaghetti dinner about clinging to the good things in life, rather than the bad. Mama G had made it sound easy, but Grace knew it took effort and a lot of love to find brightness in the middle of gloom.

As Grace drank her second cup of coffee, it dawned on her that perhaps the people of Dove Pond felt that way about their festival, that it was one of the good things that they clung to when life wasn't going well. From what she could tell, it might well be the only thing they had left. That explained the anger they'd expressed when the budget had been cut.

And so, here she was, waiting on Sarah. Grace wanted to see the archives located in the basement of the library that Kat had mentioned at the café, but it was more than that. Seeing Trav sitting at that big table in his kitchen, looking so alone, had tugged at Grace's heart. She knew he had friends, as she'd seen them coming and going throughout the weeks. But last night during dinner, she'd recognized him, one soul to another. He was private, quiet, intense, feeling everything deeply while trying not to. She was the same way. Mama G had been right about that: Grace and Trav were the same in many ways.

The door opened and Sarah stepped out onto the porch carrying her heavy tote bag. She came down the steps and had just reached the sidewalk when she saw Grace sitting in her car.

Sarah stopped in her tracks.

Grace picked up the two cups of freshly brewed coffee she'd brought with her and showed them to Sarah through the car window. Then Grace set the cups down and held up the bag of croissants. "See?" Grace said, rolling down her window. "I have snacks!"

Sarah smiled.

Grace grinned back, relief washing over her.

Sarah came down the rest of the walkway and opened the car door. "We're carpooling?"

"Yes, please," Grace said.

Without hesitating, Sarah climbed in, setting her heavy tote on the floorboard. "What's in the bag?"

"Chocolate croissants. I got them from the Moonlight."

"You drove there this morning?"

"I did. I got the coffee from there, too."

"Wow. This is nice." Sarah settled into her seat and was soon sipping her coffee. "I could get used to this."

"Me too." Grace smiled, put the car in reverse, and pulled out of Sarah's driveway. "I wanted to talk to you." *Here we go, Wheeler. Let's do this right.* "I'm going to do something I really, really suck at. I'm going to apologize. I've been an ass. That's all I can say."

"You don't owe me an apology." Sarah pulled the croissants out of the bag. "I owe you one."

"No, it was me. I just—"

"Grace, it was my fault! We should never have forced you back onto the committee. I knew Zoe was going to do something— I encouraged her to do it. I wanted you back on the committee so badly and I—"

"Damn it, Sarah. This is my apology, not yours!"

Sarah's eyes widened.

Grace gave a reluctant laugh. "We are a crazy couple of women, aren't we?"

Sarah's smile returned. "Yes, we are. By the way, I saw what happened yesterday."

"Which time?" Grace said drily. "Yesterday was a long day."

"You know . . . The truck? The puddle?"

"Oh yes. That." Grace shook her head. "Not my finest hour."

"I'm sorry I laughed."

Grace looked at Sarah. "You did?"

"Yes. I thought you saw me."

Grace shook her head. "By the time I could see anything, you had your hand over your face. To be honest, I thought you were just sending me the message that I was getting what I deserved."

"Oh no! But I shouldn't have laughed, either. It was just . . ." She shrugged helplessly. "It was a really good splash."

"Too good," Grace agreed, smiling. "I told Kat it was like a movie splash. I saw her at the café later. But look, about who owes who an apology and the committee and the festival and all of it. I've been rude to you all week and it was stupid. I don't know why I got so mad at you, rather than at Zoe and Kat. They had the most to do with it, but you . . . I guess I thought you were on my side."

Sarah groaned. "See? I knew that's what you thought. Grace, I was wrong. But I just wanted you to help us. We need you. The *town* needs you."

Grace turned the car toward Main Street. "I should be flattered by that. Heck, I *am* flattered by that. But . . . well, it hurt."

"Which is why I should apologize."

"No. You all were right when you said that if you hadn't pulled that stunt, I wouldn't have taken back the chairmanship. I didn't really give you a choice, so it's my fault. I walked into that first meeting and threw the folder at Zoe and left. At the time, it felt like the right thing to do, but I was wrong. To be honest, I'm sort of glad I'm back in charge."

"Really?"

"Now that I know the real issues with the town's finances, I have something more important to do than all of that boring data entry. I think I can help. I may not be here long enough to fix things completely, but I can at least get you all started."

Sarah's smile had disappeared. "I hate it when you talk about leaving. You should stay. You really should."

Grace shook her head, smiling. "That's not going to happen. But while I'm here, I should at least commit."

"To what?"

"To this town. To the committee. And to being a good friend." Grace turned the car onto Main Street. "I've never really had a friend, you know. Not like other women do, someone to talk to and share stuff with. I'm sort of new to this, so I'm going to make mistakes."

"But we're friends? You mean that?"

Sarah looked so happy that Grace laughed. "Yes, I mean it. We're also officially carpooling and I'll bring the snacks next week."

"Deal." Sarah put a napkin on Grace's knee and placed a chocolate croissant on it. "I have to admit something, too."

"Oh?"

"I've been a little jealous of you."

"Of me? What on earth for?"

Sarah looked at her croissant and she said slowly, "I was jealous because growing up, I always thought I was going to be the one to save Dove Pond." Sarah raised her gaze to Grace. "But it's not going to be me. It's going to be you."

"Hold on there! I didn't say I'd save the town. I said I'd get you all going in the right direction. That's all I can do. I can't save anything right now, not even myself."

"No. You're going to find a way to save Dove Pond. I already know it."

"My God. As much as I like you, and I do, although I don't know why, you're a strange one."

"I know," Sarah agreed as she unwrapped her croissant. "You'll get used to it."

Grace had to laugh. "I guess I'll have to."

"I'm glad Kat ran into you at the diner yesterday. She called me afterward."

"Why?"

"She's worried about you. She said you seemed so tired."

"Daisy's been, well, Daisy. And Mama G is a handful lately. She ended up at Trav's in the middle of the night, cooking spaghetti of all things."

"Oh dear. I knew she was there; he texted me and asked for your number."

"I wondered how he'd gotten it. Well, she made him pay for it, and me too, because she said some embarrassing things." Super-embarrassing things.

"What did she say?"

"Nothing that made any sense, but I wish she hadn't said them in front of Trav."

Sarah took a sip of her coffee. "He understands. He took care of his dad, so he knows how it is."

That was true. Maybe he wouldn't put any stock in Mama G's weird meanderings. "I just wish I knew how she got out. I had a lock installed way up high so she couldn't reach it, but after Trav texted me, I found the door standing wide open. She's not tall enough to reach the lock, and there weren't any stools nearby or anything to show that she'd figured it out." Grace shook her head. "I have no idea how she did it."

"Oosh. That's worrying."

"Very." Grace shot a glance at Sarah. "By the way, last week your sister sent some tea for Mama G."

"She said she was going to. Does it work?"

"Amazingly, yes."

The tin had been labeled AVA'S SPECIALTY TEA FOR MAMA G, and Grace had no idea what was in it. Whatever it was, it was effective. One cup at dusk, and Mama G visibly relaxed, humming to herself and willing to enjoy the moment. While it didn't seem to help her sleep, it had alleviated the anxiety she seemed to feel every evening. "To be honest, I was a little worried it might not be good for her."

"Ava's teas are safe." Sarah's tone was a little stiff.

"I'm sure they are, but I was afraid it might interfere with Mama G's medications. Of course, Linda scoffed at that. She loves all things Dove."

Sarah grinned. "Linda is a good one."

"She is. Ava dropped off her tea while I was at work, so before I got home, Linda had already made Mama G a cup. It worked great." Of course, had it been up to Grace, she'd have never allowed Mama G to try the stuff without first knowing what was in it, but that was not to be. "I called Ava and asked for the ingredients. It was just some chamomile, lavender, and a touch of magnolia bark, none of which Doc Bolton thought would be harmful."

"You can trust Ava."

"I know. And I do." Grace slanted a smile at Sarah. "Want to know something funny? The tea worked so well on Mama G that Linda decided to give it a try."

"It doesn't work like that. Ava didn't make it for her."

"You're right. Linda said she drank six cups of it and all it did was make her need to pee in the middle of the night."

Sarah laughed. "I knew she'd tried it. Linda stopped by the house a few days ago and Ava made her some special lavender tea."

"Oh, I've heard all about it. The tea is supposed to make dreams vivid. Since then, I've had to listen to Linda talk about her dreams, mostly of her naked on a hot beach with a nameless man."

Sarah grinned over her cup of coffee. "Oh no."

"Oh yes. Linda said her dreams were so real that she woke up to the smell of salt water and coconut rum." Frankly, Grace didn't want more vivid dreams. She just wanted to sleep through one night. *Just one.*

"I'm glad Ava's tea helped."

"You've both been helpful." Grace turned the car into the parking lot and pulled into a space. She turned off the car. "I can't thank you enough."

Sarah looked at her half-eaten croissant and set it down on her knee. "Look, I know I've been overeager in welcoming you to our town. And I know that made it harder on you. It's just that I have a good feeling about you moving here, and I'm glad I've gotten to know you and Daisy and Mama G."

Grace's chest tightened, a bubble of emotion near the surface. She knew it was because she was just exhausted from too little sleep, but this time she didn't fight it. "I'm glad I'm here, too. That's the one thing Mama G said last night that was true; I've been holding on to my anger way too much. I was so, so mad when I had to leave my job in Charlotte, because I've always thought of money as a measure of success. That's what I've told myself my entire life—that I would grow up, make a lot of money, and buy a house for myself and Hannah." Grace sighed, and it came from her heart. "But things haven't turned out the way I thought. Not even close. And I haven't been at my best since I got here."

"You've been great. You're being way too hard on yourself."

"Not really. To be honest, I'm not sure what I was mad at. Fate? The circumstances? Mama G's illness? Probably all of that. But I think I'm angriest at Hannah. And I think I've been angry at her for a long, long time, but never admitted it to myself." She sent a self-conscious glance at Sarah. "You're close to your sisters, so you may not understand that."

"I'm not close to all of them. Just Ava, really."

"You never had one who hurt as many people as Hannah. She had Daisy, and she never once stopped to think how it would affect her own daughter, to just abandon her with Mama G. And Mama G has given me and Hannah so much, she didn't deserve to have a kid dumped on her like that, either, even a good kid like Daisy." Grace leaned back against the headrest. "In some ways, I was just as bad as Hannah. I should have helped Mama G more. I played Favorite Aunt and swept in and handed out presents, and took her out to eat, and spent money on her, and then I just left. I never really got to know her."

"You know her now."

Grace gave a dry laugh. "I argue with her now."

"It can't be easy moving from aunt to mom. I'm sure it's been difficult for both of you."

"It's harder on Daisy. She's bored, staying at home all the time, and that's no good. I just don't know what to do with her."

"You'll figure it out." Sarah gathered her tote. "I know you will."

They were simple words. And yet they were exactly what Grace needed to hear. She sighed as she opened her door. "I hope so."

They climbed out of the car and were gathering their things when someone called Sarah's name.

Grace turned as Mrs. Jolean Hamilton limped up, her dog panting happily behind her.

Mrs. Hamilton stopped on seeing Grace with Sarah. "Well! Have you decided to undo the damage you're doing to the festival budget?"

"Aunt Jo!" Sarah said, frowning.

Grace waved her off. "It's okay. I've been getting a lot of this."

Mrs. Hamilton huffed. "You should be getting more! People around here are mad. It's insulting when someone who doesn't even know our town makes big decisions like that without so much as a by-your-leave."

"Aunt Jo, you know I'm on that committee, too," Sarah said with a touch of impatience. "I would never vote to do something reckless with Dove Pond."

"I know you wouldn't. But her?" Mrs. Hamilton jerked her thumb at Grace. "I don't know about her."

"Fair enough," Grace said. "To be honest, I'm looking into the matter today. I think I may have missed something."

Sarah and Mrs. Hamilton looked at Grace, both clearly surprised. Even Moon Pie appeared unsettled as he tilted his head to one side. Grace added, "In fact, I was going to ask Sarah if she would show me the town archives this morning."

"Of course I will," Sarah said. "But . . . why?"

"I want to see everything you've got about past Apple Festivals. I want to learn every last thing I can about them. It dawned on me yesterday that I have no right to change something without thoroughly understanding what it is to begin with. When I worked at my old job, whenever we got a new project, that was the first thing we did—we tried to understand the brand, and what it meant. We did all sorts of research before we made a single decision. Our committee never took that step and it didn't dawn on me we'd skipped it until I was talking to Kat yesterday."

"There you go." Mrs. Hamilton looked impressed. "Sarah, show her those records."

"Sure." Sarah looked at Grace. "Do you want to see them now?"

"If you don't mind. I already told the mayor I'd be in late. He's doing data entry this morning, so he can cover the office until I get there."

"The mayor is doing data entry?" Mrs. Hamilton broke into a wide grin. "Honey, I think I might like you after all."

Sarah grinned and she said to Grace, "Let's go. I've got a lot to show you."

CHAPTER 14

Sarah

"Meow."

Sarah paused in readying the conference room for the improvement committee meeting and went to peer out the window. Outside, Siegfried was turning in a circle in front of the book drop box. *One. Two.* He stopped and sat, watching the door of town hall as if expecting a mouse to dart out.

Only two circles. That's promising. More heartened than she had been in a while, Sarah rubbed her hands together. It was more than Siegfried that had given her hope, though. Grace had spent almost three hours this morning going through the town archives, and when she'd emerged, she'd been deep in thought, as if something had occurred to her.

Please let her have a great idea. A wonderful idea. A fricking brilliant *idea.*

The door to town hall swung open and Zoe stepped out, dressed in a formfitting sheath dress of chocolate brown trimmed with a Peter Pan collar. She carried a stack of folders, a pen tucked behind one ear. She glanced both ways, then crossed the street and walked toward the library.

Siegfried meowed again and then wandered down the street and was soon out of sight.

Sarah went back to getting the room ready for the meeting, setting out bottles of water and notepads.

Zoe came in. She didn't stop by her usual chair but walked straight up to Sarah. "Okay, how'd you do it?"

Sarah blinked. "How'd I do what?"

"This." Zoe held out the Italian phrase book Sarah had handed her a few weeks ago.

"Ah. That." Sarah put the last bottle of water in front of Grace's seat. "It's not easy to explain."

"Explain it anyway."

Sarah took stock of the militant sparkle in Zoe's hazel eyes. "I take it you needed that book after all."

Zoe's mouth tightened. "Yes. But don't you dare ask me why."

"Fine. But you give, I give. I'll explain exactly how I knew you needed that book, but only after you tell me what it did for you."

The mulish line of Zoe's mouth said all Sarah needed to know, so she grinned. "I'm glad it was handy."

Zoe didn't smile back. "Out with it, Dove. How do you do it?"

People had asked that before, and over the years Sarah had learned to tread carefully. Some believed, some didn't, and it was a waste of time trying to convince the nonbelievers. "It just comes to me."

"How?"

She shrugged. "They tell me, and I listen."

"The books talk?"

"Sort of. Not out loud but inside my head."

"For the love of— Here." Zoe thrust the book into Sarah's hands. "Take it back."

Sarah looked down at the book. It seemed to be laughing softly, but as it didn't argue, she tucked it under her arm. "You seem upset. Did you—"

"It doesn't matter what happened. I don't want that book any-where near me. It's— I didn't—" Zoe clamped her mouth closed and then spun on her heel and walked back to her seat.

The book was now laughing even harder. Sarah patted it. "I'm sorry if it caused you problems. I'll reshelve it as soon as the meeting is over."

"Thank you," Zoe said stiffly.

"Of course. I wouldn't want you upset."

"I'm not." Zoe sat down. "Is everything ready with Plan G?"

"Yup. I just got off the phone with Ava and she's on board. I— Ah, there's Grace. Good afternoon!"

Grace breezed in and made her way to her seat. "Good afternoon." She was carrying a new stack of folders and she smiled as she walked past Sarah.

Sarah noticed that the faded folder Mrs. Phelps had used for years had been replaced by a set of neat, color-coded binders. A sign of permanence, she hoped.

Ed and Erma walked in, Nate following, and soon the room was buzzing. Grace had just looked at her watch when Kat and Ava came hurrying in and found their seats.

"Sorry we're late," Ava said. "Kat had some unfinished business."

Kat put her folder down but remained standing. "Before we begin, I have an announcement, thanks to Grace."

Everyone looked at Grace, who appeared shocked. "Me?"

"Yes, you. After our conversation at the Moonlight, I realized I've been limiting myself. So . . ." She beamed at everyone. "I started my own business."

"What?" Erma exclaimed.

Kat grinned and pulled a small stack of business cards from her pocket and handed them out. "I'm just beginning, and it'll be a while before I turn a profit, but at least I started."

Erma held the card at arm's length and tilted her head so that she could look through the bottom part of her glasses. "'Carter Commercial Real Estate, LLC.'" Erma lowered the card. "How's this different from your mother's company?"

"Mom works in residential real estate, while I'll be working with commercial properties, both rentals and sales. Mom hates the commercial end of the business because of the paperwork, but there's a lot more money to be made there. Or"—she corrected herself—"there will be soon."

"Congratulations," Grace said. "I think you'll do great with that."

"I hope so," Kat said as she took her seat. "I'm going to try. I'll still work with my mom until I've built up my business, but I'm hoping it won't take long."

"Way to go," Ed said approvingly. "If I hear of anyone looking for commercial property, I'll share your information."

"Thank you."

"I can think of a few people you need to talk to right now," Zoe said. "May I have more of your cards? I'll need at least five."

Kat handed a small stack to Zoe, who tucked them into her folder. "Thank you."

"That's excellent news, and it plays right into what I have to say." Grace looked around the conference table. "Are we ready to begin?" When everyone nodded, Grace said, "Old business first. Did you all read the report Zoe emailed this morning?"

Ava made a face. "I tried."

"It was too long to read on the computer, so I printed it out and wow, was it thick," Nate said with a grimace. "Or maybe I am, because I still couldn't figure out what it meant."

Grace looked at Zoe. "Care to explain what we've discovered?"

"Sure. I brought copies in case some of you didn't have a chance to read it." Zoe flipped open her folder and handed out copies of her report. "Grace and I were wondering why the festivals have lost their audience. So we worked up a fiscal analysis of the festivals and, since we were there, their impact on Dove Pond."

"We dug way, way back in the financial records," Grace added. "And then I topped it off by spending some time with the archives."

"We discovered that the festivals and the town have the same problem," Zoe added.

"Only one?" Nate looked disbelieving.

"A big one," Zoe said firmly. "Large and costly, too."

"What is it?" Erma asked, looking interested.

"The town lost sight of why we had the festivals to begin with. They were originally held to benefit the residents while celebrating Dove Pond and its history."

"Those are good reasons to have a festival."

"True," Zoe agreed. "But as time went on and the festivals became more successful, the town took over and they became a cash cow for the Dove Pond coffers."

"What do you mean, 'took over'?" Erma asked.

"Exactly what I said. The town also began to charge for their contributions—use of the park and security and other things as well."

Grace nodded. "They charged vendors for booths, too."

"Wait," Kat said. "I thought our festivals always *lost* money?"

"They do now," Zoe said. "But at one time, they brought in a lot of cash."

"Just not for the town," Grace clarified. "You see, the original purpose of the first Apple Festival was to help the people of Dove Pond. So farmers and the stores in town would bring their extra stock, crafts they'd made, the last round of produce, and whatever else they had to sell, and that money would help them make it through the winter."

Zoe added, "Conversely, the Spring Fling was held to bring everyone together to celebrate the early harvests and to assist the farmers and local businesses in finding the help they needed for their bigger summer crops."

"It was a big hiring fair, in a way," Grace said.

"So originally, neither of our festivals were meant to make money for the town," Erma said. "They were meant to help the citizens."

"Exactly." Grace tapped one of her binders. "But as the years passed, the focus moved from helping the residents to establishing a cash flow for the town coffers. And as it did so, the festivals became less and less successful."

"That's not good," Kat said.

"It wasn't. Things really got bad when the festival became an official town event in nineteen seventy-seven. That decision was made under Mayor Jenkins, Mayor Moore's predecessor. Jenkins made the festival an official part of the town clerk's job."

"Jenkins was a penny-pincher," Erma said with distaste. "Getting him to pay for anything was like pulling teeth. That's why he was voted out."

Grace nodded. "Under his aegis, the festivals became stale and anemic."

Zoe returned the report to her folder. "We were left with two poorly functioning generic festivals mainly geared toward tourists, which was completely contrary to why the festivals were originally established. The further away from the original purposes of the festivals that the town got, the less successful they were."

Kat sat back in her seat. "We forgot our client base."

"Exactly," Grace said.

There was a moment of silence as everyone considered this. Nate dropped the paper on the table in front of him. "We need to go back to the old formula."

"Yes," Grace said. "Which is why I want to revisit the festival budget."

"Praise the Lord!" Erma said.

"What's to revisit?" Ava asked. "You said at the last meeting that we need to do some sort of business outreach or we're sunk, and that there's no more money."

"Which is still true, and I'm going to address that. But first I want to talk about something I discovered this morning." She looked around the table. "I went through the town archives, almost three hundred years of history. It was a fascinating history lesson. But now

Dove Pond is failing, and there are similarities to the failing companies I used to help restructure, more than I'd realized. As I told Sarah
this morning, when we'd first take on a company, we'd spend weeks,
sometimes months, getting to know who they were, what they were,
and how they were viewed. That's their branding. And of all the things
a company owns, their brand is worth more than anything else."

"Sure," Kat said. "Like Nike or Nabisco—you know what those
represent."

"Exactly. When you're helping a company restructure, the last
thing you want to do is damage their brand. In fact, you do everything you can to protect it and, if you can, build on it."

"And you think the Apple Festival is part of the town brand?"
Erma said.

"No. The town's brand isn't the festivals. It's all of you."

Sarah leaned forward. "Us?"

Grace nodded. "While I was reading through the deeds and the
old newspapers and the old flyers for references to the Apple Festival,
I kept seeing the same thing over and over. I saw the Bells, the Doves,
the Parkers, the Moores, the Carters, the Jepsons, the Tingles, the
Boltons—all of you, all your families. And you're all still here. *You're*
the brand." She tapped the binder in front of her. "The Apple Festival
was a huge event because it was a *family* event."

Sarah blinked. "And family is what Dove Pond is all about."

"Exactly. That's our brand. And that's what we need to focus on if
we want to bring the town back."

"But . . . how do we do that?" Ed asked.

"We sell ourselves on the basis of what we have, not what we don't."

Ava looked confused. "But what do we have?"

Grace pointed to Zoe. "We have a bank eager to increase its business accounts."

"You know it," Zoe agreed in a fervent tone.

Grace pointed to Kat. "A huge amount of available, low-cost commercial properties."

"Most of the owners would be willing to cut good deals, too," Kat said. "Especially for long-term leases."

"Good," Grace said. "We also have plenty of businesses interested in promoting themselves and finding new customers."

"Count me in," Nate said.

"Me too," Ed agreed.

"Oh my God," Ava said. "I'm starting to see what you're saying. We should combine the two."

Grace smiled.

"Wait. What?" Sarah felt as if she was the only one being left behind.

Zoe sent her an impatient look. "The Apple Festival could be the ultimate small-business outreach event."

Grace leaned back in her chair. "But we have to go back and make it what it used to be, a festival about this town, about the people who live here."

"How do we do that?" Sarah asked.

"We showcase who we are," Grace said. "Dove Pond is a beautiful, friendly, family-oriented town."

"*With,*" Zoe added, "a huge potential for low-cost, small-business start-ups. That's who we've always been. We just haven't focused on that. We haven't *told* anyone."

"Which means," Grace said, "that every business and every community entity in Dove Pond should have a booth."

"All of them?" Nate looked surprised.

Grace nodded.

"The churches could have booths," Erma said. "They could do a cake walk or something like that. They'll love it."

Grace added, "So will most community groups."

Ed brightened. "I'm a member of the Kiwanis and we just had the Callahan brothers make us a half a dozen corn hole boards. We got them for our summer barbecues, but we're always looking for ways to raise money for the children's hospital. People love that game, too."

"That's a great idea," Grace said.

"The Moonlight could set up a lunch tent," Ava said thoughtfully. "I could sell spring plants, and my teas too."

"The bank can hand out piggy banks and totes," Zoe added. "Dad was just saying last week that we don't do outreach the way we used to, so this would be a good start."

This is so exciting. Sarah's mind whirled with ideas. "The Callahan brothers make beautiful wood items like cheese trays and salad bowls and cutting boards. And Doc Bolton is always saying we should have a health fair, so I bet he'd be willing to host a tent for free blood pressure readings, where he can hand out some of his pamphlets."

"He loves handing those out." Ed rubbed his chin. "Maggie and I can do dog grooming and sell some of the discontinued items we've got in boxes in the back. We need to get rid of that stuff, anyway."

"You can sell new items, too," Zoe reminded him. "Just mingle it between the sale items."

"That's a good idea," Ed agreed with a thoughtful nod.

"I'll set up a summer gardening display and do some planting workshops," Nate offered.

"We could put the schedule on the website," Grace said.

"Great. I'll get that to you this week."

"Hmm." Kat tilted her head to one side. "I wonder if Lisa Tilden would be willing to bring some of her coworkers and do mini massages? It would be a great way for her to build up her local client base."

"Perfect!" Zoe said. "I'd pay for that."

"Me, too," Nate said fervently. When everyone looked at him, he flushed and said, "What? I've got a bad back."

Kat grinned. "Right. Bad back. That's a great excuse, Nate."

"What about T.W.?" Erma asked. "He's got all of those near-tame animals. They're like house pets."

"So?" Ed said.

Erma gave him an impatient look. "So he could do a petting zoo.

He's got chickens, pygmy goats, a pony named Bruce Lee, and the cutest baby donkey right now, too, as well as two lambs."

"Yes!" Grace couldn't have looked more pleased. "You see what's happening? Dove Pond is happening. *This* is who we are. And *this* is what we need to sell."

Sarah heard Grace say "we" and had to fight the urge to yell out a celebratory "whoop-whoop."

"I like this." Kat tapped her folder. "We should also invite these businesses who've left. Most are still local and would see our community as potential clients."

"Great idea," Grace agreed.

"I'll buy in," Nate said. "I don't see how we can't. But how do you envision the outreach part of your plan?"

"At the festival, we'll have a special area where we'll welcome any and all businesses. We'll treat them for what they are, prospective investors in our town. We'll have a packet of key information available for each of them when they arrive, and we'll assign a guide who will show our beautiful town."

"I love this," Erma said, beaming. "I take it you've already thought about the funding issue? You've thought of everything else."

"Zoe and I figured that out earlier this afternoon. We're going to add vendors to our fair."

Erma's smile slipped. "We've always had vendors."

"Not this many. We're going to add a lot."

Zoe nodded. "We're expanding the size of the festival—doubling it, in fact."

"My God," Erma said, her eyes huge behind her glasses. "But how will that make our festival affordable?"

"Because we're going to charge a vendor fee again."

"No!" Erma threw down her pen. "People will hate that."

"We already thought about that," Zoe said smoothly. "We're not charging a traditional fee. We're only asking for a cut of profits over a certain amount."

"A *generous* amount," Grace said. "If a vendor doesn't make a good profit, neither will we."

"Isn't that taking a chance?" Ava asked.

"I'd prefer to call it a calculated risk," Grace said. "But it means we've got to hit the ground running. We need to plump up our vendor list as soon as possible and get commitments. Erma, I was hoping you'd take the lead on the vendors."

Erma flushed but looked pleased. "Me?"

Grace pulled out a folder. "Would you mind?"

"No! I mean, I'm glad to help."

Grace slid the folder to Erma. "We'll talk about it after the meeting. Since we're going to ask for a cut of their profits, we'll need to do more for the vendors."

Zoe nodded. "Welcome baskets, a listing on the town website and on all promotional materials—we want to get the word out for them."

"Sheesh," Sarah said. "I never thought about having a welcome basket for vendors."

Ed shook his head. "Every year, we had a festival checklist and we'd just go down it and check off the boxes. And when it was done, we just sort of quit."

"Some of that was Mrs. Phelps," Ava pointed out.

"She was too busy to do more than the basics," Grace said. "The clerk's job can be overwhelming; there's a *lot* of paperwork. I daresay she saw the social club the way I did initially—as an inconvenience that needed to be gotten over with as quickly and painlessly as possible."

"Done right, it's a big job." Ed closed his folder and leaned his elbows on it, his hands clasped on top. "But shouldn't we be careful what sort of businesses we try to lure to our town? We want the ones that would be a good fit, the ones the locals would support."

Nate gave a skeptical laugh. "Can we target like that?"

"Sure," Zoe said. "We'll do it the same way you sell mulch at the hardware store. You put it on display by the front door with a lot of photos of gorgeous lawns, and you ask every single person going through the checkout line who has bought a spade or a garden hose if they need any."

Nate grinned. "It works."

"Exactly."

"But how do we know which businesses to ask?" Ava asked.

"Grace and I are working on a list," Zoe said. "Some are obvious. We lost our local pediatrician when Dr. Lynn retired, and his offices are available. He was plenty busy, too, so there's an opportunity there, if we could find a good match. And the theater has been closed since Lou Jacobs died. It's a beautiful building. After his death, Jules Stewart from the Moonlight bought it. She said she's willing to let it go for the right price, and it's the perfect place for an independent movie house."

"I love indie films," Sarah said.

Grace looked at Ava and smiled. "You're on our business list too."

"Me?" Ava looked from Grace to Zoe and back. "I already have greenhouses and an office."

"Yes," Zoe said, "but you don't have a teahouse."

Ava opened her eyes wider. "A teahouse?"

"That would be a nice addition to town," Erma said.

"I love teahouses," Sarah said. "Nothing goes better with a good book than a cup of hot tea and a scone."

Ava considered it. "I guess I could. I never thought about it, but— no. I don't know how to cook, and no one wants tea without food."

Kat shrugged. "If you're interested, we can work on that."

"She's right," Zoe said. "That's the least of your worries. And if you had the right manager, you wouldn't even have to be there. It would turn a heck of a profit without you having to divide your attention between the two places."

Ava leaned back in her seat. "I'll give it some thought. But . . . you know, I could do it. I just never thought about it."

"Exactly." Looking smug, Zoe turned to Kat. "We're going to need a list of all the available office and warehouse spaces in town and their prices. We want to include it in the business welcome packets."

Kat brightened. "I'll get right on it. May I put my company name on the list?"

"Of course. You're the only commercial realtor in town, you know."

Grace beamed around the table. "I know it seems overwhelming, but the reality of Dove Pond is that it slipped away slowly, one business at a time. We can bring it back the same way."

"One business at a time," Ava said, looking bemused.

"Do you really think it's possible?" Erma asked.

Grace shrugged. "Nothing's guaranteed, but yes, I do. I think Dove Pond will get better and that this committee will make it happen."

"And better is"—Sarah grinned—"better."

"Wow," Erma said. "Just wow." She placed her hands flat on the table and slid her chair closer. "So what do we do now?"

"First things first," Grace said. "We're going to focus on our festival planning for the rest of the meeting. We'll call an extra meeting Monday to brainstorm the business aspect. Zoe will be in charge of that."

"On it, boss," Zoe said.

"What will you do?" Kat asked Grace.

"I'll be in charge of the logistics—tents, electricity, safety. The basic setup."

Sarah thought about the town, and all her hopes for it, which were too numerous to count. She was happy to see the enthusiasm humming in the room, which boded well for the festival. But today she had a higher purpose. She cleared her throat. "Before we get into the festival planning, there's another issue I'd like to bring up."

Everyone stopped talking. As if she sensed Sarah's nervousness, Ava nodded her encouragement.

Grace, who'd just pulled her notepad closer, looked up, surprised. "What's that?"

Sarah pulled a paper out of her folder and slid it across the table to Grace.

Grace picked it up and read it aloud. "'Monday, Paw Printz for dog washing. Tuesday, help Ava package teas. Wednesday and Friday, the library for Children's Hour. Thursday, the Moonlight for pie class.'" She lowered the list. "What's this?"

"It's something the committee and I put together," Sarah said. "It's for Daisy."

"For Daisy?"

Sarah nodded. "We know you've had a really difficult time lately, and we wanted to help. So we'd like to hire Daisy to assist us with a few things. She'll get two dollars a week."

"We didn't want to pay her too much," Erma said. "That's not good for a child."

"But Maggie and I really could use the help at Paw Printz," Ed said. "Monday's our busiest day."

"And you know I always need extra hands packaging my teas," Ava said. "I have almost more orders than I can fill."

"I've been struggling to make Children's Hour better," Sarah added. "Daisy can help me select the books and then read to the other kids. It would be good for her, too, because this way she'll see at least a few familiar faces when she starts school."

Grace slowly put the list back on the table. "I— You all . . . I don't know what to say."

"You don't have to say anything," Nate said. "I'll run out and pick her up at one every day after lunch. I go right by there on my way back to work, so you won't have to leave the office."

Sarah added, "She can ride home with you when she's done. She'll be safe and busy, and except when she's helping Ava, she'll be somewhere close by, so you can check on her at any time."

Grace's eyes were shiny. "I can't let you do this."

"You'll hurt our feelings if you say no," Ava said.

"It'll be good for Daisy," Sarah added.

"And it'll let Linda spend more time with Mama G," Kat said.

Grace pressed her hand to her cheek. After a moment, her eyes bright with tears, she looked at Sarah. "You knew about this during our ride this morning."

"I did, but I didn't want to say anything until we were all together. This is a gift from the whole town, Grace. All you have to do is say yes."

"I—" Grace swiped at her eyes and looked at the people sitting around the table as if she were just seeing them for the very first time.

Finally, she met Sarah's gaze. "I can't say no. Daisy will love this." And in the softest, warmest voice Sarah had ever heard Grace use, she said, "Thank you."

CHAPTER 15

Grace

Grace pulled her car into the driveway and climbed out. Things were amazingly good. The committee meeting had gone even better than she'd hoped, and the offer to help with Daisy—Grace's eyes clouded with tears once again. The town's offer of help had been so generous, and so needed. Grace couldn't help feeling . . . hopeful. Yes, that's what it was. She felt hopeful. And maybe even a little happy.

It was funny, but she'd thought she'd never feel that way again, at least not until she'd moved back to Charlotte. *That just goes to show how little I know myself.*

She collected her purse and satchel and started toward the walk. It had been a great day, and she felt a huge sense of accomplishment about the work she and the committee had done. They could save the town, she was sure of it. *This is what I was trained to do, salvage a dying company.* She smiled to herself and had just put her foot on the sidewalk to walk to the house when she noticed Trav in his driveway, working on his motorcycle.

Grace slowed to a stop. She owed him a word of thanks for his help with Mama G's late-night spaghetti run. *It's the least I can do.*

Still, she hesitated. He really did remind her of herself, private and never totally comfortable around others. Sarah had said that before his time overseas, he used to be different, and more outgoing, but Grace couldn't imagine it. She only knew him as he was now.

She crossed to the fence, tiptoeing over the grass so that her heels didn't sink into the turf. Once she reached the fence, she said, "Hi."

He looked up, his gaze locking with hers.

And once again, it was as if an electric arc ripped between them, linking them together. A flush spread through Grace, and she realized her heart was now thundering wildly.

Oh God. This was a mistake.

He set down his wrench and came to the fence.

It was a small fence, Grace realized, noticing how he towered over it. She fought the urge to turn and run for her own front door and instead gave him a polite smile. "I wanted to thank you for taking care of Mama G when she wandered into your kitchen in the middle of the night."

He pulled a rag from his pocket and wiped his hands, his gaze never leaving hers. "How is she doing?"

"The same. She has good days and bad. But more good days."

"I'm glad to hear that." Something flickered behind his eyes and he tucked the rag back into his pocket. "Enjoy the good days."

She found herself looking at his hands. They were large and calloused. The hands of a man who knew how to work and had done so all his life. She thought of the hands of the bankers and analysts she'd worked with—soft and pale, with perfect nails, not a scar in sight. There were scars all over Trav's hands. Some of them had to have been painful, and yet on he worked.

She looked from his hands to hers. At one time, hers had been like those of the bankers she knew—soft and white and perfectly groomed. Now two of her nails were broken, while ink stained her palm where a marker had leaked while she'd been using the whiteboard at the committee meeting. She closed her fingers and wondered at the differences. She wasn't embarrassed by her efforts, but proud. She was doing something bigger than what she'd worked on in Charlotte. Her job in Dove Pond, while it didn't involve huge amounts of revenue and expenditures, was far more important than anything she'd done before. She was creating something organic and all hers, and it felt—not good. Better than good. She didn't know how to explain it.

"Grace?"

She raised her gaze to his and realized she'd allowed the silence to go on for far too long. "I just wanted to say thank you." Her voice was rushed, breathless, her words inane. *Why didn't I figure out what I wanted to say before I came over here?*

"Mama G reminds me of my dad. There were times he was normal, and then . . ." Trav shook his head. "It's tough."

There was sympathy in his voice, and she had to swallow before she could answer. "It's not easy. I still don't know how she got out of the house."

A faint smile touched his hard mouth. "They're like children, in a way, always doing what you tell them not to."

"I have enough children to take care of with Daisy." Grace looked around. "Where is she? I'm surprised she's not watching you. That has to bother you."

He shrugged and then winced, absently rubbing his shoulder. "She's no trouble."

Grace realized the scars on his shoulder and neck must have pulled as he shrugged, and she wondered what sort of horrific accident must have caused them.

She wanted to ask about that, and about why he lived alone, and about how he'd learned to fix his own truck and motorcycle, and why his house felt so small and cozy when it was large and empty, and—God, there were so many questions she wanted to ask.

But she didn't know where to begin or how, so instead she just said, "I guess I'd better go inside. Thank you again."

His dark gaze never left hers. "Any time."

Face hot, she turned and took a step toward her house but couldn't move. Her high heel had sunk into the grass and was now trapped. She yanked her foot and with a snap, the heel broke. *No! No, no, no!*

Trav hadn't moved from the fence, and there was nothing she could do but pull her foot from her broken shoe, bend down and pick it up, and then—too embarrassed to look his way—hobble inside as quickly as she could.

It was the longest walk she'd ever made and she could feel his gaze with every step. When Grace finally reached the house, she slipped inside, closed the door, and leaned against it. *Gee, what was that? If that was a headline, it would be "World's Most Awkward Woman Embarrasses Herself Without Help from Anyone."*

"Grace?" Linda came out of the kitchen. "I thought I'd heard you. How was work?"

"Better than I'd hoped." Grace dropped her broken shoe to one side of the door and then pulled off the other one and tossed it beside its mate. She walked barefoot into the living room. "How was Mama G today?"

"Today was a good day. I gave her a half cup of Ava's tea and she's been an angel since."

"That's great. Where's Daisy?" Grace couldn't wait to tell her about the deal she'd struck with the committee.

"Upstairs in her bed reading a book."

Grace's surprise must have shown, because Linda said, "I know. Will wonders never cease?" She leaned forward and added in a pointed voice, "She's reading *Little Women.*"

Grace, now halfway to the kitchen, stopped. "The one Sarah sent over?"

"I thought you were supposed to read it, but maybe it was Daisy. You never know about a Sarah book. Sometimes you're just the delivery person." Linda looked at her watch. "Since you're here, I may as well go. Mark is making a quiche."

"Of course. Thank you for your help. I don't know what I'd do without you."

Linda grinned as she gathered her things. "Fortunately, you don't need to worry about that." She headed for the door. "See you Monday."

Grace stared at the closed door for a long time. She'd left *Little Women* beside the front door on the table where she kept her satchel so she'd remember to take the book back to the library. But despite it being in plain sight, she kept forgetting it. It was as if it hid itself whenever she was ready to leave. *What a ridiculous thought. I just missed it, that's all.*

Muttering to herself, Grace went into the kitchen.

Mama G looked up from her tea. "You're home."

"I am." Grace eyed Mama G, evaluating her expression, and was relieved to see her looking like her old self. "And I only brought a very little bit of work with me."

"You and your spreadsheets."

Grace had to smile. "Excel is my friend."

"It always has been."

Grace looked around the kitchen. It was too soon to start dinner, but a snack would be nice. "Do you know what I want? Some hot chocolate." She pulled out a small pan, got the milk from the fridge, and took the powder out of the cabinet over the sink.

Mama G got up. "Here. Let me."

"Stay there. I can do it."

"Hmph. Go sit down." Mama G smiled. "I used to make you and Hannah hot chocolate after school every day. Do you remember?"

"Of course I remember." Grace let Mama G have the pan, but she stayed nearby just in case. "You always make the best hot chocolate."

"It's a gift." Mama G put the pan on the stove, poured in some milk, and turned on the burner. She pulled a spoon from a drawer and shot Grace a questioning look. "You look happy."

"It's been a good day." *Except for the part where I humiliated myself in front of our neighbor.* Except for that, her day had been outstanding. "There are a lot of nice people in this town."

"Oh? Have you changed your mind about staying in Dove Pond?"

"There's not enough opportunity for me here. The clerk position doesn't pay well enough for us to stay."

"Oh, Grace. You can't measure everything in dollars."

"I'm not. But I don't see myself being a clerk for the rest of my life. It's not enough. One day, we're going to want to buy our own house."

Mama G made her usual "I'm not commenting" *hmm*. After a moment, she said, "How are you and Sarah Dove getting along?"

"Good. I like her even though we have very little in common." Grace shrugged. "She says books tell her things."

Mama G nodded wisely. "The Doves have always been different."

"Do you believe she actually hears books talking?"

"Why not?" Mama G set down her spoon and pulled the sugar canister from the back of the counter. "Your spreadsheets do the same thing for you; you just don't call it 'talking.'"

That was an interesting way to look at it. But still . . . "I don't think that's how she means it."

Mama G added cocoa to the milk and stirred. "Sarah's mother used to say that all her daughters had special abilities."

"You make it sound like they're magicians or something."

"They're skilled. Just like you."

"And you." Grace leaned against the counter, watching the expressions play over Mama G's face. She loved this woman so, so much. Even now, she could remember that first moment when she stood on the porch of Mama G's home and knew it was where she belonged. "Do you remember how you used to read to Hannah and me when we first moved in?"

"Oh yes. So many books. Once you learned to read well enough, you couldn't get enough." She began to recall the books Grace had read.

"There were a lot," she admitted.

"Books are a treasure." Mama G stirred the milk a little more. "This is just about ready."

Grace pulled two mugs from the cabinet and filled them. She set the pot on a back burner and, following Mama G, went to sit at the table.

Mama G cupped her mug carefully and then took a sip. She didn't swallow but turned red and then spit it back out in her cup. Muttering, she stood and took Grace's cup and went back to the counter.

Bewildered, Grace asked, "What's wrong?"

"I forgot the sugar."

Grace noticed that the canister was where Mama G had left it, and that it was unopened.

Mama G pulled the pot from the back burner, slapped it onto the front one, and turned on the heat.

But then she didn't move. She just stood there, staring at the pan, her shoulders down.

"Mama G . . ." Grace stood and went to the stove and turned off the burner. "All we have to do is add sugar. It's no big deal. Here. You sit down and I'll—"

"No!" Mama G lifted tear-filled eyes to Grace's. "That's not how this is supposed to happen. *I'm* supposed to make the hot chocolate, not you. It's what *I* do. What *I've* always done."

Grace slid her arm around Mama G's thin shoulders, surprised at how fragile they felt even through both a shirt and sweater. "Forget the hot chocolate. It's not important. I love you."

"I love you, too. But I hate this. I hate forgetting and not knowing. Sometimes I feel as if I'm someone else and I can't even think—" Mama G's lips quivered.

Grace rested her cheek against the older woman's soft hair. She smelled of flowers and cooking, of comfort and safety. "It's going to be okay. I promise."

Mama G slipped her arms around Grace, resting against her. "I used to say that to you when you were little."

"I hope you'll listen better than I did."

Mama G gave a watery giggle. "Probably not."

Grace kissed Mama G's forehead. "Go sit down and I'll bring the hot chocolate. It's my turn."

Mama G nodded and turned away, pulling a tissue from her sweater pocket and wiping her eyes. "I'm making this harder on us both."

"Nonsense. You're scared. To be honest, I'm scared, too. But we're together and that isn't going to change." Grace got the sugar and added it to both cups, and then carried them to the table. "I promise."

"Oh, you promise, do you?"

"You used to promise me all the time." Grace handed Mama G her hot chocolate. "Just hearing you say it made me feel better."

"Of course it did."

"I say it to Hannah all the time, too." Grace winced. "I mean, I *said* it to Hannah. It's been months and I still can't believe she's gone."

"We were lucky we had her with us as long as we did. She never let herself grow attached to anyone. No roots, that girl. None. So when the wind blew, off she'd tumble."

Grace was so glad Mama G was lucid today. Grace had needed this talk, and the truly good moments were getting far too rare. "I'll never understand how Hannah could leave us, especially Daisy."

"Daisy has your anger. That worries me."

"I know. I've seen it."

"You have to talk to her. A lot. Even when she doesn't want to hear it." Mama G reached over and put her hand over Grace's. "The same way I did you."

"I feel like I'm just bothering her."

"That's what mothers do. They bother you until you listen. And they do it because they care. Keep at it, Grace, and don't stop, no matter what she says."

Grace nodded. "As much as I hate to admit it, I think being here in Dove Pond is good for Daisy. It's been good for me."

"I have the best memories of this place." Mama G sighed and looked around the kitchen and her expression softened. "Philomedra and I would play in the backyard while our mothers made Sunday dinner. Sometimes my other cousins would come over and there would be such laughing. So many children. So many women."

"And men?"

"Well, not in the kitchen." Mama G smiled wryly. "But yes, there were men. Philomedra's husband was very helpful."

"He cooked?"

"Lord, the things you say. Not back then, he didn't cook, but he was an excellent eater. Every singer needs an audience, and he was a very appreciative one."

Grace had to laugh. "I suppose things were different back then."

"You have no idea." Mama G sipped her hot cocoa, a faraway look in her eyes. "It's odd—when you look back, things seem simpler, but they weren't."

"Really?"

"When it's a memory, you already know the outcome, so we believe it was an easier time. Looking forward is much more uncertain, and so feels more complicated. But I don't think it is. Not really."

Grace nodded. "I wish Hannah was still with us."

"I know."

Tears stung Grace's eyes. "I keep wondering if it really was an accident, or if—" The words stuck in her throat.

"Oh, Grace. Don't. She accidentally overdosed, pure and simple."

"How do we know that for certain?"

"She wasn't the sort to inconvenience herself, and death is the ultimate inconvenience."

Grace sighed. "I just wish we knew."

"Would it make any difference?" Mama G's gaze darkened as she sipped her cocoa, holding the mug with both hands. "I knew from the moment I first laid eyes on Hannah that she would avoid anything she didn't like and that would be trouble. You could see it in her face. I'd hoped that as she grew older, something might capture her wild heart, that she'd fall in love, if not with a man, then perhaps with her own child. I've seen that happen and it can make a difference. But when she had Daisy and nothing changed, that's when I knew how she'd end up."

"How could someone not care about a child like Daisy? I don't understand that."

"She's a good one, our Daisy. I'm glad she has you. But, Grace . . . you need to talk to her about my illness."

"Why?"

"She thinks it's temporary. I heard her tell Linda that. Daisy needs to know what's happening, what to expect. I'd tell her myself, but she'll be freer to express her thoughts with you."

"I don't want to do that. She's already had to deal with so many bad things."

"The truth is always the best way to go."

"I can't. It'll just make her sad."

"It will. But you'll be there for her."

Grace looked at her cup of hot chocolate. "I don't even know what to say."

"You'll know once you start. And you need to do it soon."

The words hurt, but Grace nodded. "But right now, I need to cook dinner." She got up and set to work, making omelets for them all. She had to call Daisy three times to get her to come down to eat, but she eventually came, so determined to get back upstairs to her book that she stuffed her mouth too full and almost choked. Grace had to tell Daisy to slow down, and the command was met with a glare.

Grace took the opportunity to tell Daisy about the "jobs" the committee had for her. Daisy seemed interested but cautious, and Grace was a little disappointed at the little girl's lack of excitement, although Grace supposed she understood. Daisy didn't know the people in town very well, but she would.

After dinner, Mama G's calm began to slip away. She got irritated when she couldn't find her favorite slippers. Twice she called Grace "Hannah," and even asked where her mother was. When she began to get fretful and even her knitting seemed to irk her, Grace fixed some of Ava's tea, relieved when it worked.

Hours later, after she'd put both Daisy and Mama G to bed, Grace locked up the house and headed to her bedroom, tired from the long day.

She noticed the light was still on under Daisy's door, and she knocked softly. Getting no answer, Grace went in. Except for the small lamp by the bed, the moonlight streaming in through the window on the other side of the room was the only light.

Daisy sat in a chair in front of the window, staring at the moon through the trees. She wore a Wonder Woman nightshirt that was two sizes too big, her blond hair mussed and uncombed.

Grace had expected to find Daisy reading, but the book had been left open on her bed. "Are you okay?"

Daisy never turned her head, the moonlight giving her pale skin a bluish glow. "I'm fine."

Grace came closer. "I was just—" She stopped. "What's that cat doing in here?"

Killer, who'd been curled up beside Daisy, sat up and yawned.

Daisy patted him. "He was sleeping."

"How did he get in the house?"

Killer leapt off the chair, landing on the floor with a solid thump.

"I let him in." Daisy watched him stretch. "He likes to sleep with Mama G."

"But we don't have a litter box or anything."

Daisy shrugged. "Mama G leaves her window open for him."

"Geez. How long has this been going on?"

"I don't know. A few weeks, I guess." Daisy watched the cat meander out the door. "Mama G says he keeps her feet warm."

Grace looked at the empty doorway the cat had just disappeared through. "So that's 'Theo.' I thought she was imagining things."

"Nope." Daisy looked back out the window.

"Are you excited about your new jobs? You can start Monday, if you'd like."

"Yeah, I guess so. It'll be better than just sitting around here."

That was something, at least. Grace tried to think of something to say. Finally, she slid the book over and sat on the edge of the bed. "Is something wrong? I thought I'd find you reading."

Daisy's gaze moved to the open book. "I thought I might like it, but—" She frowned. "It's not really for me."

"I used to love this book."

"The people in the story are so different from me. I don't have sisters or a mother or anything that they have."

"I see." She picked up the book, put Daisy's bookmark in place, and looked through the familiar pages. "Don't you think that's the beauty of a book? It can take you places you can't visit on your own, lets you meet people and see things you can't in real life."

"It makes me sad."

Grace lowered the book. "I think we're all a little sad right now. It's been a crazy few months."

Daisy looked at Grace. "Are you sad?"

"Sometimes." What should she say now? *You'll know*, Mama G had said. Well, she didn't know. She had no idea. None. She sighed. "Daisy, you know Mama G isn't herself. Do you know why?"

"She has Alzheimer's. Mr. Travis told me about it. He said his father had a form of it." Daisy pulled up her knees and tucked her nightshirt over the top of them. "Mama G didn't know my name yesterday."

"That's scary when that happens, isn't it?"

Daisy nodded. "Sometimes she calls me Hannah."

"You look a lot like your mom when she was your age. She was just as pretty as you."

Daisy rested her chin on her knees.

She was becoming smaller, somehow, pulling into a tight ball.

Tell the truth. "Daisy, there may come a time when Mama G doesn't know us. Not even a little."

Daisy didn't move.

"It won't happen at once. Her ability to know where she is will come and go. But it will eventually happen."

"I know."

"You . . . you know?"

"I've heard you and Ms. Linda talk. So I know."

Grace nodded. "It's good you understand. I just—" She held the book tighter and stood, moving closer to Daisy. "Is there anything you want to know? Anything you'd like to ask?"

For a long time, Daisy didn't move. Finally, she said one word. "Why?" The sound was as thin as it was tiny, barely audible even in the quiet.

The pain in Daisy's voice cut Grace like a knife. "I don't know why." She dropped the book back on the bed where it flopped open. "Sometimes things just happen."

Daisy stared outside, not moving.

Grace stayed where she was, trying to find the words. "Listen, Daisy. Whatever happens to Mama G, you and I are going to handle it together. As a family."

"We're just two people."

"Two is enough. And I—" She took a deep breath. "I'm new at this, so I'm learning as I go. But I care so much about you and I want the very, very best for you. Sometimes I have no idea what that is, and sometimes I'm just guessing. I need you to be patient with me and give me some time to learn. Can you do that?"

Daisy looked at her as if measuring her words one at a time.

Grace added, "I don't know what to say when we talk . . . like now. But I want to do this right. I'm going to do this right. But it would help if you'd tell me what you want. What you need. I promise to listen, and I'll never, ever leave you."

Daisy turned to watch the tree outside her window as it waved in the night breeze. "Okay."

Grace tucked a strand of hair behind her ear. "I know these past few months haven't been easy, what with your mother dying, Mama G getting sick, and then moving here, and—"

"Why did Momma have to die?"

I wish I knew. "She didn't make good decisions. She never did. And her death . . . To be honest, it doesn't make sense to me, either. Mama G says it was time. Maybe that was it. I don't know."

Daisy threaded her fingers through her toes where they peeped out from the bottom of her nightshirt. "The girls in the book miss their father."

"They did, didn't they?" Grace looked over to where the book rested. "I bet I read that book a hundred times when I was your age, or a little older. Well . . . a few years older. You're a better reader than I was."

"I like books about families. I guess I like that book, too. It's just hard to read sometimes."

The wistful note in Daisy's voice pinched Grace's soul. She looked down at the book and her gaze locked on a sentence. *"I am not afraid of storms for I am learning how to sail my ship."*

She didn't realize she'd said it out loud until Daisy said, "Amy said that. I love Amy."

Grace smiled. "You look the way I always imagined she'd look, although you're not as prissy as she was."

Daisy straightened and put her feet flat on the floor. "I wish my mother had wanted me."

Up until that moment, Grace had thought her heart couldn't bear any more pain. And the growing anger she felt for Hannah flared brightly. "Daisy, I want you. I want both you and Mama G. We're a family, the three of us. And I'll always be here for you both, no matter what."

Daisy didn't say anything.

"I promise." Grace patted the bed. "Now, come to bed. It's late."

Daisy sighed but she did as Grace had asked.

"You can read a little longer, if you want." Grace tucked Daisy in and bent to give her a kiss. "It's a good book," she whispered against Daisy's forehead. "And we Wheelers are going to be a great family."

Daisy reached up and hugged Grace hard. "You might be a good mom."

Grace had to laugh. *Might. Well, that's the beginning, isn't it.* "You think so, do you?"

"You can practice on me."

Grace gathered the little girl closer and hugged her back, smiling through her tears.

CHAPTER 16

Sarah

Three and a half weeks later, Grace looked up from her list. "Let's see what you've got."

Sarah handed Grace the clipboard. "Fifty-two vendors, not counting the food and beverage area. We've never had so many." They stood in the middle of McIntyre Park, the future site of the biggest Apple Festival Dove Pond had ever seen. The warm summer wind ruffled the flowers, which had settled on a lovely purple color, vivid against the grass.

Sarah eyed the flowers with a smile. They hadn't changed colors since the day Grace suggested combining the Apple Festival with her brilliant outreach idea. And just yesterday, Siegfried had walked past the library and had only turned in a single circle. *We are getting there, aren't we?*

The grassy area had just been mowed, so the scent of warm, cut grass tickled her nose. And as they watched, Lenny Smith added bags of rubber chips to the playground area so it would be extra safe for the children. Lenny saw them and grinned, showing two missing teeth. Sarah thought the maintenance man was more excited about the festival than anyone else in town.

Grace flipped through the pages on her clipboard. "Look at this list of vendors. Erma was on fire. I wonder if we should have reined her in?"

"Heck no," Sarah said.

Grace grinned. "The Apple Festival has returned, a true two-day family event, launched with a bang thanks to Erma's enthusiasm."

"And Zoe and Ed have put together a masterful PR campaign, too. They've bought ads in every local paper within a fifty-mile radius, will be making the rounds of the local radio stations, and have flyers up in every coffee shop and library, too. Plus, almost every business and community group in town has signed up for a tent. It's going to be huge."

"I hope so. If we need to, we can put a few vendors near the food trucks beside town hall."

"Food trucks from Asheville." Sarah couldn't wait. "That was Nate's brilliant idea."

"The whole committee is rocking it."

They strolled toward the sidewalk, pausing to discuss the special electrical needs of certain vendors, and trying to decide the best place to put water stations.

Sarah handed Grace a pen so she could mark their decisions on the site map, glancing up at the sun with a grimace. "It's hot today. They say it's going to rain, but I'll believe it when I see it."

Grace wrinkled her nose. "I hope it doesn't rain during the festival weekend."

"It could happen. It gets wet in the fall."

"We'll need some of the Dove family good luck to hold it off, then." Grace finished marking the map and then she handed the clipboard back to Sarah. "Daisy can't wait to visit the fortune-teller. Linda told her about it. But I'm most excited about Zoe's booth."

"Me too," Sarah said. Zoe and Nate were hosting the "Welcome Home to Dove Pond" hospitality tent. Zoe had invited thirty-two potential business owners and investors to stop by and pick up a gift.

The committee had worked long nights putting together a high-quality investor's packet, complete with a community profile that included a list provided by Kat of the available commercial properties. Meanwhile, Kat's mother was busy making several dozen of her famous baskets, which featured gifts and coupons donated from various businesses in Dove Pond.

If just a tenth of the invitees stopped by the booth, Sarah thought she might weep with happiness. "I think that's it for the day. I guess I'd better get back to work."

Grace grimaced. "Me too."

Sarah and Grace walked up the sidewalk toward town hall.

"What's left on our to-do list?" Grace asked.

Sarah checked the clipboard. "You need to order the banner that will hang over Main Street. When the time comes, someone needs to oversee the hanging of it. Someone other than Lenny. The last time Lenny hung a banner without supervision, it was upside down and crooked."

"Ask Erma to see to that. She's a perfectionist."

"She's doing a kick-ass job on the thank-you cards. She's making them herself, and they're pop-up. I asked if I could have one to keep on my fireplace mantel."

"She's talented," Grace said. "What else?"

"Just two things. We're still waiting on confirmation of an ambulance from the county; we should have one on standby."

"That's just a phone call."

Sarah looked at the list. "Security. Someone needs to talk to Blake and make sure he has a map of the event and knows where the control tent is."

Grace stopped walking. "That's you."

"Oh no, no. I'll call the county EMS. You talk to Blake."

"Nope."

"Grace . . ." Sarah frowned. "Come on. Blake and I are . . . It's awkward."

"It'll always be awkward until you start talking." Grace tilted her head to one side. "What happened with you two?"

"It's complicated. We've had this weird I-like-you-when-you-don't-like-me sort of relationship. First he liked me but I didn't like him, and then I liked him but he didn't like me, and then— You know how it goes."

"If no one liked anyone at the same time, why is it awkward now?"

"There was this one time, just a short week, when we did like each other." Sarah paused. "Or so I thought."

Grace winced.

"Yup, I was wrong. And I didn't realize it until after I'd made a total and very public fool of myself." She scowled. "Blake didn't make it any better, either." She hated to remember that day. *Hated it, hated it, hated it.* "So you can see why you need to talk to him instead of me."

Grace shook her head. "You should do it."

"But I just told you—"

"Sarah, aren't we friends?"

Sarah said cautiously, "I think so."

Grace rolled her eyes. "Of course we're friends. If you thought I needed to do something, wouldn't you tell me? You'd be super honest, even if I didn't want to hear it."

"I suppose I might."

Grace choked. "You know you would. You've done it before."

"True."

"So I'm going to tell you this. Sarah Dove, you should talk to Blake."

One day, Sarah would talk to Blake. She'd say something, and then he'd say something, and it would be so far away from the day they'd hurt one another that it would be easy and painless.

But now was not the time. "I'll do it. Just not now. And hey, if we're going to talk about needing to talk to people, what about you and Trav? I haven't seen you talk to him since the day after Mama G's middle-of-the-night spaghetti heist. I thought for a minute the two of you were going to jump over that fence and go to it right there in the yard and—"

"Don't change the subject." Grace tapped the back of the clipboard that Sarah was now holding in front of her like a shield. "It's time you put an end to the Blake McIntyre madness."

"I will one day."

"Today."

"Why today? I don't see you jumping the fence to tell Trav you think he's—"

"It's not the same. I don't think anything about Trav."

Sarah frowned. "Really?"

Grace flushed. "Fine. I think about him a little. There's this weird spark thing, and I— Darn it, you changed the subject again! We're talking about Blake. That's gone on too long. Way too long."

"I'm not ready."

Grace smiled. "You'd better be."

"Why? What have you d—"

Grace took Sarah by the elbow and spun her around.

Blake stood Right There. And by Right There, she meant that if she bent her arm at the elbow and lifted her hand, she'd have touched him.

He wore his uniform, sunglasses perched on his head, and his green gaze was cautious but not unfriendly. "Grace said you all wanted to talk about the festival. What do you need?"

Sarah didn't have to turn around to know that Grace was already gone. *Some friend.* Irked, Sarah opened her mouth, but no words came out. None. Not a single syllable, a sigh, not even a squeak. Just nothing.

She hugged the clipboard, closed her mouth, and turned on her heel, head down, ready to bolt.

"Hold on!" Blake used his cop voice and she instinctively froze in place. "Let me see that clipboard."

She slowly turned around.

He reached for the clipboard, but she couldn't seem to loosen her grip.

He tugged on it and then muttered under his breath, "Sarah!" His voice was warm with both exasperation and humor. "Let it go."

She'd forgotten how his eyes crinkled when he smiled. And as he did so, she melted, her arms loosening. The clipboard clattered to the ground.

He sent her an exasperated look and then scooped it up. "Grace said you all are having quite an event."

Right. She needed to talk to him about security. *I'm going to kill Grace for this.* Sarah cleared her throat. "We, ah . . . we wanted you to go over the, ah . . ." God save her from a man with green eyes. It was like trying to do complex math while your favorite song played in the background. "The security plan. I need you—I mean, *we* need you to sign it and let us know if you want anything changed and if we need to have more security present or if it's fine the way it is." She said the words so fast they might as well have been one long word.

"Do you have the festival map? I'd like to get an idea of where to put my people."

She took the clipboard and fumbled through the pages, finally finding the one he wanted.

He looked at it. "Will there be any changes to this?"

She shook her head.

He studied it, tracing his finger across the page as he went.

She watched hungrily, mesmerized. He was so close. So, so close. Had his lashes always been so long? Where had that small scar on his chin come from? That was new. It had been years since she'd been this close to him. Her gaze moved down his chest, and she could see the outline of a bulletproof vest under his shirt. *He's being safe. That's good.* She wondered if he still wore the same cologne. God, how she used to dream about that scent. Right now, he was too far away for her to tell. Maybe if she just edged a little tiny bit forward . . .

He flipped the sheet over and pulled out his pen. "I'm going to mark a few things, but overall, it looks good."

Sarah leaned forward even more and took a deep, deep breath. *Oh my God, he is wearing it. The exact same cologne.* She closed her eyes as she soaked it in.

It was lovely.

Heavenly.

Perfect.

She leaned forward a tiny, tiny bit more, and her balance, already made precarious by her nervousness, slipped. She started to rock forward.

Her eyes flew open and she put up her hand.

Suddenly, Grace appeared out of nowhere. She put her arm around Sarah's waist and yanked her back upright. "Hi, Blake! Any questions?"

Blake, who'd been focused on the map, now looked suspiciously from Grace to Sarah and then back. After a moment, he shrugged and asked about the parking situation. He and Grace talked while Sarah stared. *I should kiss him*, she told herself.

Her good side said no. *What if he doesn't kiss me back? I'll look like a fool.*

Her bad side laughed. *You can't look like more of a fool than you already do. Go ahead! Do it!*

Her bad side had a point. A kiss. Just one and—

"Don't you think, Sarah?" Grace asked. She and Blake were now looking at Sarah.

She nodded.

"Good." Blake handed the clipboard to Grace. "I think we've got you covered. I can call in some of the reserve deputies if we need them. I'll make sure there will be two of us available at all times. I'll keep one on standby too, in case the crowd is bigger than expected."

"Reserve deputies?" Grace asked.

He smiled and said drily, "They're retired officers and are service volunteers. There won't be a cost to the town."

"Sorry. We're on a shoestring budget and I promised Mayor Moore I'd keep it that way."

"I understand." He glanced at the park. "From what I'm hearing, it's going to be a good event."

"Sarah was just saying that same thing, weren't you, Sarah?" Grace pinched Sarah's arm.

"Ouch! I mean, yes. You're great. You and the deputies, I mean. All of you—" She nodded. "Thank you. You're wonderf—"

"We've got to go." Grace backed up, pulling Sarah with her. "Thanks, Blake. Sarah and I have a meeting, or we'd stay and talk. I'll let you know if the plan changes in any way."

And with that, they left. Or rather Grace left, pulling an unresisting Sarah with her.

As soon as they were out of earshot, Grace hissed, "What in the heck was that?"

"I told you I wasn't ready."

"That's the understatement of the year. You were paralyzed."

"I managed to talk. A little."

Grace sent her a frustrated glance. "Did you make sense?"

"Now you're getting picky. I just didn't—"

Blake's patrol car rolled past, and Sarah stopped walking and watched it disappear down the street.

Grace stood with her. "I saw you leaning toward him, teetering like a Jenga tower. I was afraid I wouldn't reach you before you fell on top of him."

Sarah's face grew hot. "I was never in danger of falling."

Grace raised her brows.

"Okay, fine," Sarah muttered. "I was a little unstable. Do you think he noticed?" She threw up a hand. "No. Don't tell me. I don't want to know."

Grace slanted her a regretful look. "Why aren't your books helping you with this? Isn't that what they're there for?"

She lifted a shoulder. "You don't tell books what to do. They tell you."

"They sound bossy."

"If you only knew." Sarah scrunched her nose. "Maybe one day I'll find a book that will help, but I've searched, and none of them seem to have a clue."

"When you do, let me know." Grace shook her head. "That didn't work out at all the way I thought it would. I shouldn't have pressed you to talk to him."

"I told you that."

"I know, I know. I thought that if you had to talk to him just once, it would break the ice and you wouldn't have to keep avoiding him. I didn't realize that in facing him, you might also jump his bones."

"In broad daylight, too," Sarah said miserably.

"And on Main Street."

Sarah pressed her hands to her temples and moaned. "I'm horrible. Whenever I see him, I just lose it."

Grace sighed. "That one was on me. What can I do to make it up to you? How about a piece of pie from the Moonlight?"

"Pie always helps." Sarah rubbed her face and then dropped her hands. "He's my one weakness. Well, that and worrying about whether or not our town is going to make it."

Grace's expression softened. "I've never seen anyone care about a place the way you care about Dove Pond."

Sarah looked at Grace. "You like it here, don't you?"

Grace gazed down the street, taking in the sun-splashed sidewalks and the faded awnings. "I do." She sounded surprised.

"It sneaks up on you. I hope your plans help us. No, wait. I don't hope. I know they will."

"They're not just my plans. The whole committee has pitched in and is doing a heck of a lot of work. They've been phenomenal. All of you have been."

"Yeah, well, you've been a great leader."

Grace smiled. "I'll tell you a secret. I've never been completely in charge of anything before."

"What?"

"When I worked in Charlotte, I was a member of a very large group."

"Yeah, but you had to be in charge of something. Surely you were the boss of some sort of project."

"Nope. I did my thing, which was straight analysis, a sort of numbers crunching, and I turned it in. And then I did it again. And again. And again."

"Sounds sort of boring."

"It was, but what's weird is that I didn't realize it. But now ..." Grace tilted her head to one side. "Now I wonder how I'll ever go back."

"You're supposed to stay here," Sarah said firmly. "Dove Pond needs you. *We* need you."

"I would if I could, but I barely make enough to pay my bills as it is. When the year is up, I'm going back to Charlotte to make some real money." Grace caught the disappointment on Sarah's face and she added, "Look, I have to take care of Daisy's future."

"I know. How is she doing?"

Grace brightened. "So, so well. She loves her jobs, as I'm sure you know."

"She's a great help in the library. I'm not sure how I got along without her." Sarah smiled. "She's always welcome there. You know that."

Grace returned the smile. "I do. I can't thank you all enough for what you're doing for her."

"Pssht. You'd do the same for any of us. But enough of that. Did you say something about pie?"

"I did and I'm buying."

"Good, because I left my wallet in your car this morning." Sarah slipped her arm through Grace's and together they walked toward the café, the sunshine warm, the flowers nodding along. "Just so you know, I'm not giving up on you, Grace Wheeler. What Dove Pond wants, Dove Pond gets."

CHAPTER 17

Trav

The rain pattered down, running in sheets off the roof and shaking the shrubs as if trying to dislodge loose apples. Wearing a T-shirt, gym shorts, and sneakers, Trav eyed his weights and tried to find the energy to work out but couldn't. He'd managed only two hours of sleep tonight. Two lousy, unrestful hours. He was so tired that just hearing his own breath irritated him.

He might as well work out. What else did he have to do? He'd just reached the bench when the porch light flipped on next door.

Surprised, he looked at the clock on the shelf over his dad's workbench. One thirty-five. Odd to see the lights on at this time. He went to the garage door opening and watched.

Mrs. Giano stood on the porch, her tiny form lost in a huge, flowered housecoat. She shuffled to the top step and, one hand on the porch rail, the other clutching her robe tie, she looked out at the yard, peering into the rainy night as if looking for something.

"Don't," Trav muttered under his breath. "Go back inside." When Dad's illness had progressed, he'd grown confused about night and day, waking at odd hours and thinking it was time to get up. At first,

Trav would attempt to put Dad back to bed, but it had irked the old man so much that Trav had quit trying. Eventually, whenever Dad would get up, thinking it was morning, Trav would accept it, escort him to the kitchen, and fix them both a big breakfast.

God, how Trav missed those breakfasts in the middle of the night. Even now, they seemed like some of the most peaceful times he'd ever had, even before he'd gone to war.

Mrs. Giano leaned over the step, swaying uneasily. "Here, Theo!" she called.

She's looking for Killer. The cat hadn't come home this evening, which wasn't unusual, considering the rain. The animal was probably bedded down somewhere dry and safe.

"Theo!" Her voice, thin and reedy, was barely audible over the rush of the rain.

Trav looked up at the window where Grace's bedroom was. He was slightly annoyed that he knew which room was hers. One night, completely by accident, he'd seen her closing the shade. She'd been dressed in a pink nightgown, clearly ready for bed, so it took almost no deduction to know where she slept. And right now, her room was dark.

Mrs. Giano wobbled down the steps, gripping the railing as if she were trying to keep her footing on a swaying ship. She blinked up at the rain but it didn't stop her.

"Theo!" she called, clutching her housecoat tighter.

Trav must have made a noise, for she turned his way and, after a second's hesitation, began to shuffle toward him.

The rain increased, the pitter-pat turning into a faint rumble. He could see her nightgown getting darker and wetter by the second, her curly white hair lying flat against her head.

Damn it. He strode to one side of the garage, shook out a small blue tarp, and, holding it over his head, went to meet her.

She'd just crossed through the gate into his yard when he reached her. He held the tarp over her. "Mama G, it's a little late for a walk."

"Late?" She moved from under the tarp and stared up at the sky, squinting into the rain, blinking as tiny drops hit her face.

He moved the tarp back over her. "Let's go home. Grace will know where Theo is."

The sharp *tick tick* of the rain told him it was coming down even harder now. He noticed that Mama G's fluffy slippers were soaked and bedraggled. He winced, thinking of how cold the water must be.

"I can't ask Grace," Mama G said, looking astonished at the suggestion. "She's taking a nap."

"I bet Theo is in your house, hiding somewhere. I think I saw him go in there."

"You did? Maybe I missed him. We'll look again." She patted his arm, smiling pleasantly as if she weren't standing under a tarp in the middle of the night in the rain. "We can have some tea once we find him."

"Sure." He escorted her to her house. When they got there, he threw the wet tarp over the porch railing and followed her through the open door. He didn't dare leave her alone, or she'd wander back outside.

"Theo?" she called, drifting here and there, looking under pillows and in other improbable places.

Trav wiped his feet on the mat and then took a step inside, and there he stood, blocking the door, unsure what to do next. If he yelled for Grace, it would upset Mama G and wake Daisy. Maybe he should text? That was an idea. He'd just pulled his phone from his pocket when Grace appeared on the stairs.

She was dressed in a long silky green sleep shirt, her hair sleep-mussed, faint circles under her eyes.

He'd never seen anyone look so beautiful.

Grace saw him, eyes widening. "What—"

He nodded toward Mama G, who was just now coming out of the sitting room.

"Mama G? How did you get so wet?" Grace hurried down the final steps.

"I've been looking for Theo. He shouldn't be out in this weather."

"We'll find him. Here. Take off that wet housecoat." Grace helped Mama G. "You're shivering. Let's get you into a dry nightgown and back to bed."

"I can't. Theo is outside and it's raining. I thought he might be in here, but he's not." Mama G's face creased with worry. "I can't leave him in the rain. I'll go find him—" She headed back to the door.

Trav stayed where he was, blocking the way.

Grace caught Mama G's arm. "Wait! It's too cold and wet to go outside."

Mama G pulled free, her face tight with irritation. "I'm going to find Theo and bring him home."

"He's at my house," Trav lied.

Both women looked at him.

Mama G regarded him suspiciously. "What's he doing at your house?"

"Sometimes he likes to sleep on the blankets in the corner of my garage. I was working out when he came over, so he settled in." He shrugged. "You know how cats are when it rains. They find a cozy corner, curl up in it, and stay."

Grace nodded. "If he's sleeping, we should leave him alone."

"He'd hate being out in this rain, too." Trav closed the door and then went to one of the windows off the porch and opened it a little. "There. Once it stops raining, Theo will come back home. If you leave your bedroom door open, he'll find you."

"You think he'll come?" Mama G didn't look convinced.

"I know he will. He's a good cat."

"He *is* a good cat." Mama G's brow relaxed, and she said to Grace, "Theo likes to sleep on my bed. He keeps my feet warm."

He used to do the same thing for Dad. "Cats are good for that," Trav said.

"I— Goodness!" Mama G shivered and crossed her arms. "How did these slippers get so wet?"

"Oh dear. We should get you out of those, shouldn't we? Let's go find your other pair." Grace slipped her arm through Mama G's and guided her to the stairs.

As they went up, Grace sent Trav a quick, fleeting smile. "Would you mind waiting for a moment? I'll be right back."

He'd wait longer than a moment. If she asked, he'd wait a lifetime.

The thought shocked him.

He didn't know this woman, not really.

And yet, at this very minute, with one look, he knew everything she was feeling. She was worried and anxious, sad and relieved, all at once. Her feet were cold, but she didn't care, and she was embarrassed to have been seen without her robe.

He didn't know how he knew all of that, or why he was so sure. He just was.

They disappeared up the stairs, Mama G saying in a peevish voice, "I need to put a pillow on the bed for Theo."

"Of course. He'll like that."

Grace returned some time later, this time wrapped in a robe, her hair brushed and clipped up. She looked every bit as sexy as she had before, and he realized it wasn't what she wore. It was just her.

She stopped in front of him. "I just wanted to thank you. If she'd gotten lost in this weather—" She shook her head.

"I know. Dad used to wander, too."

"How did you keep him in?" She sent a worried look at the door. "I don't know how she does it, but she's getting out."

He went to examine the bolt. "She'd have to use a chair to reach that." He looked around. "It doesn't look like anything has been moved."

"I don't think she could move a chair. She's gotten weaker over the past few months." Grace tucked a stray strand of hair behind her ear. "It's frustrating."

"I bet so. Here. I'll bolt the door for you now. If she tries to get out, we'll hear her."

Grace flashed him a grateful look. "Do you mind? She's gotten tricky."

He smiled. "It's like taking care of the world's fussiest and smartest toddler, isn't it?" He bolted the door and turned to find her watching him.

"I know it's late, but I'm going to make some tea for Mama G and myself. Would you like some, too?"

He didn't drink tea. He never had. "I'd like that." And he followed her into the kitchen.

He leaned against the counter as she pulled two tins from a cupboard and set them on the table. Then she filled three mugs with water, put them in the microwave, and turned it on.

"That should do it." She stood by the counter as the water heated. "Have a seat."

He sat in a chair by the table.

The microwave dinged and she pulled out the mugs, put them on a small tray, and carried them to the table. Then she opened a tin and dropped tea bags into two of the mugs.

The smell of the tea made him think of his mom. "Earl Grey."

She smiled, her brown eyes twinkling. "Impressive. But it's Lady Grey. It's not as strong." She crossed to a drawer near the sink and returned with a spoon and a small metal ball on a chain. She spooned some black tea from the other tin into the ball, snapped it shut, and put it into the last cup, the chain hanging over the side. "That's for Mama G. It'll calm her down enough to sleep."

He picked up the tin. "Ava and her teas. I hear she's making a fortune with these."

"That one was a gift, so I'm not sure of the retail value. I asked for the ingredients, and she told me. Doc Bolton said he didn't think they would hurt Mama G or interfere with her medicine, so I use it. I have to say, it works." Grace winced. "Some days, I have to fight the urge to give it to her every ten minutes."

He put the tin back on the table. "The uncertainty can wear you out."

"Exactly." She picked up Mama G's tea. "I'm going to take this upstairs. I'll be right back."

He watched her go and wished he could tell her everything would be all right. That if she ever needed help, he could come over and— *Do what? Moon around your house like a fool? Stay awake all night and wonder what's wrong? You don't need that in your life.*

No, she needed someone who could offer real support. Someone stronger and less restless. *Someone not me.*

The urge to leave overwhelmed him. He stood, but hesitated. It would be rude to just disappear. He should write a note. Something short but nice. He'd just say that he was suddenly tired. He was, although he already knew that going home wouldn't help that.

"Are you leaving?" She was in the kitchen doorway, obviously surprised to find him standing. "We haven't had our tea."

"Right. The tea." He sat back down. "How's Mama G?"

Grace came the rest of the way into the kitchen. "She took two sips and fell asleep."

"That's a relief."

"I hope she stays that way." Grace removed the tea bags, then she pushed the sugar and spoon his way.

She sat down and picked up her mug, resting it against her cheek as she closed her eyes. "That feels soooo good."

He dumped a spoonful of sugar into his tea and stirred it, trying to pull his gaze from her. But he couldn't. Instead, he tried the tea. It wasn't too bad. Just for good measure, he added another spoonful of sugar. "You should set up a camera on that front door and figure out how she's getting out."

"I'm afraid of what I might find. Mama G believes in ghosts, you know." Grace gave a little laugh. "I'm beginning to believe in them, too."

A creak upstairs made her turn toward the door, her expression frozen as she listened.

After a moment, she stood. "Sorry. I keep thinking she might slip away. Would you mind if we moved to the sitting room? I'll be able to see the front door from there."

"Sure." He picked up his mug and followed her.

She pushed aside the lap blanket that hung over the back of the couch and sat down, wincing when he stepped on a creaky board. "Sorry about that. There are a few things that need fixed in this house and that's one of them."

He looked from the empty side of the couch to a nearby chair. It would be more polite to sit in the chair, but he couldn't resist sitting closer to her. He sat down on the couch, using one foot to move Mama G's knitting basket out of his way, careful to give Grace plenty of room. "What else needs fixed?"

"Let me see. There's that floorboard, the railing on the stairs is loose, a few slats on the fence are missing, and the sink upstairs has a slow leak." She pursed her lips. "I think that's all, but there may be more."

"That doesn't sound too bad. I should stop by one afternoon and fix those things for you."

She waved her hand. "No. I couldn't ask you to do that."

He shrugged. "It would let me spend more time with Daisy and Mama G." He laughed at Grace's surprised look. "I know. I can't believe I said that, either. But they've grown on me. Daisy would make a good mechanic. She's a fast learner."

"She's smart." Grace sipped her tea, and her eyes sparkled at him.

"What is it?"

"You. You're so big and bad-ass looking, and yet here you sit, drinking hot tea."

"Bad-asses like tea too. Ask Ava."

Grace smiled. "Ava is a lot of fun, but you're closer to Sarah."

"She's been my closest friend since elementary school."

"She believes in ghosts."

"Sarah believes in fairies, gnomes, and giants, too. She's read too many books."

Grace laughed. "You think so? I think she's read just enough. Well, except on one topic."

"What topic is that?"

She shook her head. "Nothing."

"Let me guess. Blake."

Grace scrunched her nose. "Does everyone know?"

"Pretty much. The people in this town talk. Plus, they're both friends of mine."

"That must be awkward."

"A little. I don't really understand what's going on, but they'll work it out."

"I hope so." She eyed him over her cup. "Since people around here gossip, I daresay you know everything there is to know about me."

He knew some things, sure. People did talk, and because she was new and making changes, she was one of their favorite subjects.

But he didn't know the really important things, like her favorite color, why she wore her hair parted the way she did, or if she knew how adorable she looked in her too-big robe, her bare feet flat on the sitting room rug.

He lifted his mug to take a drink, and his gaze met hers. Time froze. Something sizzled between them, something too hot and raw to be contained or described. He felt it, and he could see that she did, too.

"Trav?"

"Yes?" God, but she had the most delicious lips he'd ever seen. How had he never noticed that until now?

She flushed. "Nothing." She looked at him over the rim of her mug. "Tell me about you."

"There's not a lot to tell. Most of it would bore you."

She smiled. "Try me."

So he did. He told her about his dad. About his friendship with Sarah. About why he liked his motorcycle and the garage. He talked, and she listened and laughed, and every once in a while she'd ask a question that made him wonder why no one had ever asked it before. As he talked, the bitter heat seemed to seep away, eased by the lightness of her laugh and the coolness of her gaze.

A half hour passed and he realized he was talking way too much. Their mugs were empty by the time he paused, his face heating when he realized how much time had passed. "I've been talking enough. Tell me about you." He turned a bit more toward her as he spoke, his foot bumping against Mama G's knitting basket.

Grace put down her empty mug. "Here. Let me move that." She bent down and pulled the basket toward her. "There's not much to tell that you probably don't already know. I've lived—" Her voice caught.

Trav frowned.

She didn't move but stared at the knitting basket on the floor at her feet.

"What is it?"

She didn't answer.

"Grace?"

She took a shuddering breath, then reached into the basket and pulled out a long, ragged chain of red yarn.

As little as he knew about knitting, he recognized that it was a mess. There were tangles and knots in the frayed yarn, as if someone had tugged and pulled it in frustration.

Grace raised tear-filled eyes to his. "She's forgotten how to knit."

He recognized this moment. He'd had the exact same reaction the day he'd realized his dad could no longer recall how to put together an engine, something he'd done hundreds of times before, something that was as intrinsic to who Dad was as his own name.

Grace's lip quivered, and a tear rolled down her cheek. She hugged the tattered yarn as if it were a teddy bear, and she a child.

Trav didn't hesitate. He reached over, pulled her into his arms, and tucked her head in the crook of his shoulder. She hugged the tangled yarn, turned her face toward his shoulder, and with a shuddering sob, she wept.

Trav kept his arms around Grace, his cheek against her hair, wishing with all his heart that he knew how to ease her pain. But there was nothing he could do.

So he kept her there, holding her, rubbing her back, whispering against her hair that it was okay if she cried. That tears were good and helped heal wounds. That if she wanted to talk, he was there, and if she didn't, that was fine, too.

As he spoke, she quieted, but she made no move to leave the circle of his arms.

Carefully, Trav leaned back, pulling her against him. He found the blanket that rested over the back of the couch and tugged it over her, tucking her in.

And there he stayed.

A short time later, they fell asleep, cozy under the blanket, wrapped in each other's arms, his shirt still damp from her tears.

Trav awoke so slowly that for a minute, he didn't know he was awake. He blinked sleepily at the unfamiliar ceiling, trying to fight his way through the edges of a delicious dream.

Something was different. Something important.

It took him a moment to realize what it was. A warm body snuggled against him, a rounded arm slung over his chest, silky hair tickling his cheek.

Heaven.

But it was more than that. It was the flood of early-morning sunshine that lit the room. It was the fact he'd just awoken from a deep, deep sleep.

He blinked awake. *Oh my God, I slept through the entire night.*

How long had it been since he'd done that? A year? Two?

Grace stirred, snuggling deeper, fitting against him as if made to be there, and he suddenly remembered Mama G's knitting basket and Grace's agony from the night before.

He tugged the blanket higher over her shoulder and rested his cheek back against her hair. He would have to leave soon, before anyone else in the house was awake, but for now, he'd stay where he was, holding her for as long as he could.

CHAPTER 18

Grace

Grace pulled her Honda into the driveway and turned off the engine, the lights shutting off as the rain battered against the car roof. It was raining cats and dogs, pale flashes of lightning rippling through the air, an occasional rumble popping up now and then. *Better to wait here until it lightens up.*

Smiling, she closed her eyes and leaned back in her seat, tired but happy.

It was late, but Linda had promised to stay until eight, so Grace had ten more minutes before she had to be inside. Ten minutes to sit here and rest and go back through her mental check list. The festival was a scant month away, but she was 99.9 percent sure everything was in place.

Thunder rumbled a little closer, and rain sluiced down. This past month had been a blur. Every time she thought they were set with their plans for the festival, someone on the committee would come up with another great idea. But it was more than the festival. Other things were moving along at a terrific pace.

Daisy was sill enjoying her "job" as Official Town Helper, as Sarah called it, and Grace couldn't believe the difference in her niece. She wasn't always in a good mood, but her outbursts had disappeared and she was quickly making friends with everyone in town. Her "job" had made her transition into Sweet Creek Elementary successful too, as she already knew most of the kids from helping with Sarah's Children's Hour.

Grace was making friends as well—good ones. Ones she couldn't imagine not having in her life, especially Sarah. Grace had grown to love the quirky, book-loving, Dove Pond–adoring librarian. As opposite as they were, in some odd way, Sarah's loose, unplanned approach to life balanced out Grace's overly structured one.

And then there was Trav. Her head still against the headrest, she opened her eyes and looked at his house. His lights were on, and she had to fight the urge to text him an invitation to come over, late as it was. Since that night over a month ago when she'd had a meltdown upon finding Mama G's knitting basket, Trav had become something of a fixture at their house. The day after that dreadful night, he'd shown up with a bag of tools and set out to fix every creak and leak that made their rental less than perfect.

Grace appreciated his efforts, but more than that, it was nice having him around. He teased Daisy and was gentle with Mama G. He was quiet, but funny and smart when he did talk. She loved his wry comments.

She also liked that he'd never once put himself forward after the night she'd slept wrapped in his arms. She was aware that he watched her, though, his dark gaze following her every move. Grace wasn't sure what to make of that and she sometimes wished he would say or do something . . . more. Maybe he was waiting on her? She wasn't sure.

Well, she had time. She wasn't planning on leaving anytime soon.

Sighing, she dropped her gaze to her satchel and pulled out her binder, flipping through it to double-check the items. One month from tomorrow would be the culmination of the committee's work, Dove Pond's very own fresh, newly imagined Apple Festival, two days of stellar family fun. Grace couldn't wait.

The rain let up some, and, seeing her chance, she collected her things and hopped out of her car, opening her umbrella as she went. She tugged her sweater closer and kept her gaze on the sidewalk to avoid puddles. She was halfway up the walk when she realized the front door was standing wide open.

She stopped in her tracks. Something was wrong.

It wasn't just the door.

It was the silence.

At this time of the night, she should hear the jazz Mama G liked, or Daisy and Linda talking. But the house was completely silent.

Grace's heart tightened, and she hurried to the porch, ignoring the splashing rain as she dashed up the crooked steps. She tossed her open umbrella to one side as she hurried into the foyer. "Linda? Daisy? Mama G?" she called.

No one answered.

She dug in her purse for her phone, frowning to see that there were no messages. She called Linda, but it went straight to voice mail.

Irked, she dropped her phone on a side table and hurried through the house, going from room to room, her footsteps echoing loudly.

The house was lit as usual, the blinds drawn, table lamps ablaze, the lights in the dining room and kitchen on, as they usually were. But where were they? What had happened? Had someone been hurt? As she searched the house, she looked for the telltale marks of an accident—a broken vase, a drop of blood, a piece of furniture out of place.

But everything was as it should be. Mama G's cell phone was tucked in her knitting basket, where she usually left it and then forgot about it. Daisy's bedroom door was ajar, *Little Women* open to the final chapter. Linda's lunch box, part of her dieting efforts, still sat on the kitchen counter. A nearly empty cup of tea sat in the sink.

Nothing was off. Not a single thing.

Which was even more terrifying.

Images began to flicker through Grace's mind, her overactive imagination spurred by her growing panic.

She turned back to the door, took two steps, and then stopped. Where did she start? Had they gone for a walk? Not at this time of the night. And not in the rain. And heaven knew they wouldn't have left the front door wide open.

She should . . .

She blinked. God, she had no idea. But something was wrong. Terribly wrong.

She went back to the porch and noticed that only one set of wet tracks led inside—her own. If something had happened and an ambulance had come, it had to have been before the rain began, which was hours ago. But then why hadn't someone called her?

Where are they? Lightning flashed across the black sky, followed by the sharp crack of thunder. She jumped, her heart already pounding wildly, and hurried back inside. *Please, God, let them be okay.*

Hands shaking, she found her phone and dialed. She'd barely stammered out one sentence before Sarah said, "Wait for me there."

Grace called Trav next. He arrived before she put the phone down. He took one look at her and, in two strides, had crossed the room and enveloped her in a hug. "You've already searched the house?"

"Yes. They're not here. No one is. I tried Linda's phone, but it went straight to voice mail and I—" She looked at Trav. "What do I do? I have no idea where to start." Grace gave a broken laugh. "You know, growing up, Mama G did everything for me—packed my lunches, bandaged my cuts, taught me how to fight my worst tendencies. When I was little, she even cut my hair. She didn't do it particularly well, but she tried. And now, I don't even know where she is or where to start looking for her or Daisy or—"

"Grace." Trav's warm hand closed over hers. "Take a deep breath. We're going to find her and Daisy. Did you call Sarah?"

"Yes." Grace bit her lip. "You think a book will tell her where—"

He shook his head. "But she'll know what to do. Did you call Blake?"

"Why would— Oh. Blake, of course. He's the sheriff." She reached for her phone, but Sarah appeared in the doorway, her rain slicker dripping, Ava close behind. Big umbrellas rested on the porch behind them.

"We are calling Blake," Trav said.

"I just spoke to him." Sarah looked at Grace. "Do you have any idea where they went?"

"No. The door was wide open and the house was left empty."

Ava and Sarah exchanged glances. Sarah came forward. "We were thinking that perhaps Mama G wandered off, with Daisy and Linda in hot pursuit."

"That can't be it," Grace said. "Linda would have called me. I know she would have."

"I'm sure there's a reason why she didn't. Whatever happened, don't worry. We're on it."

"We?"

"Us. Dove Pond." Sarah's smile warmed. "I didn't just call Blake. I called the prayer chains, too."

"The what?"

"There are two churches in Dove Pond. Half of the people go to one, half to the other. They each have a prayer chain. You call one person, and they call the next, and they call the next. Everyone knows who they have to call. In about ten minutes, every person in Dove Pond will be out looking for Mama G."

"Oh, thank God."

Sarah's phone rang, and she pulled it out of her pocket. "Hi, Ed. No, no. No word yet. Okay. That sounds good . . . Yes, I called Blake. Of course I did. He said for you guys to cover the town and the main buildings. His squad car has a searchlight, so he's going to check the farms and such. He doubts they're that far away, but better safe than sorry." Sarah listened a minute and then she nodded. "Good idea. Can you do that? . . . Great. Okay. We'll start here." She hung up and looked at Trav. "Ed wants us to go up and down this street and check all the houses and sheds. They might have taken shelter once the rain started. He's already got people assigned to the other streets."

"Which streets?" Grace asked, feeling as if her world was tilting wildly.

"All of them," Sarah said. "Ava, you and I should get started. Blake asked Ed to set up a control center at the Moonlight. Zoe's on her way there, but first she's stopping at town hall to pick up the city's walkie-talkies."

"She won't have the key," Grace said.

"She's meeting Mayor Moore there. She was going to call him as soon as I hung up."

"He won't answer his phone. He gets bad reception at his house."

Sarah snorted. "Did he tell you that? He'll answer the phone for Zoe. And if he doesn't, she'll drive over and grab him by the ear." Sarah turned to Trav. "Text me the second you find anything. I can alert the others. And none of your brief, noncommunicative texts, either. We need details. It'll save you a phone call."

"Fine. Details. Got it."

"I'll need my coat." Grace started for the closet, but Sarah shook her head.

"No. You need to stay here."

"I can't just sit here while Mama G and Daisy are out there."

"You have to. Someone needs to be here when they come back."

A clap of thunder rumbled ominously. Grace found it hard to swallow, her heart aching. "I have to come."

Sarah's face softened. "You're the one they're going to want to see when we get them home, the one they'll ask for. You *have* to be here."

As much as Grace hated to admit it, Sarah was right.

Grace's shoulders slumped. It cost her dearly and tears stung her eyes, but she managed to nod her agreement. *What if Mama G has fallen into a ditch or been struck by a falling tree limb, or—*

"Grace, don't." Trav's deep voice interrupted her increasingly panicked thoughts.

As she met his gaze, she saw his concern, but more than that, she saw his deep reassurance. "She's going to be fine," he said.

"They will all be fine," Sarah said, nodding firmly, her eyes bright. "I promise."

I promise. It was an empty promise, but now that Grace was an adult, she knew what it really meant—that no matter what happened, they would be there to help her deal with it.

"We've got to go." Sarah headed for the door, Trav following. Sarah's phone rang as she stepped out onto the porch, and Grace strained to hear what she was saying as she dashed off through the rain.

Ava had stopped by the door. "Make yourself some of Mama G's tea."

"I thought it would only work for her?"

"It only works when it's needed. Make some." Ava waved, and then was gone.

Grace remained where she was, listening to the rain pouring down. Outside, thunder cracked loudly, and the lights flickered. She couldn't bear to think of her loved ones out in this weather. They must be so frightened.

Grace found her phone and sank down on the chaise.

Please let them be found.

Please let them be found.

Please let them be found.

She didn't know how long she waited. It might have been ten minutes, or it might have been an hour. She waited as the lightning flashed across the black sky and the rain poured down. She sat.

Then she paced.

Then she sat some more.

Her phone buzzed, and she almost dropped it in her eagerness to read the text. It was Trav. *Someone saw Linda and Daisy earlier. Checking it out now.*

Grace waited, staring at the phone. It was funny how time slowed when you most wanted it to hurry. As if it liked to tease the desperate into losing hope.

She raked a hand through her hair and remembered all the times she and Mama G had waited for news of Hannah, back when she'd been so young and had first started running off. *You'd think I'd be good at this by now.*

But she wasn't. If anything, she was worse.

The minutes ticked on relentlessly.

Unable to sit still, she stood and paced again, her gaze locked on the phone screen.

She didn't have long to wait.

Found them, Trav wrote. *They are fine.*

"Yes!" Grace texted back, *They? All three? Mama G too?*

She waited.

Not Mama G. Still looking.

Tears burned her eyes. *Are you bringing them home?* she asked.

Soon. They want to help search.

Grace waited, fighting the urge to ask a thousand questions. Finally, she typed in, *Any news about Mama G?*

There was no answer.

She dragged her hand through her hair, realizing she was still dressed for work. That seemed wrong, so she kicked off her high heels and ran upstairs to change. She tugged on jeans, a T-shirt, and sturdy boots in case she needed to go out in the weather.

That done, she went back downstairs.

The house was painfully silent.

Tea. Ava had suggested tea.

Grace went to put some water on to boil, wishing her hands didn't shake so much. She'd just reached over to turn on the stove when her phone buzzed.

Got her, Trav had texted.

Got who? Mama G? And what did he mean, "got"? God, didn't this man know she needed information? More than two lousy words? As if in answer, another text showed up. *Mama G might need Doc Bolton.*

Grace gulped a sob. Might? What the hell?

She'd started to call him when she got another text, this time from Sarah. *Trav is an idiot. Ankle sprained, but nothing more. Doc Bolton on way to your house.*

Grace kissed the phone as another text arrived, this time from Trav. *She's fine, Grace. She's going to be okay.*

Grace stood in the middle of the kitchen, not sure where to go or what to do, so happy she felt as if she could fly.

Blankets.

Dry clothes.

Towels.

She should get those. She ran upstairs, frantically collecting some of each, and then hurried back downstairs.

She'd just piled them on the chaise when her driveway filled with lights. Two trucks, one of them Trav's, pulled up.

She grabbed a blanket and hurried onto the porch as Trav walked up the sidewalk, carrying a bundle, Ava following. Mama G's pale face rested near his shoulder, and she was wrapped in a blue tarp, which looked far too much like a shroud for Grace's comfort.

Trav stepped onto the porch, water pouring off him and the tarp, the porch light spilling over them. He carefully set Mama G on one of the chairs and tugged off the tarp.

She sat half upright, limp but alive, soaked through and through and shivering, her chin moving as her teeth chattered. She had one hand on her leg, and she winced when her heel touched the floor.

Grace wrapped her in a blanket, hugging her swiftly. "I was so worried about you!"

Mama G tried to talk, but her teeth chattered too much for Grace to understand her.

"I'll go make some tea." Ava disappeared inside, pausing by the door to remove her wet raincoat and hang it up.

Grace looked at Trav. "Can you take Mama G inside? We've got to get her warm."

Trav nodded and bent to wrap the blanket more tightly around Mama G. He picked her up and carried her through the door and into the sitting room, where he gently placed her on the couch. He nodded toward the fireplace, which hadn't been used since she'd first moved in. "Should I start a fire? It'll warm the house faster. There's wood on the end of the porch; it should be dry."

"That would be nice." Grace put a pillow under Mama G's injured leg and tucked her in with the lap blanket that hung over one end of the couch. Mama G leaned back and closed her eyes, looking as fragile as glass.

Trav left and came back with some split logs and a handful of bark. "There's no kindling, but this should work."

Grace watched as he set the fire. "Where did you find Mama G?"

"About three blocks over, in the field behind the elementary school. I don't think she knew where she was. The lightning frightened her."

"I'm so glad you found her."

"I didn't." He reached up on the mantel and pulled down the box of matches Mrs. Phelps had left there. "The Spankles did. They live beside the elementary school."

Ava returned from the kitchen, apparently just catching Trav's comment. "When the Spankles got the prayer call, one of their kids mentioned that he'd seen a ghost out in the yard earlier."

"It wasn't a ghost," Trav added unnecessarily as he lit the chunks of bark where they stuck out between the logs.

Ava grinned. "Not this time."

"Where're Daisy and Linda?" Grace asked.

"With Sarah. They're on their way here."

The fire crackled to life, and soon the welcome warmth soothed Mama G's shivers.

Someone knocked on the door and Trav went to answer it.

"Hello!" Doc Bolton came inside, a bag in his hand.

Trav took the doc's wet coat.

"Heck of a night for a stroll, isn't it?" Doc went to Mama G and took her wrist, patting her hand as he took her pulse. "Causing trouble, are you?"

Mama G stirred, tugging weakly on her arm. She looked exhausted, although her teeth had stopped chattering. "What are you doing?"

Grace knelt beside her. "Doc Bolton came to visit and we're going to have some tea. I— Oh, the tea." She looked at Ava.

"I'll go see if it's ready." Ava disappeared back into the kitchen.

"Tea?" Mama G blinked in confusion.

"Something hot to drink would do you some good," Doc said. "But first, we should get you into some dry clothes and into bed."

Sarah looked at Trav. "Would you mind?"

"Sure." Trav picked up Mama G, swinging her into his arms as though she weighed no more than a feather pillow.

Mama G protested weakly, but Trav would have none of it. "Mrs. Giano, do you remember when you used to babysit the Parker boys?"

Mama G stared at him. "The Parker boys." A weak smile touched her mouth. "You are all trouble, do you know that?"

"I once took a cow to church, or so I've been told." He carried her upstairs, repeating the story she'd told him more than once.

Grace turned to the doctor. "If you'll give me a moment, I'll get her into her nightgown."

"Of course. She seems fine, but I should look her over before I leave."

"I will. Thank you for coming."

He smiled. "It's what I do."

She hurried upstairs. Trav was with Mama G, who sat on the edge of her bed, looking tired. "Thank you, Trav," Grace said. "I'll take it from here."

"Call if you need me."

He went to leave the room, but as he walked past her, Grace slipped her arms around him and gave him a quick hug.

He rested his cheek on her head and hugged her back.

She would have stayed like that, warm and safe, but Mama G put her hand on her nightstand and tried to get up, wincing when she put weight on her hurt ankle.

"Mama G!" Grace released Trav. "I've got to get her into a nightgown."

"I'll be downstairs. The fire will need tending."

"Thank you." She hoped he knew how much she meant it.

After he left, she helped Mama G dry off and into a nightgown. Mama G, tired and fretful, complained, but Grace kept her tone light even when her eyes filled with tears at the bruises and scrapes she saw on the older woman's legs.

Finally dressed, her damp hair combed, Mama G was tucked under her blankets, a mound of pillows behind her head. Her lip quivered as she looked wearily at Grace. "I don't understand."

Grace kissed Mama G on the forehead. "You got lost. That's all. But everything is fine now."

Outside, the rain eased. *We are almost back to normal*, Grace told herself.

Mama G plucked at her covers. "I was looking for Theo." She looked around the room. "Where is he?" She tried to push herself upright. "He hates the rain."

"He's fine. Here. We'll put a pillow at the foot of your bed for when he comes home. He likes that."

"He does, doesn't he?" Mama G settled back against her pillows. "He keeps my feet warm."

"Of course he does." Grace adjusted the covers, noticing that Mama G's skin appeared almost translucent, the blue veins visible. She looked so fragile, so delicate. Grace brushed the back of her fingers across Mama G's cheek. "Doc Bolton wants to see you for a minute, to check your ankle."

"It hurts."

"I know. That's why he needs to see it. After he's done, I'll bring you some of your special tea."

Mama G nodded. "I like my tea."

Grace smiled. "Then you shall have two cups."

Outside, a car pulled into the drive, followed by another.

Grace kissed Mama G and turned to leave, glad to find Doc Bolton waiting in the hallway. He winked at Grace as she left, but she found herself too choked up with gratitude to do more than give him a tremulous smile.

She reached the sitting room, where she grabbed a towel from the stack before she hurried onto the porch.

Daisy, sopping wet, jumped out of one of the cars almost before it had stopped. She flew up the walkway and into Grace's arms.

"Oh, Daisy," Grace said, holding her tight.

Daisy burst into tears.

"Hey, it's okay. Mama G is here and she's fine."

Daisy sobbed harder.

Grace pulled the little girl inside, settling her on the couch in front of the fire. Grace knelt in front of Daisy, holding her tight and ignoring the water that seeped from her clothes. "I was so worried about you."

Daisy, still burrowed in Grace's arms, spoke so fast that her words tumbled over one another even as shivers racked her thin body. "She w-w-was here and I opened the door and then she w-w-was gone and Ms. L-L-Linda and I l-l-looked for her, but we didn't know w-w-w-where she went and Ms. Linda's cell phone d-d-died and no one knew where we w-w-were and it w-w-was raining so hard and I—" Daisy sobbed.

Grace hugged Daisy tighter and rested her cheek against the girl's wet hair, catching sight of Trav. She mouthed the words *hot chocolate* and he sent her a warm smile, then disappeared into the kitchen, where she could hear him talking to Ava.

Grace rocked Daisy, letting the girl weep. Finally, Grace said, "Whatever happened, you're home safe now. You're okay."

This seemed to calm her, for Daisy caught her breath and pulled back. Hiccupping, she gave Grace a miserable, tear-stained look. "M-Mama G got lost b-because of me."

"Oh, honey. It wasn't your fault. She gets confused. That's why I put the bolt on the door, but she's found a way around it, so—"

"It wasn't her. It was me." Daisy gulped loudly. "I undid the bolt. I've been undoing it every night after you went to bed."

Good God. "But . . . why?"

"Killer likes it here. If Mama G's window isn't open, he scratches on the door."

Grace laughed wryly. "That darn cat." She got up to fetch another towel, wrapping it around Daisy. "So you've been unlocking the door and letting him in." She should have thought of that.

"I use a kitchen chair to reach it. But I always put it back. I didn't want you to know I was doing it." Daisy looked at Grace with a miserable expression. "I thought you were just trying to keep Killer out. I didn't know you were trying to keep Mama G safe. I didn't think—"

She sobbed again, and Grace pulled her closer. "Oh, honey. I should have told you. But it's all right. Mama G is fine. Doc Bolton is with her now and he doesn't look the least worried, so we don't need to be."

"I just wanted Killer inside."

Grace rested her cheek on Daisy's head. "It *is* raining . . . and I've heard that he hates the rain."

Daisy pulled back, sniffling. "You'd let Killer inside?"

"I guess I'm going to have to, seeing as both you and Mama G have fallen for him." She looked around. "I wonder where he is now? That poor cat."

Daisy wiped her face with the end of the towel. "He's under my bed. He doesn't like thunder."

"No one does, do they?" Grace hugged Daisy. God, but she loved this child. She remembered being at the hospital with Hannah and holding Daisy for the first time. It had been so very special. So right. *And now she's mine to care for. Mama G was right; that's a gift.* "Come Monday, I'm going to call the Callahan brothers and have them install a cat door for Killer."

Daisy looked up at her, her blue eyes reddened by tears. "Really?"

"Yes. I'd do anything for you and Mama G."

Daisy's smile made Grace think of a rainbow after the rain.

A ruckus arose on the porch and Sarah, Linda, and Linda's husband, Mark, appeared in the doorway, Ed and Maggie Mayhew not far behind.

Sarah closed the door and they all peeled off their wet raincoats and hung them on the coatrack. "We've called off the search."

"Everyone is accounted for." Mark took off his ball cap and hung it over his coat. "Jules Stewart is serving hot coffee to the rescue parties at the Moonlight."

"But no snacks," Ed said, obviously disappointed.

"She would have, if we'd been out longer." Linda looked at Grace. "How's Mama G?"

"Tired and a little bruised, but she's going to be okay."

"Thank God for the First Baptist Church prayer chain," Ed said.

Linda snorted. "You mean the Dove Pond Methodist prayer chain."

"No, I mean the Baptist prayer chain. The Spankles are Baptists."

"Yes, but Lisa Tilden saw me and Daisy at the corner and she called the Methodist prayer chain and let them know where to find us, so she was first."

Ed rolled his eyes as he went to stand in front of the fire. "You and Daisy were never lost."

"We were stuck in a doorway because of the lightning and thunder." Linda turned to Grace. "My uncle was struck by lightning. I never go out in it if I can help it."

"I hope your uncle recovered."

"It turned his hair white, but my aunt said he was an animal in the sack after that, so it wasn't all bad." She looked around. "Where is everyone else?"

"Doc is upstairs with Mama G," Grace said. "Trav and Ava are in the kitchen making tea. Would you throw me another towel? Daisy has been using this one as a tissue."

Mark picked up a towel, rolled it into a tube, and started to toss it.

Linda muttered at him, then snatched the towel out of his hands and marched it across the room to Grace. "Here."

Grace wrapped the towel around Daisy.

Linda sat down. Her hair was soaked, and it clung to her head, although small curls were already beginning to pop up. "Grace, I'm sorry we left without calling you. I gave Mama G some of her tea before bedtime and had taken the empty cup to the kitchen. When I came back, she was gone. I was out of that room a minute, maybe less. When I realized she'd escaped, I grabbed Daisy and took off, thinking Mama G would be right outside. I had my cell with me, too, figuring I could give you a buzz if it took longer than a few minutes to find her. I didn't realize the stupid thing was dead, and once Daisy and I got down the road, the thunder started up and the rain grew worse, so we took shelter under the Kavanaughs' porch. They're visiting their kids in New Jersey, so I knew we wouldn't bother anyone. I figured that once the rain let up, we'd find Mama G and bring her home, but apparently Daisy and I headed the wrong way, and the rain—"

Grace put her hand over Linda's. "I can't thank you enough for keeping Daisy safe and trying to find Mama G. I owe you big-time."

Linda blinked back tears. "I was so worried."

"Me too, but everything is okay now."

The kitchen door swung open and Ava appeared. She carried Mama G's cup of tea and a little plate with two peanut butter crackers. As she went up the steps, she called back, "There's coffee in the kitchen if anyone wants some, and Trav's making hot chocolate."

"Coffee," Ed Mayhew said fervently, heading for the kitchen.

Linda got up. "I need something warm. Grace, do you want some coffee?"

"Not right now, thank you."

Linda headed into the kitchen while Mark followed.

Sarah brought a blanket to Grace. "Daisy looks cold."

Grace tucked the blanket around Daisy. "What you need is a hot bath," she told the child.

Daisy snuggled under the blanket. "After I have some hot chocolate?"

"Immediately after."

Daisy nodded meekly, and Grace smiled. The meekness wouldn't last; the child had too much spirit.

Sarah looked at the chair Linda had just left, and she carefully pushed it out of the way and replaced it with its mate. "Wet seat," she told Grace. Sarah sat in the new chair and threw her legs out in front of her, basking in the warmth of the fire. "Whew. What a storm. The Cramers lost a tree. They're two streets over. It hit their truck but missed the house."

Grace smiled but didn't answer. She suddenly felt so overwhelmed by all that had happened, too full to speak.

As if she knew, Sarah went on to list all the different storms that had come through Dove Pond over the years, her tone low and soothing.

Grace half listened, Sarah's voice doing a lot to ease her tension.

After a while, Maggie came out of the kitchen, Ed following. Maggie handed Daisy a cup of hot chocolate. "Here you go, sweetie. Trav said you liked extra marshmallows, so that's what you've got."

"Thank you." Daisy took the hot chocolate and soon had a thin line of marshmallow crème on her upper lip.

Maggie turned to Grace. "If you don't need anything else, Ed and I are going to head out."

"You've both been such a help." Grace stood and gave them each a hug, then walked them to the door, leaving Sarah with Daisy. "Thank you."

He beamed. "It wasn't anything you wouldn't do for us."

"Ed's calm now," Maggie confided, looking at her husband with admiration. "But you should have seen him when the call came through. He was all business."

"I don't know what we'd have done without him."

Ed beamed. "Thanks. Come on, Maggie. It's getting late."

Grace saw them out just as Ava and Doc Bolton came downstairs.

"How is she?" Grace asked.

Doc Bolton removed the stethoscope from his neck and dropped it into his bag. "Blood pressure is a little high, but no more than expected."

"And her ankle?"

"It'll be stiff in the morning. She'll need to rest it, but other than a few scratches and bruises, she's fine."

"I'm so glad to hear that. I don't know what would have happened if we hadn't found her. Thank you so much for coming."

"My pleasure. Now that the county EMS is available, I don't get many late-night calls. I sort of miss them." He grinned. "Makes me feel like Dr. Quinn."

"Would you like some coffee?" Ava asked.

"Actually, I'd like some of that tea you made."

"Oh, it won't help you."

"No, but with a little luck, I'll figure out what's in it."

Ava sent him a surprised look. "I already told you what's in it."

"Did you? I tried to re-create it but my brew, while tasty, didn't have any other effect."

"Maybe you need a little magic to go with it."

"I don't believe in magic."

"That's your loss." Ava grinned as she and the doctor went into the kitchen.

"She'll never tell, and he'll never figure it out," Sarah said with satisfaction. She scooted her chair closer to the fire. "My, this is cozy."

Grace couldn't agree more. She watched Daisy drink her hot chocolate, smiling when the little girl licked marshmallow off the edge of her cup.

Linda and Mark came out of the kitchen. "We'd better get going. We don't trust our daughter to be alone this late. She's at the party-hard stage."

Linda looked at Daisy. "Don't get any ideas. She stays grounded all the time."

"Daisy knows better, don't you?" Mark asked.

Daisy nodded. "I don't party. Not yet, anyway."

Grinning, Mark gathered his and Linda's coats. "Before we go, Ed was telling me there's going to be a beer garden at the festival?"

"Featuring eight local craft brewers, no less," Grace announced with satisfaction.

"And Nate thinks he can get a few more," Sarah added.

"That's great," Mark said. "My cousins are coming up from Hendersonville that weekend. I can't wait to tell them about it. What time will the tap turn on?"

"Eleven sharp on Saturday, and one o'clock on Sunday."

"We'll be there at eleven-oh-five the first day," Linda said. "You have to give them time to set up and let a little air out of the taps. It's the only way to get a proper pour."

"Wow." Sarah's eyes sparkled. "Linda, that's some impressive beer knowledge you have there."

"Oh, I know my craft beers," Linda said proudly.

"You know a lot about everything." Grace gave Linda a big hug. "Thank you again for all you did tonight."

"I'm just sorry my blasted phone died. I need to get one with a better battery."

"Yes, you do," Mark said as he helped Linda into her coat, and then tugged on his own. "You don't answer half of my text messages because of that stupid battery."

"If you didn't send me two hundred texts a day, my battery might last longer," she retorted as she slipped her arm through his. She waved at the others. "Good night."

They left, and Sarah beamed at Grace. "The festival is going to be huge. Everyone is talking about it."

"Apparently so." She looked down at Daisy. "I'd better get Daisy into her bath and then to bed."

Daisy, who'd finished her chocolate and was now yawning widely, nodded sleepily.

Grace held out her hand. "Come on, sweetheart."

Sarah stood. "Go ahead. I'll clear everyone else out."

"Would you mind? I'm so very tired."

"Of course I don't mind." Sarah slid the fire screen in front of the fire. "I'll lock up."

"Thank you," Grace said. And although she didn't list all the many, many things she was thanking Sarah for, Sarah knew.

She smiled. "Go, put that kid to bed."

Grace bundled up Daisy and took her upstairs. She heard voices downstairs for just a bit longer, and then the front door closed and all was quiet.

After a quick bath, Grace dried Daisy's hair, pulled her nightshirt over her head, and then tucked her into bed. Daisy, so tired she could barely keep awake, turned on her side under the covers, mumbled a good night, and instantly fell asleep.

Grace, every bit as exhausted, stopped by Mama G's room. She slept, one hand under her cheek, her hair soft and curly and just as white as her pillow. At her feet, perched on his pillow like a king, lay Killer.

He opened his eyes when Grace came in but didn't move.

"Well, Theo. I guess you're here to stay."

He closed his eyes, unimpressed with her generosity.

Shaking her head, Grace went to her room and got ready for bed. As she slid under the covers, she thought about her evening. She'd needed her friends tonight, and the people of Dove Pond had come without question, without complaining, every one of them. They'd searched the wet corners in the dark, in the rain, without the expectation of being paid back in some mysterious way. They'd come because she'd needed them.

When Grace had first moved here, she'd thought it a prison sentence. She'd wanted to keep to herself, take care of Mama G and Daisy, and pass the time until she could leave.

But now . . . She looked around her cozy bedroom, listened to the sound of the rain on the roof, and knew the people she loved were all here, in this house, on this street, and in this town.

CHAPTER 19

Trav

A week before the festival, ignoring the chilly fall breeze, Blake slid his sunglasses to the top of his head. "So . . . when are you going to ask Grace Wheeler out on a date?"

"Shut up," Trav growled at his friend as he ducked his head back under the hood of the squad car. "Didn't we agree you'd never come to my house in uniform? It kills my 'bad boy' image."

"We did, but I'm here on official business." Blake leaned against his car where it was parked in Trav's driveway. "Ole Charmer needed that new headlight."

"What a ridiculous name for a squad car."

"My mother hates it, which is why I use it." Blake patted his car. "She's a good one, Ole Charmer."

"Do you want me to fix this headlight or not? I'm off the clock, so I'm only doing it as a favor."

"I know. I had to chase you down here because you'd already left the garage for the day."

"Arnie was there, which you know, since he gave you the bulb. He or one of the other guys could have fixed this."

"They could have, but you know Ole Charmer better than anyone." Blake watched Trav work. "I was surprised you were already home. It's not even five yet."

"I had errands to run."

"You were here, not out running errands. Remember when you used to work late every single night, even on weekends?" Blake looked past Trav to Grace's house. "Of course, that was before you got those interesting neighbors."

"I didn't come home early because of my 'interesting neighbors.' I came home early because I— Damn it, I don't need to tell you anything."

"You don't, but it would make me leave faster."

Trav tightened the last screw and then straightened. "Fine. I came home early because I was thinking of making a change."

Blake looked interested. "Like what?"

Trav dropped the screwdriver into his tool bag and then closed the hood of Blake's car. "I'd tell you if I thought it was any of your business, but it's not, so take a hike."

"There you go. That's the Trav Parker we know and love."

"Did you come here just to bother me?"

"No, I came to get Ole Charmer's headlight fixed and see if you wanted to watch the game later at Po Dunks. It's four-dollar beer night. Unless, of course, you have other plans."

Trav glanced at Grace's house. In the weeks since Grace had found Mama G's mangled knitting, he'd found himself visiting her house pretty much every day. At first, he went to fix the things he'd promised to—the creaky floorboard, the loose handrail, the broken fence, the leaky sink. He could have fixed them all in one day, as none of the projects was very complicated. But instead, he'd taken his time, doing one repair a visit, and always finding something else that needed fixing while he was there. He also made sure he was still around at dinnertime, which always garnered him an invite.

He was sure Grace was aware he was dragging his feet, but damn, he enjoyed being there. He felt at home listening to Grace's smart-aleck replies to Daisy's sass, and the comfort of Mama G's warm wisdom. And so he'd worked slowly and, to his chagrin, had enjoyed every blasted second.

"You going to do something about that?" Blake asked.

Trav sent his friend a frosty look. "What 'that'?"

Blake nodded toward Grace's house. "That 'that.'"

"Tell you what. I'll do something about that when you do something about"—Trav jerked his head toward Sarah's house—"that."

The humor on Blake's face disappeared. "That's different."

"Really?"

"Totally different, and you know it." His face red, Blake unhooked his keys from the leather loop on his gun belt. "I'd better go."

"Leaving already?" Trav smirked. It wasn't often that he could rattle Blake.

"Yes. Meanwhile, you'll remain here while you avoid admitting how much you like your new neighbor."

Trav pulled a rag from his bag and cleaned his hands. "It's not just her. The kid is funny and Mama G—" He shook his head, smiling. "She's tough. I like them both."

"Bonuses, the both of them. I know where your real interest is. Just don't take too long to make your move. The sharks are circling."

Trav's smile slipped. "Sharks?"

"Other men. I saw her having lunch with someone and they looked pretty cozy."

Damn it. "Who?"

"Nate Stevens."

Until that moment, Trav had never thought of Nate as a playboy, but now Trav was certain the man was a bona fide lothario.

"He seems taken with your Grace." Blake nodded thoughtfully. "He must like the highly-organized-but-still-hot type."

Trav regarded his friend with a flat gaze. "Your car's done. You can leave now."

Blake held up his hands. "I'm going. Just thought you should know there's a shelf life for this quiet obsession of yours. I hope that's the 'change' you were talking about."

"It's not," Trav lied. It was part of it, but it wasn't the only reason he'd come home early.

"Too bad." Blake opened the door of his squad car. "Call me if you want to head to Po Dunks for the game. That is, if you're free, and to be honest, I hope you're not." With a wave, Blake climbed into his car and left.

Trav picked up the burned-out bulb and the empty box and tossed them into the trash can that stood outside the garage door. Then he went inside and washed his hands. So Nate Stevens thought he had a chance with Grace, did he? Well, Trav had something to say about that.

He dried his hands and then, taking a deep breath, went outside and made his way to Grace's house. He passed by Linda's truck where it sat alone in the driveway, climbed the steps to the crooked porch, and knocked on the screen door.

Footsteps sounded before Linda swung the door open. "Hi, Trav. Grace is still at the office."

His face heated. "Is Mama G here? I need to ask her something."

Linda looked surprised, but she stepped back from the door. "Sure. Come on in. She's in the kitchen, drinking some of Ava's tea. I swear, but that stuff is the bomb diggity."

He walked inside. "So she's having a good day?"

"She's better today than I've seen her in a long time. She's not entirely sure what year it is, but she's not living too far in the past."

He'd come at the perfect time, then. "I have a favor to ask her."

"Do you now?" Linda led the way to the kitchen, saying over her shoulder, "She sure is popular today."

He stopped. "If she's busy, I can come back later."

Linda paused beside the kitchen door. "Nonsense. She's just visiting with an old friend. We ran into Aunt Jo while we were grocery shopping and I brought them and Moon Pie back here for some tea. They've been reminiscing."

He'd known Aunt Jo since he was a child, as she'd been a frequent visitor at the Dove house. Sarah sometimes called the woman her "other mother." "Aunt Jo knows everyone."

"When you've lived as long as she has, so will you." Linda grinned. "It's been nice having her here, because she makes Mama G laugh. And it'll be even nicer when you join them."

"I shouldn't. Not today, anyway." He backed away. "I'll come back when Mama G's not busy—"

"Is that the Parker boy?" Aunt Jo yelled from the kitchen. "Tell him to get his handsome rump in here!"

Linda grinned and swung the kitchen door wide open. "I guess you don't have a choice now, do you?"

He guessed she was right.

Mama G sat at the kitchen table, Aunt Jo across from her, teacups and a plate of cookies in front of them. Moon Pie slept under the table, his gentle snores just loud enough to be heard.

"Well, if it isn't Robert!" Mama G beamed as Trav gave her a hug. "We thought we heard you talking to Linda."

He supposed it wouldn't hurt him to be Robert for a while. It was what she called him most days, anyway.

Aunt Jo leaned closer to Mama G and said out of the side of her mouth, "Lord love you, but you do have handsome visitors."

"So I do." Mama G inclined her head toward the empty chair beside her. "Have a seat, Robert. We're having tea. Would you like some?"

"No, thank you." He took the seat, wishing he didn't have such an interested audience.

From where she stood leaning against the counter near the kitchen door, Linda said, "Mama G, our visitor came to ask you something."

Three pairs of interested gazes were now locked on him. *Damn it.*

As if sensing his distress, Mama G patted his hand. "You look het up. Doesn't he, Jo?"

"Like a cat on a greased floor," Aunt Jo agreed. "Maybe some tea would settle him down."

Linda straightened. "I'll make it."

"No, you won't." Aunt Jo gathered her cane and stood. "You make it too weak."

Linda snorted. "And you make it too strong. I could cut concrete with your tea."

"'Robert' is a big boy and needs his tea strong."

"I'm fine, really." Trav wished he hadn't taken the seat Mama G had offered, as he was now too far from the door to make a quick getaway. "It's nice of you all to offer tea, but I really should go. I'll come back later when—"

"Ha!" Aunt Jo limped to the cupboard, where she pulled out a cup and poured hot water from the pot that sat on the stove. "You'll stay where you are and tell us why you came."

Feeling a little helpless, he looked at Linda, who shrugged as if to say he'd be a fool to fight.

He supposed she was right. He was no match for three bossy women. One, maybe. Two, probably. But never three. A man had to know his limits and that was his.

Mama G watched him over the rim of her teacup. "You might as well tell us what you want. We're going to find out one way or another."

They would, too. "It's no big deal, really. I just . . ." He rubbed his neck, wondering if he should even ask. *I suppose it won't hurt. All she can do is say no.* His face hot, he took a deep breath. "Mama G, Grace once mentioned that you used to cut the hair of your foster kids."

Linda, who'd been leaning against the counter, straightened.

Aunt Jo, who'd just dropped a tea bag into the cup of hot water, turned to look at him.

Even Moon Pie, who was still asleep under the table, snorted as if he could feel the sudden tension in the room.

"So I did," Mama G said thoughtfully. "I was pretty good at it, too. Saved all sorts of money."

"I imagine you did. And that's why I came today. Mama G, would you cut my hair?"

Her eyes widened. Her gaze moved up to his hair, following it across his brow and down past his ears, and to his shoulders. "Son, *nothing* would make me happier."

Five minutes later, all three women had donned their sweaters and placed him in a chair out in the middle of the backyard. Aunt Jo used a chip clip to fasten a tablecloth around his neck while Linda brought out Mama G's knitting basket.

Mama G fished in the basket for her shears. They were buried under knotted bundles of yarn, but she untangled them and then waved them in the air over her head like a sword. "Behold the shears!"

"I swear, but I feel like I'm seeing the Samson and Delilah story right in front of my eyes." Aunt Jo beamed.

"There's no Delilah," Linda said with regret.

"I'll be Delilah," Aunt Jo said, dancing her way to the chair Linda had put out for her.

Linda laughed. "Oh! Wait here a moment. We need one more thing." She went back inside, the screen door banging closed.

Trav eyed the shears with trepidation. In Mama G's small hands, the shears looked like they belonged to a giant. "You're not going to use those, are you? They seem sort of big."

"I don't like the tiny little scissors some people use when they knit." She snapped the shears open and closed rapidly. "I like shears with a little gumption to them."

Oh God.

Aunt Jo rested her cane against her chair. "Those seem sharp enough to me."

"Oh, they'll cut through wood if you needed them to." Mama G snapped them in the air for emphasis.

Trav silently told his ears goodbye. *I'm dead. I wonder if anyone here besides me knows how to apply a tourniquet?* He tugged on the tablecloth, which suddenly seemed too tight around his neck, but the clip held it stubbornly in place. "Maybe this isn't such a good idea. I can come back another time—"

"Nonsense." Mama G moved behind him and, before he could say another word, she began to cut his hair.

Now he couldn't move. Not even a little. His heart racing, he remained stone-still, the snip-snip of the shears abnormally loud in the quiet.

After a few moments, Linda came back outside, this time carrying a bowl. She settled in the chair beside Aunt Jo. "Want some popcorn?"

"Why, thank you. I do love a snack while I'm taking in a show." Aunt Jo munched on the popcorn and then stretched her plump legs out in front of her. Moon Pie, who'd settled under her chair when they'd first come out, snored gently.

Mama G snipped a bit of hair near Trav's ear and then stopped. "Robert, child, you're grinding your teeth."

"Sorry," Trav mumbled.

She chuckled and set back to work. "Lord, the fun we had when you were a child. Jo, do you remember what shenanigans Robert and his brother used to get into?"

"I do," Aunt Jo said. "Like the time they snuck into the drive-in in the trunk of Lenny York's car and got stuck? Lenny thought they were demons and refused to let them out."

Mama G laughed and then began to recall various other pranks Trav's father had embarked upon. Oddly enough, the stories were soothing and Trav found himself grinning as Mama G and Aunt Jo recalled Dad's various pranks.

Trav had been close to his father, but he was beginning to realize that he had only known him in one way—as a father. There were other parts to his dad's life when he'd just been Robert Parker, prankster and who knew what else. *It's funny, but we only know the people in our lives in relation to who they are to us—a father or a mother or a brother. We never see them the way others do.*

The next fifteen minutes went by in a blur. Trav held as still as he could and although the big shears seemed awfully close at times, they never once touched his skin. Tufts of dark hair fell to the grass, the soft breeze teasing them away. He watched as they tumbled across the grass and came to rest along a small garden near an old oak.

Finally, Mama G lowered her shears. "I think that'll do it." She slowly walked around him. "Yes. That'll do just fine."

He glanced at Aunt Jo and Linda and found them frozen in their seats, their gazes locked on him, the popcorn forgotten in the bowl.

"Huh," Aunt Jo said. "I forgot how handsome the Parker boys were."

"He looks a lot like his dad, doesn't he?" Linda said.

Mama G undid the clip that held the tablecloth around Trav's neck and released him.

He stood and ran a hand through his hair, relieved to find it short, but not too much so. His head felt lighter, and the fall air seemed chillier. He rubbed his neck and winced as he realized how the haircut had exposed his scars. He'd known that would happen, but still, he felt oddly vulnerable.

Mama G patted his arm. "Don't hide, child. People who really live have a little wear and tear. But that's good. It's what makes us interesting."

"Lord, yes." Aunt Jo grabbed her cane and hauled herself to her feet. "You look good, with the scars or without. In fact, if I were about fifty years younger, I'd let you date me. Moon Pie would be jealous, but I'd do it anyway."

"To heck with being age appropriate," Linda scoffed. "If Mark wasn't such a good cook, I'd chase you down right now."

Trav'd thought his face couldn't get hotter, but he'd been wrong. To save the conversation from getting worse, he turned to Mama G. "How much do I owe you for the haircut?"

"Psssht. Consider it a return for some of the work you've done on this house." She looked at Aunt Jo. "If you need anything fixed, he's good, but good lord, he's slow."

"Hmm. Maybe there's a reason he's slow."

"That's what I think," Linda agreed.

Oh God, please don't let them start talking about that.

Mama G beamed. "He likes our Grace."

This is a nightmare. "I haven't really thought about—"

"He more than likes her, if you ask me," Aunt Jo said. "Look at how red he turned when you mentioned her name."

Linda nodded. "We should help him. Give him some advice."

"It's the least we could do," Aunt Jo agreed. "Between the three of us, we have a good hundred and fifty years of experience. Meanwhile, he's got less than thirty."

They all looked at him with something akin to pity.

Half laughing, and half dying of embarrassment, he threw up his hands. "You are being way too kind, but I think I know what I need to do."

"You'd better do it quickly," Linda said. "She says she's not staying, so you're going to have to change her mind."

"That could take some time," Aunt Jo said. "And some wooing."

"She likes flowers," Mama G said thoughtfully. "And movies, too. We watch movies every night. She and Daisy both like the old ones best. I think she might like dinner out, too, someplace not too fancy, though. She— Ah! Speak of the devil." Mama G nodded toward the street. "There's Grace now."

Trav turned to see the Honda pull into the drive, the tires crackling over the scattering of gravel on the asphalt.

"They're home early." Linda got out of her chair and looked over the fence at the new arrivals. "That's unusual. Poor Grace has had to work late a lot because of the festival. I'll be glad when it's over."

The car stopped beside the front porch. Daisy threw open the door, hopped out, and soon disappeared around the front of the house, leaving the door open in her wake. Moving at a more decorous pace, Grace got out of the car and followed her niece, pausing only to shut Daisy's car door before slipping out of view.

A moment later, Trav heard the front screen door slam and he was suddenly hit with an irresistible urge to leave. And not slowly, either, saying goodbyes and calmly walking home, but quickly, over the fence even, and back to the safety of his own house.

But before he could do more than think about it, the back door swung open and Daisy bounded out.

She stopped in her tracks on seeing everyone in the backyard. Her blue gaze went from Aunt Jo to Linda and then to the shears still in Mama G's hand, and finally to Trav. "Whoaaa! You look different." She came closer, walking around him.

He fought the urge to cover his scars. "Well?"

"You look younger. A lot younger."

That was good. Wasn't it? "Thanks. I think."

Daisy shrugged, her attention already drifting. "I'm going to— Moon Pie!"

Aunt Jo watched with a smile as Daisy dropped to her knees and hugged the dog. "Don't I get a hello?"

Daisy, still grinning, climbed back to her feet. "Sorry, Aunt Jo." She gave the older woman a hug.

Aunt Jo patted Daisy's shoulder. "That's okay. I'm used to it. That dog upstages me at least once a day, and usually more. He's—" She frowned, her gaze locked on Mama G. "Inna, dear, are you okay?"

Mama G was frowning at the shears in her hand as if she'd just seen them. "I was . . ." Her gaze drifted to her knitting basket. "Was I knitting?"

Trav's heart sank at the quaver in her voice.

Linda handed the nearly empty popcorn bowl to Aunt Jo and went to Mama G's side. "Yes, you were. I'll take those shears for you. Your knitting basket is right over here. See?"

Mama G's brow cleared. "Yes. Of course." She gave an awkward laugh. "I don't know why I couldn't remember that."

Linda slid the shears into the basket and then put it into Mama

G's arms. "Why don't we go inside. It's getting cold out here. Daisy, want to help your grandmother up the porch stairs?"

"Sure." Daisy slipped her arm around Mama G and together they walked toward the porch. "Have you been working in your garden?"

"I was waiting for you to come home, but I'm a little too tired now."

"Maybe a snack would help," Linda offered. "I could make some peanut butter and apple slices."

"I like apples," Mama G agreed, although she suddenly seemed exhausted, hugging her basket while Daisy led her to the porch.

Linda walked behind them with Aunt Jo, Moon Pie panting as he followed. "Aunt Jo, it was nice having you for a visit. We'll leave once I fix Daisy's snack. I'll drop you off on my way home."

"Thank you. I have a lot of work to do this evening. The First Baptist Church is sponsoring a booth at the Apple Festival, so I'm printing Bible verses on tiny slips of paper. We're putting them inside the wrappers of lollipops. It'll be sorta like a fortune cookie, only better 'cause it's Jesus."

Daisy looked over her shoulder. "Can I help?"

"Of course you can. Ask your aunt if you can spend some time at my house tomorrow. Moon Pie likes visitors and— Oh. There's your aunt now."

Grace had just stepped out of the house. She stood on the porch, and her gaze—which had widened at seeing so many people in her backyard—locked on Trav.

He fought the urge to touch his hair. He wasn't quite sure what to do with his hands, so he crossed his arms over his chest.

Daisy and Mama G went up the steps. Mama G, still holding her basket, went inside while Daisy stayed to speak to Grace. Trav thought she looked a little tired this evening. Her hair, which was always in a proper bun, had loosened somehow, a long strand looped against her neck.

Trav wished more than ever that he'd left. Why had she come

home early today of all days? He wasn't yet ready to speak to her. He needed some time to think things through. To figure out what to say.

He'd just head home. All he had to do was walk past Grace on the porch, and then he could make his escape through the kitchen.

Daisy gave Grace a big hug and then followed Linda and Aunt Jo inside, where Mama G waited.

The screen door closed and Trav was alone with Grace.

What do I say now? He couldn't think of a single thing. He rubbed his chin, wishing he had Blake's gift of gab.

She stepped off the back porch, her dark gaze as inscrutable as ever as she crossed the lawn to where he stood. She stopped in front of him, and the cool evening breeze ruffled her loose strand of dark hair and tugged at her blue sweater. She crossed her arms, as if to ward off some of the chill.

And so they stood, face-to-face, arms crossed, neither one seeming sure of what to say.

He cleared his throat. "Daisy seems happy today."

Grace's expression softened. "She is, thanks to the committee. She loved working in town this summer. It kept her busy and she made so many friends. When she started school, she already knew most of the kids in her class."

"Sarah said a good number of them came to her Children's Hour."

"Almost all of them. And Daisy got to help with it, which made her seem pretty cool to the kids in her class, too. She's never had so many friends."

"That's good."

"It's very good. She's changed so much over the past few months. She still has her days, but not many."

"She's a good kid and you're a good mom."

She opened her mouth as if to argue, but then closed it and shrugged, looking adorably embarrassed. "Thank you. She's everything to me."

"As she should be."

Grace smiled. "She likes you."

"She'd like anyone who let her wash their motorcycle."

"And paid her. She says she's going to spend all ten dollars at the book fair."

"That's a good place to spend them."

Grace's gaze flickered from his eyes to his hair. "You . . . you look really good."

"Mama G cut it."

Grace's eyebrows rose. "She did?"

"You said she used to cut your hair, so I figured why not mine." *Why not. Such little words, but in the right circumstances, they could mean so much.*

"She cut my hair until I got to high school, and then I decided I needed a professional." Grace tucked the loose strand of her hair behind her ear and said in a mischievous tone, "I wouldn't admit it back then, but she was way better than the girl I found."

"I used to go to the barber in town, but he retired years ago and closed up shop."

"Is that why you let your hair grow?"

"No. It just seemed a waste of time. Besides, I wasn't exactly social-izing at the time, so . . ." He shrugged.

"What changed your mind?"

You did. The thought rang loud and clear in his mind, and he moved closer. Not a lot, but enough to let her know it was deliberate. "I've decided it is time to start socializing."

"Oh."

It wasn't exactly encouraging, but he'd come this far and he wasn't about to stop. "I'd like to socialize with you, once the festival is over and you have the time."

She put a hand to her cheek. "Socialize. You mean . . ."

"On a date." Oh God, he'd said it. There was no going back now. He waited, his chest so tight it felt as if it might explode.

Her gaze moved over him, resting on his hair, his eyes. Finally, she said, "I don't plan on staying in Dove Pond forever."

"I know. Although I think that might be a mistake."

Her gaze darkened. "It might be. It's been nice here. Daisy's doing well and Mama G is more comfortable being around people she knows, but I just—" Grace looked toward the house, where they could hear the distant laughter of the women inside, and her face softened. "I don't know. Maybe." She turned back to him. "But no matter what, whether I stay here or leave, I'll always be responsible for Daisy."

"Of course."

"And Mama G, too, so long as I can." Grace's voice quavered a bit.

He fought the urge to pull her closer for a hug. "I know," he repeated firmly and without hesitation.

"I'm not always easy to get along with, either. I get irked. A lot."

He nodded. "I've noticed."

She burst out laughing. "I don't think you should agree with me about that."

"Sorry. It's true, though. I'm the same way, and to be honest, I don't mind it. In fact, I have just one question."

"Yes?"

"Should we have both dinner *and* go to a movie for our first date? Or just dinner? We might want to talk. Get to know each other a little more. And God, I love talking to you." He loved other things about this woman, but if all he ever got from her was a string of words, he'd never regret anything he'd ever done in his life.

She bit her lip, and he could feel her struggle. She wanted to say yes, he could see it in her eyes. But she was proud, and cautious, and determined to keep her independence. She could keep all of those things if she said one short word—*no*.

"Fine," she said in a breathless voice. "Let's try it."

He was so shocked that he blurted out, "Really?" As soon as he said it, he wished he could take it back. So he hurried to add, "I mean, good. Very good. I'll—I can make a reservation. Maybe the Saturday after the festival? There are some great restaurants in Asheville and—"

"No. Let's start here. In Dove Pond. Let's go to the Moonlight. We'll order the meatloaf plate and—" She laughed softly and shrugged. "We'll see what happens."

He had the ridiculous urge to pump his fist in the air and give a war whoop, but he maintained his cool enough to say, "The Moonlight it is, then. I . . . I guess I should go."

"You should. I came home early to go through the festival budget one last time. I didn't want to get halfway done and have to pack everything up and race to get Daisy, so I brought my work home and picked her up a little early."

"You're busy. I'll leave, then. But I'll see you a week from Saturday. I mean, I'll see you before then, too. I still need to stop by sometime and fix that shelf in the coat closet. But I'll see you at the festival as well, but—" *Oh God, shut up!* Grinning sheepishly, he said, "You know all of that."

Her cheeks a lovely pink, she nodded. "Of course. Later, Parker."

"Later, Wheeler." And with that, he turned and left, crossing the porch and heading inside. As he walked into the kitchen, the three older ladies looked at him, each measuring his expression.

"He did it," Aunt Jo said approvingly.

"Did what?" Daisy licked peanut butter from her fingers.

"The thing," Linda said smugly.

"What thing?"

"The one he should have done a month ago," Linda replied, sliding another piece of apple onto Daisy's plate.

"It's about time," Mama G announced.

Trav could see that Daisy was about to ask more questions, so he mumbled goodbye and hurried out of the kitchen. Then, grinning ear to ear, he went home.

CHAPTER 20

Sarah

From where they sat in wooden folding chairs on the empty grandstand, Sarah and Ava watched as Lenny Smith, Ricky Bob, and Tommy struck the festival tents and loaded them onto a flatbed truck. In the distance, they could hear music from the final event of the Apple Festival, a huge bonfire held at Dove Pond High School a few blocks over. Ed and Nate had wanted fireworks, but the budget wouldn't allow for it, so they'd settled on a bonfire and a local band.

The chilly autumn air made Sarah snuggle deeper into her coat as she cupped her hands around the warm cup of cider Ava had brought her. As good as the cider was, Sarah'd never been so tired in her entire life. The Apple Festival had been a huge success—even bigger than she'd hoped. In fact, the only complaint she'd heard so far was that it had been too crowded.

Beside her, Ava stretched her legs out, looking every bit as tired as Sarah felt. "Geez, what a weekend."

"I know. I feel like I've been beaten with a bat."

"No wonder. You were everywhere. The library book sale was a huge success."

Sarah smiled. "The books were so excited. Permanent homes for the lot of them."

"The whole festival was great." Ava looked at her sister over the rim of her cider cup. "You should be proud. You've accomplished a lot."

"No, Grace accomplished a lot. I just helped."

"I'd say you were equally responsible for the miracle that just happened." Ava lowered her cup. "When we were growing up, you always thought you'd be the one to save the town. That's not quite the way it's happening."

"Not quite." Sarah shrugged, smiling. "I was a little jealous when I first realized Grace was going to be so important in saving Dove Pond. The old stories about how the Doves have always been there when good things happened—it seemed as if that was who I was supposed to be, you know. A sort of magic heroine. But it turns out it took two of us." She looked at Ava. "Actually, it took eight of us. The committee will save this town, not just Grace or me."

"You're being generous."

"I'm being honest."

Ava sipped her cider. "Do you wonder if Charlotte Dove's journal lied to you?"

"I don't think it knew the specifics, but it didn't want to admit that little fact. It's a very proud, very cranky old book. I stopped by today to let it know how well things were going. I think it was happy, although it fell asleep in the middle of our conversation."

Ava snorted. "It's a pain in the ass, that book."

"Yup. But our town is going to be okay, and that's all that matters. Plus, I got a really good friend out of it. Grace is special."

"You think she'll stay?"

"Yes. I don't think she's admitted it yet, but she's beginning to suspect it."

Ava chuckled. "Well, she sure knows how to run a festival."

Erma Tingle came up, carrying a tote bag. "There you are! I should have known you'd be here."

"My tote!" Sarah reached for it. "Where did you find it?"

Erma handed it over. "You left it in the First Baptist tent when you went to fetch some change for them."

"I didn't even realize it was missing." Sarah peered inside the tote at the three books waiting on her. A low murmur greeted her. "I haven't forgotten," she told them.

"Are they mad?" Ava asked.

"Not yet." Sarah put the tote back at her feet and noticed that Erma was rubbing her lower back. "You should come up here and join us. Take a load off."

"Thank you, but I've got to get home. Did you see Zoe with her handsome Italian?"

"Yeah, who was that?" Ava asked.

"He owns a restaurant in Charlotte, but he's talking about opening one here."

Ava looked at Sarah. "Now you know why she needed that phrase book."

"And why she was so ticked off about it. She doesn't want to believe." Sarah shrugged. "Some people never do."

"Their loss," Erma said with a sniff. She looked around, and her expression softened. "It was a great festival, wasn't it? I've never seen a crowd like that. I sold out of everything and now I have enough cash to make it through the slow season without blinking."

"Me too," Ava said. "Zoe said she has four businesses lined up for meetings to find out more about the town, three she feels certain will come through. And Kat said she got over fifteen inquiries into town properties."

"I heard one of them signed on the spot," Erma said.

Ava finished her cider. "That was me."

Surprised, Sarah looked at her sister. "You? No way! Not the teahouse idea?"

"Tearoom," Ava corrected. "I thought about what you all said at the meeting, about investing in our own town. So I'm going to open a tearoom. Kat got me a great deal on the empty florist's shop just down from the Moonlight. I close on it in the morning."

"Close?" Sarah looked at her sister. "You're buying the building?"

"I am. I'm going to use the first floor for my tearoom and then make apartments out of the top floor. There's already one up there, but it needs updating. We think there's room for another if we move some walls."

"You can build all the apartments you want," Sarah said. "But you're not moving out of our house."

"Lord, no." Ava grinned. "Who'd do my laundry?"

Sarah sniffed. "I'm glad I'm appreciated."

"I like the idea of a tearoom," Erma said. "It'll be charming and quaint. That fits our town."

Ava smiled serenely. "I'll serve my specialty teas and I found a distributor in Asheville for gourmet coffee. I'll also sell teapots and strainers and— Oh, all sorts of things."

"No food?" Erma asked.

"Scones, tarts, and pastries. Nothing bigger than that. I'll buy those from local people. Aunt Jo said she'd make me an assortment of scones every week. I think she'll be happy to make some extra money. Mark Robinson offered to make fruit tarts. The rest I'll get from the Moonlight Café."

Sarah blinked. "Jules supports your tearoom? Won't you two be competing for business?"

"Jules offered to furnish fresh pies and cakes every week, and at a great rate too, if I promise not to serve full meals."

"Ah. That's a bargain, then."

Ava grinned. "I had no intention of competing, but she doesn't know that. We both win this way. I even told her I'd hand out flyers with the Moonlight's special of the week. She was happy about that."

Sarah nodded approvingly. "You've always been a good business-woman."

"And you've always been a good town champion." Ava's gaze was warm.

"Amen!" Erma said.

"Thanks. That means a lot." Sarah started to sip her cider, but she caught sight of something that made her instantly forget the warm cup in her hand. "Ohhh, look at that."

Erma and Ava turned to see what had caught her attention.

Grace stood with Trav beside the fountain. They were just talking, but her hand rested on his arm and he was bent close as if afraid he might miss something she said.

Sarah sighed with satisfaction. "They make a cute couple, don't they?"

"Crazy cute," Ava agreed.

"You think it's serious?" Erma asked.

"Oh, it's serious all right. Not only did he cut his hair, but last week, he asked me to go through his closet and pull out everything that needed to go." Sarah chuckled. "We went shopping afterward because there were only about four pairs of blue jeans, a stack of T-shirts, and some flannel shirts left."

"You think he did that for her?" Ava looked a little envious.

"And for himself, too. He's finally letting go of the past. He's having a yard sale next week. He cleaned all his dad's stuff out and decided to update the bathrooms and kitchen."

"Wow," Ava said. "He seemed so lost for such a long time."

"He did. But now he's been found. By Grace."

Erma looked impressed. "He's a good boy, Trav is. I hope he knows he's got himself quite a catch with our Grace."

Ava's gaze narrowed and she sat up straighter in her chair. "The flowers!"

Erma frowned. "Which ones?"

"The ones around the fountain behind Grace and Trav. Last week, for the festival, Lenny and I planted blue asters all through there. But now they're crimson."

Erma's eyes widened. "Crimson like love."

Sarah grinned. "Apparently the Dove family good luck approves of this union."

"This day just keeps getting better and better." Erma watched as Grace and Trav slowly walked away from the fountain, the asters along the pathway changing behind them. "God bless the Dove Family Good Luck. I love a happy ending."

"Me too," Ava said.

Erma nodded her approval. "Well, children, as fun as it's been, I'd best get home. But before I go, I had a thought that I wanted to share with you two."

"What's that?" Sarah asked.

"We've had a deadbeat mayor for too long."

Sarah made a face. "He was annoying this weekend. He was everywhere, taking credit for the whole festival."

"Yeah, but he had no idea what was going on." Ava rolled her eyes. "Per usual."

"Which is why we need a new mayor," Erma said. "A better one. One with a head for business."

Sarah eyed the older woman. "I'd vote for you."

"Not me! Grace."

Sarah had lifted her cup for a sip, but at this, she lowered it. "Grace? For mayor?"

Erma nodded. "I want to run her campaign. You know, when Grace first took over the committee, I had my doubts about her. But now I'm sold."

"Sign me up as a campaign volunteer," Sarah said.

Ava raised her hand. "Me too."

Erma smirked. "It's perfect, isn't it? But first, I need to convince our candidate to run. Once we get going, I'll give you both a call."

"I hope you can convince her to do it," Sarah said. "If I can be of any help, you know where to find me."

"I will. Tell those books of yours to give it some thought, too."

"I'll try, but you know how they are."

"Didn't you already give Grace a book?" Ava asked.

"I did. It was *Little Women.*"

"Do you know why it wanted to visit her?"

"Nope, but she finally brought it back last week. Whatever it was meant to do, it must have done it."

Erma shook her head. "I'll never understand how all of that works, but I'm glad it does." She tugged her coat a little closer. "Whew. It's getting cold. I think I'll stop by the bonfire and then head home."

"You going to stay for the band?" Ava asked.

"Probably not. I'm tired, plus I have money to count. Good night, you two." Erma waved and left, walking far more spritely than her age would suggest.

Sarah and Ava were quiet for a moment. Finally, Ava said in a thoughtful tone, "Grace as mayor makes sense."

Sarah couldn't agree more. "She'd make more money than being a town clerk."

"A lot more money. And then there's Trav." Ava sighed happily. "I hope I get to be a bridesmaid. I'll be mad if I'm not."

Sarah had to laugh. "I'll put in a word for you when the time comes."

"You do that." Ava stood. "I guess I'll head home. I have to get up bright and early to meet Zoe and Kat at the bank."

"Go on. Just leave the porch light on for me."

"I always do." Ava smiled and started for the stairs.

"Wait! I almost forgot." Sarah reached for her tote. "I have something for you."

Ava groaned. "Oh no. Not a book."

"Of course it's a book." Sarah pulled it out and handed it to Ava.

A confused look crossed Ava's face. "*How to Create Your Own Water Feature and Other Landscaping Gems.* Good lord, Sarah, I don't need this. No one has ever asked for a water feature and I sure as heck don't intend on doing one."

"Hey, I don't tell the books anything. They tell me. And that one said you should read it."

Ava muttered sourly under her breath, "Fine. I'll read it."

"Good, because there's one more."

"Nooooo!"

Sarah reached into her bag, pulled out another book, and handed it to Ava. The last book in Sarah's tote bag settled deeper into the folds.

Ava looked at the book Sarah had just given her and her expression darkened. "No." Ava held the book back toward Sarah. "I don't want this one."

"No one would," Sarah agreed, feeling a little guilty. "I wish I knew why it thinks you need it, but it says you do, so—" She put her hand on the book and pushed it back toward Ava. "That's all I know."

Ava's gaze dropped back to the book. After a long moment, she put it on top of the other book and tucked them both under her arm, her smile long gone. "I'd better get home."

"I'll see you there." She watched as Ava headed down the steps, pausing to toss her empty cider cup into the trash before she walked across the almost empty park and climbed into her truck.

"That was quite a day, wasn't it?"

Sarah turned to find Grace standing at the steps leading up to the grandstand. "Hail, Queen of the Festival!"

Grace laughed, her brown eyes sparkling as she climbed the steps. "It took all of us. It was a lot of work, but worth it."

"So everyone seems to think."

Grace smiled and took the chair Ava had just left. "I'll tell you something else."

"Does it have to do with you and Trav? If so, I'm all ears."

Grace flushed, but her smile didn't waiver. "No. He just went to the bonfire. Linda is there with Mama G and Daisy."

"I saw Mama G earlier. She was in a wheelchair."

"Linda thought it would keep her from getting tired. I told Trav to let them know I'd catch up with them in a bit."

"I hear you can tell a lot about a man by how reliably he delivers messages."

Grace laughed. "I didn't know that, but I'll quiz my loved ones when I see them next." She leaned back in her seat. "Speaking of which, where's Blake?"

"He's at the bonfire, I'd think." Sarah knew exactly where he was, but she refused to admit it.

Grace didn't appear the least bit fooled. "You should talk to that man, put him out of his misery."

"I'll talk to him when the time comes."

"You're impossible, you know that? Fortunately, what I wanted to say to you has nothing to do with Blake or Trav or anyone else. It has to do with the festival budget."

"Uh-oh."

"No." Grace beamed. "Zoe brought me the final figures after she'd checked in with the vendors as they were closing. Sarah, we're under budget, not over."

"Under? As big as our festival was?"

"It's under because it was as big as it was. We made enough to cover the price quoted for the tents, and the more tents we had, the cheaper they were, so . . . we're under. Once we add in our cuts from the vendors, we'll have made a good profit."

"Wow. Erma's right about you."

Grace's eyebrows rose. "How so?"

Sarah grinned. "You'll see soon enough."

"That's cryptic."

"So is this." Sarah reached into her tote bag for the last book. She handed it to Grace. "I think you need this."

She looked at the book. It was a small book, but thick. In large blue letters the cover read *The Knitters' Guide to Perfection.* "I don't knit."

"The book says you need it."

" 'The book says,' " Grace muttered, shaking her head. "You're a strange woman, Sarah Dove."

"There are stranger."

"I'll take your word for it." Grace traced her finger over the knitting needle featured on the book's cover and said in a musing tone, "Mama G must have knitted me a hundred pairs of mittens over my lifetime." She smiled softly. "Which was a good thing, because I kept losing them."

"Apparently it's time you learned to make your own."

"Or make them for Daisy." Sadness flickered over Grace's face as she added, "Mama G always said she'd teach me, but she can't now."

Sarah hated the sadness that rested on Grace's face. "Try the book. It can't hurt. All the knitters in Dove Pond have had it at one time or another."

"You really think I should learn?"

"Yes. And when you're done, you can teach Daisy." Sarah smiled. "Now that the festival is over and Mayor Moore has caught up on the data entry, you're going to have a ton of free time."

Grace laughed. "True." She patted the book. "I guess I'll keep this. I didn't think I'd have any use for the first book you sent me, but I was wrong." Her gaze grew searching. "I was never sure why you sent *Little Women* to me, but I have to admit, it reminded me of all the things I used to want as a child—a close family, friends, a simple but full life. Was that why you sent it?"

"I sent it because it asked me to. I don't get to pick the books. They pick the readers. That book picked you."

"And Daisy."

Sarah nodded.

"Part of me thinks you're kidding when you say things like that. And part of me hopes you're not."

"I never kid about books," Sarah said solemnly.

Grace smiled. "What are you going to do now that this madness is over?"

"Sleep. Maybe soak in a tub for a week."

"And after that?"

"Ava and I were talking about visiting a cousin of ours in the Berkshires."

"In Massachusetts?"

"That's where the Doves originated. Our cousin owns a Gilded Age mansion called Blantyre. He seems to think he's got a ghost problem."

Grace shook her head. "A pity Mama G can't go with you. She loves a good ghost."

"Miss Grace?"

They turned to find Lenny, Ricky Bob, and Tommy standing beside the grandstand, the half-filled flatbed truck parked not far away. "All we have left to do is the grandstand," Ricky Bob announced.

"I guess that means we should go." Sarah stood.

Grace joined her. They went down the stairs and moved out of the way. Together they watched as the men put away the chairs and then took down the stand, folded it up, and tied it down on the flatbed. With a deep roar, the truck pulled out of the parking lot.

All too soon, the park was empty except for Grace and Sarah. Overhead, the streetlamps flickered on as, in the distance, the first strum of the band could be heard, followed by a joyous yell.

"And that's that," Grace said.

"That's that," Sarah agreed. "For now."

Smiling, they walked arm in arm toward the music.

❭❬ ❧ EPILOGUE ❧ ❬❭

Just as the first snow fell softly to the ground in late January, Mama G passed away quietly in her sleep.

The entire town of Dove Pond came to the funeral. Preacher Thompson and Preacher Lewis forgot their differences long enough to give a joint eulogy. At the graveside, Grace wept so much that Sarah wondered that a body could hold so many tears and not drown. But Grace had Trav and Daisy and Sarah, who all stayed nearby. Love can't cure a broken heart, but it can hold the two sides together while they heal. It took all three of them, but that's what they did for Grace.

A few days after the funeral, Daisy showed an astonished Grace Mama G's garden. In each row, there were items—a bent spoon, a broken watch, a brooch missing a garnet. Nothing of value, and yet each one held a memory that made Grace wet the ground with fresh tears. The next spring, roses bloomed where Grace's tears had fallen—large, red, lush, vibrant roses that were so beautiful, Ava asked for some to add to a special tea she called Giano's Red Gold. It was said that the spicy scent of the tea caused people to remember things they'd long forgotten—a special Christmas or birthday, the smell of freshly made bread from the oven of a long-gone loved one, and even the whisper of a favorite but lost sweater.

To Sarah's huge relief and Trav's eternal happiness, Grace stayed in Dove Pond. And while she and Daisy never stopped missing Mama G, with the help of their friends, and the time they spent together learning to knit from a very special book, they became a family.

And in the deep crack left by Mama G's death, love found a home it would never leave.

Book Charmer

By Karen Hawkins

A BOOK CLUB GUIDE

1. The first book to speak to Sarah Dove is an old journal written by her ancestor, fourteen-year-old Charlotte Dove, who moved with her family to North Carolina from Massachusetts in 1702 and founded Dove Pond. What did the old leather journal want to share with Sarah?

2. Later on, as a librarian, Sarah Dove uses her gift to place the perfect book into the hands of the reader who needs it most. Has anyone ever shared a book with you that was particularly appropriate for that moment in your life? What book was it? How did it help? If you had the opportunity to give a book to someone that you love in the hopes it would help them, what book would it be?

3. As children, Grace Wheeler and her sister, Hannah, bounced from foster home to foster home until finally landing at Mama G's house. How did Grace cope with this uncertainty? How was it different from the way Hannah coped?

4. Much of *The Book Charmer* centers around the definition of "family." What was Grace's view versus Sarah's? How has your own view of family changed since you were a child?

5. Eighteen years later, after the death of her sister, Hannah, Grace and Mama G move to Dove Pond with Hannah's eight-year-old daughter, Daisy. They are all reeling from the changes wrought by Hannah's death and Mama G's newly diagnosed illness. Why does Grace view this move as temporary? Are her expectations based in reality? In what ways are they colored by the insecurities of her childhood?

6. Veteran Travis Parker is healing from his own wounds, both inside and out. Over the course of the book, he and Mama G bond as she is losing her memory while his haunts him. What does Trav see in Mama G that appeals to him? Why do you think he finally lets her cut his hair?

7. Until newcomer Grace arrived, the Dove Pond Social Club had come to believe that their goal was not to plan the best festival ever but to "check the boxes" and mimic the previous year's effort. This sort of stale, as-is thinking isn't a rare event for committee structures. Have you ever planned something as a group where this happened? Could a newcomer who didn't know the rules change things?

8. Because of Grace's background in business, she instantly sees opportunities to sell Dove Pond to new businesses. But what does she fail to take into account? What does she learn when she visits the town archives?

9. Sarah sent Grace the book *Little Women*. Throughout the story, this old book sparks various thoughts Grace has about her new situation. Why do you think *Little Women* was the right book for Grace? What lessons do you think that particular book could teach her?

10. Sarah desperately needs to convince Grace to stay in Dove Pond, and eventually, with the help of the entire town, this happens. Are you a member of any community? What are the costs of becoming an active member of a close-knit community? What are the benefits?

ACKNOWLEDGMENTS

A huge thank-you to Beth L., Lisa C., Jon F., and Mark C., beloved friends who spent hours and hours sharing their personal struggles dealing with mothers and fathers suffering from the devastating effects of Alzheimer's, and who read my rough drafts to make sure I stayed true to their experiences.

I listened to each and every one of you, and I wept with all of you. It's one of life's most unfair truths that sometimes love can hurt. To me, each of you are true heroes.

Keep reading for an exclusive excerpt of

Love
in the
Afternoon

By KAREN HAWKINS

A novella set in the magical world of Dove Pond.

Now available online for $1.99!

WELCOME TO DOVE POND, NORTH CAROLINA

Three weeks after seventy-one-year-old Doyle Cloyd's mysterious death, his daughter held a garage sale to beat all garage sales. Doyle's friends and neighbors turned out in full force, anxious to glean any new information about the strange details of his passing that they might have missed in the course of their incessant whispering during both the funeral and wake.

People came, they shopped for wonderful bargains, and they whispered even more. But Doyle's daughter offered no new information. All she'd say was that she'd miss her gruff dad and his wonderful sense of humor just as much as she missed her beloved and kind mother, who'd passed away from cancer six months earlier.

And so the people of Dove Pond returned home, their arms full of Doyle's things, their curiosity unquenched.

After the sale, no person in Dove Pond over the age of twenty could meet another without pointing out their garage sale bargains. Thus it was that five years after Doyle's death, the citizens of Dove Pond found themselves thinking of him often as they went about their days sitting in chairs that used to grace his porch, using tools scratched with his initials, and serving jam from his mother's vintage milk glassware.

Doyle and his mysterious death were always at the forefront of the minds and hearts of the residents. Even after Ava Dove, the sixth of seven daughters of the Dove family, bought Doyle's house and land and built greenhouses where she produced her specialty herbal teas, people still whispered about the odd circumstances surrounding Doyle's demise, about how he'd been found in his bathtub wearing nothing but a long blond wig over his flattop buzzcut hair, electrocuted by a hot curling iron that had fallen into his bathwater. As Doyle had looked enough like John Wayne to be the actor's younger brother, and had the same manly cowboy air, no one could picture Doyle wearing anything as ridiculous as a long, curly blond wig.

Only one person wasn't surprised about the state of Doyle's dress on the day he died: his next-door neighbor, Jake Kaine. And Jake wasn't about to tell anyone a darned thing, even after Doyle's annoying ghost started hanging out in Jake's tub. . . .

CHAPTER 1

Jake

During the entire course of his forty-one-year-old life, Jake Kaine told only one person that he could talk to ghosts.

It didn't go well.

When he was seven, he'd told his mother as she was tucking him into bed. She'd paused, her expression serious. He was a precocious child, socially awkward and far smarter than the other children in his class, which worried her. His mother used to say he was a "too" child—"too smart for his own good and too much of an introvert to care what that meant." Even at that young age, he was already a serious loner and the object of some brutal teasing, which pained her far more than him.

So when Jake had told his mother about the ghosts, her mouth had tightened and she'd said in a firm mom-tone, "Don't call your invisible friends 'ghosts.' The other kids will laugh at you."

When he'd started to argue that he didn't care about the other kids, she'd added sharply, "If you call them ghosts, they won't come back."

He liked his "invisible friends" and refused to do anything that might chase them off. Being smart, he'd also learned his lesson, and he'd never told anyone else about his visitors.

Later on, long after he was old enough to realize that his mother hadn't believed a word he'd said but had attributed his comment to an overactive imagination, he'd realized how unfairly ghosts were portrayed in fiction, especially in the horror genre. In his by-then vast experience, ghosts were rarely angry, they were never mean, and they certainly weren't scary. Instead, for the most part, they were occasional, drop-in-when-they-felt-like-it, nonjudgmental friends. They couldn't have cared less about the current political state of affairs, were only mildly curious about what he thought or did, and rarely stayed longer than a few days.

As friends go, he thought, they were rather perfect.

Over time, the visits got to be such a part of Jake's life that he didn't think about them. They were as normal to him as having the occasional case of hiccups. Or rather, he didn't think about them until Doyle Cloyd showed up in Jake's tub still wearing the now-infamous blond wig, a small washcloth floating in the ghostly water over his nether regions. For some reason Jake couldn't fathom, Doyle's visit was unlike any of the others.

For one, Doyle didn't just linger a few days. Instead, he stayed for weeks. He wasn't present every day, thank goodness, but he was around often enough that he was a total and complete bother.

For another, unlike with the other, quieter ghosts who'd visited Jake over the years, death seemed to have loosened Doyle's tongue. He now had an opinion about everything, and he wasn't shy about sharing it.

When Doyle was alive, Jake had thought the old man was the perfect next-door neighbor. He never had parties, rarely needed anything, and only spoke when he had reason to. Whenever he and Jake saw one another, they'd nod. And since Doyle liked to sit on his front porch after his wife, Barbara, passed away from cancer, he and Jake had nodded at one another often.

People from town might have been shocked that Doyle had died wearing the long, golden-blond wig, but Jake hadn't been the least surprised. In the months before the old man's death, Jake had frequently caught sight of his neighbor through his den window, sitting in his big green recliner in front of his TV, wearing that very wig. Jake had no idea exactly when or why Doyle had picked up that particular habit and couldn't have cared less. After all, a man's home was his castle, and whatever he chose to do within his own four walls was his business and no one else's. Thus Jake, respecting Doyle's privacy, hadn't mentioned a word about the guy's odd TV-viewing garb.

So it was a bit of a surprise when, five years after his death, Doyle's ghost showed up in Jake's guest bathtub, leaving Jake in a dour, waspish mood. To be fair, his normal mood was remarkably close to dour and waspish anyway. He'd grown from a precocious child into a taciturn, curmudgeonly man, so *good-natured* wasn't a term that applied to him on a day-to-day basis. But Jake was particularly cranky in the months after his fiancée and self-proclaimed soul mate, Heather, had left him.

Jake hadn't been surprised at Heather's departure. In his experience, women (especially pretty ones) rarely stayed with a work-from-home IT specialist and game developer who, while a programming genius, was more comfortable sitting in the silence of his own living room than making small talk over a meal out in public. But Heather had been different from the other women he'd dated. She'd talked a lot, but as she'd only wanted the occasional nod or murmured "Really?," that had worked well for them both—she'd talked, and he'd pretended to listen, and she'd been content with that. She was also flighty, reveling in her lack of knowledge with a stubborn abandon he could only admire. She'd had a flair for the dramatic, too, and had liked being in charge. In fact, she'd planned her own proposal, buying her ring with his credit card and then making reservations for a fancy dinner so that all he had to do was show up and say the words she wanted to hear.

Most men might have found that a sort of overreach, but Jake was perfectly happy to let her plan both their lives. In return for this unprecedented control, Heather had accepted his social liabilities and didn't mind that he didn't enjoy going out and thought bars were boring. In fact, she'd been perfectly happy to venture out without him and spend time with her friends, which had suited him just fine. He'd liked that she was so independent, and thought that one of her most attractive traits.

What he didn't realize was that Heather's "friends" were really just one friend, an inked-up tattoo artist from Asheville named Klaus with a thick beard and a penchant for muscle T-shirts and craft beer. And so Jake had been unprepared when, one ungodly early morning, while he was still rubbing sleep from his eyes, Heather had stood up from the breakfast table and announced in the deathly quiet tone she reserved for her more dramatic moments, "I'm leaving."

Jake didn't really believe her at first, because she'd played this scene before. It wasn't until he followed her to the driveway and saw the boxes and suitcases piled up in the front and back seats of her car that he'd realized that, unlike the two hundred and ten times other times she'd said the words, this time she meant it.

She was really going to leave.

While he was digesting that fact, she'd thrown open the car door, informed him that she'd be back as soon as possible to get her dog, Peppermint, and to please remember to feed the poor animal. And then, without another word, she'd left.

It wasn't the first time a woman had left Jake. To be honest, he was rather used to it. Once they got past his quiet demeanor, women tended to be attracted to his wry sense of humor, stay for his steady companionship and financial security, and then leave when he didn't fall wildly, passionately in love with them. They never seemed to understand that he wasn't that sort of man. Not once in his entire life had he been wild or passionate about anything, much less love.

What was really, truly surprising about Heather leaving was that even though he'd been 100 percent certain that she would eventually do just that, and he was nowhere close to being wildly in love with her, he found himself lost. Deeply, utterly, and bone-chillingly lost.

His mother told him it was for the best, that she'd never liked Heather, who'd had a tendency to dislike anyone who took his attention from her. His dad told him to "get back out there and find a real woman." His two friends Nate and Conner, both of whom he'd met in college and who occasionally stayed at his house where they'd alpha test his latest game, breathed a collective sigh of relief and told him how much they'd not-so-secretly disliked Heather and her controlling ways.

Jake wasn't surprised by any of this. He'd known his relationship with Heather wasn't good, but somehow, even knowing that, he'd found himself unable to move on. To let go. To start over. Somehow, in living with the demanding and dramatic Heather, he'd lost some part of himself, and he couldn't seem to find it, whatever "it" was.

And so he'd retreated into his own safe world. He used his sleepless nights to focus on his work, going from nine-hour days to fifteen-hour days. In doing so, he cut himself off from his parents and his friends and their perpetual and unwanted advice and sank deeper into his own world, where things were calm and orderly and made sense.

For eight months, it was just him and Peppermint, Heather's fat, sleepy bulldog that she'd left behind. Despite what she'd said, Jake hadn't expected her to return for the mutt. She'd paid a fortune for the animal—or rather, Jake had paid a fortune for it during one of Heather's depressed spells. She'd fawned over Peppermint when he'd been an adorable, wrinkly-faced velvet puppy, overfeeding him and spoiling him rotten. But as soon as Peppermint lost his puppy cuteness and entered his teenage stage of shoe chewing, trash eating, and face burping, Heather's affections had cooled. Jake supposed that he should have seen that as a sign, but at the time, he'd been too mesmerized by the astonishing ups and horrible downs of their relationship to see much of anything.

So now, here he and Peppermint were, alone together and just as lost as ever. Or they had been alone until Doyle's ghost had shown up in Jake's tub a few weeks ago. Of course, Doyle didn't stay there all day, every day. Ghosts tended to wander in and out, and Doyle was no exception. The only difference was that he kept coming back.

Repeatedly.

Over. And over. And over.

So much so that it was beginning to get annoying.

"I didn't ask to come here!" Doyle yelled from the tub, his deep, gravelly voice rumbling down the hallway from the guest bath to where Jake sat at his desk in the corner of the living room.

He's back. Great. Jake ignored Doyle, refusing to get up from his computer. He was neck-deep in developing a new game, a fast-paced battle-royale game called *Strategy X*, and the deadline to deliver it to his publisher was looming.

"He can wait," Doyle announced loudly, as if that settled everything.

Jake sat back, trying to remember the line of code he'd been getting ready to enter before Doyle interrupted. But for the life of him, Jake couldn't remember it. *Why, oh why, does he keep coming back?*

"Ha!" Doyle hollered. "I don't come for the fascinating conversation, that's for sure!"

Peppermint, woken from where he'd been sleeping under the desk, snorted noisily. Jake, who'd grown to love the bulldog since Heather's dramatic exit, reached under the desk and tucked Peppermint back into his bed with his special blanket. The dog gave Jake's hand a fond sniff and then snuggled deeper into his bed.

"You know you can't ignore me!" Doyle's gravelly voice cracked through the silence once more.

Jake rubbed his forehead, where an ache was beginning to grow, and leaned back in his chair, staring out his window. Not that he could see much because of the thick leaves that blocked most of the late-afternoon sunlight.

When Heather had first moved in, she'd announced that she loved roses and wanted the yard full of them. He'd protested, because he liked his simple, Craftsman-style home and its large, square yard the way it was—neat, clean, and uncluttered. Of course, that had led to a scene that had begun when Heather'd claimed he didn't care about her and then ended when she'd looked at him with tears in her eyes, her lips quivering as if he'd yanked out her heart and stomped on it.

He'd never been able to say no to a crying woman and so he'd lost the argument. Over the ten months he and Heather lived together, he'd lost a lot of arguments.

All of them, in fact.

After Heather left, his peace still shattered, he'd decided to hack down the roses and burn them in a pile in the backyard. But they'd seemed to realize his intent and had fought back, scratching viciously and ripping at his clothes. After a two-hour battle, which had left him bleeding and his clothing in shreds, he'd left them alone, thinking they'd die over time without any care. But, as if they were determined to thwart his dark wishes, the roses instead began to grow at a shocking, unfathomable rate. Over the course of the past few months, they'd grown into a thorny thicket, surrounding his house, climbing up the walls and covering the windows, nearly cutting him off from the world in general.

As much as Jake hated the roses, he liked that a shield now grew between him and the rest of the world. In fact, he'd decided that his mower would remain in his garage forever, unused and unneeded. Let everyone pass him by. He and Peppermint didn't need people. They were fine where they were, as they were.

The sound of water splashing made him glare in the direction of the bathroom. Doyle always appeared in the tub, and while the water he sat in might look ephemeral, somehow it still soaked the floor.

The splashing sound increased, and Peppermint, stirring under the desk, snorted in his sleep.

Damn it. Jake got up and went to the bathroom, stopping at the door. "What do you want?"

From where he sat in the tub, Doyle said, "A good steak would be a nice start. I miss food."

The ghost was a sight to behold. When he'd been alive, Doyle had never been what one would call a physically fit specimen. The best one could say was that he was taller than he was wide. But that was about it. Added to his roundness and the accompanying folds, he was as hairy as a chimp and, except for his wig, every bit as naked. Every time Jake saw the old man in the tub, he gave a little prayer of thanks for the small washcloth and puddles of bubbles that floated on the water and hid the worst parts from view.

Doyle propped his foot on the side of the tub. "You're lucky I can swim. I could have drowned in the time it took you to get here from the living room."

"You're already dead. Besides, I have a job. You remember those, don't you?"

"I try not to, but yes, I do. I daresay you need a break, so come on in and sit down a bit." He nodded toward the wicker hamper that sat in one corner. "Take a seat and let's chat."

"I have to finish coding this section. I'm on deadline." Besides, the last thing Jake felt like doing was talking, now or ever.

"Come on. You can take a break." Doyle sent Jake a sly look from under his shaggy gray brows, where the fringed bangs of his blond wig rested. "Or should I say *another* break? What was that YouTube video you watched about an hour ago? Something about Batman, I think."

"It was an exposé on superhero origins," Jake said stiffly. "And yes, Batman was included. I was stuck on something, and it helps if I do something distracting, like watch a video."

"Or have a chat with your neighbor."

"Ex-neighbor, who is now a ghost hanging out in my tub while wearing a ridiculous blond wig." Jake eyed the wig now. The ends of it clung to Doyle's hairy shoulders, a few curls floating on top of the water. "Do you have to wear that thing?"

Doyle grinned. "Why? Are you jealous?"

"Hardly." Jake sighed, his shoulders aching. "I don't mean to be rude, but I'm really busy and I need to work. Can you keep the splashing down to a minimum?"

Doyle tucked a strand of his wig behind one ear. "Nope."

"You—" Jake clamped his mouth over the rest of his sentence. "I don't understand. I've had ghosts visit me since I could remember. Some stayed a few days, sure, but none of them ever returned like this."

Doyle leaned back against the tiled wall and nodded thoughtfully. "It *is* different, isn't it?"

"Very. And I want to know why."

"Don't look at me." Doyle rubbed his chin, where gray stubble grew. "I just do what I'm told."

"By whom?"

Doyle arched a heavy brow at Jake.

Jake scowled. "Fine. Still, you're interfering in my life. Surely that's a no-no."

"I don't think there are any no-nos."

"Really? You guys don't have rules?" Jake's programming soul was rightly outraged. Rules were everything.

"Not that I can tell, but then again, I'm new to this whole ghost business. I'm learning the ropes, you might say."

"New? I hate to tell you this, but it's been over five years since you kicked the bucket."

"What?" Doyle looked shocked. "Five years? Are you serious?" At Jake's nod, Doyle shook his head. "Huh. Doesn't seem like it. Wait until I tell Barbara about that."

That caught Jake's attention. He wanted to ask so many questions, but the last thing he wanted to do was encourage Doyle.

Jake's curiosity won. "You get to see Barbara?"

"When she's not busy, sure." Doyle twisted a strand of blond hair around his finger. "She never liked you, you know. Said you were odd."

That stung a little. Everyone liked Barbara, including Jake.

"But," Doyle added, "I told her you were a good neighbor for me once she'd gone. Quiet, kept to yourself, didn't cause any harm, and you were very sympathetic."

That made Jake feel a little guilty. "We didn't speak often."

"No, but after she died, you got my newspaper every day after and put it on my porch."

Jake shifted awkwardly from one foot to the other. "I didn't think you'd noticed. I made sure you weren't up yet."

"Oh, I saw all sorts of things. I don't know much, but I do know that these other ghosts you've seen wandering through, they're on their way somewhere else, so they don't stay. But me? I'm here because I'm supposed to be." Doyle lifted his feet out of the water, crossed them, and rested them on one corner of the tub, water dripping on the floor. "I'm just guessing here, but I think I'm here because I'm to make sure that something that *might* happen *does* happen."

That was alarming. "Like what?"

"Lord, I wish I knew. I haven't figured all of this"—Doyle waved his hand in a vague circle—"out. But I will." He settled down a bit and closed his eyes, the wig slipping to one side as he rested his head against the wall. "Barbara says it takes a little getting used to, having an assignment. And you're my first."

"I'm your *assignment*? Are you kidding me?"

Doyle opened one eye. "Why would I do that? Do I look like I like being here?"

Nate eyed the steaming coming up from the water. "You don't look like you hate it."

Doyle sighed and opened both eyes, but he didn't sit up. "I suppose it could be worse. I could be sent off to someone I don't know. At least we know one another, although I knew your dad better."

"He said you guys used to work together."

"A long, long time ago." Doyle raised one eyebrow. "How are your parents, by the way? You should visit them more."

"I see them plenty when they're not out RV'ing around. They don't stay in one place long, now that Dad's retired."

"Rick always had an itch to travel." Doyle eyed Jake sourly. "I guess I should be grateful I got you and wasn't assigned a total idiot. It's a plus that you can see me and we can talk. Barbara says that's unusual. Apparently not many people can do that."

"Great." The last thing he needed right now was a ghost "assigned" to him.

"Yeah, and about that girlfriend of yours."

"Fiancée," Jake corrected absently.

"Whatever. What was her name again? Pester?"

"Heather. 'Pester' isn't even close."

"It's a better name for her than Heather." Doyle made a face. "I don't know what you saw in that one. I mean, she had a nice ass, I'll give you that, but she talked a blue streak and made no sense at all. I don't get it."

Jake's face heated, and the familiar lost feeling weighted down his shoulders. "I don't want to talk about it. I need to get back to work." To prove it, he turned on his heel to leave.

"You do that," Doyle called after him. "And say hello to those new neighbors of yours, too, while you're at it."

Jake stopped and turned around. "New neighbors?"

Doyle's thick brows rose, disappearing behind his blond bangs. "You didn't know? Ava Dove rented my old house, so you have new neighbors. A woman and a kid."

Ava Dove was one of seven daughters of the family that had founded the town of Dove Pond a long, long time ago. After Doyle's death, Ava had bought his house and two acres for her landscaping and herbal tea business. She'd turned the small house into an office and had built two huge greenhouses out back, which meant cars and trucks came and went all day long. Jake hated that. Even worse, the smell of her herbs drifted into his house every time he opened a window.

It wasn't a bad smell, even he had to admit that. But it was different and thus irritating, and Jake hated change. About a year ago, flush with success, Ava had purchased a larger tract of land on the other side of town, where she planned to grow even more herbs. The new place had a bigger house on it, so she'd moved her office there and had put Doyle's old house up for rent, although there were no takers, which had suited Jake just fine. He didn't need annoying neighbors, especially one with a kid.

He realized Doyle was waiting for a reaction, so Jake hid his irritation behind a shrug. "They're quiet, I'll give them that. I didn't even know they were there."

"They've been there for two whole weeks and you didn't even notice." Doyle shook his head. "You've become a hermit, you know that?"

Two weeks? Doyle must be mistaken. "Are you sure it was two weeks ago?"

"Hell yes, I'm sure. You know that, too, but you can't see outside your own windows because of those damned rosebushes. You're like Sleeping Beauty in here, surrounded by a thorny wall and waiting for your princess to come. Well, she ain't coming, and you need to get a grip, boy, and move on."

Jake's jaw ached from clenching it. It stung to be ordered to "move on" when he'd been trying to do just that.

Doyle's gaze suddenly moved past Jake, and the ghost tilted his head, one end of a long tress of golden wig dipping into the water. "Oho! That's unexpected."

"What's unexpected?"

Doyle looked back at Jake and grinned. "Sorry, kid. But whether you want to or not, it looks like you're about to meet your neighbors."